
Kindle   ISBN 978-0-9961615-5-8

EPUB   ISBN 978-0-9961615-1-0

Thanks to my Dad, Mom, and my little sister for all the
wonderful support you've given me. Your love, time and
effort means more to me than I could ever explain. It feels as
though it goes beyond the universe itself! It's that strong! I
greatly appreciate and love you all!
This is for you!

UNNATURAL

RACHEL F. WILLIAMS

Copyright © 2014 Rachel F. Williams

Chapter 1

Dmitri Vladoiu's journal
September 16th, 1907

I cannot bear it any longer, for I have learned—the one whom I once considered an angel sent to me from the very heavens above—Rozalia—is more like a fallen angel! A demonic woman, she is. I have been blindly led along these past weeks; been too entranced and infatuated with her. Each time we are together, I feel abnormally diminished afterward. I am such a fool to not have realized this before! Perhaps leaving my home country of Romania for Albany, New York in '95 was a mistake (sarcasm)—or vice-versa for Rozalia. Maybe when uncle Corneliu told me he decided to move his architectural company to America, I should have told him I wanted to remain in Bucharest to finish my studies in Mechanical Engineering. But America is the land of opportunity; such happiness and fortune we have gained by living here. I received my engineering degree and also finished my schooling in business administration. I decided to leave my job as a mechanical engineer and start my own company in that field. So perhaps, I really cannot complain—as far as that goes.

This brings me back to the previous subject . . .

Today at Rozalia's apartment, I saw it at last; the monster she is. I was leaning in to give her a kiss when suddenly, we heard the paper boy shouting in the street below, which distracted us

6

both. I saw her eyes were glowing extremely bright brown. Never before have I seen her like that. She caught me staring as she turned back to me. I looked away but she stopped me and said, "No Dmitri—look at me!" She demanded I look into those unnatural orbs of hers, expecting me to obey immediately as if I were nothing more than a loyal pet or servant! I moved away from her, bewildered by her sudden immodest behavior. She snatched my cravat and growled yet another demand; "Kiss me now!" The tone she had - I will never forget something so malicious-sounding.

Because of my studies in Mythology and the occult, it was in that moment, I realized she was either possessed by an evil entity or was most definitely a succubus herself. "What are you?" I remember shouting at her; just to be sure I had judged her correctly. She was stubborn with me; took my mouth and forced herself on me. I remember very little after that, for now it is all but a blur to me. I must have fallen unconscious. When I awoke, I was alone and nearly exhausted. I finally realized she was draining my very life energy from my body. I knew that if I simply left her, she would find another 'victim'. For the good of all mankind, this leaves me with only one other choice - kill her!

According to the books I have studied, there are many ways I could destroy her but I am having a difficult time deciding what I should do. Note: Succubae are powerful entities—more powerful than demons. This would be a very dangerous undertaking to say the least. I must think on this some more.

Dmitri Vladoiu's journal
September 19th, 1907

Late last night . . . I drew Rozalia away to an island in the Sound, making her believe it was a special place for us to go. I distracted her and took her life. I cannot go into detail now; I feel too terrible. This memory will never leave me . . . Never.

In that moment after I killed her, I distinctly recall falling to my knees with a sudden stabbing pain in my head....It was so overwhelming, I fell unconscious. I awoke a couple of hours later still reeling from a severe headache.

I think it is quite cowardice of me, but I must admit that, as I sat beside her lifeless body, I mourned and cursed myself many times for what I had done. However, I reminded myself then and continue to remind myself now that it was indeed most necessary and there is no reason to think otherwise. Finally, I regained my composure, put her body in the boat and went back out onto the sound. I put her over the side into the depths before sunrise as I journeyed back to the mainland.

For committing such a heinous act, I feel just as horrid as she was. May she never find peace! May god bless me and have mercy on my soul for doing such a terrible thing! What else could I have done? My hands are now forever stained with her blood.

Dmitri Vladoiu's journal
September 24th, 1907

I hope I am not going mad. I noticed that after I killed Rozalia, strange things have been happening to me. For one, my appetite has increased immensely—unnaturally. I have been unbearably hungry for the last few days. No matter what I eat, I can never satisfy myself completely. Also, this morning, I looked in my bedroom mirror and thought I saw her face instead of mine! Surely it must be guilt overwhelming me to the point of having hallucinations. I felt my face, pinched myself a few times; I even slapped myself. And still, I saw her in the mirror. I broke down for a moment. I knew time was ticking, so I put my emotions aside and hurried out; I had a business meeting to attend. When I returned home to Corneliu this evening, I assisted him with preparing dinner in the kitchen. And yes, I have yet to give word on what happened with Rozalia. He has been curious but does not pry.

Something very tragic happened this evening. While helping Corneliu with dinner, I offered to finish preparing it all. He agreed and went to sit down in the chair near the door. As he did this, the chair gave way, and broke into pieces. He cut his arm on a shard of wood. There was much blood seeping from his injury. I moved as fast as I could to help him. I frantically made some bandages but because I was so upset, he slapped my mouth with his bloody hand. I glared at him and almost yelled, but as I pointed at him, I licked my chapped lips and tasted his blood. My eyes suddenly widened and I touched a finger to my mouth. I was instantly astounded by the euphoria I had gotten once I swallowed the bloody saliva. My senses tingled; my mouth watered, my stomach jumped in delight; I was oddly desirous for more. All I could do was stand in place with a blank expression. I looked at him again, then down at his bleeding arm. I needed more—I truly did! I then formed a plan.

"Corneliu," I said as I stepped closer, "Saliva heals wounds, I know. If I licked your wound, it should be more likely to heal faster—believe me or not; I learned this." He did not trust the idea but eventually, with much hesitance, he allowed me to take his arm and run my tongue over it. I too was unsure about this. Again, my stomach leapt with excitement. I felt as if many, many strands of energy streamed through my entire body like a rapidly flowing river. I pulled his arm closer to my lips to get more blood. I remember him gasping at me, "Dmitri, stop!" I couldn't though, for something was pushing me further, and his voice was quieting. The entire room was becoming completely silent to my ears. There was a familiar voice in my head. It sounded like Rozalia. No it WAS Rozalia! I was absolutely stunned; she told me over and over, compelling me, "Bite him. Bite him. Bite him Dmitri! Do it! You want this—you need this—you are very, VERY hungry! DO IT! BITE HIM NOW!" I suddenly clamped my jaw down on his arm and sucked away at his blood like I hadn't had anything to drink or eat in days. I felt Corneliu try to pull away. I could tell he was in severe pain but I did not care at all; the blood was *more important to me.*

The next thing I knew, I threw my head back, letting out a great terrible pained scream. My eye-teeth—I could feel them growing! Rozalia spoke again, "Ignore it! You need to heal Cornelius!" I then snatched him by the neck and looked into his eyes for a long time, focusing on them. After a while, I could start to see his thoughts. I felt as if someone else was using my eyes and mind to give him the desire to drink my blood. Could it have been Rozalia doing this? He then got a knife and slit my wrist and thoughtlessly drank from me. I did not try to stop him and panted from the stinging sensation but I let him because Rozalia said, "Good. He will be fine now."

I close my journal with a smirk, "The old days when I was so young." How could I have ever imagined living this long and not age a day past that fateful night so long ago? I had to invent a way to explain it in passing to anyone who might ask. My alternate self is now a very old man no one ever sees and me being the younger they do see. Now it's September of 2014…

My eyes rise from my table, then I look over my shoulder at the door of this coffee shop 'Lounge 'n Sip' and find many people coming inside. I run my tongue over a fang in want of them as a snack—or so I should say, Rozalia wants their blood for life-energy to keep her strong and 'healthy'.

Last time I came here, it was 1998 and this was a small ice cream parlor. I thought I would see what has changed. Well, not much.

'I just wanted some coffee and fresh air.' I sneer lightly after my thought to her, now turning back around. 'Notice where I am sitting—the far end of the shop—with my back turned to the door.'

Rozalia chuckles at me in a mocking way. I roll my eyes but then notice as I look back again at that crowd of people one person in particular; a thin beautiful woman about 20-years-old with wavy strawberry-blonde hair, an oval face and a cute shoe-nose.

"Hmm... she looks... so familiar." Rozalia is immediately interested, and surprisingly not in a wicked way; she is more astounded and taken back in memory. She's not just looking at her; she's making me stare at her in a long gaze now. I slowly turn my chair and bring my cup of coffee up to my lips. "How so?"

I don't get an answer.

Instead, Rozalia makes me grin and whisper, "Look at me." The young woman turns her head and blinks at me with a preoccupied look. Rozalia gasps. 'What?' I ask, annoyed. There's silence.

I'm becoming curious... She never behaves like this. She's always evil and manipulative—it's part of her revenge.

Before I ask again, she forces my lips into a sinister and makes my light-blue eyes glow softly, "Dear girl... dream of this man; dream of him as if he has been in your thoughts for many years." Why on earth is she saying this?

"Rozalia, what are you up to?" I question under my breath. Again, no response...except quiet chuckling, and she whispers, "She reminds me of *me*."

The woman continues to stare in my direction. I leisurely drink my coffee, Rozalia keeping my glowing gaze on her.

She blinks again and quickly looks away, bemused by what just happened. After that, I look down at the table with a sudden frown, "No, leave her alone. I won't keep doing this to satisfy your needs Rozalia." She makes me smile in a wicked way, "You know you want her." "What interests have you in her besides a meal? And stop making me talk to myself!" I scold.

"In time, you shall see." I hear her say in my mind.

"Hmmph," I ball one hand into a fist. I do really like that girl but I won't act on this. 'Rozalia...what is on your agenda now?'

She laughs at me and I grow more agitated. Luckily for me...my only thoughts she can read are the ones directed to her specifically.

I look up for the woman again and find her standing in line to get coffee. "Look at me." I say. She turns her head and locks eyes with me again. I narrow mine and brighten them, "Forget my face." As she's staring at me, her mouth opens slightly. I raise an eyebrow slowly.

The woman barista says, "Can I help you?" To hearing her, she closes her mouth, turns to her and nods the positive, stepping up to the counter.

I sigh and rub my lowered forehead, "La naiba." I wish I could put an end to it all. I watch her take her coffee, a little brown bag and glimpse at me while turning her nose up and walking to the door. My eyes follow her, slowly falling from her long wavy hair, her curvy back to her nicely shaped bottom and then her long beautiful legs. I lick my fangs absentmindedly, 'Good lord she's gorgeous... I have to meet her.'

Just then, a brown-haired woman disturbs my train of thought by walking up and asking, "Excuse me, could you help me with some directions? I'm new here in town and I'm looking for the closest grocery store." I blink up at her for a moment and immediately stand. Rozalia purrs, "Oh, lovely... a snack." A slow grin traces my lips, "Sure." I offer her a place to sit, "Please, join me and I'll tell you." She sees my eyes beginning to glow as I offer my hand. She takes it and notices my temperature. Her eyes widen, and in a small voice, she says, "Oh my, you're so warm... Okay..." she sits down.

I smile, "I'm Nicolai Francis."

"Elizabeth Reynolds."

"That's a beautiful name."

Rozalia tells me, *"You will charm her, take her to our castle and drain her of her blood."* As I hear this in my mind, I smile genuinely at the girl. 'Rozalia, no more. Please no more.' I mentally beg. *"I want her!"* Rozalia hisses, making my ears focus on Elizabeth's heartbeat. It's so torturous. The temptation is taking over. I shouldn't have come here.

As I bite my lip, grinning, Elizabeth slowly smiles back at me and blushes, "Well thank you! Your name sounds fancy." She giggles. I prop my chin on my left hand and gaze into her eyes almost lovingly, "Yes…anytime dear."

My womanizing skills never fail.

*La naiba
Damn it

Looking in my bedroom mirror, I tuck my dark red cravat under my vest, occasionally glancing at the bed where Miss Elizabeth lay, naked and lifeless. Poor, poor girl…and her family. I pause with a forming grimace and say to Rozalia, "Satisfied now…" I cock my head sideways, "bitch?" She makes me smirk halfway, "I feel like–what's the expression?" She inhales comfortably and contently, "Like a million 'bucks'." I roll my eyes, 'Now I need to figure out what to do with her body. This hasn't happened here in at least 50 years.'

"Don't forget that girl in 1983–Ivana." She coyly says. A memory pops into my head of a pretty woman whom I tried to love but Rozalia made me kill her in the same way as… the girl lying on my bed right now. It was an act of jealousy and disgust…as always.   In the corner of the room, Elizabeth's spirit is on her knees, holding her weeping face. I try not to pay any attention to her, but it's hard.

Just then, there's a knock at the door. I turn my head toward it, "Yes?"

"It's Walter sir." My butler. Looking back over at Elizabeth's body, I murmur, "Meet me in my office."

"Yes sir." He walks away from the door, back up the hall.

As I'm gazing at her body, I begin to think to myself; 'I just can't keep living like this. I have given up trying, but think somehow there is still hope.' Hope. What 'hope' though?

I have come to a fork in the road.

I could turn down the road where nothing matters anymore, or I could take the other; the path to risks of many sorts–again.

I look back in the mirror and see Rozalia staring me down with the same appearance she had before I killed her. My eye twitches, disturbed. All that I would have to lose is everything. I need something great to happen; something big and extraordinary. In this moment, I plan a party… "I'll have a great masquerade party…"

"Oh, I love those." Rozalia makes me say. I blink and then smile. "Yes, me too." I flick my shirt cuffs, nodding my head in arrogance, "It will be a lot of fun. Many people will come… more this time hopefully." At that, she purrs in delight.

"What about me?!" Elizabeth cries. I lose the smile and stare at her for a moment, then I walk up to her and kneel slowly, "It isn't my fault." I reach to touch her face and my hand goes through her like moving through smoke. She jerks away with a sob.

"*Ridiculous!*" Rozalia suddenly contorts my face into an ugly scowl, brightens my eyes to all-white and shoves my hand into her head. She tenses my neck as we both watch Elizabeth become completely immobilized. Then suddenly, she shifts my hand down and Elizabeth vanishes with a loud, nearly glass-shattering scream that only the spirits, Rozalia and I can hear.

I shut my eyes and turn my head down as if in shame. Now she's gone. I reopen them and stand. I step to the bed and pick her body up, position it over my shoulder and take it over to a closet. Opening the door, I carefully go in, press my right hand to a square in the finely detailed wall and then ahead of me a space in the floor opens up to a rectangular hole. I approach it with Elizabeth and stand in silence for a moment, then I let her tumble off my shoulder, down into the oubliette far below. Momentarily, there's an unnerving slice and crunch noise, followed by a big splash of water.

"And soon, her remains will drift to the depths of the Sound." Rozalia chuckles. I tense up, very upset and disgusted.

'I've had enough. I've had ENOUGH! I have just killed another innocent person for you. How many more? Will you ever leave me in peace?!' My hands clench into tight fists of rage.

"What will you do?" she scoffs and laughs, *"Try to commit suicide again? You don't have the will!"*

'No, you don't deserve an answer to that.'

"Ahh...but that is not the case Dmitri; I already know you have no idea. I know how you operate." She says, humored. I grit my teeth, then punch the square in the wall and make a swift exit out of my room and head to my office.

When I get there, Walter is patiently looking out the window. I clear my throat. He turns and bows his head, "Sir." I nod once and walk to my desk, "What is on your mind?" "The staff is growing curious about your 'guest'."

I stop tapping my fingers on the chair.

Scoffing, I say, "What is she to them? It's not their business. The staff are not my concern... they are yours Walter." I even manage to chuckle.

"Yes sir... of course." He nods before looking down with a faint laugh of his own, "Personally sir, I would call myself...one of those staff members as well." He slightly lifts his quizzical eyes back up to me. I arch an eyebrow, "You are using them as an excuse?" He nods carefully.

I remove my hand from the chair, "She is just a guest." An innocent smile fills my face. He says nothing; just watches me.

I take a deep breath and then look past him at the doorway, "Mr. Vladoiu will be throwing a masquerade party on the 19th of October. I will be hosting it for him." Momentarily, I glance at him, "I need you to send out invitations to people we know who earned over a million dollars last year. No politicians, doctors or people of the press. Hire the ferry to run from 6 to midnight. And of course you know, no photography or recording devices will be allowed." Still watching me, he says, "Of course sir... Will that be all?" I nod my head at him and he goes out.

Lacing my hands together behind my back, I stroll up to the window and those memories return about Elizabeth, my terrifying past, the future...that beautiful woman I saw before I met Elizabeth–I wonder what her name is–and Rozalia...

In the time my maids and Walter are setting everything up for the party, I will form an idea. "An idea...yes." I absentmindedly whisper to myself.

"An idea?" Rozalia asks. I then realize what had just slipped out of my mouth.

Nonchalantly, I nod while looking out at the many arched trees leading to the front of the castle, "Yes...a rather...exciting one." I smile slowly, now staring. She hums in an almost ideological way.

Chapter 2

Name: *Ivy Summers*

Journal entry date – *September 26, Friday*

I just woke up to my super loud radio alarm clock playing Led Zeppelin. I forgot to turn the volume down, and what did I get for being so forgetful? It scared me into trying to turn it off in a hurry. It tumbled off my nightstand as I put my feet down on the floor. Damn thing landed right on my toes! Ouch! Miss Ivy Summers, you can be an idiot sometimes! Oh well...I was tired last night. I wonder how long that mark will stay there? It sure took some skin off! Anyway... I had that same dream last night that I've been having since I was a teenager... the one where I'm standing in front of a mirror, wearing a white Victorian dress. I was at a castle that I supposedly "live" in with an extremely handsome guy from Romania. I still don't know why I keep having this dream. I continue to think it may be a message...but I don't know. Mom always says I read into things too much. Maybe so. Like always, he came up to me, pulled my hair away from my neck and started kissing it. I leaned my head back and pulled his head closer; it felt so good. It's strange that... I love a man in my dreams and never have an interest to actually meet one. I keep hiding this secret and it's killing me; the great desire for him. Yeah, I know - it'll never happen. That's okay though - these dreams always put a smile on my face.

I put my journal down and look out my 2nd story apartment window with a sigh, "If only…" I pull my hair back into a pony tail, and stare at the buildings across from this one. Gales, NY… I've been here for about a year now working at the local hospital. It's a small city on the coast of the Sound. I moved out of my parents' house about 40 miles away from here to be on my own. Annnd…I still miss my friends. I have a couple around here… sort of, but the silence is good. The only ones I'm closest to is a 27 year old nurse named Gina and an old friend of my parents'–Eric. He's about their age. When I was a kid, I'd go fishing with him and dad in the Sound and Nancy (his wife) and my mom would go out shopping together a lot too. He and Gina met at one of my birthday parties and have gotten along greater than I thought they would, which is something I still chuckle about. Gina is a real people person. Overall, my social life is visiting with them and my parents, and this journal that I've had since I was 12. Weird I know, but that's me.

Suddenly, my eyebrows come together. I quickly look back at my clock, then again out the window, worried. The sun never comes up a 5am! Oh no! It's 6:35! I forgot to reset the alarm for 5am. I have to be at the hospital at 7 today! "Shit!" I jump from my bed and scramble around for my medical tech uniform. I find it, throw my pajamas off, slide into my work clothes, and out the door I go. I didn't even have time to bathe or fix my hair!

Clocking in just in time (7am), I stand in the hall listening to Gina talk about a movie she's going to see. I chuckle at her, "Gina, to enjoy a horror movie at the theater properly, you need someone to go with you. You know that." In case you're wondering, she's a thin, brown-eyed brunette that has the most innocent face you could ever imagine someone to have.

She nudges my shoulder and mockingly winks at me, "Then why don't you come with me, huh?" I roll my eyes and lie to her amusedly, "I don't like going out much."

She tilts her head from side to side at me, "Well ok then! Maybe I should ask this guy I've been noticing at the Lounge n' Sip." Oh? I smirk, "Is he hot?" She nods slowly with a forming grin, "Very. Almost unnaturally hot. He has a sexy Russian-like accent too; I overheard him talking to a barista, flirting with her. She–like every other girl around–was drooling over him, if ya know what I mean." She winks again. I laugh, "I was in there yesterday afternoon and didn't see anyone like that… Hah, well, you better ask him out before he's taken! Anyway, what's going on here? Anything major yet?"

"Yep." she folds her arms, "A guy came into trauma with a broken leg. There was a metal rod stuck in there pretty deep. He's stable now though." I take a deep breath, "People just don't know how to stay out of harm's way, do they? It's like they go looking for trouble every time."

She nods, "Exactly."
I pat her on the shoulder, "Well, I'll be in triage then. See ya later." We go our separate ways.

As I walk to that part of the ER, I say some friendly hellos to most of my coworkers. I don't know if it's just me or if they really are never very cheerful. Some of them only mumble something or utter a sound in reply. I prefer to be chipper here at work. I'm happy with the life I have; single with no strings attached to anything. I'm 21, have my own apartment, and a job that allows me to see some interesting things and meet interesting people from all over the world. It's always exciting for me.

I get to triage and see the place is almost deserted, except for a few people in here. There's an old man in a wheelchair bent over one side, a woman lying half-asleep on three chairs, a guy trying to talk on his cell-phone while holding his leg in pain, and another lady with a particle mask on her face. I look at them all for a minute, and then go into one of the small office-like rooms to begin the day.

There are four paper slips in front of my computer, all having the names of the people in the waiting room. I set them down and check the computer to see who's working triage today. A tech named Bob, and then there's me. Hopefully it won't stay this way for very long. The waiting room can fill up in the blink of an eye. I take one of the slips of paper and walk out of my room and loudly call the name, "John McAdams!" He's the one with the hurt leg. He filled his name out on the paper an hour and a half ago. He's before everyone else. Yikes! It sucks to be him! His leg is probably throbbing terribly by now.

He waves a hand in the air while hanging up his phone. "Can you walk sir?" I ask. Before he can answer, the old man in the wheelchair roughly, rudely says, "You better hurry up in there! I feel like I'm dyin'!" I puff out a small sigh and nod at him, "Yes sir, your name will be called shortly." I look back to the one with the hurt leg and offer a hand to help him into the nearest chair with wheels. He takes it and sits down with a soft moan, closing his eyes. I push him into my triage room to be seen.

Lunchtime. Thank goodness! Well–sort of. Since I didn't take my own lunch today, I have to see what's available in the cafeteria. I had to wait until 2pm to be relieved. The ER got quite busy today, but that isn't anything new. I wouldn't bother trying to eat if I was on an 8 hour shift instead of 12. I did have some things I got from my car to snack on during the small bits of time I had while working where I was. I continue to scold myself for keeping a dirty car, yet today–it turns out that junk food was a lifesaver for me. I guess I always (unconsciously) have a back-up plan.

I go through the big open doors to the cafeteria and see there must be some kind of conference going on today. It seems like the whole hospital is in here (metaphorically speaking of course). There's no way I'll be getting anything from the grill today! I know I have an hour, but I don't want to wait that long just to get a burger or whatever they have over there! Instead, I grab half of a turkey sub and make myself a small salad.

After I pay for my food and find a table at the nearby coffee shop, I sit, unwrap my stuff and start eating. I keep my head down. And believe me, it's for a reason. Sometimes, a pharmacist named Liam will find me and sit at my table. He always beats around the bush, asking me out. And I always give him basically the same answer: No.

I have a nice way of doing that though. However, I must say, it's getting to the point that I just might be a little less friendly next time.

"Well," I muse as I search around for him, "at least I have my ear-buds in my pocket today." I plug them into my phone turn on 'The Who'. I'm going to be in the ICU (Intensive Care Unit) after this. What a joy that'll be. I think I'm happiest in triage, to be honest. I have time to surf the internet (there are some limitations to what I can do on there, sadly) and time to snack when no one is in need of me. The ICU is a hopping place. It's crazy. But don't get me wrong, I do love the insanity that goes on in that area of the ER–to some extent. Ah well, hopefully everything will be alright. I can always hope, right?

Finally–finally it's time to clock out! I came in today, happy and optimistic, but yes, as I expected–the ICU and other places I worked today have managed to make me want to yank ALL of my hair out!

I swipe my card through the clock and march down the long halls on my way out of this godforsaken hospital. I'm so ready to go home, eat dinner and just kick back and watch some T.V. I may even conk out on the sofa. There's no doubt that'll happen… But not before I make some T.V. dinner Chinese food!

I check my makeup in the rear view mirror–looks good–start the engine, and haul-ass home.

Chapter 3

My cell-phone rings. It startles me enough to make me jerk and fall right off the couch. BAM! "OOMPH!" I grumble as I snatch the phone off the coffee table and answer it, "*Yeah*?" That came out impolitely…

"Ivy?" It's my mom–Bess. I throw my head back with a little sigh, "Hey mom, good-" I look at the wall clock and see it's 5:58am, "morning… Shouldn't you be asleep? We already talked about you getting plenty of rest."

"I can't sleep past 6, you know that. So, you got any big plans for today?" Big plans? Like going to work? I look around my room, then I say, "Mom, it's Saturday."

"Ivy, you told me you're off for the next few days." Realization hits me.
I pause yct again and turn around to look at the calendar on the other wall. Wow, she's right. I have no plans at all actually.

"C'mon Ives, do I have to remind you that you'll have your 22nd birthday in two days?" She tells me. I lay back down on the couch, "Yeah…I'm just trying to do more than one thing at once, I guess."

"Stop doin' that. Now, how about we go out for some coffee and do a little shopping? I need some new stuff." She snickers after saying 'stuff'. A small smirk appears on my face. I close my eyes, resting my head farther down in the big fluffy pillow, "Mom, you know I have things to do today. I gotta go pay some bills and go to the post office. And you know I still hate clothes shopping. How about some coffee and a little sightseeing?" I so prefer that over going inside crowded clothes stores.

She sighs, "Yeah, I forgot. Ok–sightseeing sounds good."
"So, where do you wanna meet?" She asks.

"The coffee shop at the corner in that strip-mall we go to sometimes; Lounge 'n' Sip. 8 o'clock ok?"

"Yep! Sounds good!"
Alright then.

7:47… I turn my stereo down as it plays Blue Oyster Cult and check my red lip-gloss in the rear view mirror. I've always liked dark lip-gloss…

I put on my aviator shades and lean back in the seat. After staring at the empty parking space next to me for a few minutes, I see my mom park there. It looks like she's rocking out in her little SUV. I try not to laugh. "Hmm," I get out of my '68 Jaguar and readjust my black sweater, nodding a hello to her. Gosh it's cold out today! I sure am glad she suggested we get coffee!

She walks up to me, gives me a hug, then sort of guides me into the shop, "Come on before we freeze." "Yeah," I snicker, following her.

As we step inside, I take my glasses off and look around at the people there. Mom sways her head like telling me to hurry along behind her. She always does this. It's annoying but I know I can't change her.

As we're heading for the counter to order our drinks, my eyes suddenly lock onto a guy at a small table in the far back corner. He's writing in a small book that looks pretty old. That's interesting… He looks strangely familiar to me. His hair is short and nicely groomed, he's built, and he has an extremely handsome face. He has a nice five o'clock shadow and his eyes are a hazy greenish blue. My goodness… he's very, very charming looking. His face, that behavior–all so quiet and mysterious… like the world around him doesn't even exist but his eyes show he's hiding a huge secret. I can't stop staring at him, reading him. There's something about this guy that seems off–but also intriguing. As a matter of fact, he kind of reminds me of the man in my reoccurring dreams! But, that would be absolutely crazy and out there to think that! He could be someone I saw at the hospital recently. Yeah… probably so.

"Ivy?" I hear mom say. I blink a couple times, but just as I do, the guy's serious-looking eyes flash up from the pages at me. My mouth falls open just a tad. Whoa... what intense eyes! Quickly, I look at her, then slowly back to him. He smirks and returns his attention to the book. Wow... freaky. I release an uneasy breath before turning to the woman barista at the register, "Yeah, a pumpkin spice latté please." The lady gives me a strange look, but I ignore her. She rings us up.

We get our coffee and head out the door, because I strongly recommended it. I'm in a bit of a hurry to get inside my car–not because it's cold out, but because I'm oddly on edge now.

I motion across the top of my car for my mom to get in the passenger side as I unlock my door. She's decided to leave her car here; it would make things easier. It's about the gas.

"Ivy, what's the matter?" She exasperatedly asks. I look up at her, opening my door at the same time, "I don't know, I'm just cold. Don't worry about it." I glance over to peer in through the window at him. He's standing up, tucking the book away in his long fancy gray trench-coat, and boy, he's quick about it. I notice he's giving everyone a smug expression as he does this. It's like he thinks he's 'above' everybody.

I turn back and get inside the car, "Let's go to the coastline." I start the engine and drive us out of the parking lot.

When we approach a red light, I lean my head back on the headrest. Now I'm getting the feeling I'm being stared at. I look out of the corner of my eye at mom, "What?"

She folds her arms after putting her hot coffee in the plastic drink holder hanging from the door, "You wanna talk about earlier? Girl, you gotta stop being scared of everybody. You're 21– not 13."

I sardonically tilt my head at her, "Mom, I'm ok. I just saw someone I'm tryin' to avoid. It's a guy I know from work who's very annoying." Hopefully that's a good excuse. But, wait... I'm not avoiding anybody. Crud... How am I going to back that up if she asks who I'm speaking of?

"Oh." She says, then looks ahead again. "The light is green." Wait, that's it? My eyes have widened shortly in amazement. Oh thank goodness! "Yeeahh..." I check the traffic light and hit the gas.

We arrive at our destination and I've gotta admit, I've never been to this part of the coast. Neither has she–I think. She's 44yrs old; she should know about some nice places to go. There's lots of rocks and a few trees around; typical NY scenery–the quiet side. There's a big white statue behind me of a man standing on a mound looking through a telescope. He's Harold Gales II–the founding father of the town. All of this is something I never get tired of. I'm a city girl who wants peace and quiet every once in a while–and this–this has that. The only bad thing about it at the moment is the weather. It's getting cloudy and possibly colder.

I sink my head lower into my sweater and push my hands farther down in my pockets, then glimpse back at my car thinking I should've brought my coffee with me.

"Wow... Ivy, look out there!" Mom says while walking up to the guardrail. She's pointing out at a small island filled with all kinds of trees. I walk up beside her and study it, "It looks like there's something there." It's about as big as Hart Island (among the thousand islands here in New York).

She momentarily says, "Yeah, it looks almost like the top of a big building or...hmm...that's odd. It looks like a castle, but I'm not sure if it is."

What's that about? I push up against the railing while my eyes narrow in interest, "You think it has anything to do with the government?" I can only see the tops of it. Towers–it looks like it has two towers with dark coned roofs.

"I don't know...but whatever that is, it's shielded from the public for a reason, don't ya think?" She says. I look at her.

That's a good question.

Chapter 4

Well, mom and I have parted ways; she's gone home, I've paid my bills and done all I needed to do today. It's 5:02pm and I believe now is the perfect time to figure out what that island is all about!

I turn on my PC and get on the internet. There is a granola bar halfway hanging out of my mouth and have a cherry soda to wash it down. So, to start things off, I type in the search engine, 'Islands in the Long Island Sound'.

There are many suggestions. Over a matter of say… 40 minutes–I end up clicking on all of them, but none of them are about that Island. Why? This is really starting to confuse me. I can't even find an aerial shot of it. I'm beginning to really wonder about that place. Undaunted, I spend another hour looking. Gosh, this is just nuts!

I throw my hands up and scoot back in my chair real fast, "Geez!" I turn the monitor off, shoot up from my seat, and stomp away into the kitchen to prepare a T.V. dinner: Lasagna. I get it out of the fridge and put it in the microwave for 15 minutes. While that's warming up, I'll go watch the news. So, as I go back into the living room, I stare straight ahead at my two windows. It's storming pretty good out there. That'll make for a good night's sleep…

There's a woman reporter talking about the bad weather. There are a few people with umbrellas scurrying behind her. I notice right off she's standing in the same spot I did with mom today–where we saw that island! My mind strays away from the TV into deep thought. Those trees…those trees all over there are so dark–it's like they're hiding something evil, something horrific. Something is going on there. There has got to be more on that island than meets the eye… and that building…

I pause the TV and lean forward until I'm on the edge of my

seat. From the way mom was talking about the condition of the island, I'm beginning to make myself believe it's abandoned and NY hasn't decided what to do with the property yet. There weren't any signs of life when we were looking over there, and there aren't any now that I can see. An idea then pops into my head. I'll check the local newspaper on the net and read some stuff in their archives to see what's going on! They might have something about it.

I get back to my computer and start typing the name of the local newspaper into the search engine. I find the site and start a search of their online archives about the island. I come across an article about a local businessman named Dmitri Vladoiu (Vlad-oy-u) who had a big party there at his castle in 1923. Lots of rich people, I'll bet. Hm, pretty cool guy… I love studying history.

It turns out looking here was a good decision. I wish I had thought of it first! So maybe I'm right; maybe the land is abandoned and either up for sale or the state doesn't know what to do with it yet. Now I've got something to do this weekend. And that is: go to that castle! I've always wanted to go to one. To have one so close–of course I'd want to go!

The microwave suddenly beeps, startling me. My stomach lets out a growl in expectation and I give it a pat. "Yes yes…" The microwave is all steamed up and ready for me to pull my food out. "Let's Eat!"

About an hour later, I come out of the bathroom drying my hair, still in a towel. I'm hearing a commotion outside my window. Sounds like a guy and a girl are fighting. That's not very unusual to hear, but since the noisiest neighbors moved out about 2 weeks ago, I can't figure this out. I guess some other annoying people replaced them. I really hope they finish up soon. People gotta sleep! One last thing for me though…

I get out my journal. I always stare at the star-sticker-filled cover for a second before opening it. I hug it close, then slowly open it and continue writing inside.

28

Name: *Ivy Summers*

Journal entry date – *September 27th, Saturday*

Well, two things happened to me today... One: I was getting coffee with mom and I saw this guy who I think I recognized, but I just can't place him. Everything I did in Lounge 'n' Sip, I could feel his eyes on me like a hungry wolf. That's weird to say, but it's how I felt. I can STILL feel his eyes on me. It sounds crazy - coming from me anyway. And two: When I was out with mom today, we went to the coastline of the Sound to do a little sightseeing. We did that for sure! She pointed out a small island that seems to have a strange building on it. Who knows what else is there? I feel like I need to know more about it. I looked it up countless times when I got home, and always - I got nothing on the place. It really aggravated me. But guess what? I turned the news on and I saw a lady giving the weather report at that very place we went to. Right then, I got an idea from watching that broadcast. I went and looked up the local newspaper, then I typed in 'Islands in the Long Island Sound'. Some businessman named Dmitri Vladoiu owned it back in the 20's. I'm assuming it's not inhabited anymore. I couldn't get any more information on the place than that. So since that's the case, I feel strangely determined to go there. It's like... I don't know - like I HAVE to go there. I've seen many shows where people would see some places and automatically feel drawn to them; they'd want to go back to them. Well I have that feeling. It never really turns out good for the people that have this experience, but as for me - I'm not going to let that happen.

Before I even make this special trip, I should see

about borrowing Eric's boat. I don't know if that's a good idea yet though. Once I get the transportation issue out of the way, I'll be off to that island.

I set the book down on my nightstand and get under the covers. For a while, I stare at the ceiling. A small part of me wanted to talk to that guy–but I was very intimidated by him. I've seen some intimidating people at the hospital, but they don't affect me the way this guy did.

"Pff…" I reach out to cut the light, "What am I thinking? I probably won't even see him again. He's just a regular dude who likes Lounge 'n' Sip's coffee." I roll over, cuddling my pillow now, "I've got other things to think about." I close my eyes…but after a minute, they fly open and focus on the wall. "But gee…he sure was hot." I snort… then laugh.

Chapter 5

As the alarm clock goes off, I gently reach for the button and hit the snooze bar with my eyes shut. A full minute goes by before I actually see it.

It's 7:31am. I have a long day ahead of me, yes I do! But first... some yogurt! Now, usually I stop by Lounge 'n' Sip in the morning for a quick snack, but I don't know if I should do that today. I don't want to see that guy today–if he's there. Oh who am I kidding; why am I being such a child! I need something to get me moving! I need some caffeine and sugar damn it!

I toss my empty yogurt and go out the door. On the way downstairs, the friendliest neighbor I have asks me why I'm in such a rush. I just wave him off; telling him it has something to do with my birthday. He doesn't say any more; just smiles at me as I go by. At least he's not nosy like a lot of other people here. The good thing about him is he keeps things in confidence pretty well.

It's a little ways to my car so I'm walking fast and not really paying attention to anything. I start to unlock my door when my ears pick up someone with heavy footfalls coming toward me. What the hell? This better not be one of those thugs I saw a while back. I'm tired of their crap. I yank the keys out and position them tightly in my fist. "Come any closer, I'll gouge your eyes out."

"IVY!" A woman gasps. Huh-?! I whirl around and look her up and down. It's Gina! Gosh... and I said THAT to her! I shake my hands defensively, "Gina, I'm so so so sorry!" She laughs somewhat nervously, "Wow... I didn't know you had a dark side!"

I frown a little, slowly looking back to my car door, "Sorry, I just get a little uncomfortable when people sneak up behind me." She walks a little bit closer with a small laugh, "Sorry...I should have thought about that." I face her again, "So...what brings you here at-" I check my phone, "9 this morning?" Though that's not really early...

"I thought I'd come by and surprise you with something for your birthday! I saw on a bulletin board somewhere at work that your birthday is coming up real soon, so... forgive me when I say I almost forgot." I'm stunned. "It's okay!"

She smiles, "For the surprise, come with me." She gestures me to follow her over to an old white Lincoln, so I do.

She opens one of the back doors and starts digging something out of the backseat. "Wow, so you got a Lincoln, huh?" I ask. "Yeah, it was my grandma's." She backs out with a big red box that has a gold ribbon on the top, "Happy early birthday!" She smiles at me. Wow, it looks beautiful!

I take it with a smile of my own, "Aw, thank you..." Slowly, I peer up from it at her. She really didn't have to do this...

She puts her hands on her hips and cocks her head with a smile, "What's with that look?" I form a small 'o' with my mouth and quickly look back down at the box, "Oh, nothing!" I shake it a few times, "No rattle... Hmm... I'm curious." I grin at her. She gives me the go-ahead to open it. I untie the ribbon and open the box. It's a beautiful bed comforter! Looks soft and cushy! It's red and black with a big Victorian pattern. "Aww Gina, I love this!" I giggle.

"I figured you would! I saw it and thought, 'You know what? She looks like the kind of person who likes Victorian stuff!'" She winks at me. I stop smiling all of a sudden and make a blank face. **Wait... I do?**

"What's wrong?" She asks.

My eyes slowly rise from the box and I realize I'm behaving strangely, so I immediately say, "Oh um, no never mind! I just remembered something I forgot to do. You reminded me." I smile reassuringly at her. She gives me a quiet unsure 'Ohh', then looks at her watch, "Well, I gotta get going. Hope you enjoy your gift Ivy!" I wave at her, "Yeah! Thanks again!" I watch her get in her car and then start driving away. She almost beeps a final goodbye but I figure by the way she jerks her hand away from the horn she doesn't want to piss off my neighbors.

I hum in thought, gaze down at the box and decide to put it in the trunk. There... it fits. I start the car and toss my journal into the passenger seat. Now I really need that coffee!

Every now and then, I look in the rear-view mirror while I think over all this stuff that I'm 'reading into' as mom likes to say. It keeps my mind busy and I like that–but it sure can get annoying at times when there really is nothing to it. This obsession over Victorian things, it started when I was a teenager. It never left; it's just gotten more intense. I know that wasn't long ago, but it sure feels like it. Ever since then, I've been seeing many different things from that era, more and more, day by day. My eyes always find them before I see anything else. A good example of that would be: Yesterday, I saw a guy writing in a very old book that seems like it could be from that time (why it wasn't falling apart, I don't know), and Gina said I look like I fancy Victorian things. Those are two things. However, worrying about what she said– that's probably going a *little* too far, so maybe I shouldn't give this stuff much thought.

I pull into the lot and park. "Really... am I pushing things too far?" My eyes gradually rise to the rear-view mirror. A memory of a dream I had pops into my head; one where I'm wearing a Victorian dress, standing in a large main entrance of a castle, facing some big medieval-looking doors. The man I always dream of comes up behind me and hugs me, whispering something I don't understand–but I'm supposed to in the dream. Not far from him, stands a butler with folded arms. He's happy to see us close like this. Everything is Victorian styled–everything.

Ivy, wake up. I blink twice as I come back to reality. My gaze drops to the dark red lipstick in the empty space below the stereo. This is crazy.

I take it and put some on. Calmly, I walk inside Lounge 'n Sip and look around at the few people in here. Business will pick up soon. I check the table I saw that guy at. It's empty. "Of course," I mumble under my breath. I'm relieved, yet maybe… a little upset. I move to the counter to order a mocha latte, and that's it. I've decided I'm not really hungry after all. I'm just determined to get that boat!

With my drink in hand, I go back out the door. As I step over the threshold, I glance to my right and see a neatly dressed man with a jet-black trilby hat slowly lift his head up to look at me. In that moment, I recognize him as the one I saw at that table yesterday. He smirks at me as he did before. I jump with a gasp, spilling my coffee a little bit, then somebody walks in front of me. I swerve around them to look at him again. He has the same outfit– but a different face. It's an old man with a close white beard. I blink repeatedly at him. He forms a bemused expression and raises a hand. I quickly shift my head away and go to my car. That doesn't make any sense! I drop my keys in the middle of trying to unlock my door, "Fudge." My shivering is most likely the cause of that. I see a man's arm come close to my legs. As I step away and turn, I hear, "Excuse me." I dart my eyes over to the person. It's the old man. He's holding my keys. I look up from them to his face as my eyebrows curve inwardly.

"Are you alright miss?" He asks. I give him the deer in the headlights look, but then I nod and lower my eyes to the ground, "Yes, I'm okay. I just…" slightly, I look back up to him. He smiles at me warmly and pats my shoulder, laughing kindly, "Maybe you woke up too early. Here," he hands me my keys, "you'll be alright. Have a good day and enjoy your coffee." He winks at me as he tips his hat and walks away. Well, a perfect gentleman, he is…

After I watch him go inside the coffee shop, I squeeze the keys in my hand and get inside my car. I shake my head, "Infatuation… This is nuts." I'm thinking so much about that guy, I hallucinated. I shove the keys into the ignition, back straight out of the parking space and leave.

Now at Eric's house, I shut my car door carefully as I scan his yard. I know he and Nancy go on vacation around this time of year to spend about a month with their grandkids down south. They come back the day after Halloween usually. I'd hate to do this... I'll leave a note explaining that I stopped by just in case. The good thing is he doesn't mind me borrowing his boat and truck. He's told me where the spare keys are and that I can use the boat whenever I want–as long as I return it the way I found it.

Their house is an average one with the single car garage on the right. The front yard is small and the backyard is medium-sized. None of it is fenced in. I clear my throat and walk toward the house. Everything's quiet. There are no cars in the driveway, and they never park in the garage, so I guess they aren't here. The doors are locked and the drapes are shut. Yeah, they've gone on vacation.

I go back to my car and drive around the garage to the backyard. The keys are in a decorative plastic rock by a flowerpot on the porch. As I go for the keys, I see the truck and boat are still hooked together from the last time he used them. Good for me! They are covered in leaves, so it's been a little while. I start the truck and check the lights. Good to go. I grab my journal and lock my car. If I do this right, he'll never know I used them. Before I 'venture to the island' though, I need a snack or two. A little grocery shopping is in order!

Chapter 6

Now that I'm walking down the chips aisle, I keep wondering to myself if it's ok that I parked in two parking spaces. Oh well... if anyone has a problem with it, they can kiss my ass! I smirk at the thought. Just when I stop at the potato chips, my cell phone rings. On the screen it says 'Mom'.

"Yeah?"

"Hey Ivy, how're you?"

"Hey mom. I'm fine... just shopping for chips. What about you?"

I laugh a little.

"You can't live on chips girl!"

"I'm ok."

It sounds like she's smiling.

I snicker as I snatch the ones I want and turn around to leave, "So what's up?"

"I'm just callin' to let you know your great aunt from Georgia will be at your birthday party this year. She's coming to our house, of course you know."

"Oh... she's gonna stuff us all with lots of food... like she always does."

"Yep! Alright Ivy, I'm just letting you know who to expect."

"Ok, thanks. I gotta go now, talk to you later."

"Love you!"

"Love you too mom."

I get back to Eric's truck and get in. As I look in the mirror at the boat, I think about the trip I'm going to make. Yeah, it really wouldn't be wise to go alone. Someone needs to come with me. I need to go there. The urge to visit it is so strong. I've never wanted to go somewhere so badly before. True, I've always had the desire to see new things, new places, but this–it's an obsession.

Who will come with me...? Let's see who's on my call list.

There are at least five I think I can trust, but they're all talkers and nosy; busy bodies pretty much. I hardly speak to them. "Tch… why do I even have them in my contacts list?" I scroll some more until I end up on Gina. Why didn't I think of her first? I bet she would love to go.

Before I do anything, I look at the clock at the top of the screen. It's 10:52am. Still a little early. "Hope she gets this soon." I text her: 'Gina, it's Ivy. Call me when you can please.' I set the phone down on the dash. It sucks that I have to wait. And stupid me, I didn't plan things out before I got this boat.

My phone goes off. "Hello?"
"Hey Ivy, what up girl?"

"Hey. You on a break?"
"Well, I'm actually home right now. I came in and they said I had a day off. Hah, imagine that! It was a bit of a mix up."

I smirk slightly. Wow, this must be my lucky day!-Sorta.

"Well uh…wanna meet up?" I ask.
"Sure! I'm not doing anything at the moment."

"Okay, cool." I almost say something else but she cuts me off.
"Yeah! How about we meet at Lounge n' Sip?"

Ok, that's just- I just don't feel right about going there! Why! I shake my head in disapproval, "No, the last time I went there, the coffee and food made me real sick. How about we meet at the local diner or something?"
"It did? Oh my gosh! That's terrible!"
"No, it's ok!" I instantly assure; how she says that is a little weird to me.

"Ivy…" she sighs, "I have to run by there anyway to drop something off for my brother. He works there. I'm really sorry you got sick. I have a strange phobia you see, and whenever I hear of some restaurant or something like that making someone sick, I have the feeling it will do the same to me."

That's really weird… but, ok.
"Yeah, I'm fine."

"...When do you wanna meet?"

I look at my phone, "Considering I'm about 10 minutes away from there–how's 15 minutes sound? You're about that far from there anyway, right?"

"Yeah. Sounds great!"

"Kay, cool."

"Alright, see you then!"

...Oh boy.

As I stand outside of Lounge 'n' Sip, repeatedly looking at how I parked the truck and boat in the middle of the parking lot. I hope nobody hits it. "I'm so gonna get chewed out for that." I look over at the door to the shop. People are going in and out of there. Just pulling into the lot, I got that overwhelming feeling of those eyes of his on me again. I really don't understand what is unsettling me so much. There's no telling until I walk through that door if he's there or not. I'm watching every man I see closely. *Even the ones with females*. Those ladies by the way give me nasty looks for 'ogling' at their men. I can't believe them. I wasn't staring at their guys in that way at all! Geez–most of them are the ugliest things you could ever lay your eyes on. I sarcastically say, "Surre..."

Suddenly, I hear, "Ivy!" I glance over. Gina's walking toward me, smiling wide but also looking at the truck oddly. I gotta be quiet about that. I dip my head and meet up with her. We hug and she says, "Isn't that Eric's truck and boat?"

"Yeah," I say, "we can talk about that inside. It's cold out here." "Right. Okay, come on, let's go get some coffee. I'll make some for you." she winks at me, "I won't make you sick, I promise." I try to smile at her, but it's not really possible at this point.

We go inside, and what do I do? I look at that stupid table. Oh my gosh–I see him. There he is, writing in that old book, obviously stuck in his own world again; nothing's distracting him. This time, he's wearing a regular long-sleeved navy-blue shirt, which accents his muscles… perfectly. He's wearing black jeans and formal shoes. He looks very pale in this lighting. His hair's the same. What is it about him that makes me feel this way? I'm extremely attracted to him but something doesn't seem right at all about him.

"What?" Gina looks at me. I give her a side-glance, "That guy over there–I've seen him before. He just intimidates me real bad and I'm trying to avoid him." I slightly look over at him again. Is this really intimidation? She does the same as me. He flips a page like he's bored and his enticing eyes shoot up at us for a split second, then he looks back down at the book. He seems annoyed.

I slowly bite my lip. What is he writing? Is that a journal? Gina scoffs a little in disgust and says, "He's the one I told you about at work. I talked to him and he was very short and couldn't wait for me to leave. Asshole." "Oh...really?" Yeah, I don't know what she just said to me. He's so calm, so smug, so... His eyes flash up at me. I lose my breath as my heart skips a beat. It feels like he's drilling that captivating gaze into my soul. I… don't think I can look away. Everything around me has all of a sudden disappeared and he has put me on the spot just by staring at me. How I'm feeling and thinking makes me feel 15 all over again.

I then hear Gina quietly ask me, "He really does get to you, doesn't he?" She's amused.
I sigh almost exasperatedly, "Yeah… yeah, he sure does."

She scoffs and chuckles, "Come on," She guides me into the empty restroom, then she starts talking.

"Do you know him?"
I shake my head, "No."

She raises an eyebrow. I think she had advice for me, but when I said that… she became speechless. "What…?" I ask. Seeming curious and confounded, she murmurs, "…You said you're avoiding him." she starts pacing the room, then stops and throws her hands up, "Well, I don't know what to tell you. I was going to give you some advice, but… I don't know why you'd be intimidated so harshly by someone you've never met. It looks like it's affecting you pretty badly girl." I put my hands together. I'd explain what happened to me earlier, but I don't want her to think I'm crazy.

I just shrug at her.

"Well," she smooths back her ponytail, "how about we forget him and I buy you some coffee?" "Um actually-" I quickly say while raising my hand a little, "Can I ask you something?" "Sure, what is it?"

I stiffen as I get ready to ask her about coming with me to that island. Noticing my change in behavior, she slowly leans against the sink counter. Her features are becoming more interested.

"Ok." I say, "Right off the nearest coast of the Sound, there's an island filled with many trees and a castle-like building is on it. Have you ever seen it?"

She makes a thoughtful expression, "Hmm," she rubs her chin, "Yeah... Yeah I think I have." she nods. I nod back, "That's why I have Eric's boat-" She quickly leans forward, "You're going out to this island alone?"

I sigh, "No... I don't want to go alone. I don't have anyone to come with me. Will you–if you aren't too busy...?"

She smiles at me, folding her arms, "Well... I don't really see why not. I mean, I'm not working today or tomorrow. I think you forgot I'm very adventurous–I told you I am, didn't I? But, how long will this be for, and when do you wanna go?" Whoa, she's so quick to accept!

I grab her hands, "Thank you!" I snatch her into a hug. She starts patting my back while laughing uncomfortably, "Um, Ivy? Are you okay?" I open my eyes and move away, "Oh!" I tug on the sides of my sweater to readjust it, "Yeah, sorry. It won't be for long. I just want to do this before tomorrow." To be honest, I'm really not looking forward to my birthday tomorrow, because my family likes to get together and celebrate it like it's a huge holiday; there's a lot involved. I'm their only child, yeah–but I don't need all that. I also don't want to wait a whole week before I can go to that island.

"Ivy, how much time do you think is in one day? How could you pull this off? How far is it anyway?" She's amazed.

I frown slightly, "...Not far. It won't take long."
"But you want to do some exploring, right? And what about getting through those trees?" I inhale deeply. Maybe it's too unrealistic for someone to go there. I might just have to go alone anyway. "Yeah..." I grimace to myself and walk over to the door, "No no, it's ok. You have more responsibilities than me anyway. It was wrong of me to do that." It really was. Selfish too.

I open the door and go into the shop. I don't see that man at the table anymore. If I had the chance, I might've gone up and asked him what his deal is–but that opportunity is gone.
"Ivy..."

I turn around to her. She puts her hand on my right shoulder and nods, "I'll go with you. I never said no. And I need an exciting adventure to be able to look back on one day. I'm ready when you are. When do you wanna go?" A smile tugs at the corners of my lips.

"...After the coffee should be fine." I say.

Just when I was feeling down and out, she managed to brighten my day yet again. Thank you Gina, the wonderful nurse I 'threatened' this morning.

She also smiles, "Alright then."

Chapter 7

While dropping her car off at her beautiful white two-story house, she comes out with two bags; one filled with snacks and the other has a few sodas and teas in it. I didn't think we would need that much… Apparently, she did. After fighting the lunch hour traffic, we finally launch the boat.

Gina is patiently waiting in it while I park the truck and does a pretty good job at keeping it close to the dock so I can get in. "That wasn't too hard!"

I chuckle at her, "So far so good! All is in check." She nods and moves away from the wheel.
I take it and start driving us off.

She looks up at the sky. I do the same and see it's getting pretty cloudy out. More rain? The weather guy said it should hold off for hours… It's already cold out.
"Better hurry up with this." She mutters.
"Yeah." I agree.

So here we go… We have our snacks bagged, we're determined and mostly fearless, and we have our phones charged and ready to take plenty of pictures. I'm not telling mom and dad a thing about this. No one but Gina knows what's up. Oh, and I brought along Eric's tire iron–and my journal. We're well-prepared indeed!

"Why did you bring a tire iron anyway? Are you expecting trouble?" she asks me. I smirk, "Well, it was convenient and I would rather have it and not need it than the other way around. I didn't bring anything else because I was in such a big hurry to do everything at once. That's a bad habit of mine. I've had it for as long as I can remember."

She warily smiles at me, "That could really put you in a bad position, you know."
"Yeah I know." I mumble, then look away from her to the island ahead of us. It won't be long now; I'd give it about 5-10 more

minutes and then we'll be there.

"So what's making you want to do this?" She asks. I start to turn my head but pause midway. Do I tell her it's because I have a serious obsession over castles and stuff like that or do I make something up? Would she judge me as a closet-Goth and tell others about it? She strikes me as a person who wouldn't want to be associated with a Goth. The last thing is what worries me the most. I care too much about what other people think of me–that's the truth. I don't want to be somebody I'm not.

I look at her. "Well, I'm like you–I'm adventurous and I want to experience something new." I smile innocently. There: the truth–In a way.

She nods slowly at me, "Ohh... ok... Well-" Before she can finish talking, raindrops start to pepper us. She makes a troubled face and looks up. As do I.
"Oh man..." I muse. This is not-

Just like that, the rain starts pouring down on us like crazy. –Good–This is not good!

There are a few loud crashes of thunder and lightning. Definitely not good for us! CRAP!

"Aww, c'mon!" I whine, trying to speed the boat up. I wish it'd work, but sadly enough, I can't manipulate things with my mind. "I knew this was a bad day to do this!" Gina complains. I see a sandy place with a big 'no trespassing' sign where we can land, so I move in closer and pull the motor up.

As the boat slides up onto the sand, I jump off the bow with a rope and run to the nearest tree to tie off the boat. I tell Gina to throw the lunch hook off the stern to keep the boat in place while we explore. The rain is coming down steadily now. Gina grabs the bags and other effects, throws them to me on the shore, then lowers herself from the boat and wades in the water to me. She looks a little pissed as I pick up the bags.

"We can't go back right now, and do you see that sign Ivy?" I look at it. Yes, it certainly is a big sign.

"Well that's just for people passing by at a distance." I quip. She looks past me through the leafless trees and points, "We need to go that way. I can see the building towers from here." Great. We really have to keep our eyes peeled; the only way we know where we're going is by looking up at those towers. "Keep your voice down!" I quickly warn her. She nods at me.

Soon, she points to the north-left, "Look! A stone trail!" We run that way and follow it. Now that we're doing that, our way to the building is becoming clearer; the trees are arched over our path like someone has been keeping the branches trimmed. It's nice but we don't have much time to admire it. It doesn't make sense to me that everything around us now looks so neat. Perhaps someone works or lives here...?
Interesting...

We stop as soon as we're out of the trees, right in front of this- "Oh... my... god." I breathe, also shivering from the cold rain. It's a beautiful Gothic castle! Three stories high, majestic, nicely manicured from top to bottom, has a large fountain in the center of a white brick roundabout with a woman holding a pot full of spilling water, and there's a big overhead with a black lantern hanging from the ceiling. My god–it's *magical*...

I don't care that it's raining anymore or about how chilled I am. I could stand here all day! I'm not usually this emotional, but I have to confess that I have tears welling up in my eyes to seeing such beauty! I never thought I'd be able to stand in front of such a magnificent structure!

"IVY!" I hear Gina cry.
I refocus my attention to see where she is.

She's under the overhead, trembling, soaking wet, holding the bags impatiently. I check my hands and see the tire iron in the right one. I look back up to her and hurry over.

When I approach her, I wipe my face and try to catch my breath, "Hey, sorry!" I turn my gaze up to the ceiling, then back down to the big dark-brown doors with black iron holding the wood together (they're medieval-styled doors). There's a strange hybrid beast holding the doorknocker in its mouth, I think. I give it a good examination to figure it out, but I can't.

"What were you doing out there?" she scolds.
Quickly, my eyes meet hers again, "I'm sorry! I don't know what came over me!" She huffs and shakes off some of the rainwater, "Well, we have to get inside somehow. This is not good for our health to be out here like this." She reaches for the doorknocker and suddenly, we hear one of the doors' handles being jiggled. She quickly withdraws her hand and we take two steps back.
The left door opens. Right away we feel a gust of slightly cool air. I shiver.

There, peering through the opening is a tall, thin, older man with salt-and-pepper hair. We can only see his face. He looks at us with a sort of dismissive curiosity.
Holy shit...

"I don't believe we are expecting any guests today." He says in a sinister low voice.
Oh my... that's creepy.

He's looking down his nose at us, also noticing the tire iron I have. His expression is authoritative and very intimidating.

"Um, well, uh," I stumble over my words. What a fool I'm being! Gosh this is so embarrassing! He raises an eyebrow.

"Well..." Gina starts saying, "The weather got bad and we had no choice but to land-" He cuts her off by asking me, "What is that for?" He's talking about the tire iron.

"Defense... against animals." I carefully answer.
He stares at us for what seems a long time, then he steps aside and waves his hand toward the dimly lit interior, "Well then... that is, I suppose... a good reason. It seems you both are in some difficulty and require something to dry off with. You may come inside if you'd like." his eyes move past our shoulders, gesturing that he's speaking of the rain. I drag my own eyes away from his face and peer inside. It's dark but I can still see everything. There's a large

white marble set of stairs straight ahead through the foyer. To seeing it, I get a little red flag in the back of my mind but I ignore it. It seems most of the stuff I'm able to see in there is illuminated by firelight.

I give the man a strange yet emotionless look, "Alright." But don't try anything with us, I feel like adding.

I motion the unsure Gina to follow me in. "Ah, ahh," he stops me. I look at him. He asks for the tire iron and bags. I slightly turn my head to the right as I try to understand his intentions better. I'm not so keen on giving this tool up.

Sighing frustratedly, Gina gives him the bags and tells me, "Ivy, hand it over. Just do it." I don't look at her; my eyes are locked on his. But, I soon do it…
I give in and let him take it from me.

He smiles–Very, very faintly and bows his head; "Carry on then." Though I am suspicious of him, I calmly proceed through the foyer into the main room, gesturing Gina along. Just like me, she makes a face at him as she trails behind me. I think we've seen far too many movies…
He arches an eyebrow again while watching us, then he slowly follows us.

I stop walking and look all around me. The things I look at first is the ceiling, which is very high up, the huge white marble staircase that splits in two at the top and has grayish, gold trimmed statues of women at the bottom on each stair post, holding things, the giant rooms with arched doorways on both sides, the floor that's–like I said–white marble and actually has hints of blue and yellow in its large tiles, the dark red walls that have really beautiful large paintings on them, and last but not least, I see the GIANT fireplace glowing, where the biggest painting in all of the room is; it's of an old dark-haired aristocratic man posing authoritatively–like the famous George Washington's portrait. He's posing just like Washington! At the fireplace, there are 3 elegant Victorian styled sofas. They're red fabric with crafted golden metal trim along the edges. There's a loveseat at both sides and a long couch directly in front of the fireplace. I must mention that there are old-fashioned lights on the walls. This place–it feels shockingly, creepily, and amazingly familiar to me. I don't want to find out why; I might scare myself!

I'm not sure where I am, but I was right to want to come here!-I think. This castle is just...WOW!

As I'm standing off alone, lost in awe, the wary and astonished Gina asks the strange man, "Is this your castle?"

After putting our items down on a big empty table in the closest corner to the doors, he says, "No madam... Dmitri Vladoiu II is the master of this castle."
Master?

I abruptly stop right in the middle of enjoying the views and turn to him. The 'master' of this castle? What is this–1800 something?-Or even before that for that matter...
So, it isn't just one person that lives here, but surely there are many employees...

"Master of the house, eh?" I ask with a small scoff.
"Indeed miss." he moves past me. "I shall fetch a few towels for you two. Please wait here; I will return shortly." He goes into the large room on the right, leaving us alone. I look at Gina, who then uneasily shrugs at me and wanders over to stand by the fireplace. I nod and join her.

For a minute, we stay quiet. There are only the sounds of the crackling fire. It's quite echoic and awkward in here–pretty wild. Soon though, Gina looks at me with a disbelieving shake of the head. "Wow... you sure know how to pick them. I didn't think places like this existed in the United States." she spreads her arms out, "This is incredible... I would've never thought of coming here! Fear would've driven me away from the idea." My unmoving eyes remain on her. Again I almost tell her that ambition and obsession made me do it. I wanted to do something different this weekend. I found that 'something' and wanted to explore it before my birthday.

I lower my head, "Well, that's what makes me so different from anyone you've ever met–I suppose. When I see an opportunity to do something out of the ordinary that seems really cool, I go for it– I take that opportunity. Isn't that what most people should do?" "I...guess so." she says, "Yeah, that does make sense. I wouldn't have become a nurse if I didn't want that job badly enough." I smile at her, "Precisely."

She asks, "...Hey Ivy? What time do you think it is?" she quickly grabs her phone from her back pocket to check it, "Great. Dead battery. Never mind." she puts it away.
"Hold on," I look at my own, "Mine's dead too... That's odd... I had a full charge before we left the boat dock."

"Ladies," We hear. We look back and see the butler coming back into the room with white towels draped over his arm. Gina takes hers with a shy gratifying smile and I do the same. He straightens his posture and clears his throat, "The rain is very heavy... Perhaps you would like to wait here until it dies down a bit?" I slowly move the towel away from my face–By the way, it smells like lilac. Very nice.

"That would be a good idea...but," I glance at Gina. Well, apparently she's okay with this–The face she's making says so. "That would be most preferred." she agrees.

I look at him again. He's just standing there, lips pressed in a thin line. He's kind of
emotionless. Really creepy, I must say.

"Okay...I guess we'll stay for a bit. So...what's your name?" I ask.
"Walter." He says through his teeth.

"Well... nice to meet you...Walter. I'm Gina Lewis and she's-"
"Ivy Summers." I quickly say. I don't like our names being revealed but they have to be.

He bows, "Likewise. It's a pleasure to make your

acquaintances. I apologize that I've not asked before... Would you both like something to drink?"

After being out in the rain in the Sound? Ohh-kay...

"Water..." I uncomfortably chuckle.

"Yes please–water." Gina says.

"Alright then." he cracks a quick smile, which looks sort of like a type of grimace. "Make yourselves comfortable. I will return in a moment." he bows again and walks away.

Gina looks at me and whispers, "I think we should get out of here. Something's not right. This is just too easy."

I whisper back, "I know, but not yet. It wouldn't be wise to leave now anyway. The weather is bad."

She doesn't understand why I say that, but she'll get it pretty soon, most likely.

Chapter 8

A woman dressed like a maid enters the room carrying a silver tray with two fancy empty glasses and a pitcher of water on it. She is about 30 years old, wearing that classic black and white uniform that you'd see in the movies. And her brown hair is pulled back into a bun. She barely looks at either of us as she puts the tray down on a small table near us. She steps back from the table and almost comes to attention. She stands motionless and says nothing. Her eyes give the impression she has quite a mean streak. Gina thinks her clothes are interesting while I'm trying to understand why she is behaving like this. Walter returns and walks to the tray. He carefully pours the water into the glasses and hands us our drinks. "Is there anything else you would like?" he asks.

"Thanks…but no sir." Gina whispers once taking her water from him. He turns to the maid and says, "That will be all." She bows her head slightly and quickly leaves the room. Gina and I look at each other like 'Wow!'

Walter clears his throat to get our attention.
I redirect my eyes to him as I sip, and say, "So is Mr. Vladoiu out of town or something?"
He nods at me, "Yes–for a short while."

Gina then asks, "So what does he do?" For a long few seconds, he stares at me in a most unnerving way–like he's reading me or something, but then he turns to Gina and seems to regain that sort of professional but friendly attitude he had before. "He owns a heavy machinery corporation." My eyes grow. I know I should've expected something fantastic like that but it still shocks me. Gina is making the same face as me.

"Oh," she is quieter all of a sudden. A little shy smile graces her lips.
Walter turns his attention to the rain-soaked windows, "It seems the weather has gotten worse. It would be dangerous to cross the

sound under the current circumstances and I don't imagine it will be getting better any time soon. Mr. Vladoiu's executive assistant, Mr. Francis, has asked me to suggest you consider staying the night."

I glance at Gina in an almost expectant way.
She does the same to me.

...So I'm left to answer.
Ohh, I don't like this idea! I look at a window.
It's raining cats and dogs. We don't have a choice.
Damn it.

"Okay, that sounds alright." I agree.
Gosh, I could just hear my mom right now.

"Our phones..." Gina says, "They don't have any life left in them; do you by any chance have a way we can-"   "I'm afraid the lines are down at the moment. I'm sorry."
She blinks at him, "Because of the weather?"

"Indeed." He says.
"Damn..." I mutter to myself. This feels bad.

He then walks to a telephone on a nearby desk and picks up the receiver. I see him push 2 buttons, wait about 2 seconds, then he starts talking. I can't understand what he is saying. After a couple more seconds, he hangs up and looks toward the door on his left. Gina looks at me and starts asking Walter about the phone. "You said the phone was out." Walter smiles at her and says, "This castle is equipped with internal telephone communications madam. I assure you the lines to the mainland are down." The maid returns to the room and stands still. Walter bows his head and gestures Gina to look at the maid, "Maria will show you to your guestroom and I will show you to yours Miss Ivy. She will also provide each of you a robe while your clothes are laundered and pressed." Oh...! Well...that's quite nice! Wow!

Gina and I give each other the 'are you okay with that?' look again. She nods at me and starts walking away with Maria.

"Wait," I say to Walter, "What about our stuff? And what floor will this be on?" Gina and Maria stop and peer over their shoulders at us.

"Of course. Your belongings will be taken to your rooms momentarily. The guestrooms are on the second floor madam." He says.

I nod carefully, "Ok then." Second floor sounds easy enough. My eyes slide away from him to Gina who seems to get what I'm thinking. Her gaze says 'stay safe–I'll see you soon'. I purse my lips at her in a likewise manner. Maria leads her up the left staircase and I look at Walter again. He motions me to follow him, so I do–carefully.

We go up the right side. I continuously peek back for Gina but she has already disappeared, which I find a bit odd. I don't give it much thought though.

The hall is long and narrow, with blood-red trimmings, has many oil paintings of people and old-fashioned lamps on the walls. This place feels eerier now. The atmosphere is also becoming strange in way I can hardly explain. The best I can do is to say the air is getting heavier. And even that sounds crazy.

"Alright Miss Ivy…" he stops at a door and gently opens it, "Here you are; the Windsor room." I look in. Whoa! There's an old dark brown canopy bed with white drapes and a burgundy comforter–How heavenly! The room has a very beautiful 19th century English twist with many different antiques and an amazing dark brown grandfather clock. The nightstands, table lamps, dressers and doors have a dark yet exquisite look. I really love that. The two windows at the right side of the bed are tall, pointy at the top and dressed with burgundy curtains. Mr. Vladoiu sure has taste!

"Windsor room…like Windsor castle?" I quietly ask–almost like musing it. "Yes indeed." he says, "Each guestroom represents a castle Mr. Vladoiu has visited." Oh my!

Well if that's the case, what kind of room does Gina have? I'm sure it's amazing. "That's absolutely beautiful and clever." I look at him with a smile. He is amused by that, and he says, "Yes, yes it is." He looks back in the room shortly after that, "Maria and another maid, Christine, will come with your belongings and your robe momentarily."

I nod an okay, but also ask, "What room does Gina have?"
"The Mont-Saint Michel room; fashioned after the castle in Normandy, France." He says while stepping into the hall.

I smile again, "Wow..."
He dips his head, "Now, if you'll excuse me."

"Of course," I agree, and as he starts walking away, I slowly shut the door.
With a sigh, I rub my arms and wander over to the window. For a worrywart, I think I'm doing pretty well so far. I wonder what Gina is doing right now, or my family for that matter. I hope they aren't fretting over me too much–or at all.

I slowly bring my eyes up from the wavering trees to the darkened sky, watching the rain. Then the heavy feeling from the hall returns, as if something is slipping through the seams of the door. This makes me turn to look. But nothing's there. I raise an eyebrow as I scan everywhere around me. It feels like there are many people in the room with me, watching me, staring at me, planning to do something...possibly bad. Because of that, my stomach is starting to twist. I back up slowly to the window. Suddenly, I jump to hearing someone knocking on the door. I put a hand on my forehead, "Yes?" Wow...that was intense.

"Miss Ivy?" It's a woman's voice. It could be Maria. I go and quickly open the door. I see her and another maid–Christine, I assume–with my stuff and a very soft-looking red robe. I can't wait to wear it.

I step aside, letting them in.
"Hello, I'm Christine. I'll just set this robe on the bed here if that's alright."
Maria puts my bags on a table. I'm a little shy and tell Christine, "Yes, that's just fine, thank you."

"I will return for your clothes in a bit." Maria says. Man, even her voice has a little attitude about it–or maybe I'm just quick to judge her. She adds, "If you need anything, you can use the phone over there on the nightstand to speak with the maids' quarters. Just push 11."

"Oh…ok…thanks." I say. She and Christine nod and leave the room.

I walk over to the bed and start removing my clothes. "God, I didn't realize they would stick this bad!" Taking my shoes off nearly knocks me off my feet. I don't want to sit on the bed; it'll mess it up.

I glance over at a door, thinking it must be the bathroom. I wonder what it looks like in there… I need to wash off but I'm shy about the idea of using someone else's shower/tub. I can't exactly make myself comfortable–even if I tried. Plus, I don't know when Maria will be back.

Well, regardless of how I feel, I need to do something about this nasty clamminess, so I walk up to the door. Before I touch the knob, I jerk away and look around. A couple strands of my hair were just tugged on! There aren't any cobwebs. It doesn't really make sense to me that there would be…

It was something else. It had to have been. What was it? Rubbing the back of my head slowly, I stop searching the room and proceed to open the door. My eyes grow in awe.

The walls are light yellow with white royal-looking trim, the stone floor is a grayish yellow, there are a few tables and chairs spread around and there's a beautiful tub in the center of the floor. The two windows to my left are fairly small with no curtains, but instead are stained glass, and of course, they're European-styled. Wow… How I would love to take a bath in that… But I can't, sadly… Maybe in the morning?

There's suddenly a knocking on the door and someone calling my name. I turn and quickly go out to answer it, snatching my clothes along the way. "Just a second please." I open it in a hurry.

Maria takes a step back in surprise.

"Sorry..." I lightly chuckle.

She looks down at my clothes and reaches for them, "It's alright." As I hand them to her, I say, "I'm kinda clammy..."

"You can take a bath." She nods at me.

"Oh..." Thank goodness!

"Your dinner will be brought at 6, and by then, your clothes will be finished." Whoa, dinner in here rather than in a dining room or something? "Not in a dining room?" I ask.

"Well," she slightly smirks, "we wouldn't want our guests roaming the castle..."

Oh, I see. "Right... Okay."

I then ask, "Can you tell me where Gina is?"

"She's down the other hall." She starts going for the door, "Enjoy your bath." Before I can ask which room Gina's in, she goes out. That's weird...

Slightly puzzled, I go to take my bath and run the water hot. Once I settle in the tub, I rest my head back and let out a long relaxed sigh; the uncomfortable feeling of using another's bathroom isn't bothering me at the moment. However, speaking of 'uncomfortable', I slowly open my eyes and scan the room. Something might happen while I'm in here; this place has an unnerving vibe to it. I stop lounging and hurry up with my bath a little. With these supernatural occurrences on my mind, I don't want to give anything any chances.

When I come out in my robe, I look around the room for a television or radio. "Nothing, hmmm..." Well, maybe they don't get a lot of guests and that's why? I go pick through my stuff and take out my phone and journal. It's unfortunate that my battery is dead, but at least I have my book. I begin flipping through it as I walk to the bed. I soon realize that I've only made a few entries about that man I have dreamt of for years. Why is this? I am so much in love with this figment of my imagination yet I haven't written anything about him? That doesn't seem like me. It's like I just started dreaming about him, but I know that's not true! Or maybe…maybe I have either been too embarrassed or shy to put it down on paper. My dreams can get graphic sometimes…

I blush, slowly smiling to the thought. Lifting my head, I put one hand on the part I was about to read and stare off into space as I look back on a certain dream I had of this guy. I remember us laying together in a meadow under the midnight sky, holding each other, watching how the stars glistened like diamonds. There wasn't anything else there–it was just us. It was one of those dreams that you would be so sure, it would last for eternity. I wanted it to; therefore I thought it would. Waking up is always the most dreadful part.

"One of those innocent dreams." I close the journal and lie down on the bed. The covers are so comfy! Comfy like clouds. If I were at home, I would fall asleep immediately. This place though… I search the room once more, still trying to shake off the feeling of the unseen studying me. "No. It's got to be my imagination." I sigh, then look over at the nightstand on my right, near the windows. There's an old-fashioned clock there, showing it's 4:30 now. I took longer in the bathroom than I thought.

Well, I have a little while before dinner. I wish I could go see Gina. I can't though; I'm wearing this robe and I'm in someone else's home. What if Walter saw me walking down the hall in just a robe? I shudder to the thought. Well, there's no television in here. All I have is my journal and a lot of things to admire. "Ahh, that must be why there are so many antiques in here…" It's so the guests don't get too bored! I laugh lightly.

For the first 30 minutes to an hour, I examine the pictures, lamps, chairs, tables, the amount of detail in the walls and their panels–just about everything. Then after that, I look through my journal for a while. Most of the memories held in it make me laugh. I was so silly when I was in my early teens; so emotionally driven. Once I started working at the hospital, my way of thinking drastically changed. I got serious. But some of the goofiness has never left me, I will admit that.

I hear a couple knocks on the door. I put the book down and go answer it. Maria is standing there with a cart that has a plate with a metal top on it, and I tell you, something on it smells absolutely delicious! It smells like lobster.

She comes inside, I follow her, and she removes the top. I'm hit with a blast of warm, great-smelling steam, which makes my stomach rumble. It was already doing that before but now I'm *really* hungry. I see lobster, corn and mashed potatoes all surrounded by lettuce in that fancy way high-dollar restaurants do.

"Compliments of Mr. Francis." She says.
I look up at her, "Wonderful…! Thank you!" I smile wide. She nods and puts the plate on a table. I watch the door shut. Then I turn and quickly go sit at the table.

"I'm really wondering who this Mr. Francis is now…" I say aloud. This night is going to be a long, quite possibly sleepless one. But I'll try to sleep through the creepy feelings this place gives off.

I begin my meal and wonder what Gina is eating.
"Oh, this is heaven!" Such scrumptious delight this lobster has! I can't wait to try the potatoes and corn! YUM!

Damn Mr. Francis has awesome taste!!!

-Nicolai-

"Walter, tell me… which rooms are they in?-The girls that had just arrived." I ask, setting a cup of tea down on my office desk.

Putting his hands together behind his back as he stands in front of the door, he says, "Miss Summers is in the Windsor room and Miss Lewis is in the Mont St. Michel room."

"Hmm…" I lower my head and stare into my drink, the memory of when I stood in the darkness of the southwest tower, watching them journey to the island flashes in my mind. I left the tower for my office, called Walter in and told him to invite them inside. He questioned me on that and Rozalia slightly snapped at him. "Ivy is important to me!" And suddenly, I knew her name. Rozalia knows the unknowable and reveals things to me quite unexpectedly.

"Ivy… sir?" he asked. I sighed and covered my face with a hand, "Excuse me… Yes–the strawberry blonde woman." After that, he became even more curious but left without saying another word. Rozalia made my special sight stray from the office to the main entrance to observe everything between him and those girls. I almost scolded Rozalia. However, once I saw 'Ivy' again, I too was distracted by her being here. I had nothing to say in that instant.

"Sir?" Walter says, bringing me back to reality.
I flick my eyes up to him, raising a brow in question.

"Are you alright?" He asks. I blink, then form a smile and nod, "Yes yes, I'm quite alright." He becomes more puzzled. First he's silent, but eventually the great curiosity overcomes him. "I've noticed…" he says, "You behave as if you know Miss Ivy quite well." He slightly smiles in a teasing manner.

I start to grit my teeth a little.
"Ohh, this is uncomfortable. We cannot have him noticing this interest in her."
My smile ***almost*** vanishes.

Despite Rozalia's attitude on this, I say to him in a friendly tone, "Only in passing when I visited the mainland…"

"Ahh," He says, yet wonder still remains in his eyes. He doesn't comment any more than that though. I tilt my head, glancing at the clock on my desk, "Do they have cell phones with them?"

"Yes sir…"

I look up at him, "Are they dead?"

"Yes, they are." As expected.

I nod slowly, "Ah…" This is good–no photo snapping or phone calls. He studies my face almost intently.

"Will you bring me another cup of tea please?"

"Yes of course Sir." He walks out.

Once he shuts the door, time slows to a stop in the room. I grimace down at the desk and rub my forehead, "This is foolish."

"I have an agenda; one that will benefit both of us."

"You are vain. I know what you want and I will not provide it. She may be familiar to you but all you want is a drink."

"You are beating yourself over the head trying to understand, Dmitri. Just drink your tea." She makes me pick up the cup and stare into it like looking down a well.

I quickly put the cup down, "No control tonight!" She laughs and tries to pick it up again. I snatch that wrist and start cackling in her way. The door opens, and time returns to normal. I stop laughing when I look at Walter standing there, giving me a strange expression. I frown, removing my hand from the other, "You're back."

"Yes Sir." He walks up and places the cup on the desk, then he asks, "Excuse me sir, but I heard you shout and then I saw you-" I wave my hand at him, "I'm fine. It's nothing."

He steps back a little and shoots me a quizzical look, "Are you taking your medication?"

At that, I draw my brows down at him.

His own rise, as well as his hands, "Very well sir… I apologize."

I move my eyes over to the door, then back to him.

He nods at me and starts to leave, "Have a good night sir."

After he goes out, I hum to myself, "Mâine dimineață va fi interesant, fără îndoială."

I close my eyes.

*Mâine dimineață va fi interesant, fără îndoială.

Tomorrow morning will be interesting, no doubt.

Chapter 9

-Ivy-

I put my hand below my neck as I take in the beautiful view. But I somehow know I'm not alone. Slowly, I turn, then a smile graces my face. The man I love is walking toward me, wearing a dark-gray vest, black pants and a white shirt with the sleeves rolled up. His eyes are glistening. I notice he's holding something with a small chain.

He approaches me, "Ivy, my love."
I happily wrap my arms around his neck, looking from his lips to his eyes. He glances down at mine, then gestures me to turn around. I playfully do as told.

"Keep your eyes closed." He says. I giggle as I feel him gently put the warm chain around my neck. "Now," he grabs my hand, turns me back around and looks down at the necklace. I take it in my fingers to see the pendant, then I gasp. It's my favorite color; blue sapphire! He snickers and lifts my chin up with a finger, "How ravishing you look." His accent is so heavy. I love it. My lips part as I gaze into his eyes. He leans in and presses his lips to my neck, above the necklace. My heart skips a beat. As he embraces me, I grab and squeeze his shirt.

My eyes fly open as I feel my stomach leap and my heart about to jump out of my chest. I hear my door quickly shut along with faint male whispers in the hall. They sound aggravated. I don't remember seeing any other man besides Walter and that didn't sound like him. Automatically, I assume it's either a ghost, or perhaps…maybe it's Mr. Francis? Why in the world would that be though? It doesn't seem right at all. I blink oddly at the thought as I rub my neck and try to calm down. What is going on? I reach for the covers and see they're nearly about to fall off the end of the bed. "What the-?" I hope this weird stuff happening to me isn't some kind of supernatural stuff. Turning my head toward the windows, I see the sun is already up. The clock says it's 8am. It feels like I just went to sleep.

All through last night, I heard female whispers and banging in the walls and in the hall. I know they were in the walls; I put my ear to the one behind the bed. It sent shivers up and down my spine and made me go into a cold sweat. I felt so cornered and defenseless.

I called the maids' quarters twice in regards to the strange occurrences but both times one of the maids told me no one was up here except Gina and I, which completely threw me off. I know Gina wouldn't do anything like that. She'd have to be nuts first. So I accepted, and luckily by 4am, things started to calm down. They were at their worse between 2:30 and 3. I laid there curled up in a little ball with the blankets over my head. That's when I finally shut my eyes long enough to fall asleep.

There are a couple knocks on the door.
I pull the blankets up close and lie back down, "Yes?"

It opens and there's Christine, holding some towels and a washcloth.
"Sleep well?" She asks.

"Yeah…" **Not really. I'm tired and freaked out.**
"I brought you some fresh towels." She stands there watching me with a kind of passive concern for a few seconds, then gives me a nod and walks over to the bathroom, "I'll just put these in here for you."
"Thanks."

I sigh and look straight up at the bed canopy. That sure was a long night. If only I could just go back to sleep…

She comes back out and asks me, "Would you like some coffee?" I look at her. Boy that sounds great right about now.
"Yes please!"

She smiles, "I'll be back."
I glance at the window again and stare out at the trees. The weather is nice. It reminds me of what I just dreamt of. What a wonderful

dream that was…

"Hmm…" For a few minutes, I lay here like this, lost in my thoughts, then I get up and put my robe on. At the same time, I hear Christine come to the door again, but she's not alone. I think I hear Gina talking to her.

I go to the door and answer it after Christine's first knock. There I see Christine with a coffee cart and Gina is behind her, dressed and ready to go. I feel sloppy because I'm the only one who isn't dressed. I'm pretty happy to see her though–it's a real relief she's here.

Smiling a little, I step aside. As Christine leads her in, she says, "Good morning Ivy. Wow, what a room!" I suddenly lose the smile.

Yeah… what a room.

Christine pushes the cart over to the table near the window and then turns to us, "Enjoy your coffee. There are some croissants on the side." She goes out with a friendly smile. After watching her shut the door, Gina shoots me an ecstatic smile. I take a deep breath, trying to do the same…but I can't. She and I step up to the cart, take some croissants, then sit at the table and start drinking our coffee.

"Well, how was your night?" she asks.
"It was…" No, I don't want to tell the truth. She'll think I'm crazy.

"It was…?" She's looking at me expectantly. I keep my eyes on the table. What would I lose if I told her the truth though? Nothing–but maybe a friend. However, I think I'm forgetting she's a very outgoing, open-minded woman. I put my croissant down and meet her gaze, "It was interesting."

She leans back a little, slightly confused.
I say, "All last night, I heard a woman or a few women whispering and some banging in the walls and in the hall. To be sure of what I was experiencing, I put my ear to the one behind the bed. It scared the shit out of me; made me go into a cold sweat. I felt so cornered and defenseless. I called the maids' quarters twice about this

strange stuff happening but both times the maid in there told me no one was up here except you and I, which really unsettled me. I didn't want to seem childish. Instead, I just sat here, and luckily by 4am, everything calmed down. They were most active between 2:30 and 3. I laid here curled up in a little ball with the blankets over my head. Finally after a while, I shut my eyes long enough to fall asleep."

Now she's staring at me in a most bewildered way.
After a couple seconds, I suddenly smile, "You think I'm crazy don't you?"
Still, she stares at me.

"Yeah…" I look down at the napkins beside my coffee, "I expected that reaction."
"Um, no! I don't think you're crazy… It's just–I didn't experience any of that. I mean, I fell asleep right away and didn't hear a thing."

I search her face warily.
"What?" she says.

"I was right… The noises only happened around the Windsor room and nowhere else. I didn't want to think that at first but it–it's true." I sigh and take a sip of my coffee, which by the way is definitely nothing like Lounge n' sip's coffee…

"Well don't worry," she says, "we'll be getting out of here real soon. The weather is nice now." One side of my mouth slightly quirks up in a relieved, agreeing way. She finishes her croissant, hurries the last few sips of her coffee and stands up from her chair, "I'll be waiting in the grand room, alright?"
"Ok. I'll be there soon."

As she goes out the door, I look around the room cautiously. It feels like I'm still not alone. No, I'm not going to tolerate any more scary occurrences. This room has done enough for me. I finish my croissant, grab my clothes and decide to dress in the bathroom and also wash my face. I come out to see a woman walking across the room to the window. She has dark hair and is dressed like it's the 1940's. I gasp, eyes widening a little. She slowly looks at me and disappears. Oh hell! I blink quickly, then rush over to the window and look out. I see an older man down below with a shovel, wearing overalls and an old tattered coat. He is wearing an unusually large hat. I watch him lean the shovel up against the fountain and take his hat off to fan himself. He's looking at something off to his left. What could it be? My eyes zip over in that direction. There's a dirt path that leads behind the castle I think, then I see a wooden wheelbarrow filled with dirt and flowers. I don't think that lady was trying to show me anything, but who is she and why is she here? No, I really don't have time to concern myself with that.

I start looking for my journal. I check everywhere in the room, even the bathroom, then a different sort of concern begins to overwhelm me. I can't find it anywhere! If it isn't in here, maybe Walter or the maids know something.

I check myself in the mirror and give the room a last look before leaving. Just as I'm heading down the hall, I feel a gush of cold wind blow past me. A sudden feeling of anxiety, anger, hunger and great sorrow fills me. It's so bad I lose my breath and feel like breaking down on the spot. "Oh my god…" What happened here? Man, I really need to leave this place!

I start walking again until I get to the stairs and see Walter at the bottom talking to 6 maids standing in a row at attention. **I wonder what's going on down there...**

I slowly go down the stairs, and as I do, the first maid on my left looks up at me and then to Walter. She clears her throat and looks back to me.

Walter turns around and says, "Good morning Miss Summers." I look at the maids, "Good morning."

Walter looks at them and says, "Ladies…please introduce yourselves."
The first to speak is Christine. "Good Morning Miss Ivy, we met last evening." I nod to her and then Maria speaks up. "Good

Morning. We also met last evening." She smiles warmly while raising a brow.

"Yes, I remember..." I mutter.

Then Pamela; a petite red-head about 25 with high cheekbones, blue eyes and round-rimmed glasses. Next is Angel; a taller, slender woman about 35 with brown hair and brown eyes. She looks Italian. Then Lucy–she seems all-business and has a stare that's a little unnerving. But when she speaks, it's pleasing to the ears. A high-pitched tone from a large woman. She is about 30, has black hair and blue eyes. And lastly…Beatrice…whom seems to be happy no matter what. She has a small frame and a big smile with perfect teeth. Green eyes and red hair. She's about 21 or 22, I'd guess. When they finish, Walter dismisses them and they go in different directions. We're alone now.

"Sleep well?" he asks.

"Yeah…thanks." I look down and away while I collect my thoughts, "I have a question."

"Yes madam?"

"I had a journal with me when I came here, but now I can't find it… I left it on the nightstand in the room you put me in, but now it's gone. I checked everywhere possible for it. It has star stickers all over the front cover." I tell him, voice getting stern by the last two sentences. He raises an eyebrow and says, "Indeed… Well, Miss Summers, I will see if I can have it located right away."

I sigh gratefully, "Thank you so much," Looking up the stairs, I see Gina watching us curiously. I motion for her to come down.

When she reaches us, she gives me a hug and then starts talking to Walter.

"Good morning Walter, may I ask you a question?"

"Yes Ms. Lewis?"

"Will we be able to meet Mr. Francis?"

"He is out at the moment and won't be back for a few hours…" He says.

I frown slightly.

"Oh…" Gina shakes her head and looks at me. "Well I can't stay much longer; I have things to do."
"I understand." He agrees.

She gives me a questioning expression. I look from her to him, then get the feeling of something warm shooting up my spine. It feels internal. It doesn't freak me out either; rather, I stand quietly with a preoccupied stare. I was going to leave, but now I really want to stick around. No, not 'want'–I *need* to stay a little longer. Something is changing my mind… I don't know what it is. No, I won't leave yet. I've just formed a plan.

"Ivy…?" Gina says.
I blink finally and say to them with a small smile, "Well, if it's okay, I'd like to meet him."

She looks up through her eyelashes at me, "Are you sure?"
"Yeah." And then I face him. He inhales deeply as he stiffens; giving me the impression he really wants us to leave. But then–he smiles in a kind way and says, "I have no instructions from Mr. Francis concerning your departure… Very well then." I watch him for a minute.

"Well what about the boat? You know I don't know how to operate it." Gina quietly asks me. Now I can explain my plan. But before I speak, Walter says, "I think I know what you want to do. Our boatman's name is Leonardo. He and his sister Esmeralda are in the boathouse at the moment. They can assist you in moving your boat. Now that Ms. Summers wants to stay a bit longer, he may have to tow it." he looks at me, "Do forgive me for not mentioning it sooner but, I had Leonardo put your boat in our boathouse to save it from the weather."

I'm amazed. "Thanks… When did this happen?" I ask.
"Last night, after you decided to stay." he says.
"Oh… But how did you know where the boat was?"
He smiles a little but doesn't answer the question.

"Would you like to do what I suggested?" He asks.
Without a second thought, I agree to it. After all, that was my plan.

Gina is looking at me a little oddly–probably because I didn't ask her opinion on this.

"Well alright, I'm fine with that." She says.
"Okay… Gina, I'll give you the keys to the truck and my car."

As she accepts, Walter clears his throat, then says, "Very good, very good. One moment; I'll fetch your bag Miss Ivy." He goes into the foyer, gets my stuff out of one of the closets, then comes back and hands it to me. I fish around and find the keys and give them to Gina.

"So…I guess this means goodbye for now." She mutters while looking down at them. I slightly smile and hug her, "Stay safe, alright? When you take Eric's boat back, park it in his backyard. You can tell where it was when I got it. Please try to put it there. I didn't ask to borrow it. Oh, and keep the keys for now." She gives me the 'oh shit' look and says, "Yes, of course…will do."

Walter waves his hand out, "Let us be on our way then, shall we? Miss Summers, please wait here while I escort this young lady to Leonardo's boathouse. I will return shortly."

"Yes, ok." I kindly say. Gina collects her grocery bags, gives me a last wave and nod, and I smile calmly at her. Watching her go out the front doors sends many different thoughts through my head–mostly questions about why I had a sudden change of mind.

I find myself staring after her a little too long, so I go over to the sofa in front of the fireplace and sit down for a while. My eyes rise to the big portrait of the man posing like Washington. Who is he? Or perhaps…who *was* he? For a long time, I stare at him. That's the thing about these kinds of pictures; if you look at them long enough, you start to think whoever's in it is looking back at you. Freaky–just…freaky.

Suddenly, a breeze of cold air brushes over my neck. I immediately turn around with a shiver, rubbing my arms up and down and searching everywhere. There's nothing here.

"*Corneliu*…" A male voice sighs into my ear, having a heavy Romanian accent. I jump away from the sofa. Just then, a maid comes in. It's Pamela. She notices the look on my face and then looks around the room in a bit of confusion.

"Miss Ivy, are you alright?"
I only stare at her. She doesn't move.

Her nose goes down as she peers over her glasses. She expects an answer–but she never gets it. A few tense seconds go by before she nods and says, "Excuse me." She leaves the room in silence.

I let out a huge sigh and look toward the doors. "Hurry up Walter."
Turning back to the portrait, I examine the man's face further. He doesn't exactly look like the average American from the 1800's or early 1900's–or if he's American at all. His nose, eyes and lips say some kind of European all the way. This may seem crazy but…was he the one that just blew on my neck or said that name in my ear? I shudder again.

One of the front doors opens. I quickly turn to see who it is. It's Walter! Finally!
I wait for him.

When he approaches me, he says, "Your friend is safely on her way back." Suddenly, my stomach growls.

He begins to smile, "Hungry?"
I briefly roll my eyes, "A little but I'm alright."

"Miss Ivy, I insist that you have something to eat. After all, you are here for a little while longer and it's time for breakfast, isn't it?" I look around the room for a few seconds and answer. "Yes, I believe it is." I snicker.

"Well then…right this way."
I follow him toward the stairs.

"The dining room is upstairs?" That's different…
"Yes. Mr. Vladoiu has two dining rooms."

"Wow… That's cool." I smile a bit as we head up and turn right.
"Yes…very cool." He does a very brief smile. **I can't wait to eat!**

-Gina-

As I stand back in Leonardo's amazing 2-story boathouse, watching him and his sister Esmeralda finish getting the boats ready, I stare at Mr. Vladoiu's boat. It's pretty big. It has a gray finish with a single red stripe on both sides and a shiny black bow. I'm usually not one for boats but this sure does look nice! Leonardo and his sister must have years of experience working with boats. They certainly seem to know exactly what they're doing.

I'm also wondering about the weird stare Ivy had when we were trying to make a decision in the grand room. It's almost like she forgot I was talking to her and she remembered something she was supposed to do. I hope everything is alright for her.

I look out the window at the tops of the castle. Yeah, it's really a beautiful place… It must have tons of history.

Leonardo rubs his hands together while looking over the boats, "Alright, we're ready to go–the J. Wagner ramp, right?"

"Yes sir." I say, then look from him to Esmeralda, who smiles a little at me, motioning me to get in Vladoiu's boat while she starts the other boat's engine. I board it and he starts his engines. He presses a remote control button on the boat dashboard to open the large metal doors, then we carefully start heading out.

It takes about a half an hour for us to get across. The wind is a little strong today, which means the cool air is harder to tolerate. I see in the distance there are hardly any boaters out today on the Sound. This is something I half expected.

"How far do we have to go?" I ask.
"About 3 miles. We'll be there in a few minutes."

Not bad. I'm a little relieved. I look back and see Esmeralda is close behind and keeping up. She waves at me. She seems to be a happy woman.

During our trip, I hide my nose in my shirt and squint to the wind. He doesn't mind it much–he just puts up with it. After a little while, I feel the need to talk.

"So you work for Mr. Vladoiu?" I have to almost yell. He turns his head slightly, "Yeah. My sister does too. I've been working for him for 5 years and she has for 3."

"Do you two like it?"
"I sure do. It's a good living. Esmeralda loves it." His answer makes me smile.

"What about you?" He asks.
"I'm an RN–a registered nurse."

"Oh, that's handy."
"Yep, my dream job you know." I say with a small laugh.
"Well I'm happy for you!"

We slow down as we approach the ramp. Immediately, I look for the truck. Everything looks just how Ivy and I left it.
"That old white truck over there is what we used." I point at it and hand him the keys. He puts them in his pocket and nods as he pulls up to the dock. He shuts off the engines and says, "I'll be back." Quickly, he jumps across from the boat to the dock with a rope and ties the boat up.

"Keep the boat here." He says. I watch him walk away to the truck, then look back and see Esmeralda waiting for him to back the boat trailer into the water. As soon as he does, he jumps out of the truck and walks on the trailer. Esmeralda slowly drives Eric's boat close enough to it that Leonardo can attach the winch cable and pull the boat up onto it. I'm so glad they're here. I couldn't have done all this alone!

Leonardo drives the truck back up the ramp so Esmeralda can get out, then she helps him finish securing the boat to the trailer. He comes back to Vladoiu's boat and extends his hand to me. I take it and jump a little to the dock.

"Ok, you're good to go!" he says.
"Thanks guys," I gladly shake hands with both of them, "I owe you!"

Esmeralda waves it off, "Nah, it's alright."

"Haha…ok." I get in the truck and salute them both.
They head back to Vladoiu's boat and I start the engine.

Now I have to drop this off in Eric's backyard and use Ivy's car
to get home.
"Okay…let's get this show on the road."

I carefully go on my way.

Chapter 10

-Ivy-

Walter pulls out a chair and I sit down at a very nice antique dining table in a room that doesn't appear to be a dining room. The windows are long and the drapes are red, and I see there are more paintings here, but most of them are of nice scenery rather than people. Around the table, there are 8 dark chairs with high backs, and at the far end there's a larger, more important-looking one; it's nicer than all of them. I already figure that's where either Mr. Vladoiu or Mr. Francis sits. This most definitely isn't the main dining room. Why someone would have more than one though, I don't know.

Pamela comes and sets a nice plate of pancakes, bacon, eggs and some toast in front of me. For a drink, she gives me a glass of orange juice. This is so beyond what I would have asked for. I don't know if I can eat that much! The table is beautifully set up; a large fruit bowl in the center with a candle on both sides. After she leaves, I jokingly ask Walter, "All of this–just for me?" I look up at him with a faint grin. He bows his head slowly, lacing his hands together at the front, "No, the table is always set like that."
"Oh…"

I pick up the fork and knife. Hey, they're fancy too!
Of course they're fancy stupid…
Gosh, where did this stuff come from?!

"Walter, why don't you sit down?"
"Oh no Miss Ivy, I wouldn't do that."
"Why?"
"It's inappropriate." He says.
"Oh…" I lift an eyebrow. "I'll talk to you while you stand there and watch me eat…"
He nods at me once, permissively.

I start cutting the pancake. "I want to talk about last night…" I take my first bite. Wow…it's amazing! This is great food.

"About last night?"
"Did you hear anything last night–like banging on the walls or something?" Maybe he heard it...

"What do you mean?" Great, that's not a good sign.
"Well, call me crazy but, I heard female whispers and banging in the walls... I called the maids' quarters last night but the maid that answered the phone said no one was up here."
"Perhaps you were imagining things." No! I know what I heard!

Narrowing my eyes slightly, I say, "Perhaps..."
"Things are quiet here."

He says that, yeah–but he's talking about the rest of the castle. Oh well...I don't live here. It's not my problem if it's haunted, but I'm always going to be unnerved about this place. After this, I don't think I'll ever come back.

Now the journal... "That still doesn't explain it." I mutter.
"I beg your pardon?"

I look at him again, realizing my thoughts were a little too loud. "I'm just trying to figure out the issue with my journal."
"We'll find it." He assures. Then he goes silent.

"Ms. Summers..." he finally speaks, "What was that back there in the grand room earlier? You seemed...distressed, when I saw you before your friend departed." Wait, the face I was making was that noticeable? Man, that's not the only thing that occurred...

I look at him, almost astounded, "You saw what happened? And please, just call me Ivy." I slightly smile at the last sentence. The formalities are actually getting a little annoying, to be honest. He nods seriously at me. I drop my gaze to the plate, "Well...have you ever suddenly been overwhelmed by many emotions at once?–Like you absorbed what someone else feels or felt in a matter of say– less than a second?" His eyes go thin in thought. He quietly says, "I'm not sure what you mean." I place my chin on my hands, "I don't know... It happened to me on the way to the grand room just before I saw you with the maids. I felt loss, anger and starved at the same time. I know it sounds crazy but...that's what happened." "Hmm…" He looks skeptical but his curiosity is growing at the same time. "This place can be overwhelming at times, I suppose. Maybe that's it?" He says.

Suddenly, we hear a phone ring. He walks to the corner of the room and answers it. I watch as he says, "Yes, thank you." and then he hangs it up. He looks at me and bows a little, "One moment please; I'll be back." he quickly leaves the room. **No, don't go!**

I sigh, but then get the feeling that must be Mr. Francis. My stomach leaps. I instinctively fix my hair, getting ready to finally, hopefully, meet this guy.

I suddenly hear a woman's voice; "You should be careful," I move around to look for her. She's the same one I saw in the Windsor room earlier! I'm able to see her face this time and I see it's kind and warm, but a little blurry. In fact, her whole body is slightly in and out of phase! This is creepy! I almost ask her who she is but the words can't seem to leave me. Anxiously, I watch her quickly walk up to me and put her hand on mine. I don't feel her touch me. There's nothing–nothing at all! She looks deep into my eyes as she tells me, "Big things are going to happen." Slowly, she fades to nothing. I quickly pull my hand back and press it on my chest. My heart is thumping madly now. I'm surprised I haven't jumped out of this chair! What did she mean by what she said?

For a few minutes, I sit here in a frozen position. This is the second time I've seen her. What's next? I look at the walls and down at my plate of food. Slowly, I move my attention away from it to the silverware. It had better not start shaking. I've seen that shit in movies and somebody ends up getting killed! "Miss Ivy," I whirl my head around again. It's Walter and he's alone. He still calls me 'Miss'.

His brows furrow, "What happened? You're paler than sheep's wool." Well duh! If only you knew!

I shake my hands as I stand up from the table, "Walter, please just tell me what's going on here, will you? Is this place haunted or what?" No, that's a stupid question. I already know it is! He makes a strange face at me. Evidently, he doesn't believe in that stuff. "Madam, please calm yourself." I nearly say something else, but instead, I purse my lips in frustration.

"Mr. Francis has returned, and is in his office at the moment. I have to speak with him before you meet him." he turns away. I take his hand, stopping him, "Ok, but please don't leave me alone in here; let me come with you." He quickly looks down at my hand, then back up to my face. "Please." I repeat. He scans the room slowly, "You really are afraid, aren't you? ...If it makes you feel better Miss Ivy, you can follow me." I frown and trail along behind him like a puppy. Yes, I'm afraid... Very afraid.

We go up a hall almost identical to the one he took me down earlier and then, he stops and turns to me. "Wait here please." he says. I nod at him. He goes a little bit farther and then enters one of the rooms. I wait and listen. I can't hear anyone.

I sigh uncomfortably and rub my arms while searching both ends of the hall for ghosts or whatever might appear. The light from the window ahead of me is dimming down, which means bad weather. I'm sure people are really wondering about me right now.

I hear a door open, and out comes Walter. Good, good! "Well?" I whisper. He waves his hands like pushing me away, "Go go go—Go back to the dining room." His tone is barely audible. At first, I'm confused, but I do as I'm told and cautiously rush back to the dining room.

When we get there, he shuts the door behind him, and I give him a very strange look. "Walter, what's going on?"

He faces me and sighs heavily. He stiffens his posture to seem sterner. "Miss Ivy, he would like to dine with you. Sit down please. He will be here shortly." he dips his head and quickly goes out of the room before I can say another word to him. Oh my god, I finally meet Mr. Francis!

I'm getting nervous again. I gingerly walk over and sit down.

My eyes stop at the area I saw that ghost woman and stay there as I begin to rub my clammy hands together on my lap. I'm too uncomfortable to even blink.

The door opens and I see Lucy and Beatrice quickly come in with a servant's cart and almost slam the door shut behind them. They immediately start preparing a place setting for Mr. Francis. They place a plate with a tall stack of French toast with fruit and bacon there for him, pulling his seat out, setting up the silverware and positioning the napkins perfectly by the plate. They both stop at the same time and stand side-by-side, still as statues to the right of the door and wait. "Wow!" I say under my breath. And man, this guy must have an appetite…

Just then, I hear coming up to the door, "Sir, I must tell you though, she is a little unsettled." then I hear another person say, "You didn't call the police yet…did you Walter?" It's a man's voice. It's deep and very smooth. Sounds foreign to me too but I might be wrong. He's a bit muffled. Walter doesn't answer.

Oh god. I sink low into my seat, more nervous than before. I watch the doorknob turn and then I see the door open. Instantly, I gasp. The butterflies have just gotten much worse! "No," I whisper under my breath. I can't believe my eyes!

Chapter 11

There he is. 'The one.' The one from Lounge n' Sip. He's right there in the doorway–smiling at me! Walter is behind him. I was certain my day was ruined already, but this made it–this made it BEYOND HORRIBLE!

He walks into the room almost gliding. Smooth as glass it seems. With every step, he never takes his eyes off me. I gulp. He stops just 2 steps away from me and looks at Walter. He nods once very slightly. Walter nods back and looks at the maids. They slightly bow to Mr. Francis and me, then quickly leave the room. Walter follows them out and closes the door.

"Miss Ivy…" he bows slightly, takes my hand and gently kisses it while looking into my eyes, "Welcome to castle Vladoiu." I let out a small breath as a bolt of electricity rushes through me. Him being so close and his mere touch; it causes me to nearly squirm in my seat and my heart to beat faster. His lips are really, really warm–Almost unnaturally. Oh god… My face…at least I'm able to keep it as straight as possible. I was correct before; he does have an accent! It sounds…Romanian. I blush. This is so awkward…!

I then ask in a slightly shaky voice, "Excuse me, but…how do you know my name sir?" I see that he's wearing an 1800's-looking white shirt–you know–the kind with the big sleeves and the fancy cuffs? Yeah–like that. He has black pants and I noticed earlier that he has black rider boots on. Fancy–very fancy. Why is he wearing this? He was wearing casual everyday clothing at Lounge n' Sip and now this?

He smiles, and while saying, "Walter has informed me about your visit and your difficulties." he gently sits down in a chair directly across from me. "You're having breakfast... I hope it is to your liking." he says. **To my liking? Hell yeah, it's delicious!**

"Oh yes... it's very good thank you." I reply.
"You know... I am hungry myself." he says while looking into my

eyes. He looks at the food in front of him and lets out a sigh. "Please, don't let me interrupt you." he waves a hand out, "Go ahead–enjoy your meal." Gosh...the way he talks...and that smile... Wow. Whenever he looks at me, I automatically want to turn away. I feel like I can't handle his gaze; it's too captivating.

I slowly move my hand over the silverware and grab my fork. I cut into some of my breakfast and bring it up to my lips. I'm hesitant...because he's watching me. But then, he smiles again and continues, "Miss Ivy, I do understand why you are so nervous...and you have my most sincere apologies..." he pauses for a second. It's like he's thinking about something. Then he starts talking again, "Now that we are face to face, I believe a proper introduction is in order. After all, that is what you've been waiting for, yes?" he stands and bows a little, "I am Nicolai Francis, executive assistant to Mr. Vladoiu II, but you may call me Nick if you wish." he slowly sits back down with an artful glint in his eyes. Now I can't stop staring at him.

I dip my head softly, carefully in response, "I'm...Ivy Summers, sir. But you can call me Ivy." I swear...that smile has my full attention. He has some nice eyeteeth...

Such a pearly white fanged smile! Am I exaggerating or are those truly sharp fangs? If I'm blushing redder than before, curse me.

"Beautiful name–Ivy." he says. My lashes flutter, then I avert my eyes down to my plate, "Um, thanks..." I slowly look up at him again, "I see you like to wear Victorian clothing..."

"Yes... A cousin of mine came here from out of town and had brought along a trunk of clothing from that time. Heirlooms, you know. Plus, she is quite a history buff. As for me, it is quite comfortable. You can wear whatever you like where you live, can you not? I like this style and enjoy wearing it around here." His little laugh becomes contagious for me; I broaden my smile. "Yeah..." I'm a little embarrassed by that.

He tilts his head, "...We do not normally have unannounced

guests. It is unusual."

"Sorry. You live in an amazing home." I say.

He hums in amusement, "Why, thank you. I…" he looks around somewhat mysteriously, "Do not stay here much though…" he leans back in his seat, "I am always too busy." My cheeks flush again. "Oh… Part of being Mr. Vladoiu's executive assistant, huh?"

"Indeed." He winks at me. My mouth opens a tad, then I quickly close it and swallow, "Well that's… that's amazing." I smile shyly.

"Hmph." he scoffs, "What is amazing, is you." My eyes flash up at him, "What?" He waves his hand at me, "Well, as I said before, we don't have many unannounced guests and here you pop up out of nowhere." he grins.

I blink. **Right**.

"Oh. Um, yeah…" I tuck my hair behind my ear and shake my head a little, "It's a little confusing how this all happened. I'm sorry–really, I am."

"Nonsense Ivy…a little surprise once in a while is what we all need, don't you agree?"

It depends…

I nod slowly, "Yeah, I s'pose."

"Indeed! So…why have you come anyway? And what type of work do you do, might I ask?" I take a deep breath, pause…then release it, "Well, I saw this place and…it looked uninhabited. So I-" He suddenly starts chuckling at me. I give him a strange face for that. He claps his hands together, "Is that right? You must have missed the very large 'no trespassing' signs." he laughs quietly, "Well Ivy, it's rare these days for people to come to this castle. You see-" He turns his head down and away with a brief daring smile, "Hai sa ne distram putin. Sperie-o." he suddenly grimaces, "Noi nu vrem asta. Deoarece asta ar indeparta-o!" He clears his throat and straightens his back and looks at me again, "You're not eating…is the food not any good now?" I turn my head to the side just a bit, feeling uncomfortable about him now.

*Hai sa ne distram putin. Sperie-o.

Let's have a little fun. Scare her.

*Noi nu vrem asta. Deoarece asta ar indeparta-o!

We don't want that. That would push her away.

"It's... good... thank you. I'm sorry but, what was that you said? I didn't understand you." **What is he... schizophrenic?**

His brows rise, "It was nothing. I was speaking română. Continue, continue–please." He smiles encouragingly.
Oh my...

As he begins to eat, I watch how he savors his food and think to myself: it's like he's so at home here... it's sort of strange. I wonder how Dmitri feels about that–or if he even knows?
Surely he would...

He notices me observing him. He grins and puts his fork down, "Changing your mind, are you?" I quickly shake my head, "No sir, I'm not.–I mean–Nick." I purse my lips. He forms a somewhat smug smile, "Alright then."

"So, where were we? Ah yes!" he points up, "Do continue!"
I try to smile as I bite my lip, then I still my eyes on his mouth, "Well..." Oh I can't tell him what kind of job I have. He'll think I'm a piece of garbage!

"Yes...?" He slowly sips his orange juice.
I close my eyes, "I work at the local hospital in Gales."
"Oh, lovely," I know he's entertained when he says that.
"What do you do there?" That last question decreases my confidence. The suspense of what his reaction would be is killing me.

I take a quiet deep breath, "I'm a medical technician." I hear him chuckle. Slowly, I open my eyes. He has his hands in his lap while keeping an amused and admiring face. "You speak of that in such an ashamed way–Why?"

What did he just say? Wow...I didn't expect him to say

anything like that!

"Um… Well…" I look around, "It's not exactly a big deal–not as much as being a nurse or a doctor anyway."

"Ahh, but it is something. Say–if I ever fell ill and had to go to the emergency room there, my life would be in your hands, yes? I would have to depend on you to keep me alive." He seems very certain about his words. "Yes…" I say.

"Then you are a lifesaver. That is quite something if you ask me." He winks as he picks up his silverware again and eats some of his French toast. I am speechless at this point; stunned by the fact this man with all his responsibilities and title has such a positive attitude about a person like me.

He adds, "You will always have a job because there will always be a need for someone like you." I agree…

I nod definitely, "…That's very true." This guy has a very interesting way of talking. I like it…a lot.

He slowly smiles, "You dream of becoming a nurse one day, don't you?"
"Yeah, that's what I'm aiming for." I figured he would ask that. Most people do if the subject ever comes up.

"Wonderful!" He's proud. That makes me feel happy and very glad for some reason.
"So Ivy…" he says, "I'm actually quite surprised that you came here… There is a reason why this castle looks the way it does from afar." Oh?

"Why is that?" I quietly ask.
"This castle was built many years ago among the trees in the interest of privacy. When you arrived…I almost called the harbor police. We've had to do that before." He's so amused. I somehow have the feeling he's joking and not telling the truth.

"Wow…I'm sorry about that…" I say.
"It's alright. You appear to be harmless." He grins.

I slowly look around, "…This place does have quite a vintage look to it." I chuckle lightly while in the back of my mind I'm also wondering if what he just said means 'get out'. That would be quite a sudden change of atmosphere.

"Yes…but since I have met you, I would very much like us to learn more about one another." My cheeks heat up.

"Alright…" I slightly smile, "I have some questions of my own, if that's ok."
"Sure, go on."

I move around in my seat to get more comfortable as I form a more serious, less-intimidated face. "I…notice you seem quite comfortable here in Mr. Vladoiu's castle."

"Yes…my employer grants me certain liberties when I am here."
"Sounds like a real nice guy." I say.
"I agree; he's a fine old gentleman." He sips some juice, eyes narrowing in that glintful way again. I study his actions, unaware that I'm actually staring at him in a growing sort of adoration. But then I clear my throat and say, "Well then…it's kinda funny…I saw you at a coffee shop not too long ago."

"Yes…" he hums, "Coincidental that we find each other yet again, and here we are dining together, talking freely and laughing with one another." **Ooo…'talking freely'–that's fancy. And yes…it's freakishly coincidental.**

"It seems a man like you would have someone shopping for him rather than going out himself to find what he needs." I say. With a large inhale, he laces his fingers together above his stomach, now leaning back in his chair, "Well, it is usually like that, yes…but I do enjoy a casual trip out from time to time."

"I'm sure anyone would–despite the mad traffic of New York." I scoff. He laughs and raises an eyebrow, "You have not seen my country in these times." I give him a questioned look.

"The cars…" he does a few zooming motions with his hands, "The traffic goes every which way. It is nothing like India though." I start to smile and snicker at him, "Wow, you must have been everywhere to be talking like that."

"I have done a lot of traveling." He winks at me.
I blush in admiration.

"So where are you from?"
"Bucharest, Romania." He says with great pride.
My eyes widen a bit, "Wow…"

"You like Romania?" He asks.
I nod, "Yes, yes I do. It's beautiful from what I've read and seen in pictures."
"It is quite magical… Sometimes I get homesick but I chose to live here. I wanted something different, so here I am."

"Do you ever consider moving back there?" I ask.
"I used too, but since I live on this little piece of land in a castle built with a Romanian design, I feel somewhat close to home. So it is fine with me. Do you like it?"
"Oh I love it," I nod certainly. He enjoys hearing that. The room falls silent for a moment. We stare at each other; I'm astounded and he has a sort of sinister smile as he studies me–I think that's what he's doing. Then he slowly looks down at the table and slightly flares his nose. He seems to be bothered by something going on in his mind. I get the urge to ask what's wrong, but before I can, he lifts his head back up with a genuine smile. "I must say…you have lovely eyes Ivy; light blue–like the waters along the most *beautiful* tropical islands…" My eyes grow again. That was unexpected… What a compliment too. Him saying that… I blush again.

He reaches for his orange juice and gently swishes its contents around as he gazes at me. The room is getting even quieter all of a sudden. Again, he's just sitting there, watching me, sipping from his glass occasionally. He's preoccupied or something–with what, I wish I could know. I hesitantly look around with a small snicker, "Why, thank you…"
His eyes narrow intensely, "You are *quite* welcome…"
I make a bit of a surprised face at his sudden change of behavior.

"She will stay here. Ivy will sleep." He then stands up, puts the

84

glass down and walks around the table, then stops behind me. I stiffen, "What are you doing…?" My heart is beginning to beat faster.

"How fun this will be." Rozalia chuckles.
"Don't do anything." He says in a soft but husky voice.
"Oh don't worry…"

Suddenly, I feel two very warm fingers gently touch the pulse point of my neck. I gasp softly. Why is his hand so hot?

"Look at me dear," My stomach goes into a knot.
"Nick, what are you-"
"Look at me now…Ivy." I slowly tip my head back and everything starts darkening around us. What is going on? His eyes–They're glowing bright, bright blue. They're like diamonds; extraordinary, captivating, unusually beautiful blue diamonds in a dark room. That's the best I can describe them, and that's not enough. It's just him and nothing else. He's perfect–like an angel.

"Nick, your eyes-" Gosh they're so…breathtaking…
He whispers, "Relax Ivy…" Now he's fading from my sight. No! Don't go–Please don't go! "Nick…?" I try to keep my eyes on him but they continue to flutter, desperate to close. I don't feel the same–I feel so exhausted and I can't figure out why. I watch him form a slow wolfish smile, then I gasp as I realize the smile is murderous and insane, and I feel a sudden adrenaline rush.

I snatch his hand and his eyes flash brighter. My mouth falls open, almost letting out a scream. I fall out of the chair and try to crawl. He grabs my foot and pulls me back, making me cry and struggle. Suddenly, he takes a hold of my jaw and zeroes his eyes in on mine. I try to fight him but he's too strong. The room is getting so much darker as he stares at me. Squeezing his arm tightly, I cry, "Let me go!" He laughs in a low baritone voice, a weird sort of cackle. I gasp again as I steady my attention entirely on his eyes and begin to feel lost in them once more. Everything is fading again, maybe even quicker now. I can't fight back. Soon, the room goes pitch black; everything disappears from my sight.

I can't hear anything!

Chapter 12
-Nicolai-

I stop cackling but Rozalia's haunting laugh is still in my head. As I remove my hands from Ivy and slowly stand, I ball my hands into firm fists. "Cum îndrăznești...? How dare you do this to her?!" I wrinkle my nose, step away from Ivy and angrily pace the room with a low throaty grumble. 'You want her to stay yet you manhandle her? Explain yourself!'

"Dmitri, you are wasting your energy. You know what that means." She makes me lick my teeth. I stop and grit them. 'No. You answer my question NOW!'

"She will not remember anything but think she was supposed to lie down for a nap. And I needed a laugh."

"I know she won't remember anything!" I slam a fist down on the dining table, "You stupid bitch, you are so dense you NEVER understand how the human mind truly works! Disturbing her rest this morning, forcing me to nearly bite her–You have gone too far already! She can't stay here any longer. She heard us arguing!" She swipes my hand across the table, pushing the plates and glasses off, *"I have lived **many** human lives–I know the species **thoroughly**! That incident this morning was nothing!"* She stresses the arteries in my head. I gasp and almost shout, quickly taking a hold of it.

*"Do not speak of something you are **unfamiliar** with!"*

I shift away from the table, "Vile...you are vile! You are the bane of my life! You jeopardize us BOTH and you tell me this benefits us!" I go out the door, my infuriated expression suddenly switching to calm and collected, and the headache is suddenly gone.

I find Pamela coming up the hall. "Pamela," I approach her, "I need you to find Christine and help Miss Ivy to the Windsor room. She is in the small dining room." She furrows her eyebrows, "Sir?"

I wave a hand, "She just fell asleep at the table. She is exhausted. I may have put her to sleep with my talking." I lightly chuckle at her. She nods slowly, "Of course sir…right away." As she quickly walks up the hall, I put my hand on my mouth. "I will make you pay…" I whisper. Rozalia lowers my head and tilts it, "The fun has only just begun." I snap my head back up with a ferocious hiss, eyes glowing as they dart over to Maria coming out of a room.

She halts, gasping to the sight of the intense glow. Slowly, I beckon her, "Maria…come here." She stares into my eyes, Rozalia luring her in, putting her into a trance-like state. I suddenly turn my head away. Maria approaches me. I stop her with a hand pushing against her shoulder, refusing to look at her. "…Where is Walter?"

"In his office…sir." I inhale deeply, lift my head back up to stare at the wall, then I walk past her on my way there. Rozalia growls at my resistance but I ignore her.

When I reach his door, I open it carefully and see him looking at his bookcase. He turns around, "Yes Sir." I proceed inside with a serious face, shutting the door gently, "Walter, when the clock reaches 4pm, inform Mr. Leonardo that Miss Summers is ready to return to the mainland, and have his sister drive her to wherever she wants to go." He nods and says, "Yes sir." He is curious about what I tell him but doesn't pry. I turn to leave and add, "She will be sleeping for a while. She is exhausted and I want her to rest here."

He raises an eyebrow. "Very good sir, I will make sure she wakes up by then." I nod and go out.

"Well done…I look forward to the events to come."
"You are making a fool out of us." I lightly sneer, "Think of that."

*Cum îndrăznești?

How dare you?

88

-Ivy-

As I am surrounded by darkness, it feels like it'll be forever; where nothing exists and never will. I don't even see myself. But...I start to see a little pearl-white dot slowly manifesting in the distance. Curiously, I focus on it. "What is that?" Once it gets big enough, I notice it has formed into a rectangular doorway. I see through it a part of a traditional Romanian-styled bedroom, and I hear a man laughing in a quiet sort of way. It sounds...like my dream guy.

Carefully, I walk toward it, then move even slower when I'm close. I peek inside and suddenly I'm lounging on a canopy bed with him. My eyes grow and he smiles, having his hand propping the side of his head up. Behind him is a window with no drapes, giving a beautiful view of blue skies and a flock of white birds flying out in the distance. I look at him again. He forms a somewhat surprised face as he asks, "Are you alright?" My mouth opens but nothing comes out; my eyes fall and see his bare muscular chest. Oh my...

He tucks my hair behind my ear, "You seem unsettled."
I shut my eyes, lowering my head slightly, "I don't...know why."

He scoots closer and lifts my chin up with a finger, his gaze very serious, "Ivy, you are worrying me." Staring at him, I really find myself wondering where we are 'relationship-wise'. This is like we're married. Oh but I can't complain about this; this is great. I smile softly and put my hand on his face, "I'm fine. I'm really happy to be here with you." And I hug him, laying my head down on his chest. He embraces me and kisses my hair, "I'm glad too. Don't ever go."

"I won't. I'll always be here." I whisper. A small tear streams down my cheek as I start to think; 'But I will wake up and there's always a chance you won't be here with me again'–because after all, dreams change.

He sighs in content, "The wedding will be soon."
I look up at him, surprised. So we're fiancés in this? Oh my gosh,

how lovely! He smiles again, then kisses me on the lips. Astonishment still filling me, I grin into it and murmur in the middle, "I can't wait." But the thought I have…it still lingers. Why can't I just stay here forever with him? "I love you so much," I say as I bury my nose in his neck. He hums.

"Miss Ivy?" There are a few hard knocks on the door. I open my eyes. I'm in the Windsor room. Quickly, I scan around me in search of him. He's not here. This is reality and I'm not in the same place. Frowning, I look at the door as it opens. There's Maria. She has a straight face.
"Miss Ivy…sleep well?"

I sit up and rub my head, "Yeah... Man, I was exhausted."
"…I'm glad you feel better. It's now 4 in the afternoon."

I put my hand down on my leg, "Wow, 4 in the afternoon! Did you come to wake me?" Where did the day go? I feel like I just laid my head down and got plenty of rest! I've never slept all day before!

"Yes ma'am I did." she nods, "Mr. Francis will be waiting for you in the main entrance."

"Oh!" I quickly get up, "I'm so sorry!" I check my clothes and wish that I had something better. She bows her head and leaves. Everybody bows here… Hm.

Immediately, I check to see if I left anything in here, then I head out into the hall and get to the main staircase. As soon as I do that, I see Nicolai at the bottom, wearing quite a handsome black suit now. First, he's lost in thought but quickly becomes aware that I'm here. He smiles up at me, "Bună dimineața, dragă mea. You look vibrant." I blink as my lips part, a little confused by the first thing he says and stunned by the last. "Thanks…" I see a book in his left hand. It looks familiar. My journal?! My eyes enlarge.

He tucks it in his jacket, now walking up the stairs to me, "I said good morning if you are wondering… Did you sleep well?" I close my mouth and bring my eyes up from his hand to his face.

He tilts his head as he studies my expression. I nod, "Yes, yes I did–Thank you." I point to where I saw him put that book away, "I see you carry books around..."

"Oh! Why yes, I was going to give this back to you. Walter explained to me that you misplaced it." He takes it out of his jacket and holds it out to me, "He said it was underneath your bed." I carefully take the seam of it, observing his body language all the while. He puts his other hand on mine. Whoa, he's so warm! He inches a bit closer and whispers, "Leonardo will take you home now." I stare into his eyes, starting to lose awareness of everything around us. But–But I don't want to go yet! He takes my other hand, puts it on my journal and smiles. His eyes are brightening in color, and as I watch, I'm beginning to feel like I don't have any reason to stay here anymore and that I really should get back home.

Suddenly, we hear four maids walking into the main entrance behind Walter, complaining about something. Nick blinks and looks over in annoyance. I flutter my eyelashes, then do the same as him. He says, "Stay here for a moment." He walks down and meets up with them. It's interesting to see how disturbed they are. I wonder what's wrong. Maria and Christine seem to be bothered the most.

I go to them anyway and stop a few feet behind Nick. The ladies are talking about a mad ghost that was terrorizing them as they were cleaning. Walter is a little aggravated yet he keeps a calm voice. So they deal with it too...but how bad is it for them?

Nicolai looks away from him to the maids, "Don't mind Corneliu ladies. We have already discussed this." Corneliu?! Oh my gosh, no way!

"But sir, he broke a few plates in the kitchen." Maria says. "Maria," he places his hand on her shoulder while looking around at all of them, "I will deal with him...and all of you should remember... we have a guest here." Deal with him? What does he mean by that?

He turns his head some, acknowledging me, then he waves his hand in a gesture to Walter and stares slightly at the maids. After that, he tells me, "Walter will escort you to Leonardo." He slowly brings my hand up to his lips and kisses it while his slowly glowing eyes focus on mine. In a soft, low voice, he says,

"A fost cu adevărat o plăcere sa te întâlnesc domnișoară Summers. De abia aștept sa te văd dinnou . Poate ar trebui sa avem o mica discuție în casa mea verde." He thumbs over my bottom lip, "Lungă pentru mine…" I inhale slowly as I stare into his shocking bright blue eyes narrowing almost darkly. I'm starting to get the feeling that I will be seeing him again, very soon–but where–I don't know yet.

He then says, "I bid you good evening." I blink repeatedly, blushing, then I quickly move on behind Walter. As I go, I constantly look back at him and watch how authoritatively he stands there, smiling at me in a way that seems confident about something. It's mysterious and sinister.

Walter guides me into the foyer and presents the grocery bag I brought along, the tire iron, which he stows away in a different bag, and then he asks for my journal. Though I don't want to, I hand it to him and he puts it away. "Alright Miss Ivy… on to Mr. Leonardo."
"Yes…" I quietly agree, "Of course."

*A fost cu adevărat o plăcere sa te întâlnesc domnișoară Summers. De abia aștept sa te văd dinnou . Poate ar trebui sa avem o mica discuție în casa mea verde.

It was truly a pleasure to meet you Miss Summers. I cannot wait to see you again. Maybe we should have a little talk in my greenhouse.
*Lungă pentru mine...

Long for me…

As Walter and I follow the rocky path among the calmly wavering trees, I look up at them and feel the cool wind blow past me. It was refreshing at first but now it's getting uncomfortable. I would hug my arms together if I didn't have my hands full. After another few minutes of walking, I see a two-story boathouse and hear metal clanking. It's extraordinary to look at; much like the Boltd castle's boathouse…

When we approach it, I see a middle-aged man who I assume is Mr. Leonardo coming around from the garage area, dressed almost like that farmer I saw; only he has a fisherman's hat and a fairly long coat. He spots us and walks our way.

"Mr. Leonardo," Walter shakes hands with him, also nodding his head toward me, "This is Miss Summers." Leonardo looks at me with a smile, "Good evening." I smile back a little and nod once. Then we return to Walter, who says to me, "Well then Miss Ivy, it was a pleasure to meet you. I bid you farewell and a safe journey home." He gives me a warm, almost grandfatherly smile.

"Thank you… I really appreciate all that you and the maids have done for my friend and I."
Seriously, it was wonderful.

"Bye now." He lowers his head, then starts back for the castle. I look at Leonardo. "Miss Summers, right this way." He waves me along with him to the boathouse, so I go. As soon as we get inside where the boat's parked, I'm immediately awestruck. This boat in here is big and extremely beautiful! I wish it was mine! I love the colors and design!

"Mr. Francis's boat?" I quickly ask, not looking at him.
"No, this is Mr. Vladoiu's boat but he allows Mr. Francis to use it. I think he has a bigger one somewhere else."

I slowly gulp, "Wow…that's amazing…"
"He knows what he likes." He says with humor in his voice.

On our way to the mainland, I see on that side yet another boathouse, but it's a bit smaller. From what I can tell, it's really eerie around it… I mean, it's surrounded by dark leafless trees. Some of them have lanterns hanging on strings that go from one tree to another. They're not lit. Another thing that makes it ominous is a flickering light in one window of the boathouse. He said Esmeralda will be waiting for me. She is supposed to help me with my transportation.

He parks the boat in the boathouse, gets out first and ties the boat. He offers to help me with my bags. I politely refuse as I step off. We walk outside and around, up the steps toward the main house. I instinctively inspect the windows of the main house and I don't know why, but I feel unwelcome here. It's not because of Leonardo–it's something or someone else. Or maybe I'm just freaking out for no reason.

I swallow a bit harder than planned and ask, "So uh…the lights are flickering in your sister's place." I look at him. He raises an eyebrow, "Well that's unusual." Hmm…

Just then, a woman comes out of the house with a set of keys in one hand. She's middle-aged too, wearing a t-shirt and light blue jeans. Her hair is short, in a ponytail and her face is serious. I figure this is Esmeralda.

Leonardo looks at her and motions her over–though she's halfway to us. When she stops beside him, she says, "Hi–you must be Ivy. I'm Esmeralda." She reaches out to shake hands with me. Carefully, I do, "Yes…nice to meet you." She smiles brief and kindly, "Likewise… So, I'm driving you to..?"

"To my friend Gina's house. My car's there. I'll give you directions." I quietly say. Of course I'd give her the directions… What was I thinking?

"Okay then!" She points with her chin over toward the side of the house, "The car's this way. Follow me." As she walks away, I give Leonardo a last glance and trail behind her. He tips his hat at me. "Thank you." I say. He smiles back.

Once she and I make it to the side of the house, I see that everything is nicely decorated and beautiful instead of dark and eerie. I was just freaking out after all. There are flowerpots and shrubs everywhere, including some that line along the white concrete driveway, which leads to a double garage. She opens it with her key fob, revealing a black mustang and another car that has a cover over it. I lift an eyebrow, "…Hm," I wonder what's under that.

Chapter 13

While on the way to Gina's, I take my journal out and read through it a little. After Esmeralda told me she's familiar with this area, I asked her to look for a 2-story house with a white Lincoln outside. Now as I stare into the pages of my little book, the thought of calling Mom crosses my mind. I might not be able to get in touch with her until tomorrow, judging by the time and the fact my phone needs time to charge.

Esmeralda glances over, "What's that?"
"My journal...had it since I was a kid." My voice is quiet, concentrated. I'm curious...
What did Nicolai see if he looked through it? Did he see anything about my dreams? He really unnerves yet intrigues me with the similarities he has; it's his looks, his castle, and the fact he's Romanian–just like the guy in my dreams...

Something really tells me I will run into him again. I seriously wish I knew how and when. I know that right now, I need to find some way to clear my head. It's going to be pretty hard. When I can, I will make some phone calls to assure everyone I'm alright.

We pull into Gina's driveway and park next to my car. She asks me, "Is this it?"
"Yup...you got it!" I say. I give her a relieved smile and thank her. "How much do I owe you?"

She shakes her head, "Nothing at all." She looks out past me at a light in one of the windows of the house, "Have a goodnight." I nod at her, get out with my stuff and watch her drive away. I set my bag on the hood of my car and look toward Gina's place.

The porch light comes on as I approach the door. In this moment, I wonder to myself what everyone else I talk to is doing; if they're thinking of me. Any calls I make to those closest to me will all be the same; which would be anxious yet relieved. I'm not calling anyone until I'm absolutely ready to do it.

I see the door open and her head poke out. "Ivy!" Her voice is a loud whisper.

With a slow smile, I walk up and give her a hug.

"Here, wanna come in?" She steps back. I shake my head, "No thanks, I mean it's getting late and I just want to go home. How did it go with the boat?"

"The boat... No problems; it's back at Eric's, parked in its spot. "You sure you don't wanna come in? I want to hear about what happened after I left."

"I'd tell you how everything went between Nicolai and I but there isn't much time."

She pats my shoulder, "We can talk about it tomorrow at work then. You are working tomorrow, right?" I think about it. I'm in a daze right now; I can't even think straight. Why is this?

I close my eyes and the memory comes back to me. "Yeah, I'll be working."

"You need some sleep. Here, let me get your keys." She goes inside for a minute and comes back out with the car and truck keys in her hand. Taking them, I puff out a sigh, "Thank you." You know...she says I need sleep but I'm not tired.

"No problem. Get some rest."

"Alright. I'll see you tomorrow." I wave at her and start for my car. She cups her mouth, "Have a safe drive!" "I will!" I get in, start the engine and slowly back out her driveway.

Now home, I turn the lights on and look at the microwave clock. It's 7:10pm. After putting my phone on the charger and turning it on, I go to the bathroom to take a long hot bath. My apartment seems so quiet and empty all of a sudden. I don't remember it ever having this amount of silence. By the time I was halfway home, I started feeling depressed and I don't understand why. I'm not sure if it's because I'm overwhelmed with what has happened to me or what. Lounging in the tub is extremely relaxing but so...so...lonely. For the longest time, I have a towel over my eyes as the image of Nick's face stays in my mind. I see his stunning smile, I hear his smooth, alluring voice, I think of how he kissed my hand and looked at me the way he did. He made me feel the same way I do whenever I dream of that beautiful man; he shares almost the same exact charm as him.

I take the towel off my watering eyes, frowning slowly. I really want to see him again…so much. It's the same feeling as if I'd left home and miss it more than words can explain. I'm not where I'm supposed to be? "And I have to work tomorrow." Maybe after that my head will be cleared up.

I finish up in the bathroom, get dressed in my pajamas and look at my phone. It's too late to do anything now. Nobody I know would want to talk at about 9pm on a weekday.

Setting it aside on the nightstand, I go make some precooked chicken and noodles. Back to TV dinners. This night is so strange…

I arrive at work and clock in at 6:58am. The sadness that came over me last night has gotten worse. I'm in a daze; not a tired daze—a preoccupied daze. The first thing I do today when I have spare time is begin a small search for Gina; asking around and so on—doing whatever I can to find her. I need someone to talk to; someone I would consider close. Everybody here is behaving as they normally do. However, they're wondering about my strange mood. I don't tell them much—if anything at all. I check the whole ER, and STILL—she's nowhere in sight.

Finally, I stop in the hallway and then start to get lost in my thoughts again. I don't want to be here. I want to walk out the door and go back to that castle to spend more time with him—Nicolai.

"Ivy?" That voice comes from behind me. I turn around and see Gina. Instantly, I hug her. "Gina, I'm glad to see you!" I know this is inappropriate, but I don't exactly care right now.

She pats my back, "Hey Ivy…! Are you okay?"
"Oh," I say while taking a step back, "Sorry…yeah, I'm okay."
She looks at me closer, "You seem stressed. Did you get any rest

last night?"

I look at her almost warily.

"No...?" she frowns. I lower my head and shake it slowly. Now she's really starting to wonder about me.

"Oh... I see." She quietly says. I look up at her in question. "You are sad about something, aren't you?" I don't answer; I only watch her.

She quickly places a hand on my shoulder and whispers, "Did that Francis guy do anything to you?" That, makes my eyes widen. "No! Not at all!" I can't believe she said that!

"Look," I say, "we don't really have time to talk about this and we're in a bad place to do that anyway. I'll tell you later. Maybe at lunch." Right here, I'm questioning myself why I even thought of trying to talk to her during a small break. I should have waited a little longer. I'm being insecure.

She removes her hand and nods carefully at me, "Okay. You're right."

I try to smile at her, "Let's get back to work."

"Of course–Later then." She says. As she starts heading off down the hall, I let my head down again with another sigh, and I say to myself, "Can't wait for this day to end. I need something else to do." Why didn't Nick and I exchange phone numbers? ...Why?

It's lunch time now. I've amazed myself today; I've been pretty antisocial to the ones I normally talk to. I don't know what's up with me. I'm not worrying about the things I should be worrying about either; I have Nick on my mind.

I'm not sitting in my usual spot either because Gina knows about it. I've chosen to do nearly everything alone today. So I'm sitting outside at a picnic bench. And then, a memory pops into my head of a dream I had last night where my dream-man and I went to his greenhouse and sat down at this little concrete-table-set-up-thing. He told me to follow my dreams; to do whatever my heart desires most. I knew he was very serious because his eyes never left my face; they were always unmoving. That really said something to me. I have never been encouraged like that by anyone. He asked me what I wanted. I told him I wasn't sure; life is going too fast. He was amused by that, and then he leaned across the table and gently, slowly, kissed my lips and murmured in between those kisses, "I can give you anything you want…" he slowed down to a pause and lazily reopened his eyes with a slow smile, "That is…if you let me." In that moment, I felt warmth washing over my body and jitteriness filling me. I was stuck in that bewitching gaze of his. It was as if I was then standing in a dark room, staring into light-blue diamonds that were so very, very striking–But no, they weren't glowing as I thought they were. That was merely a thought. There was nothing I wanted more than to hold him close and stay there in his arms forever.

I know that this morning I woke up teary-eyed. I was very happy. What does all this mean? I love him so much…and I don't even know him.

I sniffle, wipe a tear away and think to myself how much I wish for this dream to come true. Though at the same time…all I want to do is try to forget about it because it's not healthy to be obsessed with dreams. It's not real and it never will be. I push my salad away and put my head down on my folding arms. How could I understand this? I don't think I'll ever be able to.

"Ivy, right?" I hear. I look up past my arms and see a lady about 20-something-years-old holding her lunch, looking at me questionably. I blink, then sit up straight, "Yeah." I pull my lunch closer to me, "There something you need?" Her lips look like she's going to say 'Well' but then she shakes her head, "Um, no. I'll just-" she chuckles uncomfortably and goes to sit somewhere else. I raise an eyebrow at her. Weird. Ok…

I get up and throw away what's left of my lunch and head back to work. Oh yeah…I remember now–she's new in the ER and needs friends…
No thanks.

I'm home now.

Leaving work wasn't much of a hassle and when I pulled into the apartment complex's parking lot, I noticed tonight is quieter than usual. I'm not giving that a second thought though; I'm enjoying this while I can.

As I take my uniform shirt off, I walk around the living room, planning the phone calls I have to make. Then...after that, and most importantly, I'll kick back for a few minutes with my journal in hand and write about what's happened to me lately–because it's really bugging the hell out of me. The first thing I do is go into my room where my phone is and speed-dial my mom. Here' goes...

Just as I imagined; she picks up on the 3rd ring.

"Ivy!" I run a hand through my hair and sigh with a small sheepish smile, happy to hear her voice. "Mom, hey..."

"Why haven't I heard from you?" Now she's scolding me... "I'm sorry. I didn't want to..." Think Ivy–think. "I know this sounds bad, but...I didn't want to do anything with the family on my birthday." I squint, gritting my teeth, ready for an earful of 'Ivy, we had plans! Ivy, that was very wrong of you! Ivy this, Ivy that!' Here it comes...

"Ivy...you never say stuff like this. What's wrong?" She asks. I reopen my eyes to stare ahead at my bedroom window.

Well, how do I tell a good lie? I don't like to do that, but it's quite needed at the moment.

"I just...got tired of the same thing." I say.
"...You ok hun?" She asks. Yeah, she didn't like to hear me say that.

"Fine–I'm fine. Everybody likes a little something different once in a while." I remember Nicolai saying something like that...

"I suppose. I mean...you just got up and left us all hanging. Your dad's unhappy. We just wanna know what's up. Is there any particular reason-" "Mom, remember–I'm not a kid. I'm not a teen either. That's why I didn't want any big celebration this year. It's nothing personal."

"Ahh, so you're telling me you're not our little girl anymore…is that it?" I take in a big breath, then puff it out, "You have to understand!"
"I do Ivy, I do. Here–your dad wants to talk to you." She hands the phone to him.

"Ivy?"
I close my eyes, "Hi dad…"

"What's going on?"
"Nothing." I say, "I'm sorry about yesterday–sorry that I didn't call or anything."

"Ivy, we couldn't call you at all. That's why your mother was so excited when she got your call. We called a lot of times."

"It went dead and I lost my charger." That's easy for me to say. I hear mom telling him something.

He says, "Your mom's telling me that you didn't want to celebrate your birthday like we usually do because you're growing up…" It's almost like a question how he says that.

"Yeah, that's right. Don't worry dad, everything's fine!"
"Hold on, let me put you on speakerphone. Your mom's having a fit." He sighs. I wait.

"Ivy, what'd you do yesterday? Did you do anything on your birthday?" Mom asks. I roll over onto my back on my bed with the phone pressed to my ear, "I went sightseeing with my friend Gina. We went to different shops and small landmarks." There–close enough.

"Shoppin' with the nurse… Well that sounds fun. Why didn't you invite us?" Dad asks. Oh boy, something else I have to lie about. This is a harder one.

"Well," I begin, "do you like jewelry stores and yogurt shops? Also, do you like seafood? What about crowded places? How about-" "Ok, ok!" Dad stops me, "I've heard enough!" I can see him now, turning to mom as he says, "That's a perfectly good reason why we weren't invited Bess." Right here, she probably rolls her eyes. "Oh shut up. You're no fun!" she says. I hear her smack him. I grin faintly at this. My parents: two grown children.

"Ivy, don't do this again ok? You had us really worried and you had your dad all up in the air." Mom says.

"Mom, I told you everything is alright. Again, I'm sorry. And I won't do it again, I swear." No, I can't make that a promise… Why did I even say that?

"We'll tell your aunts and uncles that everything's fine, kay?" She assures, "Because they were wondering too."

"Fuck our siblings! They're busy-bodies." Dad suddenly grumbles.
I try not to snicker at what he says.

"You have a goodnight." Mom tells me.
I nod, "Alright mom. You too." "Love you sweetie." Dad says. "Love you too Dad. Love you both!" After I say that, mom tells me the same thing, and then we end the call.

I set my phone down with a long sigh, then I go into the kitchen to make some shrimp stir-fry and turn on some music. If I'm going to make this a 'good night', I'll go beyond that and make it a GREAT NIGHT!

Chapter 14

I sit down on the couch with my steaming hot food, turn The Who–'We don't get fooled again' down with a remote and then open my journal to see where I left off. Ah yes, the entry about my desire to go to that island. Dad once told me never tear out or erase the pages with stupid, sad, or terrible memories, because after all– those are pieces of history. I almost did that one day when I was extremely angry. I stopped myself before I could destroy anything. Right now, seeing anything that mentions the castle makes me sad–a longing kind of sad.

I take a pen from the end table on my right and start writing.

Journal entry date – *September 29, Monday...*

I'm late to write in you journal. I've had a very strange weekend. Sorry I haven't kept up. This wouldn't be the first time though. However, something way different than anything that's ever happened to me - happened. I did go to that island. And guess what? It IS OCCUPIED! There's a butler guy named Walter living there with - you won't believe this, but - the guy I saw from LOUNGE 'N' SIP! And by the way, you know how I'm always talking about the guy of my dreams? Well, the 'executive assistant' to the owner of the castle (who is named Dmitri Vladoiu II) is Romanian and looks almost exactly like the guy I always mention. His name is Nicolai Francis. This freaked me out big time! It still does. Everything there just screams 1800's - it's so very beautiful! There are maids there too who wear old-time maid outfits. Nicolai had an aristocratic look to him. He said a relative left those clothes there at the castle and he likes to wear them because they're comfortable. I have absolutely nothing against that. He's hot in those, I must say...

Ahem, anyway... You know, I don't feel the way I used to about him now. Here's why I say that, and here's the kicker: I am drawn to him; desperately wanting to be around him again. It's unreal and feels stupid in a way - could say it's 'immature' of me. There is something about him... Though we only talked a little bit, I feel attracted to him like he's a magnet and I am a piece of metal. Ever since I left this castle, sadness has been eating me up. It's getting bad - worse than I could have ever imagined.

...I must also mention, the place is filled with ghosts. I think I had one go right through me and give me the feeling of anxiety, anger, hunger and unbelievable sadness. Gosh it was intense...

That isn't the only thing I experienced while there (ghost-wise)... A ghost lady dressed in something from the 40's (I presume) came up to me and said something about 'big things are going to happen'. It was freaky as hell. I thought I'd faint, to be honest!

Well anyway... I'm here now. I'm home. Everything is back to normal now - or so I hope. I have to get my head out of my ass and get with reality now.

Journal, I hope to write in you tomorrow. Right now, I'm going to eat my food and have a beer...

I close it and do just that; finish my meal while watching television for a few hours, lost in la-la land, then I finally go to bed.

I drift off into a dream where I'm in a dark hallway with many gothic windows on the left and dimmed lamps on the right. I'm wearing a dark-green Victorian dress with a black vest, black evening gloves and black shoes. Automatically, I know I'm in a well-kept castle. The end of the hall is completely dark. There's a gentle, cool breeze blowing my way. I look at the windows. They're all closed. There aren't any vents in the walls or ceilings that I can see either. I don't think I should turn around. There's something behind me–I can sense it. I suddenly hear an organ start blaring downstairs. The melody is very serious; it's being played with rage like the organist is depressed and really wants to turn everything around in his/her life but doesn't know how yet. How do I get this vibe from hearing that? The odd feeling behind me is getting stronger.

I quickly begin walking up the hall, toward the dark end. I don't feel as scared as I think I should be. Just then, two male hands take my torso and pull me back. I scream, "NO!" Oh my god! I writhe wildly. "Get away from me!" I scream again and fling my head back but don't hit anything. There's a loud clash of thunder, and in that moment, the organ abruptly stops and some of the lights toward the end start burning out. I gasp, eyes enlarging in fright. Wind blows past my ear, and within it a male voice says my name. I struggle even more to break free. There's another snap of thunder and a blinding flash of lightning. I blink quickly to refocus on the dark end and suddenly see my dream man marching toward me with a scowl on his face, glaring up through his lashes. Each light he passes burns back on; all are really bright whenever he's close to them. I lose my breath to the frightening sight of him. But I know it's not me he's looking at.
I manage to break out of the man's grip and run to him, shouting his name.
My voice is muffled–I don't know why!

When I reach out to him, he instantly envelopes me in his arms and pushes his nose into my hair, "I've got you. Shh, I've got you." Then he slowly looks back up the hall at the one that held me in place and viciously hisses, baring fangs.

I wake up, heart racing like crazy. First, I look around the room, then I sit up and put my hand on my chest. What in the world just happened? That was just insane! Whose hands were those on me? I'm so glad my dream man showed up, though I already somehow knew he would be there. I'm thrown off by the fact he hissed at my attacker like a wild animal. Now with this on my mind, I begin to conclude the reason behind his actions. Maybe I have been fixating on eyeteeth whenever I picture Nicolai smiling, and perhaps that's why my fantasy love did that. Yeah…I suppose that makes rational sense…

I sigh, "No more thinking about this right now–I've gotta go to work."
I go take a quick shower.

Chapter 15

I arrive at the hospital, clocking in 5 minutes early and hurrying to the first place I'm scheduled today–the ICU. As I'm walking quickly down the hall, I see there are stretchers that need cleaning. Wonderful! Someone hasn't been doing their job. If I could, I'd make them up. I can't though–not until I get the opportunity to. I go around a corner and run into that pharmacist, Liam. He's probably going to ask me out again.

He smiles at me, "Ivy."
I smile back, briefly, "Hey Liam. How's it goin'?"
"Good, good. It's a busy day." he says, "What about you? What are you up to?"
I dryly tell him, "The ICU. That's what I'm doing."
"Oh, fun… So uh, Ivy…you doin' anything this weekend? I got tickets to…" I give him a cold stare like I just ate a piece of glass on purpose. "I have a lot do and can't think about the weekend right now. Maybe we can talk later." He stiffens a little, not expecting me to behave this way. **Good!** He grimaces, "See you at lunch, okay?"
I look away and say, "Yeah…sure." As I walk away, I can feel his eyes on me.

I can remember the days I enjoyed coming here, but now I can't seem to stop feeling unhappy about everything and questioning everything.

As soon as I'm in the ICU, I'm stopped by a nurse who asks me to take blood specimens to the blood lab. It's a short walk that I've made many times, but when I get there I don't remember the walk. I get a page to go to the ER where I hear about a guy that arrived at the trauma center after getting into a car accident. I take the time and go check on him.

The trauma room is full of empty beds. There's hardly anyone in here. It's quiet too. This is normal. The one I'm looking for is all

the way in the back corner. I ask one of the nurses about him. They say he's in pretty good condition–now. He has a broken arm with a bad slice in it, and he's scratched up in different places. Now, as a tech, I don't normally come over here. None of us do. It's usually only nurses, doctors, environmental services, and the administration desk. Security is always outside the door that the fire dept. and ambulances use to bring people in.
I walk toward him.

When I meet his bedside, I'm stunned. I know him! It's that old man from Lounge 'n Sip that handed my keys back to me! He's amazed to see me too.

"Well well…" He says.
"What happened to you?" I quietly ask.
"Ah, well…I almost hit someone. My car swerved off the road and hit a tree. I fell unconscious after that. The fellow I almost hit saved my life by calling an ambulance. He should be here still." he looks around. "Oh wow…" I mutter. I fix his blankets and look at him again, "Are you ok?"
"I'm numb. Can't feel much'ah nothin'. I got a broken arm I think." I give him an empathetic frown, "I'm sorry you went through that… What's your name?"

"Henry." he smiles lightly at me.
"I'm Ivy."

He moves a little and says, "I'd shake your hand, but I…can't move much without a stinging pain." I nod in understanding, "Oh no Henry, it's ok. I'm glad we finally know each other's names." I smile at him, "Maybe if we're lucky, I can help ya out." He nods and then looks over past my shoulder at someone, "He's outside there talking to those security guys." I arch an eyebrow, then look back and see a man talking to the guards. Maybe I should speak with him.

I tell Henry, "I'll be back. There anything you need?"
"Some of that Lounge 'n sip coffee." he mumbles.
I laugh lightly, "Don't have that back here, sorry."

"But there's some other coffee in the café."

A male-nurse approaches us and says to him, "Sorry buddy but you can't drink anything yet; doctor's orders." That makes Henry grimace at him. I don't think he likes this guy. The nurse quietly tells me, "Sorry to cut things off for you two, but he needs to go to cat-scan again."
I nod, "Ok." I guess he's going to get double-checked; evidently somebody was being an idiot. I look at Henry again, "I'll be back later." "Alright." He's a bit annoyed. I smile at him and go out.

As soon as I get through the door, my body tenses up; the memory of last night's dream comes back to me in a flash. It's Nicolai. I'm lost at the moment, unsure if Henry was talking about him or not. I hope he wasn't!

He's wearing regular everyday clothing; fashionable gray buttoned-up coat with a black scarf, black slacks, and those black expensive-looking formal shoes.

Finally, he looks at me and then smiles, "Well hello." My stomach twists.
I utter a faint nervous hum to myself before saying, "Hello..." My voice is quiet and stunned at the same time. He then nods once at the guards and does a gesture like asking me if we can talk. I give the trauma door and the clock above it a glance, then I say, "Yeah, there's time." He blinks a glad 'okay' expression at me.

We go into a waiting room and he shuts the door. As he turns around to me, I hold my arms close. All I see right now is that same man who rescued me from those hands holding me hostage...

"What's going on? I heard from a guy in there that you rescued him." I ask. He looks around before telling me, "Yes...well it is quite a strange story to say the least..."
"I'll say!"
He half-smiles at that, then says, "That man in there almost ran over me this morning. I was on my way to the store when I saw an animal in the road, so I got out of my car and went to rescue it. It was foggy outside. He saw me at the last second and swerved off

the road, hitting a tree." My eyes widen, "What? You almost got killed?" And he saved something's life! Holy crap!

He waves his hands, "Everything is fine now. I called an ambulance. He is in good hands now." I sigh in surprise, "Wow… Yeah, I talked to him. What about you? How are you doing?" I know he'll be okay. I'm more worried about you!

He lifts a shoulder, "I got out of the way in time. I'm okay." My attention drops from his face to his neck where I spot a little bit of blood around his scarf. It sends a shiver up my spine. "Nick," I almost take a quick step closer to him but then I suddenly feel uncomfortable about doing that. "What?" He tilts his head, confused. While eyeing the blood, I compare the fact he's hurt (or maybe not) with the dream I had last night even more. I was a damsel in distress and he came to my rescue. Today, here he is at the hospital, possibly needing help… Amazing!

He takes a step closer, "Are you alright?"
"Yeah…" First I shake my head but then I nod. He becomes slightly puzzled, then checks his scarf and touches the area I keep looking at. "Oh," He sees the blood on his finger, "Well I was unaware of that…I'm sorry." I watch him take a puff of sanitizer cream from the dispenser on the wall and rub his hands together. He frowns to the feel of it. Before he does anything else, I say, "Yeah, it feels disgusting, I know."

"I prefer the traditional washing of the hands under a faucet." He mutters in amusement. I move closer to him, no longer able to resist the want to see if he's cut. "Excuse me, I'm sorry," I pull his scarf down his neck a little. What the–? There's no injury here. What happened? He grabs my hand, startling me. I lift my eyes up to his. He then smirks, "It isn't my blood; it's Henry's. I just had an itch and scratched it before I washed my hands." I blink repeatedly at him. He whispers, "Why don't you have lunch with me?" I gulp slowly, making him chuckle.
How sudden of him… And that little suave laugh of his…

"But Nick, I don't know when I'll be relieved."

I hate having to say that…

His response is a warm smile. He takes a card out of his coat pocket, "Then call me. I'm taking off work for a while so I have some time on my hands." He winks at me. I take it and hesitantly look down at it. It's his business card–a finely detailed one at that.

"Okay," I start tucking it away in one of my scrub pants' pockets, "What will you do while I'm working…?" Wait, that isn't my business…

As he wipes the blood off his neck, he says, "For now, I'm going to sight-see around the hospital and perhaps play the piano in the lobby." Oh my, he plays the piano? That's lovely! He sees the light in my eyes and a wide smile graces his face. "Yes, I play the piano Ivy."
"I wish I could watch." I frown slightly. He takes my hand, "Maybe one of these days, you can." He kisses it. My cheeks flush. "Call me when you can." He says. I nod and watch him open the door for me.

We go out, he gives me a last wink and then he walks up the hall like he owns the place. Wow…

He turns around a corner and a bleach-blonde female doctor walking past him looks him up and down. He doesn't pay any attention to her though. Suddenly, my eye twitches a little. "You…know him?" A security guy asks me from behind.

I didn't even notice him standing there.
Quickly, I tuck some hair behind my ear and proceed back through the trauma center.
"Yeah–sorta."
Sorta…

Chapter 16

'Lunchtime'

As I'm walking to the cafeteria, I pull my phone and Nick's card out. You know, I've always been terrible at making phone-calls–especially when I have to call someone that breathes authority. Now that I'm thinking that way about him, I begin to stare at both the card and my phone. I lose track of where I am and stop in the hallway. While leaning against the wall as if I'm waiting for a bus or something, I suddenly hear, "Hey Ivy!" Gina.

I look up at her and see she's checking out the card in my hand. "What's that?" she asks. I quickly put it away, "Nothing. It's just a business card." She folds her arms, "Riight…I saw the name 'Francis' on there." She looks expectant now. I'm expressionless–For the most part. "So…?" I shrug slowly. She rolls her eyes, "Okay fine, I'm going to get some coffee. Just so you know, I won't be in the cafeteria this time–I've got a date with Doctor Michelson." Oh... I grin. He's only the hottest doctor in the entire ER…

"No no no," she laughs, "It's not like that."
"Okay… Sure. If you say so." She then glances ahead of us at the cafeteria and grabs my shoulder, "Look." "What?" I follow her gaze. Oh my! There's Nicolai–Walking out, drinking a red power drink, seeming deep in thought. Has he really been here that long? What has he been doing for the last few hours? Playing the piano as he said? If he didn't leave, I must say he has tons of patience.

I inhale deeply, the jitteriness returning.
"That guy from the Lounge n' sip; I wonder why he's here…" she says.
We watch him throw his drink away and then I whisper to her, "I'll see you later."
"Oh! Yeah, okay. Let me know how everything goes." She says.

I walk up to him and he bows his head in greeting.
"Ivy, good afternoon." I study him, a smile shortly appearing on

my face.

"Hi...good afternoon to you too."

He smirks at me, "Has it been a long day?"

"Hm," I barely laugh while turning my head down a bit, "It's been interesting. And yeah, a little."

"You must be starved." He waves his hand out, gesturing me to lead the way.

"Yeah." I nod briefly and start walking.

The room's crowded–just as I thought it'd be. Nick seems to be either excited about it, or he's just happy we're eating lunch together in a place he would consider close to being normal–or 'casual', he'd probably say.

We go to the grill, and before I can order what I want, he orders the most expensive things on the menu; lobster salad with some steak. The last thing is the main course. I look at him like 'are you out of your mind?' It's not because the food is expensive, it's because he's buying me lunch. I'm so not used to that. The girl behind the counter gives us our food and me a *wow* look as we go pay. **Oh, whatever lady...**

Nick glances at me like he wants me to lead, so I pick a place for us to sit. Just to see what he would do, I choose a romantic-looking place where there are lights over our heads. He doesn't really notice it; instead, he behaves like this is just a random place to sit. I'm a little bummed by that but I don't let on.

He smells his food and smiles, "Hmm...smells delicious."
I smirk at him, "Yes...thank you again." He raises an eyebrow in a 'you don't need to thank me' way. I merely smile in reply to that.

"So..." he says as he takes his Styrofoam cup of tea, "How are you doing?"

"I'm fine... and you?" I drink some of my cola, not actually fine; I'm ecstatic to be with him and I feel complete again.

"Quite well... I played the piano as I said, took a trip into the gift shop and bought a few little neat trinkets." I slowly smile, now becoming amused with the idea of him 'shopping'.

"What'd you get?" I ask. He grins down at his food, "It is rude to present things at the dining table…" he raises his eyes up to me, "Isn't it?" My smile vanishes; now I'm a bit taken aback.
"I suppose you're right." I say.
"Indeed." He takes a bite of his food and then hums in satisfaction, "This is good for hospital food." Seeing that he's happy with it, I lightly giggle.

"Eat, eat!" he tells me. "Okay!" I take a forkful and try some. Instantly, I feel like I'm in heaven. **Oh, this is so good!**

He leans back in his chair in a proud sort of way, holding a fork in one hand and a knife in the other. With another giggle, I wipe my mouth and notice his eyes are glistening with humor. It's almost like he hasn't made this face in a very long time. I don't understand why.

"You know, I didn't get to thank you or Walter for letting Gina and I stay for the night and for the great hospitality that was shown to us." I pick through my salad.

"Oh," he dabs a corner of his mouth with a napkin, "You are quite welcome."
"If Dmitri were there and you weren't, do you think things would've been different?" I ask.
He takes a deep breath, "Mr. Vladoiu can be a generous man but he is very, very private…" he then smirks, "He does have a soft spot for beautiful women though." Oh does he…? I blush.

"Is that so?" I ask, "Well…what if a woman that could be a supermodel shows up for the same reason I did?" **I *gotta* hear the answer to this one…**

He puts his silverware down and leans forward a little, eyes darkening in a devilish way, "I don't think you would want to know what he would do with her." My cheeks redden even more. He looks at my mouth as I bite my bottom lip. He stares at it until finally returning to his meal, "Bah… he is an old man. He is just nicer to women. But he is rarely at that castle, so it is I who deals with the 'uninvited guests' when I am there, that is–If they get past Walter."

I start to laugh.

"What?" He doesn't get it. I slightly point at him, "You make Walter sound like a mean 'guard dog'."

"Oh…" he thinks for a moment, then he shakes his head in amusement, "Yes, I see what you mean now…" He laughs with me.

When we slow down to a stop, I say, "So you're surrounded by old men; how old are you exactly?–If you don't mind me asking?"

"I'm 32. How about you?" He says. Whoa, he's 10 years older than me! I expected that, yet at the same time–I didn't.

"22–I'm 22."

"You are a baby." He teases. I roll my eyes, "If you say so."

"A cute baby." He winks. I smile stupidly at that, "Thanks…" I'm being sarcastic. A fox-like smile curls up at the corners of his lips, resembling a hungry wolf, and his eyes are even more intense now. He looks down at his food and says, "I bet you would be tasty." Wait, what?! "Excuse me?" I lightly gasp. How forward! And that look! **Whoa...**

He clears his throat, "I mean my lobster salad." He takes a bite of it.

I turn my head slightly to the left, staring at him strangely, "Oh…?"

"Yes, it's delightful." He says. Ohh-kay…

"So, do tell me, how was the boat ride back home?" He asks. "...It was good... Leonardo didn't talk much but his sister was a little friendlier. Thanks." **They're a little weird in my opinion.**

"Hm," He sounds like he expected me to say something like that. Yeah…well I'm still wondering about what he said just a minute ago. My cheeks are hot and I have to admit my stomach jumped. That smile he showed sent shivers all up and down my spine. Yet again I'm trying hard not to squirm in my seat.

My phone goes off. Both he and I look around.

"Hang on, I'm sorry–I need to check this." I glance down at it and see that Gina left a text about her date. Here I thought it was important, but no–It's not.

As I go to tuck it back in my pocket, I feel him grab my other hand. I quickly look at him. His eyes are glowing bright blue. "Oh my-" He tilts his head slowly. "Morning coffee at Lounge 'n Sip?" His voice is quiet and smooth. I gasp, and oddly…the air is feeling slightly heavy all of a sudden. His eyes… They're so…

His lips move but I hear a woman's voice replacing his, "Of course you want to agree…Ivy…" She's very soothing to the ears. So soothing–It's like a tender caress.

"Of course…I'd love to." Slowly, I smile. He smiles back genuinely, "Great. What time do you go to work?"
"I clock in at 9 tomorrow."

"Wonderful. How about 7:30?" He calmly asks.
A bit surprised, I say, "You get up early…"
"Oh," he laughs, "I have a bit of insomnia. It's something I am used to."
"…I couldn't really sleep last night." I mutter, still staring into his eyes, and he slightly tilts his head. "Bad dream…?" He asks, voice seeming quieter... and deeper.

"Yeah…it was frightening yet quite an interesting one." Wow...

His eyes stop glowing as he says, "Hm, that's unfortunate... maybe you can tell me about it later." I blink slowly in awe of him, "Okay..." I form a puzzled face. I feel like something just happened but my mind was elsewhere when it took place. What could it have been? I know I agreed to meet up with him at the coffee place but there was something about it that was spectacular. Damn, what was it? And I really want to tell him about that dream I had but now isn't the time.

"Good." He says as I look around in a baffled way.
"Nick, did something just happen?" I turn back to him.

Finishing his food with a few more bites, he says, "What do you mean?" I watch him, then slowly do the same. There is something really strange about this guy. I wish I knew what.

He pushes his plate aside and smiles at me, "Well! I'm finished." "Me too." I say. Time to come back down to earth perhaps...

"Allow me," he takes my plate while standing up, pushing his chair in. "Oh! Thanks."
"Not a problem." he gestures me to follow him away from the table, and I do. We go to the trash conveyer belt and put our leftovers there, then find our way out of the cafeteria.

We stop outside and he takes my hand, and quietly says, "I look forward to our first official date Ivy," he brings it up to his lips and kisses it softly, looking into my eyes all the while...just like before at the castle. My heart flutters–Not only because of his hot touch, but because of his mannerism. I gulp as my throat goes dry, "...Me too." He straightens his posture and smiles at me; that warm genuine smile that takes my breath away. He nods once and walks on. I put my hand on my chest and rub the place he kissed. My mind is in a whirl right now.

"Oh my gosh..."

Chapter 17

I'm home now, thank goodness. After lunch, the rest of the day went back to being in a daze. When I found time, I went to see Henry. He'll be fine. He went home this afternoon with a cast, a few stitches and a prescription for pain medication. When we last spoke, he kept telling me that he felt drained of energy as he rubbed his shoulder. I asked if I could see it but he told me it was probably arthritis bothering him and that he'll be okay. All I could do was accept and move onto another subject, and I told him to buy himself a good-sized cheeseburger, and get plenty of rest. He gave me his number, which I happily accepted.

At the moment, I'm looking through my mail. I've got bills, brochures–and more bills… I toss them on the counter with a sigh. The clock says 7:32. It's dinner time.

Ivy Summers: a girl that lives off TV dinners and coffee. I wish I could have something different…

Gosh… Nick has the ability to buy expensive things whenever he wants. It must be nice. One day, I might be able to do that–but I surely won't have the things he has. "Well Ivy, it depends on which direction you choose to go. It isn't impossible to follow your dreams; you just have to believe and know how." I tell myself.

I take out a small frozen pizza and toss it on the table. Gotta preheat my oven first. "Yeah, I'm a go-getter. But I don't know if I want to be a doctor." What if I looked into starting a business? I've always liked learning about that.

I walk into the living room and turn the PC on. I wonder which will be ready first…the oven or the computer. Tick…tick…tick. For a few minutes this goes on–Until the oven beeps. You win.

I put the pizza in and come back to the computer. I really need a new computer! The pizza should be done in about 20 minutes. Now then! Researching…

A couple hours later…

I come out of the shower, put my tank-top and shorts on, then grab my journal and begin writing in it. Ahh yes…my standard everyday procedure. Nothing abnormal about this! I open it and put pen to paper.

Journal entry date – October 1st, Wednesday

Today went interestingly. I went to work and found out an old man I met at Lounge 'n Sip a few days ago (his name's Henry) came into trauma after getting into a car accident. I went to see him and found out why he was admitted into the hospital – he almost hit Nicolai, who was on his way to the store early this morning. Henry swerved his car and slammed into a hillside.

I had to talk to Nick about it of course. Well, he wasn't far. He was outside, talking to the security guys. I went to see him and then we went into a waiting room. There he explained to me he was trying to save an animal from getting hit and Henry saw him at the last minute, which is why the accident happened.

I saw blood on his neck. It made my body tingle with worry. I had to see for myself if he was okay because I believed he would just blow it off; I pulled his scarf down a little and saw not a scratch. He grabbed my hand suddenly, which got my full attention. "It isn't my blood." He said with a smile. It was Henry's… Of course, being this close and him doing that took my breath away. I wonder what I would've done if we got any closer than that. The thought makes my stomach turn with excitement. He asked me to go to lunch with him. Oh I had to! I agreed – definitely. 12 o'clock rolled around and we met up outside the cafeteria. Lunch went awesomely. We had a wonderful conversation. I say, it wasn't as awkward as I thought it'd be. However, he did do something strange. The subject of age came up; he *told me he's 32...yeah 32...and I said I'm 22. He called me a 'cute baby'. Well that made me blush. As I went into la-la land over that, I heard him say, "I bet you would taste delicious." That was the hottest thing EVER! I was absolutely stunned to hear him say that. He took my reaction different than what I thought he would though. I mean, he must've thought I was totally weirded out or something.*

Oh, and another exciting thing: Tomorrow morning, we're going to have coffee together. It's gonna be an early date; 7:30am. I probably won't sleep tonight because that will be on my mind. Gosh, I wish I wasn't so infatuated with him. I barely know him! It's so weird!

I close my journal and look out the window. The moon is high, bright...like at the castle. I put the book down on the nightstand, set my clock for 6am, pull the covers up to my neck and shut my eyes. Can't wait for tomorrow morning...

"Ivy, I have missed you." I hear his voice behind me as I stand in the foyer of the castle, looking at the front doors. I turn my head slightly, noticing I'm in yet another Victorian dress–A white one. Before I move, I feel his hands wrap around me and his hot breath brush across my neck. His prickly 5 o'clock shadow tickles my skin, making me giggle and then bite my lip to suppress the sound.

"I've missed you too." I say.
"Not as much, I know." He snickers and suddenly pushes me up against the wall. I gasp. He takes my hands and puts them above my head, then moves my hair out of the way of my neck. "Hm, not wearing the necklace I gave you?" My eyes widen, "I-" "Shush," He presses his lips to my neck and I feel him bite a little. I inhale sharply, saying his name but it's muffled.

"I feel unappreciated. You are coming with me." He snatches my hand and takes me through one of the doors, into a dark, narrow stairwell. "Where are we going?" I quickly ask.

"My bedroom." He laughs darkly. Oh! I gasp again.

My alarm clock goes off, making me jump. I breathe in deeply and look at the clock. It's 5:30am. I sit up and rub my forehead, "Oh my god," That was hot and–damn, it was startling too!

"Wow, he looks just like him." It's so scary. What am I going to do when I see Nick again? All I'll see is the man in the dream I just had. Oh geez...

I begin the morning with a quick shower, some primping, a quick snack, and then I'm gone.

I go through a bit of traffic and show up at Lounge 'n Sip 20 minutes early. I didn't do much with my looks before I left home. It's a work day anyway; there would be more to take off at work if I made myself up. Besides...I'm overwhelmed with that dream and I just can't have him staring at me. I fix my dark red lip-gloss, get out of the car and go inside in a hurry because of the cold. My eyes immediately search for that spot he sits in and–My heart jumps. There he is!

He's early...and he looks amazing. He's dressed pretty much like he was yesterday at the cafeteria, but he doesn't have the coat. He has a black long-sleeved shirt with that same scarf, some gray pants, and those shoes that he wore before. I wonder what he would look like without a shirt...? Oh my god...

I also see he's writing in that old book again. I can't help but grin.

As soon as I get within a few feet of him, he closes his book and smiles up at me. There's that smile again... Instantly, I remember my dream man nibbling on my neck. Gosh, I have to stop thinking about that so much!

"Hey...good morning." I say. Keep calm Ivy–keep calm. Yes yes, I was right–All I see now is the man in my dreams.

"Good morning," He stands, walks over and pulls a chair out for me. I blink at him a couple times, then I slowly sit down, "Thank you."

"You are quite welcome." he joins me at the table. His attention goes to my lips and stays there for a second. What? Does he like the color? A quick smile graces his features as he returns his gaze to my eyes, "So…would you like a pumpkin latté?" **Ohh, pumpkin…yummy!**

"Yes, thank you…" I say, "That's actually my favorite drink from here." A small unintentional laugh slips past my lips, which makes him smile again. He stands again, "I will be right back." I watch him go to the counter to order. He left his book at the table. Hmm... I momentarily look down at it, "What is that?" For the longest time, it seems, I keep my eyes on it. So old…there are definitely a ton of secrets in there. I would love to read through it…

I look up and see him returning with our drinks. He hands me my drink and I instantly take a sip. Ohh, such delight! Just what I needed! As he sits, he raises an eyebrow at me and looks down at the book, "It's a journal if that is what you are wondering."
I smirk, "You keep one, huh?"
He does an amused sound and nods, "Yes. I have had it for many years. It is a family tradition." **Whoa. Really?**

"Do you write in it daily?" I ask.
He takes his coffee, and before he drinks any, he murmurs, "I write in it whenever something I consider notable happens."

Well, causing a wreck is something I'd consider notable...
I make a face.

He suddenly cracks a wry smile, "What is that look?"
I shake my head, looking away from him, "Nothing. Nothing at all." I tuck my hair behind my ear and slightly look at him, then at his coffee, "Is that your favorite too?"

A thoughtful expression adorns his face, then he says, "Not exactly…I mostly enjoy the raspberry mocha drink." Ohh, that's a good one too. That's a Valentine's Day drink though…so it's seasonal.

"You know it's only around once a year." I say.

He nods, "Yes I know, but years are like days to me."

"How so?"

"Well," he sighs, "for me...days, months, years–they don't seem to matter much. It's more about paperwork, business, social politics, and money. Other things are involved of course, but I do not wish to speak of them at the moment." he grins, "...Time flies when you are having fun, yes?"

I blush faintly, "That's true."

"So..." he says, "You live around here?"

"Hm," I smile slyly while bringing the coffee up to my mouth, "I'm not telling."

He watches me put it back down, and flashes an entertained smile, "Very well... So what about hobbies?-Things you like to do with your spare time?"

"Well, you know I have a journal–that's one of the things I like to do. I like to listen to music while I cook... And I like sightseeing– you know that too." When I mention the last thing, I chuckle.

He leans back a little in interest while listening to my words and blinks slowly as if in thought. "I have the same interests as you."

"You do?" I ask.

"Yes I do."

"What are your hobbies?" I'm curious to know.

"Heheheh..." he laughs under his breath, "You ask me what my hobbies are... Well they are quite simple actually. I am an organist, I like horseback riding, I do a little bit of painting, and I enjoy music. Boating is good fun as well. I like to throw parties sometimes and I also love to read. But I do all of this when I am not working and have time for it, of course." I give him a long gaze in awe.

He sure knows how to live... Those aren't simple hobbies at all! It takes skill to do the things he's suggesting! "You are very imaginative it seems. But I can't help wondering... no Mrs. Francis?" I ask. He smirks secretively yet jokingly, "I really don't have time for a wife, and you see why I don't have guests often.

There is so much to do; very little time to spend with others."

"Yeah…" That does make sense.

Why Victorian?" he asks.

"What?"

"You like Victorian architecture. It intrigues me that you are also fascinated by it. I would like to discuss that more with you." he sips some of his coffee.

"It's just something I studied a lot about when I was in school…and it just stuck with me." I say.

"Really?" He's stunned. "You don't look like that kind of person." I look down, "No…but you do."

He does the same amused noise as me and says, "What is that supposed to mean? Most people say I'm 'unnaturally' gorgeous." He flashes his brows flirtatiously. My mouth falls slightly open as I watch him, then I shake my head with a disbelieving laugh, "You are very sure of yourself."

He raises his hands, "Of course I am! I am godly handsome. Now you Ivy…" he props his hand underneath his chin, "With a face and body like yours, you are complimented constantly… I'm right, aren't I?" I tilt my head, silent as he waits for my answer. His words, 'I bet you would taste delicious' are replaying in my mind. And he's so arrogant, but it's really hot.

"Not really, no… I don't talk to anyone; I keep to myself. I don't usually give anyone time to talk to me." I say. He hums in an agreeing way, "Well, I understand why you feel that way."

Suddenly, my phone goes off. I sigh agitatedly, "I'm sorry– excuse me." I look at it and see it's 8:10 now. Whoa. Time has gone by too fast! Gina left me a message, asking me to join her for lunch later.

"Text message?" he asks.

I put it away, "Yeah…and a time reminder." I frown.

He puts his hand on mine, "It's okay, don't let me keep you from your job." he stands, "It was a pleasure having coffee with you Ivy." he reaches for my empty coffee cup, I give it to him, then he

asks, "Would you like to meet again?" I stand still for a moment while looking into his eyes. Oh god, I would so much love for that to happen. I nod, "Oh yeah, definitely." And I smile. He slowly grins and takes my hand after setting one coffee cup down, then he whispers close to it while his slowly glowing eyes focus on mine, "How wonderful... I cannot wait. Very soon, I hope." I feel my heart skip a beat. He kisses my hand. "I..." I breathe. "How about...tonight at 6, we can meet at a place you can see my home from afar; the statue of Harold II...we can admire the glistening Sound at sunset together." I touch my hand below my neck, still captivated by him, "In uniform?"
He smiles slowly, "Wear whatever you wish."
My cheeks redden. "I would love to," I'm very quiet, hardly audible.
"Perfect." he flashes a quick wolfish smile. Gosh, that smile! His eyes, his smile, his face...he's so mesmerizing! I blink quickly.

"You're blushing my dear." he simpers.

Am I? I bet I am!

Quickly, I say, "Ahem. Well ok!"
"See you this evening...Ivy." He winks at me, his voice like rich hot chocolate truffle. Yes, it's really delicious like that. I nod at him and start for the door, slightly tripping over my feet as I go. What the hell am I doing? Walk normal!!!

Glimpsing back, I see him standing in the same spot, grinning at me. I turn back and go out the door, get in my car and drive off. GOSH HE'S HOT!

When I approach the light, I happen to look back and see Henry walking up to the shop. He's probably getting his morning coffee. I wish I could stick around to ask him how he feels, but I really have to get to work. He has a cast in a sling on his arm and he's limping only a tiny bit from the scratches. Ohh, I hope he doesn't stay there long! He should be at home resting!

The light turns green. I hit the gas and hurry off. I have no idea where my head will be today.

Chapter 18

Now I'm back at work and doing my thing; I'm in the ICU again. It's busier than usual. I was just reminded…Halloween is getting closer. One of my favorite days of the year! I hope I don't have to work that day. Well…like yesterday, the first few hours of the day I'm only thinking about Nick and our date. It went…amazingly. I can't get over that last dream and I can't get over this morning. I really want to go back to his castle and spend time with him there. Every time I'm away from him, I'm sad. But when we're together, it's like I've explained before–I feel complete.

Another person I'm thinking of is Henry. He's healing up but I'm still concerned about him. I go on lunch break and call him when I go into the break room. He answers on about the fifth ring. Momentarily after the hellos, I ask about his health.

"I'm feelin' much better than yesterday. I'm more tired during the day though. I think it's the medicine the doc put me on. I'm fine other than that… How about you? How you feelin'?"

I smile kindly, "Well I'm glad to hear you're getting better. You gotta be careful taking that medication Henry."
"Yeah yeah, I know."
"Hey, I bet you didn't know I saw you at the coffee shop this morning."
"What? No, I didn't! Where were you?"
"At the red light." I laugh, "I was there earlier than usual to have a morning cup o' Joe with your savior." Let's see if he talked to him.

"My savior…? Oh! Yeah–Nick. I saw him. We chatted a bit. It was for a short time though. We just talked about my arm and the weather."

"Oh…" I say, "Well listen," I turn slightly once seeing Gina coming into the room, "I have to go. It was nice talking to you and I'm glad to know you're feeling better."

"Alright then! Good talking to you too Ivy. Don't you work too hard now, ya hear?"

I smile, "Ok Henry. Take care." I hang up and look at Gina. "Ready to go to lunch?" she asks. I nod, "Yeah." We go out of the break room to the cafeteria, get some salads and find a place to sit.

"So, how was lunch with Vlad the Impaler? Mr. vampire-man Dracula-" I stop her right there. "That's not funny Gina." She grimaces, "What's the problem with that?"
I start eating again, "He may be Romanian-" She gasps, "He's Romanian? Dude, Romanians can be hot!" I sigh, rolling my eyes, "Yes he is. Just please don't label him as Dracula–Like that."
"Why not? Dracula can be hot too." She grins. I stare at her. She shrugs, "Okay sorry. So how did it go?" I'm quiet for a moment, thinking back on the conversations he and I have had, and those dreams are returning to my thoughts.

"Ohh…Ivy…did you two 'do it'?" WHAT! I suddenly snap my plastic fork, eyes now huge, "What? No!" I shake my head, "Gina!" She bursts out laughing, "Well you're blushing redder than an apple!" I narrow my eyes at her, "That's not funny either." She folds her arms, "Yes it is. What happened? You have me confused. I mean, one minute you're all depressed and then here you are today, lost in infatuation or something. I can see that in your face, you know. I wasn't going to ask, but what about our little lunch date that time you seemed stressed out?" I sigh and put my hand on my forehead, "I'm sorry about that. I was in my own little world and pretty much felt unsociable. It's nothing to worry about; just trouble in the family. As for Nicolai, it was nothing but a couple casual rendezvous dates. We had lunch here yesterday and then drank coffee together this morning at Lounge n' Sip."

And tonight I'm meeting him at the coastline.
Geez that's close.

"Whoa… He must really like you, huh?"
"Yeah, I think…"

"Girl what do you mean 'you *think*'? Who asked who?"

I slowly look up from my hand at her, "He asked me."
I'm amazed by everything that's happened so far.

She gradually smiles, pushes her salad aside and puts her hand on mine, "Well if this is the case, take it one baby step at a time. But be mindful of him; some rich guys spot pretty girls and wanna jump in their pants the first chance they get."
I snort, "Yeah, I don't think this guy is like that, but alright–I will."
"Good." She smiles, moving her hand away to continue her lunch.
I look away from her, "Yeah..." What would Mom and Dad say? How would they react if they knew I'm talking to this guy? If this were some normal guy, I would go straight to Mom, looking for relationship advice. I have to be quiet about this one. I can't tell anybody. Gina only knows because of, well–she's a victim of circumstance. I sigh, now coming back into reality–sort of–and I smile nicely at her.

-Nicolai-

I arrive at my island and follow the stone path to the front doors where my gardener is trimming the shrubbery near a window. He tips his hat to me, "Mr. Francis,"

I smile curtly at him, continuing up to the doors. They open, revealing Walter. "Welcome back sir." He says. "Hello Walter," I step inside, give him my coat and look ahead at the stairs. Maria is standing at the bottom with Pamela, staring at me. I take a deep breath and say, "What's going on?"

"Not much. There has been a lot of talk among the maids though."
I look at him. "About what?" He lowers his head, giving me serious eyes. I narrow my own and return to watching the two at the stairs, "I want to speak with Maria…in my office in 5 minutes." I start to walk forward. He grabs my shoulder, "Sir." I stop and shoot him an aggravated look. He lets off with an apologetic pursing of his lips, then he carefully says, "They are wondering about the woman you brought here not too long ago." I blink emotionlessly at him.

"That's not a problem."
'Rozalia, consider what year this is. Nowadays, people aren't as trusting.'

"I will not let you move again."
I grind my teeth gently.

"I do not see why they are so concerned. She left that night." I say. At that, his face turns slightly exasperated. "Sir, I think it would be best you at least speak with Maria."
"Fine, I am alright with that." I walk away from him to the staircase. Maria watches me pass her, then she looks at Walter oddly. He sighs slowly, folding his arms.

While I go up the hall, I'm confronted by Corneliu.
I don't look at him as he says, "Your next victim will have people at your doorstep Dmitri. Luck is always at your side."

"Leave me." I growl.

"What will you say? Or will you leave? Destroy Rozalia before it is too late!"

I stop at my office door and glare at him, "I cannot leave... I *will* *not* leave!"

"FOOL! DON'T TEST ME!" Rozalia raises the electrical tension in the hall, forcing Corneliu to drop to his knees in pain as the lights glow brighter. He wincingly looks up at me, "FIGHT **HER**! You have no choice but to leave! What keeps you here? Is it that girl–*Ivy*?!" He then points at me sternly, "By now, your heart should be stone. There is nothing different about this girl! You are only damaging yourself!"

I hiss in his face, "I do not have the mind of a child; I know what is at stake here. Now leave me be!" I whip the door open and slam it shut.

I march up to my desk and squeeze the edges of it, "Why is she so important to you...? Who is she really?"

"Love..."

"No! It is not love! It is something else!"

"Look in the mirror."

I squeeze my eyes shut.

*"I said **LOOK**!"*

I reopen them and slowly turn my head to the mirror on my desk. There she is–staring at me.

She tilts my head, "You are just going to have to cooperate if you want the answer to your question."

"Why won't you tell me?"

She smiles wickedly, *"Life is not always easy–especially for those who have done wrong."*

"All I did was save lives!"

"It would not have disturbed the natural order of things had I stayed where I was."

There's suddenly a knock at my door. I shift away from the mirror, "Yes?" It opens and I see Maria standing there in question.

I wave her in, "Yes yes…" Rozalia makes me smile darkly, "Come inside…" I clear my throat softly.

'No, not yet!'

"Take what you need and then I will have a small drink."

'I *really* despise you.'

I motion Maria to sit. As she does, I say, "Walter informed me there has been some talking going on about a guest I entertained recently. As the head housekeeper… I would like you to tell me what you and the other maids are concerned about." She watches me sit down in my chair and rest my chin down on my hand, then she says, "No sir…it's just…well…I know it's not my business, and I don't want to offend you sir, but… no one ever saw that other woman leave the castle. The one that was with you before Ivy and the other woman came here together. We're just curious."

"Ah, I see. You are correct…it is not your business. However… I will tell you she decided to leave late that night. I escorted her myself."

She leans forward in her chair, "But we didn't see her…or you around the castle either."

I drop my hand, now having a sardonic expression, "This is a large castle and there are very few of you. Even less at night…need I say more?" Her eyes shift back and forth while she thinks, then she sits back. "No sir."

I see in her features there's something else on her mind. "Is there something else? What is it?" I ask. She looks at me, "There's also some questioning about what happened to Ivy–when she passed out."

"No one explained it to you?"

She shakes her head.

I sigh, "Miss Summers had a very hard night. Of course she nodded off from exhaustion. She came here tired too." I pause, then continue, "It was nothing. I talked to her just this morning. She's fine now." In this moment, I start to notice she really does hate mentioning Ivy. I know because of the way her face twitches

here and there in disgust. But I don't react. Instead, I smile in a gradually teasing way, "What, are we...*jealous*?"
Her brow creases, "I don't know what you mean sir."
"Really?"

She nods, "Yes, really."
I turn my head down with a small laugh, "No, I think you are."

"Sir-" "Stop." I raise my hand and then look at her again. This surprises her. I stand, walk around to her and gently lift her chin up with a finger, "You have no reason to be jealous." Her jaw falls slightly agape as she stares into my eyes. I brighten them slowly, "Would you like me to show you proof?" She gasps. I laugh quietly and offer my hand, "Come with me." She looks at it, then with hesitance, places hers in mine.

I lead her over to my desk, help her up on it and gently ride my hand up her leg. She grabs it, "Mr. Francis!" I lean in close to her face, eyes brightening more, "How could you resist something you want so badly?" Her mouth falls open in shock. I slowly widen a dark smile. She watches me and her breathing quickens. I carefully tilt my head and start kissing her neck. A sigh leaves her as her head gently falls back. I grin against her skin and Rozalia opens my mouth.

'No! I can't bite her neck!'
*"You **will**!"*

I grimace and lick her instead, making her grip on my wrist tighten.
Rozalia growls, *"Her heart is not beating fast enough! I need more energy!"*

I snatch her hand and yank it away, then clutch her hips. She gasps, holding me closer.
'Then I will do it this way!' I claim her lips and bite the bottom one, drawing blood, receiving a pained, yet pleasured moan from her. Rozalia is stunned by my actions, but she laughs loud and wildly in my head. *"Wonderful!"* Maria pulls away to feel her bleeding lip, "Oh, my lip! Oh my-"

I see the blood and gulp hungrily. *"I need **more**."*

She looks at me in worry. With one shake of the head, I flare my nose, "Ohh, I need ***MORE***!" and I lunge at her again. These words aren't mine. "Mr. Fr-!" She gasps again. I take a firm hold of her head, now kissing her with great, great passion for the blood. She moans into it and tries to pull my shirt off, but each time she does this, I restrain her.

"Alright, not too much now; you know better."
'No no, you started something–I'm going to finish it! No one can dislike Ivy!'

"Your reputation is important for me!" Rozalia abruptly forces me away from Maria just as Maria tugs on my bottom lip with her teeth and it punctures my skin. I pant heavily, licking my lips and absentmindedly wiping them off on my sleeve. Just then I realize what just happened. "Oh god…" I whisper to myself. No, she didn't just get a taste of my blood. I lick where she bit and taste my own blood and it makes me cringe. It's the most disgusting thing I've ever tasted.

"Now…" Rozalia says.
'No, you don't understand!'

She ignores me and makes me march back up to Maria, brightening my eyes, forcing her to forget my animalistic behavior. When she finishes hypnotizing her, Maria tastes the blood and becomes confused. I take a deep breath and calm myself down. "Perhaps we got a little…carried away." She looks at me, still puzzled. But then she starts to blush.

I point at her, "This is between you and me."
She pats her bottom lip and nods, "Yes sir…"

'Why didn't you let me compel her to forget everything that just happened? I can't fool around with the maids Rozalia–that's insane. Look what just happened! Now I have to kill her before she becomes a monster.'

"It doesn't matter."
'She will cause severe problems later.'

"I don't care. We will worry about that later."

I start for the door, grumbling under my breath, "Fuck you!" How could she not care?!

"Excuse me sir?" Maria says.

I open it, "Nothing–just a thought." I motion her to go before me, "Everything is fine." I watch her walk out and then I scowl down at the floor, "I will have to go in a few hours. You had better behave when the time comes to meet with Ivy." Rozalia makes me smile coyly, "I promise. Now go change your bloody shirt."

I ball my hands. "God damn it."

Chapter 19

-Ivy-

Here I am now, hours later at the coastline where I stood with my mother and spotted Dmitri's castle; near a statue of Harold II. The breeze is cool, parents and their children are sightseeing, and the sun looks amazing on the sparkling water. I have my black scarf and white coat on. Oh my gosh, that comforter Gina gave me is still in my trunk! I sigh, looking back at my car by the road, "I'll take care of it later."

Something tall and moving on my left catches my eye. I see Nick coming toward me, wearing a navy blue short-sleeved turtleneck shirt and gray slacks. Always gray... His hands are in his pockets. He looks so very dashing. It seems he's not bothered by the temperature very much. When his eyes find me, the sun shines in them, giving off a silver color. Oh my god, they're breathtaking… I bite my lip.

He meets up with me and smiles, "Good afternoon." His tone is deep, warm–Delicious. "Hello again…" I quietly say as I watch how the sun reflects in his eyes. He halfway smirks, "You seem preoccupied."

"Oh," I smile and look down, "Sorry–It's just your eyes…you have nice eyes."

He grins, "You look very handsome in this light too." **I'm handsome?**

He raises his hand in a matter-of-fact way, "There was a time men would call women handsome. It isn't very common now." **Ohh… Yeah, you're so old you would know that Nick.** I quietly laugh.

He sees the expression I'm making but doesn't do anything; he just keeps the smirk, then he turns his head and points toward the railing with his chin. "Come." He walks ahead of me, mumbling something to himself–I think. It sounds sort of like he's arguing with himself about 'behaving'. It's weird…

When we reach the rail, he leans against it, staring off into the distance—or maybe toward the castle. I start studying him. How pale he is…it's almost unnatural, but wow, it's very stunning. His nose is long and straight—perfect. His lips are beautifully shaped… how gorgeous. That sexy black five o'clock shadow… His eyes really, really give off such an intense feeling. I blush because I'm looking at him so closely. Quickly, I avert my attention to the same direction as him.

"Ivy…"

"Yes?"

He looks at me, "There is something on your mind that you are dying to ask me, isn't there?"

In the beginning, I'm too nervous to speak. I am suddenly intimidated by him once again. Somehow though, the words manage to slip out of me, "Are you a psychic?" Now I know why I was scared to ask! Who asks *that* question casually?

He forms a strange face as he lets out a small laugh. "Oh, wow…" he turns around and leans his back against the railing, "That is a good question…" he smiles, "What if I told you…I know what you want to hear?" **He knows what I want to hear?**

I fold my arms on the railing as I give him a serious, daring look, "I would listen."

His smile vanishes, "Oh really?"

"What—does that surprise you?" I ask.

"Well…I don't normally talk about things like this to anyone…" He's quiet all of a sudden.

Well, if it makes him uncomfortable…I'll ask later, I guess.

I quietly say, "Look, there is something else that has actually been eating away at me since we met."

"What is it?" He begins to pace a little and gives me the impression like he is impatient. I swallow down my nervousness. How do I explain this to him…?

"Okay… You are an executive assistant to a man who is extremely wealthy and I'm nothing more than an ER tech."

That's right–just let it out.

He stops and stares almost coldly at me.

Ohh, I should've expected that.

"Ivy…" he takes a step closer. I back up until my backside hits the railing. "Wait, stop." I say. He goes on, "It's not what you do; it's what you are. You are a feisty, extremely beautiful woman; fearless and modest, yet surely, I can see in your eyes that you do have a dark side. I admire these things in you." he blocks me in, now drilling his eyes into mine. I gulp, heart starting to pound like before. "I want to know you." He seriously says. I let out a small nervous 'ha' and say, "But…of course there are other girls like me out there."

"Oh no no… You are a rare sort." He says. **I'm a rare sort…?**

"Perhaps… I am, yes." I bite my lip. He slowly brushes a finger across my cheek. I blink once, slowly. I'm not even thinking clearly. He smiles gently, "I will give you the answer to your question now. I am psychic–Yes. I can see spirits and I can talk to them whenever I want." My brows slightly lift and my mouth opens a little. Oh my gosh, I was right all along… He sees supernatural things. I lean back a little, coming out of the daze he's put me in and I notice how close he really is. "Nick," I say with a hint of warning in my voice.

He grins lightly, "I've had this ability for a very…***long***…***time***. You see, I wasn't born with it…it's my little secret." his eyes trail down to my neck as he gently takes a few strands of my hair into his warm fingers touching my skin, "Ivy," I softly breathe in. He raises his gaze up to my eyes, "Does this unsettle you? …Do I?" My god...I can't talk! He smiles, "Hm," My cheeks redden more. I feel like I should run away but another part of me refuses that idea.

"Nick," I repeat his name with more warning this time. "Yes?" he almost hums. I take his hand and move it away, "Please…don't…do that." He becomes more serious again as he says, "There is something Walter told me about you…"

What…? What could it be?

"You told him you had a paranormal experience during your stay at the castle." He says. He told him that? Wow, apparently secrets aren't kept there. "Yeah…" I look down and away.

"Though I would very much like to know what happened, you don't have to tell me. But, I do know by the way he explained it to me, it was not pleasant." I give an expression of slight amazement. He lowers his head, then looks past me into the distance, "Sometimes I don't see them. But I still feel them…" he looks at me, "Like you did." I stare at him for a long while.

He says, "They are attracted to you Ivy. You are special to them also." My eyes grow. He nods, "Yes…yes you are. That's how you were able to feel what you felt so quickly."
"How do you know that?" I warily ask. He moves forward to whisper in my ear, "I have abilities…" He slowly takes my hand and intertwines his fingers with my own, "I can feel this about you." I almost lose my breath, now looking into his eyes again as they appear to start glowing. What an odd illusion…

"If you don't believe me, I will show you… but you have to agree."

I think over his words and one side of me wants to think this isn't right while the other, stronger side is urging me to agree–and it's pushing the resistant half out of the picture. I stand silently for a few seconds, my sight never leaving his glistening diamond-like eyes. All of a sudden, this is all I want; to leave everything and go with him.

I blink slowly, "…I want you to show me."
A smile traces his lips and he delicately takes my chin in two fingers, "Haide la castelul Vladoiu… Ivy." He says this but I hear his voice tangled with a woman telling me, "Come to Castle Vladoiu… Ivy." then she adds, "After all, that is what you **want**…" I feel my whole body relax and nothing matters more than that voice and his completely bewitching gaze.

"Perhaps…very…soon…" How could I resist? I've missed him terribly.

"I must go now Ivy," He brings my hand up and kisses it, "It was a pleasure seeing you again and now I bid you goodnight."

Finally I blink, now back down to earth. I glance down at his hand leaving mine, then I quickly reach for him, "Wait, please don't go yet!" He stops and turns back to me. Frowning, I say, "I…miss you…" Now that I've said that, I feel childish. He studies how upset I look and it seems to bother him. He's behaving like he's holding himself back from something. He says, "Don't worry Ivy, we will meet again soon–I promise." I lift both of my hands up under my chin, making a slight sad expression.
He bows his head at me, "Until then."
I smile faintly at him as he walks away.

I can hear him scolding someone. The words are faint, but I'm able to pick up a mentioning of the castle and something about keeping control. One minute he was all about the idea of me going there and then he hates it afterward. What is wrong with him? Once he leaves my sight, I turn around and realize the sun has disappeared almost completely. I put my hand on my chest, eyes dropping to the water, "I can't go yet…but I really want to."

I wonder what will happen when I return?

Chapter 20

-Nicolai-
'Early this Morning'

For minutes, I stand stiffly at my bedroom mirror, glaring at Rozalia. "I will not let you do this."

"Dmitri, you will make the phone call to the administrator of the hospital now. We cannot have any more obstacles in our way."

I shake my head with a grim look, "No, you can shove that 'it's for a good cause' up your ass."

*"How **DARE** YOU!"*

"AH!" I drop to my knees, grabbing both sides of my now aching head.

"Stand!" Rozalia shouts. I slowly rise, breathing heavily. *"Stop being foolish!"*

As the excruciating migraine slips away, I rub my forehead, "Damn."

"Now!"

I clench my hands into fists and punch the wall near the mirror, "JUST STOP ALREADY!"

She growls at me and looks at my hand where we both see blood seeping out of the cuts from my nails. She brings it up and licks it slowly, causing me to flinch to this stinging, beyond terrible taste; she is making my taste buds react in such a horrible way I can barely take it anymore. 'Oh please! Stop!' I beg. She continues. Now my hand is feeling like I have a cat's tongue licking a burn mark. While she laughs madly in my head, I'm forced to swallow the blood and my stomach abruptly jerks and tightens. Suddenly, she stops; now satisfied with my desperate pleas and whimpers.

She says through me, "Go–*Now*." I squint my eyes, now feeling defeated, and head out for my office. My midsection is extremely numb.

-Ivy-

Today went slow... Same old stuff happened. I almost got attacked by a mental patient though. His complaint was shortness of breath. We were all nice to him even though he was violent with us. Now, thankfully, I'm finished for the day.

As I go to clock out, my Supervisor Mr. Sanchez comes up to me and whispers, "Bring your time card into my office after you clock out please." What? What's going on?

I don't question him...I only nod. "Ok." I clock out and go to his office. When I get there, I'm very careful about every move I make.

"May I see your card please?" he asks. This is not good...
I hand it to him.

"Thank you," he puts it down on his desk, "Ms. Summers...I've noticed as of late you have been preoccupied, and as a result, your job performance has suffered." he sighs, "This cannot be tolerated in this field. I have no other recourse but to let you go." My mouth drops. Now I feel like someone just grabbed me and squeezed all of the air out of me.

"Mr. Sanchez, I-" This can't be happening to me! I don't even get a warning?! Instead, I get booted out the door! I've been a good employee–Why is he saying otherwise? There has to be another reason why he's doing this to me!

He shakes his head with a very faint apologetic expression, "I'm sorry Ivy, but 'your' services are no longer required. Please clean out your locker. You can turn in your badges tomorrow afternoon when you pick up your check. Have a nice day." I grind my teeth together slowly, unsure about everything right now. What will I do now? My head lowers as I turn and go out of the office.

I go to the break room to get my things out of my locker. There is no one in here at all. Just silence. I start to tear up a little because I'm gonna miss these people. I put my stuff in an old paper bag I forgot to throw away and quietly shut the locker door. "Man this sucks!"

I completely ignore every person I pass as I leave. I can say my goodbyes tomorrow. When I get to my car, I open the back door, throw my things into the seat, and then, after a minute of standing here in the cool air, I form the ugliest look I can and slam the door shut.

I lean my back against the car, sniffling–sobbing even. My job– Gone. My hands tremble as they ball into tight fists, just itching to punch something. I gush out a breath and get in the car, start it, then burn rubber on racing out of the parking lot, headed for my apartment.

Same as the hospital–I ignore everything outside and march up the stairs. There is a door hanger on the knob from somebody from the apartment office. "What the hell is this?" I don't bother to read it and put in the bag. Keys can become a real pain in the ass when you're upset. Finally I get the door open and rip my scrub top off and throw it down on the couch. I begin to pace the room like a caged animal and think about how I don't want to tell anyone about this. What should I do? I knew I should've had a back-up plan! I knew it!

I sit down at my pc and put my face in my hands.
You know what…? Maybe I do need something to calm my nerves. I peek through my fingers and look down at my lap at the pocket my cell phone is in. "Hmmm… Gina…" I take it out and find her number, then bring the phone up to my ear. I would rather talk to her before anyone else. Even if she is a co-worker, she is the only real friend I have that I can count on at the moment.

She answers, "Ivy?"
I wipe an eye, "Yeah, hey."
"What's the matter? You sound stressed out."
My head slumps down as my fingers run stiffly through my hair, "Yeah…are you busy?"
"No, why?"
"Can I…come over?" I can't believe I'm asking this.

"...Sure. Sure!" She says. **Oh, thank goodness!**

"I'll tell you what's up when I get there, ok?"
"Ok..."

As I pull up to her house, I automatically feel more at ease. I knock on her door and can see her look through the peephole. She opens the door. "Ivy!" I try to smile at her...but it's hard to do. She looks me over and starts to make a concerned face, "Here, here," she takes my arm and guides me out of the foyer into the living room. I look around and see how clean it is. Last time I was here, she was remodeling. Beige stone tiles, white walls and ceiling, big open-paned windows where the door to the back patio is, and there's hardly any furniture in here; just basic stuff like two couches, some chairs, a few small tables, a couple little trees and some stand-up lamps. It's beautiful.

She walks me to a couch and sits down with me, asking, "What's wrong? Why are you so upset?" Treating me like she's my mom...hah.

I tuck my hair behind my ear, sighing, "Gina...you're worrying way too much."
"But Ivy, look at you!" she slightly looks down her nose at me.
"No. Look," I say, "I just need a girl's night out." Boy that sounds weird coming from me. She shuts up right then.
Oh no.

"Gina, what are you thinking?" I warily ask.
She shakes her head and then grabs my shoulder and looks at me seriously, "I'm not going anywhere, but I do know what would make a perfect girls night."

Um...I think I have some bad feelings coming on...

Chapter 21

Gina and I are eating popcorn as we watch another suspense/horror film about a serial killer who murders people in the middle of the night in a small California neighborhood. An average sort of movie, I know. Actually, they aren't too bad. I've managed to smile and laugh a few times here and there. I have to admit–I think I'm enjoying this. Gina has done well not to nag me about my issue. Thank you Gina for sparing me the aggravation! I'm dying to tell her what is wrong with me but I don't think it's such a good idea. So, I'd rather not do that.

Glancing at the clock, I see it's about 12:30 in the morning. Oh my gosh, I have to get home! I check my phone. No calls or messages...from anyone. That's depressing.

I stretch and look at her, "Gina,"
"Hm?" she won't take her eyes off the T.V.

"I have to get home."
She looks at me, the clock, then back to me, "You...sure you want to be out at this time of night? The wackos are out at this hour."

I give the clock another look. She's right...and I don't have any patience for them. These movies haven't taken away my frustration; they've only sidetracked me for a while. My eyes are droopy too.

I raise an eyebrow when looking at her again, "You would let me stay here...?"
"You're not a thief or an insomniac are ya? I don't get that vibe from you." she dryly says.
"Thief? No!" I scoff.
"Then you can stay the night." she smiles.
I force a smile of my own, "Ok...thank you."

She tips her head to one side, "You're not used to people outside your family being nice to you, are you?"
I shake my head, "No, not really. I usually keep to myself, you

know."

She gradually grins, then turns the movie off and gestures me to follow her, "Come on."

I go along with her upstairs to a spare bedroom. I take in the surroundings and feel right at home. It's so cozy-looking with that queen-sized bed in here. I've never been up here. I smile at it softly, gratefully. Then I turn and hug her, "Thank you Gina for being there for me. You're the greatest friend I could've ever asked for."

"Ohh…" she chuckles, hugging me back, "You're making me blush. Stop it." We stop hugging and smile at each other.

"There's a bathroom down the hall there if you need it. I'll see if I can find something for you to wear." I back up and she shuts the door.

"I'll be back Ivory!" Ivory, she calls me. Tch, crazy girl.

As I look around the room, I start to think about today, this evening, and what I would've done if I didn't have her in my life. I would've either stayed at home and looked all night for a job, or stewed over it until I fell asleep. I would never depend on someone for anything, and that's what I'm doing now–I consider it an act of desperation and insecurity. But I need this; I need this comfy bed, I need a friend to assure me everything is alright. I would do the same for her. I would.

I lie down on the bed without covering up, and soon, surprisingly, I fade into a dreamless sleep.

"Ivy?" Bang, bang, bang. "Ivy?" My eyes slowly open and slide over to the door. I yawn and stretch, "Yeah?" I notice she left a soft white nightgown on the end of the bed. The door opens. There she is–Dressed and ready to go somewhere, it seems.

She puts her hands on her hips, "You didn't cover up and you're still dressed?" I blink, then look down at the pillow and covers, "Uhh…" I look at her again, "I didn't want to mess it up. And yeah." Though I did mess it up a little bit…

She rolls her eyes, amused, "You're so shy. Come on, wanna go to Lounge 'n' Sip? It's 7:30." 7:30? Oh my gosh! I'm late for-Work...

"Oh..." I press a hand to my forehead. Ivy, how could you forget that you don't have a job now? "Yeah... Coffee sounds great. Just let me freshen up a little and I'll be ready." Maybe Nick will be there... If he is, I need his company, and I need it badly.

"Alright. I'm going to get in my car. I'll see you in a minute and please lock the front door, ok?" Before I can answer, she leaves the doorway and goes downstairs. Hmm...

I go into her bathroom and look in the mirror. "Wow...I'm schlumpy." Nothing I can't fix though; a little fresh water, a towel, a brush, and some of her lipstick. "There we go."

When I close the front door, I see her standing against her car waiting for me. We get in our cars without saying much to each other and we're off to Lounge 'n' Sip.

The drive is smooth, and a bit refreshing. Somehow. We arrive at the coffee shop and go inside. First thing Gina does is lean close to me and say, "Hold on, there's something I wanna look at on that shelf over there." I nod at her, and as she leaves my side, I look at that table. My heart jolts with excitement yet again. Nicolai–He's there. **Oh thank god!**

He's looking at his journal, eyebrows down in concentration. Without a second thought, I go to him. He slowly lifts his head up and closes his book, the expression he had before–Gone.

"Ivy," his voice is quiet. He looks at the empty chair ahead of him, then back to me.
"I have to stand." I say, "I'm with a friend."
"Gina, I presume?"
"Yeah..." I gently nod. "So, What have you been up to?"

He starts to smile a bit, "Meetings...lots of meetings. How about you?" He somewhat seems to be in a joking kind of mood. I put my hands in my pockets, "Nothing really. Same old stuff." He takes his latté and brings it up to his lips, arching an eyebrow, "That seems a little dishonest." **What? How can you tell?**

"What makes you say that?" I ask.
He inhales deeply while putting his cup down, "Your behavior says that."
I sit down at the table, "Oh? Then…what do you think is wrong?"
He sits there for second with a poker-face, then he does that smile again, "I don't know. Would you like to enlighten me? Maybe I can help brighten your day somehow." My eyes grow a little, "How so?"
"I could take you out." he winks at me–artfully.
"What-!" **I'd love that!**

His eyes narrow in that dark way as he smiles at me, "Ahh, you're difficult aren't you? Two days ago you didn't want me to leave your sight. You are an interesting creature." I only stare at him.

"Ivy?" I hear Gina behind me. I smile briefly at Nick and turn to her.
"Excuse me…I'm sorry but I can't join you for coffee." She says. That… makes Nick slightly more entertained. He abruptly stands and bows a little while saying, "I am Nicolai Francis; I'm sorry I could not meet you when you stayed at the castle." Whoa, I didn't expect that!

Gina looks at him, then smiles a little, "Oh... me too! My name is-"
"Yes I know–You are Gina Lewis." he says, "We have briefly met before. I apologize for my attitude at the time; I was preoccupied. Please forgive me." He bows his head a bit. Her small smile starts to broaden in understanding, "That's alright. Nobody's perfect." He blinks at her once, gladly. I quickly look back to her with excited eyes, "Why can't you join us for coffee?"

"I just got a call... My brother is having some sort of problem with his girlfriend. But I can get you two some coffee real quick before I go." she says while winking at me. Oh sure, and I didn't know she had a brother… I slump in the seat and Nick nods pleasurably, saying, "That would be delightful of you as far as the coffee is concerned. I think I'll have another raspberry mocha latté Miss Lewis and a pumpkin latté for Miss Ivy please." Wait, what if I didn't want that? She blinks at him, nods back with a faint blush and then leaves our table. I thought she didn't like him…

Nick and I look at each other again.

Unbelievable… just unbelievable.

"You have an affect on all the ladies, don't you? You ordered my coffee too."

"I don't know what you mean." he sits and puts his hands together on the table.

"Your mannerism…" I say.

He smiles halfway, "You mean being a gentleman?"

"…Yeah."

"That is just how I am." He murmurs.

A couple minutes later, Gina comes over with our coffee. We both thank her at the same time and Nick hands her a twenty for it. She shoots him a surprised look, then smiles, "No, you keep that." He leans toward her, looking up into her eyes in a daring sort of way, "No…no–I *insist*." She stares at him. And it's for way longer than I thought she would. Slowly, she accepts the money and I clear my throat.

She looks at me, "Ok! Right! Well uh, enjoy your coffee, and um–I'll see you later, ok Ivy?" Nick stands again, bows a little and says, "It was nice to meet you Miss Lewis."

"Likewise…" she gives me a big smile with a glint in her eye. "I'll see you later."

"Okay bye! Good luck!" I say. How weird…

She nods and goes on her way.

The moment we take our first sips, our eyes lock; intense against wondering ones. But the staring lasts only for a few seconds. I have to turn away–It's too much.

"Ivy…" he says, "Why do you look away?" I look at him a

little. **Let's see...you are intimidating and you're a mystery to me, Nick–You really are.**

"Because..." I say–And that's the only thing I'm able to say.
He rests his chin on his hand, "You are beautiful and you shouldn't hide your face away from anyone." I blink at him.
"I have my reasons."
"Sure you do. We all do." he drinks some of his coffee. There's silence between us for a minute.

Curiosity about him taking me out on a date forces me to ask, "Where would you take me...if I agreed to go somewhere with you?" He puts his coffee down and looks at me in a serious sort of way, "Wherever you would like." No way...!

He starts to smile, "You have doubts...?"
"There's no way that could happen."

He leans forward and whispers, "I have the means to take you anywhere." I blush.
"To another country...?"
He raises his hands, "If that is what you wish!" **No way!**
I shake my head, laughing, "No..."
He nods, beginning to laugh also, "Don't doubt me Ivy. That would be such a mistake."
"Would it?" I ask.
"Yes." he says. I cover my mouth, trying to hold in my giggling. He grabs it and looks into my eyes. I stop everything and stare at him. "Your smile–don't hide that either." he says. I slowly let my hand fall to the table. He whispers, "Go out with me." I look down at his extremely warm, pale hand holding mine, then I slowly look back up into his eyes. He winks at me, "Come on Ivy...you know you want to." I shut my eyes with a small laugh. He's so confident. "Well..." I sigh in amusement, now looking at him, "you don't need to take me to another country or anywhere spectacular; take me to the castle, and that itself would be great. I'm not working today...we could go this evening–before the sun sets." He studies my face, slowly starting to grin in an almost wicked way. He brings my hand up to his mouth and lingers there, "That sounds

delightful." he gently presses his lips to it while watching me. I gulp. That mysterious gaze of his...

He gently puts my hand back down. "Tonight..." I blink at him as he winks at me in an agreeing way and drinks some of his coffee. Oh...he's mesmerizing.

I reach for mine, then slowly look away while taking a sip of it, "I suggest tonight because I have some things to take care of this afternoon."
"Oh?"
"Yes..." I look at him, "It's a...personal matter."
He seems interested, but I can tell he won't ask me what I mean.

"Very well, when you are finished, call me."
"Alright," I say with a warm smile, "I'm gonna get going now. Talk to you soon. And thanks for the coffee." I stand with my half-empty cup, "Oh, my address–of course–I forgot. Do you have a pen and paper? I'm sorry." Watching me with that amused glint of his, he takes a black pen and a small notebook out of his jacket pocket and gently hands it to me.

"Oh, nice pen...!" I comment.
"Thank you."

I carefully write it down and then give them back to him. As he stows it away in his pocket, he says, "I look forward to this evening Ivy."
"Yes...me too." He watches me with a sort of unreadable smile that unsettles me a little deep inside. Does he have something up his sleeve...?

I purse my lips while taking a small breath, then I tuck my hair behind my ear and start for the door, "See you then."
I get halfway to the exit and he lowers his head and simpers to himself, "How cute... Shut it!"

Chapter 22

After Lounge n' Sip, I went to the hospital to turn my badges in and get my paycheck. I got stuck talking to Liam, who by the way once finding out I lost my job, asked me for my number. Of course I didn't give him anything. That particular conversation lasted for about 3 minutes. Then, I came back home and called Mom. I almost told her about my situation, but thank god I paid enough attention to keep that secret. Her being quite a talker, she kept me on the phone longer than I wanted.

Geez–Finally I get all these phone calls; it's just when I get busy with things people start trying to get a hold of me. Actually people, I intended to spend the rest of the day looking for a job! But they can't know this happened. No one can–Not right now anyway. I did manage to look around a little bit... but then I got a headache.

Here I am now, standing up from my pc with my cell-phone in my hand and Nick's card too. I check the clock and see it's 4pm. Well, he'll need time to get here. I need to call him now. So I start dialing his number. It takes a few seconds before he answers.

His voice is deeper on the phone. It makes my belly suddenly clench.
"Nick? It's Ivy." I swallow down some of my jumpiness.

"Hello there… You are ready to go now?" He sounds like he's smiling. I do just like him and say, "Yeah."

"Alright, I will be there between 5 and 5:15."
"Ok, see you then,"
"See you." He hangs up.

Again, I feel jumpy as I look at my phone. I better take a bath right now! But first I need a snack. I hope I don't drop any chips in the tub!
Well I do...

Just a few minutes later, I come out, and wow…I really needed that bath! Now, I have a little catching up to do. I grab my journal and look at it. I really haven't kept up like I usually do. "...Sometimes life is so stressful you can't do everything in your daily routine." I sigh, "But, I will write in you now."

Journal entry date – *October 3, Friday*

Ok...last time I wrote in you was on the 1st. I think I'm getting lazy. A lot has happened since then, actually. It seems whenever I lose track, something major happens in between then and when I write again. The big things this time are: I lost my job, Gina and I are getting closer (she let me stay at her place last night because I was so stressed about losing my job) and I'm building a relationship with this Nicolai Francis guy. There's definitely something strange about him. I say that because every time I go to the coffee shop, he's there. I'm not sure if that's coincidence or not. He's a businessman and lives on an island; surely he wouldn't be there as often. But then again, that's where everybody goes. It's a meeting place. No...I need to say that not once in any of those times have I seen anybody sitting with him. He's always alone - reading that old journal of his, which is an item he holds extremely close. Could I ever understand this guy? Should I just give it time and then try to understand? Maybe I should do that - give it time.

Well anyway, tonight I'm going back to his castle! I'm super excited! So very excited! I've wanted this so badly, you know. He's picking me up at 5. I bet his car is top-of-the-line expensive! We'll see!

Ok, I just looked at the clock; it's 4:45, and I've noticed I've been writing for a while already. I have to throw some dressy clothes on. I'll write more when I can!

I pick out a 'black at the bottom and white at the top' cocktail dress. It has a false diamond on each side of the halter straps. For a minute, I look at it and try to decide if it's good enough.

"It'll have to be… It's the best looking dress I have for an occasion like this." I lay it on the bed, check my hair in the mirror and brush it out. I put the dress on and fix my hair and face in the bathroom. My hair looks just right; put up in a bun with little bits of hair dangling on the sides of my head. I have long diamond earrings and my makeup is not too much, but I still use dark red lipstick and some light-brown eye-shadow. I think I look pretty good.

Suddenly, I hear a knock at my door. I look over my shoulder and walk out of my room, go through the kitchen and then peek through the peephole and see Nicolai with his hands behind his back. Seeing him makes me suddenly bite my lip. Black suit, red tie, black silk undershirt and a red handkerchief. I nearly lose my breath. How gorgeous he is… So dark and mysterious!

I open the door. His eyes flash a bit as he looks me up and down, trying to make it a brief examination though to be gentlemanly.

"Miss Summers…you look absolutely beautiful." He grins at me. I blush, "Thank you…" He bows his head and then slowly moves his hands away from the back of him, presenting a blood-red rose and a box of dark chocolates. I place my hand just below my neck, stunned. "Yes, of course…you're welcome," he laughs quietly. Still stunned, I take them and look back up into his eyes, "How perfect…" I didn't expect this!

"Here, come in," I tell him to follow me into the kitchen. I didn't want him to see how I live, but evidently, I couldn't avoid it.

He stands in the doorway, watching me as I place the chocolates in the fridge and then put the rose in a throated vase filled with warm water.

"You keep it nice here. I like the décor."
I turn to him in a slight bit of shock, not sure if he means what he says or just compliments me to be nice. "Thanks," I lightly giggle. "Of course."

I rub my neck gently, smiling, "Compared to where you live though, this is nothing."
His head gently falls to one side, humored yet again, then he walks up to me and quietly says, "But that place is not mine." I stare up at him speechlessly. He sees my sweater behind me hanging on a chair. He picks it up and hands it to me. "It is cool outside; you may need this."
"Oh," I take it, "of course… Thanks." I place it over my arm as he gazes at me.
"Is there anything else you would like to bring along in case you decide to stay the night?" he asks. "Oh, well I'm not sure…" I say, "I didn't consider you asking me this."
He makes a matter-of-fact face, "It really isn't safe to cross the sound at night, but Leonardo will do it if you wish." That's a good point.

"Let me grab a few things in a bag and I'll let you know my decision later." I smile a bit. He does the same back, "As you wish." He waits for me by the front door as I pack an overnight bag. I don't bring my phone this time. It'd be pointless.

When I come out, he opens the door and places his hand on the small of my back, leads me out and shuts my door, making sure it locks. All the way from my door down to the first floor, he holds my hand. My inner self can't stop smiling like an idiot.

Once we're outside, he guides me in the direction of–what looks like–a red Aston Martin. I immediately get the idea that's his vehicle, and I gasp out, "This is your car? Wow!" I was right in that journal entry!

He opens my door, saying in a humored way, "Get in Miss

Summers–Allow me to spoil you." I watch him wink at me as he shuts the door, then he walks around, gets in and looks at me with a handsome smile. I stare at him in amazement. Geez his world is drastically different from mine.   He lifts my chin slightly with his finger, "Trust me, you will have a wonderful time." He starts the car. **I'm sure I will!**
Oh my! What an amazing purr this engine has...

Gently, he backs out of the parking space and then we cruise our way out of the complex. I look in the side-mirror as we go and I think to myself 'we're leaving a shithole for a piece of heaven...YES!'

During our drive, he continues to glance at me every now and then. It's kind of funny to me. But I'm also wondering what he's thinking. He continues to clear his throat too. It's like he's about to say something but stops himself by doing that. The last time he does it, he asks me, "Does my driving make you...nervous?"
I look at him, "Not quite."
He smiles with a shake of his head, "Not quite?"
I form a sort of questioning expression, "It's very smooth. I thought you'd have a lead foot."
"Hm," he looks out the windshield with the same smile, "Not quite." he glimpses at me knowingly, "What fun would it be to ride slow all the time when you have speed at your fingertips?" That is so true... If I had this car, I'd drive it like that too.

As I think this, he notices my contemplative features and then he gets this wild look in his eyes. I realize it and quickly grab the armrest, "Nick, no." He begins to laugh like a madman and floors the car. "NICK!" I scream. He keeps going; his laughter and his crazy driving.

We arrive at a place I am now familiar with–Esmeralda's boathouse and cabin.

As we pull into the driveway I see Leonardo and Esmeralda standing in front of the garage. Nick stops the car just up the drive and gets out. He tells me to wait in the car because he wants to talk to Leonardo. He walks a little ways to them, and after a little conversation, I see him hand his phone and keys to Esmeralda. I don't understand why he did that, but it doesn't concern me much.

He comes back to me in an all-business way and opens the door, saying, "Alright... Leonardo is going to take us to the island." he offers his arm to me. I take it, he shuts the door, and we start walking behind Leonardo. I glance back at Esmeralda, "What's she gonna do with your car?"
"Park it in its proper place."
"Oh...ok." Wherever that is. I wouldn't think she'd park it in her garage... Or maybe–maybe his car is the one that had the cover over it...?

Leonardo guides us down to the boat, we climb aboard and he starts the engine, then we're headed for the island. The air is becoming brisk as the daylight fades from the sound. I feel Nick take my hand in his and say while keeping his eyes on the forest and castle ahead, "Calm down." I curiously stare at him. He looks at me, "You're jittery." Yes...yes I am... But I can't help it.

He kisses my hand, "You'll be alright." I watch him. He turns back with a soft smile. I follow his actions. We're almost there. It's a bit strange how he knows I'm jittery. I usually hide that very well...

When we reach the island, he helps me out, salutes Leonardo with two fingers and escorts me to the castle. We approach the big front doors and he uses the doorknocker. Sooner than I expected, a door opens. There's Walter. I'm actually quite happy to see him.

"Mr. Francis. Miss Summers." He bows, stepping aside for us. Nick takes me inside the foyer as Walter shuts the door, then politely takes my sweater. "Thanks Walter." I say.
"My pleasure madam."

I then walk beyond the foyer and see the fireplace where Gina and I stood. I remember studying the paintings mounted on the walls, admiring the shiny marble floor the firelight illuminated and the large set of stairs in front of me–and I remember…all hold such strange memories. I hold my arms, taking all this in. Nick comes up behind me, "Ivy, would you like to see the antiquities room?" Whoa…I bet that would be amazing! I turn to him and look up into his eyes, "That would be wonderful," He offers his arm. Gently, I take it and we start walking down the right corridor. I find myself unable to breathe yet again as I look around us at the arched mahogany-brown ceiling and walls with finely carved squares. Along both walls, there are paintings of mountains, sunrises over creeks, rivers and many other scenic landscapes. The doors are dark-brown with very fancy Romanian designs.

He notices my silence and starts chuckling right away. I look at him, "What? Mr. Vladoiu knows how to live." "Yes…yes he does. Many people have said he spoils himself as if he were a King." He says. Oh, those people know what they're talking about for sure!

This brings me to the question, which I can't believe I have yet to ask. "How old is Dmitri?" We walk up to a door, and as he takes the knob, he says, "In his 80's." My jaw drops. "Shouldn't he retire soon?"

He smirks, "It's on his bucket list to work until he dies or cannot do it any longer." I stare at him, then start to laugh while he opens the door, then I peer inside and see a large amazing room with many different things–All look very old. There are ancient Greek sculptures in tall cases, a couple suits of armor that seem like they're from the crusades–which are also encased–some pieces of furniture that most likely date back to the 1600's and there are a few things from the 1800's. "Oh…my…" He only smiles at me. "Come come," he takes my hand and leads me farther inside, "Let me show you something." I watch his face, a gradual grin curling up at a corner of my lips.

We stop at a heavy shelf that has a few colorful vases and plates, and he tells me, "This is traditional Romanian dishware…from 1880." he pauses, then says while turning back to me, "You know…the other day when I was playing the piano at the hospital, I noticed an old man pushing an old woman in a wheelchair…it was so nice to see. Sometimes you feel as if you could never grow old. Most people never imagine themselves elderly."

"…Why would anyone want to be old?" I quietly ask. He takes a deep breath, "Because with age, comes much more beauty." I tilt my head a little.

"Come–let me show you more." He waves his hand toward a case that has a Grecian-like statue of a man with no arms, looking right. As soon as we walk up to it, he starts explaining about it; "This was in a French museum in the early 1900's. The building burnt down and this statue was recovered, though in the tragedy, his arms were destroyed by debris falling on them. His head was almost smashed too. Mr. Vladoiu's father purchased it in 1928 while in France and here it remains to this day in that case." Staring at it in amazement, I murmur, "Wow…that's extraordinary…" I look at him, "How old do you think it is?" "Mmm… Roughly 3 thousand years old." He points to the bottom of it. I see a golden plaque with some information about its age and where it came from. Greece 900 BC...

"Oh!" I say, making him laugh.

"I have something else I would like to show you, but it's not in here. It's in a different room." At that, I give him a look of curiosity. He tilts his head toward the door with a strange smile. I don't know how to react to it other than return it with my own innocent, wondering one.

Chapter 23

We're headed down a hallway on the first floor and soon approach a single mahogany door with a golden chipped-looking doorknob. Nick reaches for it, looking back at me with a boyish grin, "Have you ever seen a real castle atrium before?" Castle...atrium? Him asking me this...? I'm feeling uneasy now; this brings back that memory of sitting at a stone table with my dream guy.

"I believe I haven't... No." I say. He turns back and opens the door. I peer in past him as I delicately grab my arms. He steps aside, "Ladies first," I glance at him and cautiously walk through. Suddenly, an overwhelming feeling of Déjà vu strikes me as I look around at the tall, glass domed ceiling allowing bits of moonlight in. The trees with their fall leaves dropping from their limbs spread out everywhere and the big, white, illuminated fountain ahead is spitting water gracefully. But...what really gets my attention is a stone table and chairs–just like in that dream!

"Oh...my-" I bring my hands up to my mouth. He comes up behind me, "Beautiful, isn't it?" I quickly look at him, shocked. "I-I can't-" Shaking my head, I look from him to the room, back and forth. "What's wrong?" he asks with a concerned look on his face. "I can't believe it." I say. "What do you mean?" "I had a dream of a place that looked just like this and-" I almost mention the rest of the dream. "And...?" He asks. I steady my gaze on his face for a minute. If I told him what happened, who knows what he'll say or do. He might think I'm crazy! I just look back toward the fountain again.

"It feels so strange..."
"Maybe you were just very excited about coming here."
"Yeah...maybe that's it." **I would like to think so...**

He takes my hand in his, "Come–let me show you off to Mr. Vladoiu's roses..."

"Oh?" Well, that's flattering…! I have to smile at that.

He guides me past the fountain and soon turns right to follow the path until we approach a long bed of rosebushes surrounding a white statue of an angelic woman holding a harp. At her base, there are small lights pointed up at her, illuminating her beauty just perfectly and also ricocheting off her to make the red roses seem to glow. The sight of all this has taken my mind straight to fantasy land; it's quite like stepping up to a part of a movie set. Come to think of it, this whole place does that to me.

He leans down and picks one of them, then slowly offers it to me as he gives that intense, yet amused glimmer in his eyes. "For you," It looks like the reddest one in the bunch! Is this where the other rose that I put in a vase came from? Carefully, I take it and smell it; the whole time, I'm watching him with a shy, gratified expression.

"You know…" he says as he puts his hands in his pockets and looks around, "I do like it better this way…at night. The moon…" he smiles and looks at me, "It makes everything more beautiful." Leisurely, I move the rose away, gaze still not leaving his face. He points up at the ceiling, "Look there Ivy," he walks up and gently moves me to where he just stood, then he points again, "The clouds are clearing… Look at how beautiful the sky is. A few stars are already out."

"Wow…" He's right… Though there are some trees in the way, I can still see how wonderful the view is. Night does seem better than day…

I feel his hand slide down to the middle of my back and stop. It sends a shiver up my spine. I turn around to him and look up into his eyes. How the light from the statue shines in his face makes me want to never lose eye contact with him. He has such beautiful eyes and such a handsome face. I'm so close to him, and for once, I feel more at ease.

He smiles and gently strokes my cheek, tilting his head a little, "Did you truly believe me when I said I am psychic?"

"Yes I did…I do believe you."

"Are you sure?"

I focus on his lips, "Yes…I'm sure."

He slides his hand down to my neck, giving me a more intense shudder. Why does he have such an affect on me like this? He looks up from it, back into my eyes, "If only you knew what I see from day to day."

"…What do you see?" I'm hardly audible. His lips twitch into an abrupt grimace that lasts only half a second, then he's serious again, "Many things. They are everywhere–Good and evil."

"How do you deal with this?" He pauses for a moment as if going into thought, looking past me in a preoccupied way. Soon though, an odd sort of smile adorns his features as he looks at me again, "I…have my ways…"

…What does that mean?

He sees my confusion and coughs lightly to get rid of the awkward moment. "Well then, you see…this wasn't always an atrium."

"Really?" I look up at the ceiling, "Yeah…that does seem fairly new."

"After Mr. Vladoiu's father died, this was built… in the late 90's." He says in a quiet voice while studying me. I look out of the corner of my eye at him, then I face him with a small smile, "How long have you worked for Mr. Vladoiu…the second?"

"For 8 years now." He smiles back.

"Long time…!" I say, astonished.

"Yes, well it doesn't feel like it has been that long. It's like a blink of an eye for me." He winks. "Wow," I say, then after a moment, I ask, "What about Walter?"

"He's been here for 5 years." That surprises me.

"He seems so experienced! I mean, I know he's old but…"

"Hahaha!" He's now thrilled. "Ivy, he has been a butler for most of his life."

"Well how old is he exactly?" I ask. He lightly crosses his arms,

"He's 64."

Oh man...

"He's in good shape..." I say in a sort of amazement. His arms fall and he frowns slightly, placing his hand over his chest, "Yes...but his heart is not so good." My brow creases. He waves a hand at that, "No worries though... He's fine." he suddenly halfway grins, "He lives here." I look down my nose at him, humored, "So you're saying this is heaven?" "Mmm...I'm not sure how to answer that. I will say that Mr. Vladoiu understands luxury, but the man would never stay through the day. He hasn't been here in four years actually."

"Four years?" Whoa! That's quite a while for someone to stay away from a place they own! "Four years..." He confirms, then adds, "He has other homes. This is not his favorite..." he stops talking for a moment. "Is there something wrong with this place? It's beautiful to me." I say. He looks at me again and faintly smiles with a small shrug, "It must hold too many memories for him. After all, I believe he grew up here."

"Ahh...I see." I slowly say. Then I look around and up again, "Well...this is a very intriguing atrium...I love it. Thank you for showing me." I smile at him. He lowers his head, "It was my pleasure." He slowly grins up at me through his lashes. I blush. How evil and secretive he looks...

He straightens his posture and asks, "Ivy...are you hungry?" "I am." I nod. "Here," he waves his hand toward the path we followed, "let us go to the grand room. By now, the fireplace will be lit and Walter will be along. We will find out if our dinner is ready then." He gives me his arm, I daintily take it and we head out through the door we came in.

The walk is for a little ways, though it doesn't seem long as he tells me about the paintings that Mr. Vladoiu had hung on the walls of this large corridor. Some have been hanging here since the castle was finished. The ones near the entrance are the newest. I must say the old paintings are easy to lose yourself in.

I ask him, "You think people aren't as creative as they used to be?"

He makes the sliest smile, "People don't change, Ivy–Dates do. However, when it comes to art, people are more likely to paint pictures of whatever is happening during the era they live in. A good example is the Victorian era, if you understand my meaning."

"Yes…" I say, "I understand…perfectly."

When we get to the grand room, we see Walter standing by the fireplace deep in thought. There is a nice fire going.

"Walter!" Nick brightly says. Walter straightens himself and tips his head to him. "Sir." We approach him and Nick asks him about dinner. "Yes sir, the maids are nearly finished preparing the table."

"Perfect." Nick says, then he looks at the rose in my hand, "You know…just for now…Walter, will you put this in a vase for Miss Summers?"

"Of course," Walter bows at him, politely takes the rose and walks away to the right corridor. Then Nick leads me over to the sofa and joins me.

"So, Ivy…did you enjoy that little tour I gave you?"

"Oh it was lovely, thank you." Beyond lovely, actually. He grins toothily.

That…makes my cheeks turn pink. I really have never blushed so much in my life!

"I'm glad you had a wonderful time." He says.

"Me too. I really enjoyed it."

His expression darkens, "After dinner, I could show you a much better time-" he clears his throat, "I mean I could give you more of a tour." I almost choke, "What?" He laughs and shakes his head, "I was joking. You don't like jokes?"

I stare at him and then finally say, "Yeah I do… Sorry, I didn't get that one." Actually, I did.

And I can feel how hot my cheeks are getting. "It's okay."

He winks at me. I gulp slowly.

"...Do you like magic?" He asks.

"Magic?"

He nods at me.

"It's interesting..." I say.

"How about hypnotism?"

"I...don't know. I've never thought about it." He pauses at my response, a smile suddenly spreading across his face for a brief moment, "Well, I know a few tricks." I give him a smug expression, "No way... Hypnotizing isn't real."
He leans in close, "Is that doubt I sense? I can hypnotize you. No, I suppose I would have to show you to make you believe me."
"Then show me." I say as I uncomfortably try to move a few inches away from him. "Hmm..." he starts to form a devilish face toward my behavior, "you're tempting me Ivy." **Am I?**

"I am." I questionably admit. He leans back, throwing an arm on the back of the sofa, "Well, I will have to show you tomorrow." **Tomorrow?**

"Oh! Well...how convenient for you." That gets his attention. "What?" He says, then suddenly moves closer. I back away, getting anxious. He keeps moving. "Nick, what are you-" He crawls up over me, causing me to practically lie down underneath him. "Nick!" I quietly panic and then turn my head as he inches closer to my face. "Look at me." he says. I slowly look at him. He's very, very close! And his eyes are glowing! Or so, it sure looks like they are! "Get off me!"

"When I say I will do something–I mean it." He whispers. I nervously watch his every facial movement. "Well what are you going to do now?" My heart is beginning to race madly now. He smirks contemplatively. "That...should be left unsaid."
"What?!" I squeak, granting a soft chuckle from him. He leans down and suddenly licks and kisses my neck, making me gasp. He moves away from it just after. "Calm down Ivy–I won't do anything to you." he laughs quietly and then backs off. As I'm

breathing anxiously and my heart flutters, I touch the place he licked, wide eyes watching him intently.

He stands up tall, fixing his shirt and looking around in an authoritative way as if scanning the room for anyone. He looks back down at me with a dark grin, "You shouldn't think twice about this." His eyes are still glowing. I can't help but to focus on them. After a moment, the last thing I remember is us talking about magic. I sit up slowly and then see Walter coming back in.

"Sir–dinner is served." Nick looks over and smiles with a dip of the head, "Very good." He turns to me, "Let's eat, shall we?" I nod at him and carefully stand, grab a hold of his arm and let him guide me to the right corridor after Walter.

As we walk, I glance at him in a questioned way. He may look out the corner of his eye at me and smirk here and there but that's about it. I can tell there's something going on in his mind though; something seems to be bothering him, yet he's masking it very well. The silence lasts until we near a door, then he tells me as Walter opens it and goes inside, "Any questions you may have, can be answered at the table, during our meal." He points toward the dining room with his chin. Hesitantly, I look away from him to see what's in there. Oh my goodness! It's the grand dining room! Wait–Of course it is! The small one I sat in before is upstairs.

In this dimly lit one, the table is long, the tall windows ahead of it are dressed with dark red curtains; there are about 4 of these windows and just like that other dining room, the chairs have the same setup with the most important-looking one at the very end. Not too mention, the table is romantically decorated… It's very romantic, indeed. There are white candles on it and some are on the walls as well.

"Let's sit down." He leads me inside. As I walk behind him, I notice a fairly young male chef is in here standing beside Walter near the door on the right wall. Neither of them are talking; they're just standing there in a professional way. The chef has a cart with two hotel-styled stainless steel plates, a bottle of expensive-looking

champagne and two fancy glasses. As soon as we get close to the table, Walter comes up and tries to pull Nick's chair out. Nick waves at him, "No, I've got this. Thank you Walter." Walter steps back with a bow of the head, "Yes sir."
Nick smiles lightly at him, then pulls my chair out and motions me to sit down. I look at him and slowly take a seat, quietly saying, "Thank you."

After joining me at the table, he looks at the chef accordingly. "Mr. Fitzgerald." He says this like it's a greeting. Fitzgerald approaches us with the cart and sets our plates on the table, removing the covers at the same time. "Filet Mignon with mushrooms and sauce pinot noir." He announces. The sides are fresh steamed asparagus and mashed potatoes sprinkled with parsley and pepper. My mouth is watering now. I watch closely as he also pours the champagne into our glasses and places them by our plates. "Dom Perignon." He says as he smiles at us both. "Thank you good sir." Nick smiles up at him. Fitzgerald nods and backs away, leaving the room with the cart. Then Walter says, "Sir, if you will excuse me, I have duties to attend to."
Nick waves at him again, "Of course."
"Enjoy your meal." He tells us as he gives a final bow and heads for the door we came in.

Now that the room has found some silence, I feel more comfortable. I'm able to admire the style of this place better. And man, I can't wait to eat! The smell of this food is making my hunger become almost unbearable.

"So…" Nick says. I look at him. He picks up his drink, "I see you like this room."
I give the room another quick study and smile, "I do. It's quite beautiful."
He lifts his glass, "Mr. Vladoiu has good taste in champagne, does he not?"

I do the same in agreement. "Yes he does," He takes a drink and savors it for a few seconds. He swallows and hums like it's from heaven. That look he does tempts me to hurry with my first sip.

And just like I imagined, it tastes pretty damn good. I bet this stuff is really expensive! I would ask how much it cost, but it might be a bad idea right now.

As he sets his glass down, he asks, "You have not traveled outside of New York, have you?" I gently dab a corner of my mouth with a cloth napkin, "I haven't, no. It's my dream to travel and eventually go to other countries, but right now... I'm still beginning my life…" There is a little unsteadiness in my voice at the last sentence. He smiles, picking up his knife and fork, "You sound a little unsure of yourself." My lips part; he just put me on the spot. And this, he notices. "Forgive me…" he cuts into his meat, "Where would you like to go?" My eyes drop to my plate, my silverware, then I take my knife and fork and cut some of my filet Mignon. "The one place I want to go most is Romania."
"Why is that?"
"The mountains, the people, the villages…" I slowly look up at him, "The history."
He stares at me in a thoughtful way. What is going on in his mind? I wish I could read it… But it doesn't take him much longer to speak.

"I have not been there in some time now, but I do know some of its history from the late 1800's…" he pauses, then adds, "As I have read a few history books that Mr. Vladoiu keeps in his library."
I'm quiet as I watch his eyes and mouth, but then I suddenly make an entertained face and take a bite from my fork, "Interesting... This steak is amazing! Oh my gosh!" He smiles wide and laughs at my words. "Well... I am pleased you like the steak." I blush as I chew.

"Seriously though," he says, "I think it is good to know about other places in the world."
"I agree." I say as I raise my glass, "But I'm wondering how you've managed to accomplish so many things in such a short amount of time."
"What do you mean?" he asks. I shrug a shoulder, "I never imagined how much a person can do in such small amounts of

time. My days feel short when they are actually long." He puts his silverware down, now giving me a knowing look, "You would be surprised how extraordinary life can be; you just have to apply yourself first."

"That's true." I sadly think of my job.

He becomes a little puzzled at my behavior. "Is something wrong?"

"Excuse me?" I say. He sits there silently, observing me–Then he hums slowly.

"What?" I say.

"Nothing…"

I bite my lip at his thoughtful expression.

Something comes to my mind. Something I wanted to ask a moment ago.

"Where did you go to college?"

"Out of state. A private college in upper Connecticut" He says.

"Oh…how was that?"

"It was…interesting. Everyone I met; my friends from there, they are all spread about the country now. I haven't talked to them in quite a while."

I halfway frown, "That's how life is."

He nods slowly, "Indeed. That is how life is. Did you go to college?"

"Yes. Before becoming an EMT, I had a year of nursing school."

"Did you like it?" He asks, taking a bite of his asparagus.

"Oh yeah, it was fun for me."

"Fun…" He laughs.

"Yeah. But like you, all of my friends spread out. They were never more than acquaintances anyway."

"Oh well." He says with a smile, "People come and go; all living their busy lives." I nod definitely, "They are. What is your job like?"

"Well, it's very demanding. Very busy all the time."

"Phone ringing on your hip constantly?" I ask in amusement.

Looking down at his plate with his eyebrows rising, he says, "Oh, you can't imagine. You haven't really seen it yet, but yes." He eats a bit of his mashed potatoes. I do the same with mine.

Momentarily, he lifts his chin at my drink, asking, "Are you drinking that?" I arch an eyebrow, "Yes…?" He reaches for it. Quickly, I stop his hand and we make eye contact. He grins, "I take large sips and mine is almost gone…" I look at his, and sure enough, that sip he took earlier lasted longer than I thought. I take my glass and slowly drink from it. Amused, he returns to his meal. The quietness fills the room.

"Tomorrow morning…" he looks at me, "come horseback riding with me." My eyes widen. I've never done that before! Where would we be doing that? And I'm also hoping to talk about his 'magic tricks'.

"What is it?" he asks.
"Well…" I slowly begin to speak but he stops me with a laugh and asks, "You've never rode a horse before, have you?" I shake my head at him, "No. No I haven't."
"Oh trust me Ivy, it is quite good fun." He says with wickedly excited eyes. Oh my!
I let out an, "Uh-hmm…"

He suddenly changes the subject, "There is something else on your mind, isn't there?"
"Well yes…" I say, "You promised you'd show me a few of your magic tricks."
That sounds so dirty.

"Ahh…you thought I had forgotten?"
"I didn't think you forgot; I assumed that you were hoping I forgot." Wait a minute…when did I get cocky all of a sudden?

"Ohh really?" he halfway smirks. "Um…" I blink at him, "Yeah…really."
"Ohh…" he lowers his head with a quiet chuckle, "Nu voi accepta acest comportament."
"I beg your pardon?" He looks up, eyes bright and aglow–fiery too. My jaw falls slightly open, letting out a gasp. He stands up,

putting his napkin down on the table. I jump out of my seat and rush toward the door. When I get to it, I hear him start to laugh quietly in a deep voice.

Quickly, I turn back around and–Holy shit! There he is! Almost in my face! "Nick?!" I gasp. He hushes me with a finger to my lips, then he whispers close to my face, "I will show you now...yes?" I search his eyes quickly. He looks down at my neck and smirks, "Your heart is racing." he looks into my eyes, "Have I frightened you?" How can he see my heart beating so easily? "Hm," he snickers. Suddenly, he sweeps me up into his arms, making me gasp again and squeak. "No! No!" I struggle in his arms. He takes me to the other side of the room, goes through a door and shuts it with his heel. Now we're in a sitting room; a blue sitting room. He drops me on a small sofa and I quickly try to sit up but he straddles me and holds my hands down on either side of my head. My eyes are huge and I'm on the edge of hyperventilating.

*Nu voi accepta acest comportament.

I will not accept this behavior.

Chapter 24

He leans down only a little as I fearfully stare up at him. "Because you doubt me, you only intrigue me more Miss Summers." His voice is entwined with a woman's! She doesn't even sound human! I try to push him away and he snatches my jaw, glowing eyes zeroing in on mine, "Don't struggle *Ivyy*... there is no need for it. All is quite well. This is, after all, a show just for you–You will see!" Slowly, my mouth falls open. He looks at it and I completely freeze as he hovers his fingertips over my lips. His features show concentration and determination but his quivering hand means he is hesitant and . I am losing myself under his gaze...and feel...safe? "A show just for me?" I ask. He blinks, then lifts his hands off, still straddling me, "Indeed–Only for you. Watch, Ivy–Watch." he leans over the couch and I hear a buzz noise. I recognize that right away.

He says into the intercom, "Angel, could you step in here please?"
"Yes sir."
"What's going to happen?" I ask.
"Just watch." He snickers at me.

A moment later, the door opens. I glance over and see a maid who notices my position and shoots Nick a shocked 'Why are you doing that?' look. He rolls his eyes at her, "Come closer." She hesitantly obeys him. He snatches her by the collar of her uniform and focuses on her eyes, "Angel, I'm holding this young lady against her will–What will you do to save her?" I watch how she begins to stare at him blankly, how her mouth slightly opens, and then he lets go of her and she slowly looks at me, then back to him. Her brows curve in as if she's beginning to reason something out.

She suddenly lunges forward in an attempt to yank him off me. He winks at me as she does this and then he's suddenly pulled away and pushed down to the floor with a painful sounding BOOM! I gasp as she gets on top of him and tries to take a swing at his head. Her face is blank the entire time. Why? Why is it blank? She has no emotion whatsoever within her actions!

He snatches her hand in midair and quickly leans forward and stares into her eyes. She instantly stares back and stops moving. He has a very entertained, wild look on his face. He tells her with a bit of humor tracing his voice, "I think you've made your point Angel." I flutter my lashes at all of this, unable to move a muscle. This is the most extraordinary thing I've ever seen in my life!

He releases her, she rises and calmly walks out, then he gets up and brushes himself off. Speechlessly, I watch him walk over and kneel in front of me, just a few inches from my face, and finally, I give him all of my attention. Geez, I'm completely stunned...

Taking my chin in two fingers, he tilts his head with a gentle smile, "What did you think of all that?"
"I...don't know what to think!" My response makes him chuckle quietly in that deep, dark sort of way again. I sit up more, moving closer to him, "You have to tell me how you did that! I want to try!"
"Ah ah ahh..." he shakes his head slowly, "Magicians never reveal their secrets. You should know that. But this 'trick', however, is not quite finished yet."
"What do you mean?" I ask, shocked. He holds a finger up and then presses the button on the intercom again, "Angel."
"Yes sir?"
"Come in here please."
"Yes sir."

He walks a little forward and folds his arms at me while I watch in confusion. The same door as before opens and Angel comes inside.

He smiles at her, "Angel, were you just in here?"
She eyes the room, "No...sir."
He looks up through his eyelashes at her, "Are you sure?"
"Yes. Yes I'm sure." She says, "Is there something wrong?"
"No." he shakes his head, "All is well. You may go."

"Yes sir…" she nods once at him and leaves.
He and I look at each other again.

"Ok, what was that?" I immediately ask. He smiles, "Maybe in the morning, I can give you a few hints." He offers his hand. I look up at him and carefully take it, "…Sure. Okay." He then turns his head as if he heard something. "Excuse me for a moment," he walks over to the dining room door and peers inside, "Walter." Wait, I thought Walter wasn't in there. How did he know he was?

I watch him say, "Yes, everything is alright… Tomorrow morning, we are going horseback riding. Make sure Eduard has Amelia and Stelian ready." Then I hear Walter say, "Yes sir. Will that be all?" Nick suddenly looks down with a very serious stare. It's like he's trying very hard to remember something or maybe he's scolding himself for something he forgot to do. His eyes are locked on the carpet. "Sir?" Walter says with concern. Nick twitches his head a little with a growl. He raises a hand and suddenly looks back to Walter. "Yes, that will be all for now." "Of course…sir." Walter apprehensively says. What…the heck? I'm not sure if I should ask about that or not… It's probably not a wise idea at the moment.

Slowly, Nick turns to me with a soft expression now on his face, "Are you still hungry?"
I shake my head, "No…but I'm tired."
"Would you like to sleep in the Windsor room again?"
I quickly give a disapproving look, "No, no thank you." He behaves as if he doesn't understand my anxiety–For a second.

"I see… Then allow me to show you to another. How does that sound?"
"Sounds good." I lightly smile. Gosh I hope this will be a more peaceful room. It's sad that looks can be deceiving.

He presents his arm, "Right this way…Miss Summers." He winks at me. I love that…
He takes me out into the corridor and we turn right, headed back to the grand room.

I just can't get over what happened earlier. Nick sure has talent! But I can't tell anyone I saw that; that's his special secret no one will ever know about. We cross the grand room and head upstairs, following the right hall until we're near the end of it. Before he opens the dark door, he tells me, "This is the Bojnice room; based on the Bojnice castle in Bojnice, Slovakia."
"Oh my…"

He reaches inside for the light switch, "Please, go in and see if it pleases you."
I take a hesitant step forward, peering in at the intriguing architecture. The walls have dark-red wood halfway down; and halfway up, soft green wallpaper with fine details. Everything in here is dark red or soft green. The furniture is very square, and also, I'd say–Intricately styled. And the bed…looks absolutely amazing. It's extremely romantic; has a comfy red comforter and pearl white sheets underneath it. The two windows have red curtains as well, and they're long. All the curtains I've seen in this castle are long.

Finally, I say, "This is really magnificent…"
"Yes…indeed."

I look at him as he stands in the doorway. "You say I can sleep in here?"
He bows his head slowly as I turn my head, "Yes of course…and…if you feel uncomfortable in here, I will be nearby…" He forms an evil ear-to-ear smile.

"Wow…" I say, looking the windows, "Thank you."
"You are quite welcome."

"Well, I should get my bag." I smile at him and start for the door.
"I can bring it if you'd like." He says. I stop in my tracks.
"Really?"
He nods, "If that is what you want." I look around the room for a moment, trying to make a decision. "You can go ahead and take a nice hot bath. You seem a little tense." At that, I make a puzzled

face at him, "I look tense…?"

"You do, Ivy…" He slowly walks in. I look up at him curiously.

He moves around me and gently places his hands on my shoulders, "Here," Oh! They're so warm…! I take in a quiet breath, heart suddenly leaping. He starts to massage my shoulders.

"Before I go, I will tell you a little about this room." I close my eyes, now relaxing and starting to feel like melting on the spot. Wow, he is very good at this…

"This is one of the newest ones, believe it or not. It was styled like this in the late 80's. Before that, it was just a regular room; Romanian design. It was Mr. Vladoiu's son's room, I think." I feel his hands gently move up my neck. I start to bite my lip. "Now look at it…" he pauses, hands sliding back to where they were before, "Beautiful, isn't it?" I swallow slowly, "Yes, very beautiful." He slowly moves in close to my neck, looking ahead, "So beautiful that you could stand here forever, gazing at it all…yes?" I breathe in as he opens his mouth near my pulse point. And then I feel his warm lips touch there. I gasp softly, "Nick-" "Relax…Ivy," he murmurs. Sighing quietly, I let my head fall back a little and he carefully wraps his arms around my midsection, allowing me to rest my head on his left shoulder. His teeth run over my skin. The bolt of energy spikes throughout my body. "That…tickles," I breathe. "Does it feel good?" he says, hardly audible. I utter a hum. "Listen to you, Ivy…you need rest…" I hear him say with a small laugh. Momentarily, he stops and leisurely removes his hands, "You are quite relaxed now." As he walks around to face me again, I put my hand below my neck, heart fluttering.

"Enjoy your bath, and…when you are done…just use the phone. It's on the nightstand by the clock." He bows at me and calmly walks to the door. As he shuts it on his way out, he lowers his head with eyebrows rising, "I will return then…" Whoa…

I let out an anxious sigh. Wow…what just happened? Seriously, it seems time just stopped and the only thing I was paying attention to was the feeling he was giving me, which has left me wanting more. But I can't want more. I...hardly know the guy! That's not like me to be so inviting! I think I forgot what I was supposed to do next. The last thing he said was...what?

I look around and stop at the bathroom. "Right...take a bath." I roll my eyes at my stupid behavior. Hold on, he said he will be back... I have nothing but a towel to wear! My cheeks redden. I see what he did there. Well then—We'll just see about *that*!

In the moment I open the dark red door, a very warm and welcoming feeling washes over me. It's heavenly. This is a beautiful bathroom! Same style as the bedroom of course; lots of dark red and soft green, and the squared-off furniture (meaning the few tables, counters, chairs and other odds and ends) with very interesting detail.

I make myself comfortable right away, drawing a hot bath and dropping my clothes to the floor without a second thought. It's a little strange to me how welcoming this room feels. It's different than any of the others—Even when I was with Nick, things felt awkward. Maybe I should sleep in here instead! That's a thought that makes me smile a little.

Speaking of which, Nick said he'd be back soon...with my clothes. I look over at the door. Thinking of him, I lightly rub my neck—and blush—again. What will it be like for me when I see him again? I would probably be motionless as I look at him, and secretly be yearning for more but I am too shy to say or do anything. Yes, it'd definitely be like that.

I finish bathing, wrap a towel around my body and peek into the bedroom. Everything is so quiet. It's a little eerie. Ah, I forget that's something I should expect...

I go over to the phone on the nightstand by the bed and reach to touch the buttons but stop midway and linger over it. What's going to happen? I'll call, he'll answer, and then what? Ivy, you are being extremely paranoid. Just do it. What would Gina say? Wait, why am I even wondering that...? I shut my eyes and press 11.

"Yes Miss Summers?" My eyes fly open; I'm relieved. It's Christine. Christine! Did I actually think Nick would be there waiting for me? How ridiculous of me!

"Um, yes...I didn't bring my luggage up here with me..."
"Yes, of course Miss Summers, we know. Your belongings will be there shortly." She says.
"Thank you." I sigh with a faint smile.
"Of course."

I hang up and start pulling the blankets back on the bed. I can't wait to get some sleep. A part of me assumes something supernatural will happen during the night, but this room–It feels nice. It doesn't give the feeling of eyes watching my every move like the Windsor room did. I somewhat wish I'd brought my journal along so I can have something else to put my mind on if I can't sleep. There's a doubt that problem will happen though. I'll probably be thinking of Nick and his astounding ability to hypnotize... It's really the weirdest, most intriguing thing I've ever seen.

I hear someone knocking on the door.
Putting a small smile on my face, I secure the towel around me and go open the door, being mindful of my appearance as I slightly hide behind it. I don't see anybody out in the hall. "Hello...?" I move forward a bit and look around. I gasp. Nick! He's leaning against the wall on the left of the door completely still like a statue...staring right at me. He lowers his head in greeting. I gulp and nod back. He raises my bag, "May I put this in there for you?" I stand silently for a moment, then start backing into the room slowly. He smiles a little and follows me in. I watch him put the bag on the table, being careful not to look at me too long.

"I see you are ready for bed." He says.
"Yeah...this room is pretty nice." I quietly reply. He pauses and turns his head slightly, showing his profile. I observe him as he stares ahead of him. Why is he doing that? He's focusing on something that's not there. Could he be watching something or hearing something? Whatever is going on, I don't think he likes it.

I ask, "Why did you want to give me my bag when you have maids and a butler to do things like that?" He blinks, finally…and turns to me with a softer expression. "Well I just wanted to make sure you were comfortable in this room… Are you?" I look from left to right in thought, then nod, "Yes, I'm comfortable in here. Thanks."

He smiles, "Good to hear. I wanted to hear it from you." He raises a finger, "I will see you in the morning. Be ready. I promise you, you will have good fun. Sleep well Ivy." He walks to the door. "Wait." I say. He stops and turns his head slightly, pointing his ear in my direction.

"What were you staring at just a minute ago?" I ask. He faces me again, also raising an eyebrow in a matter-of-fact way, "Nothing in particular. A thought just came to me; something I was supposed to remember." he suddenly grimaces, shifting his head away, "Curva proastă… Ştiu ce face ea!" I quickly back up to the bottom of the bed. He slowly looks at me. I study him from head to toe, "Are you ok?"

He sighs and shakes his head, "The thing I was supposed to remember…I missed it."

"What was it?" I ask.

He waves a hand, "Nothing major. It was just something I wanted to do."

"Oh…" I glance away for a second. Geez, he was quite grumpy about that.

"Yes yes…I will get over it though." He begins to smile at me, "Have a good rest Ivy." He nods once and heads out the door. That was so awkward.

Once I have my teeth brushed and my nightgown on, I get into bed and automatically feel like I'm lying on a big puffy cloud. A large sigh of contentment leaves me as I shut my eyes.

I notice it's snowing outside as I stand in a closed spiral stairwell, gazing out a Gothic castle window in a long dark green

Victorian dress. My hair is down, curly and nicely done with diamonds in it. I stop looking out when I feel someone is nearby. Turning to the right, I see him–my dream man–leaning against the wall with folded arms, smiling at me in a warm way. I have to return that loving expression of his.

"How long have you been there?" I ask.
He uncrosses his arms and approaches me, "Longer than you think."
"How long is that?"
He laughs at me, "A while." As I watch him take my hand and put it on his chest, he says, "I am always here…watching you, protecting you."
"…Protecting me from what?"
He looks down and whispers, "From dangers you would never imagine exist."
I furrow my eyebrows at him, "What does that mean?"
He flashes his eyes up to me, keeping his head down, "Darkness…negativity."
I fall silent, speechless and curious.

"Don't question any more of it." He says.
"But I want to know."
"If you know, you'll let them in." I get quiet again. This time it's for real.
He brushes a finger across my cheek, "You are light Ivy; shine– Shine no matter what happens."
"How can I if I don't know what you mean?"
"I won't tell you but I can protect you. And I will." I only blink up at him. That doesn't feel fair. He pulls me into a hug, "Come here my love." I rest my head below his neck and breathe in slowly, "I love you."
"I love you too, my Ivy."

Chapter 25

-Nicolai-

I shut my bedroom door and toss my jacket down on my bed, "I don't know how. I don't! Rozalia, how can I do this?" I plop down in a chair, letting my face fall into my hands.

"We will find a way. We always find a way."

"What do you suggest? All you do is cause pain!"

"Quiet Dmitri! She is among us, lest you forget!"

I get up from the chair, "Oh, I know that!" She walks me over to the mirror and there I see her glaring at me. Without moving her lips or mine, she says, *"Right now, Jennifer is playing nice and making things comfortable for Ivy. She has done no harm to her. We know this game, as we have played it all these years."*

I shoot my finger at her, "You have played it–Not me."

"Stop splitting hairs you fool! This is a situation we need to keep a close eye on! I am more aware of her lingering around Ivy than you. We must let this play out for now…then we will act when the time is right."

"What do you think I should do in the meantime? Stay in her room? I can't do that." I say.

"As I told her; I will be nearby."

"Who is Ivy to you? You say she reminds you of you but what does that mean? Why can't we just let her go?"

*"I'm getting tired of this conversation. How about…I show you your **true** face?"* She curls my lips into a crooked smile and I watch wrinkles slowly begin to spread across my face. I start to pant anxiously as I see age spots filling my forehead and my nose and ears growing larger. "No no no no NO!" She's forcing me to watch this. I'm growing older and older; so old that I'm shaking in the mirror, almost unable to stand anymore.

"Do you think Ivy could love you like this?"

"Stop! Please don't do this to me!" I beg.

"Without me...you could never have her."

Suddenly, I'm back to normal. I blink many times at myself and bring my hands up to feel my face. Gradually, I become very enraged. She's right, and I hate that with a passion. I growl, snatch both sides of the mirror and throw it down, "RAHH!!! DAMN YOU!"

"Dmitri," I hear behind me.
Huffing, I glance back at the door. Corneliu.

"Go to bed...you need sleep. I have been listening to you. I will do what I can to keep Jennifer away from this...girl–Only for you. I cannot do much though–You know that." Still shaking with anger, a tear forms in my eye and rides down my cheek. I am unable to say anything to him. I take in a deep breath and let it out, then slowly pick up the mirror, go clean my hands in my bathroom and take a long hot shower. As the water falls over me, I stare at the wall.

"You will be rewarded..."
"For what?" I sigh.
"I just might let you keep this one."

I shut my eyes with a small twitch of the lips that turns into a smile and I chuckle under my breath, "Your words...do not faze me...one bit."

"Go on and think that. We have a big day tomorrow. I will be good."
"Oh lovely, another sweet lie."

"I don't like your attitude."
"I don't like *you*." She makes me growl and punch the stone wall, denting it. I gasp to the pain.
"Now go to bed."

I grit my teeth, inhaling deeply.

I look at the clock as Christine returns to the maids' office. It's 6:46am. My stomach is growling–It hurts. I have to eat again...but I can never be fully satisfied. Since night before last, when I had that extremely terrible pain in my eyeteeth, this has been happening to me. It's strange but I think they've grown and they're sharper. I'm most likely exaggerating. This is beginning to feel very unnatural.

"Good morning Maria; I'm here. Wow, why is it so dark in here?" I hear her say as she turns on the light. I don't react–Not even move an inch. But when the light comes on, I immediately flinch and cover my eyes. I can't handle the light without it hurting either. I could've rested them and slept in the small bed in the corner but I can't sleep.

I have been alone in here, staring at the wall ahead of me, eating nonstop as female voices whisper to me from all directions. First, they were not comprehensible but as time went by, they became clearer and clearer to me. They only say one word–'Nicolai'. Since the voices started whispering to me, I feel more and more persuaded to have an even stronger desire to be with him in private; it's so strong that it will be the next thing I do. Nothing is more important. He needs to know I'm the one for him–Not Ivy. If anyone asks where I'm going, I will tell them I have to clean his room.

"Maria, are you ok?" Christine asks, walking around to the front of me. I didn't know she was talking to me. My gaze rises to her face and a gradual smile spreads across mine, "Yes…yes, I'm fine." I stand and walk past her to a storage closet and get a cart. She watches me strangely. "See you later." I say as I leave the room. She doesn't say anything. She is probably wondering why I took the cart because my shift will be over soon.

During my preoccupied walk down the hall, the voices are quieter now, but seem as if they're in my head and no longer in the walls. They would be echoic if they were in the walls. I make a right turn to the elevator, open the doors and go inside. As I close the doors, I hear a woman's faint laugh. I press 3.

The other maids and I have never liked the 3rd floor; it feels so heavy and dark. The only way to understand that feeling is to experience it yourself. Lately though, after Ivy showed up, I have

felt less and less uneasy about it. Everywhere has felt like this–
Even the basement, which is the second most unsettling place to
be. No one goes down there much.

When the elevator stops, I open the doors and quietly walk the
hall to his office door. I press my ear against it and listen. I never
know when he is working or sleeping. It's quiet as a mouse. Hm…
I step over to the kitchen door and listen. There's nothing. I put my
hand on the knob and realize the door is slightly ajar. This is very
unusual because this door is never unlocked. I listen once more,
and don't open the door yet; something makes me feel I should
wait first. Absentmindedly, I reach down into my pocket and pull a
spiral notepad out, then start unwinding the metal part of it,
keeping a blank face. When I'm done, I carefully push the door
open and daintily walk inside with the cart, also tucking the
notepad back in my pocket and holding the unwound coil firmly in
one hand.

I push the cart to one side and walk to the adjoining bedroom
suit. My sight stops at Nicolai lying in his messy bed in a peaceful
sleep. He seems to be dreaming. I also see he doesn't have a shirt
on. Suddenly, I hear my name shouted in a whisper in my head. I
move forward until reaching the foot of the bed, where I stand and
stare at him. "*Maria*…" The voice says, slower and clearer this
time, and unconsciously I say, "I need more of it; I must be
perfect."

I step away from the cart and steadily crawl up the bed as he
inhales deeply, then I stop moving, hovering my face over his. He
turns his head and utters a quiet hum. I watch his mouth. How I
would love to kiss those lips... How I would love to be his. I have
more and more hatred now that I think of him and Ivy being
together, and I really, really think she should go to hell. She's
nothing. Just garbage!

I lift my hand with the coil in it over his neck and bite my lip
slowly, then drag my eyes over to the spot I press the sharp end of
the metal to. My eyebrows slowly lift in concentration, "I must be
perfect-" I touch him, and suddenly he emits a deep inhuman

growl, eyes flying open as he grabs my left hand, then the other and flips me over onto my back with great authority. I gasp, frightfully fluttering my lashes up at him as he straddles me, having an extremely malicious, deathly glare on his face. His eyes are brightly aglow and his teeth are gritted! Instantly, my breathing sharpens. His teeth! His eyes! My god! I am face to face with a pure evil monster!!!

"How dare you interrupt my slumber?!" he viciously snarls, sounding almost demonic. "N-Nick! I-!" I don't even think this is Mr. Francis! "Don't stutter girl!" He throatily hisses. Suddenly, he stops and pats his neck, surprised. The voice screams in my ears and a sudden sharp pain shoots into my back. "AH!" I try to escape his grip but in that same moment, something makes me grab his face and get a taste of his blood on his neck. Oh god, the taste! It tastes terrible! I don't have control of myself! What's going on?! He gasps my name loudly, then growls and snatches my hair, yanking my head to one side and clamping his gaping mouth on my neck. I clench the sheets in my fists. Before I can let out a scream, he throws me off the bed and bites me again in the same spot, cupping my mouth with one hand. I try to hit him and push myself away with my legs but something makes me laugh at him, saying, "You damn COWARD! This is all?!" He takes a strong hold of my jaw and drills his glowing eyes into mine, "This will not happen again! You will not POSSESS! I continue to laugh at him until suddenly I feel something baseball-sized tear out my back. I belt out a cry and try harder to break free but I can't; he's too strong! I'm beginning to realize everything is disappearing from my sight. Everything is getting dark! I don't know what's going on! Am I dying? Oh my god, my neck! The pain; it hurts so bad! Why is this happening to me?! NO NO NO! HE'S KILLING ME!

-Nicolai-

Slowly, I stand over her, wiping my mouth with a scowl. *"This is unacceptable. I will have my revenge. Only I can possess here."* My still-glowing eyes narrow hatefully as the fearful Maria lays there, unable to move. I watch the anxiety drain from her face to a blank stare. I now have full control of her.

As I slowly turn my head toward the door where she came in, she carefully rises from the floor and walks out of the room. I follow her and watch as she goes to her cart. Like a robot, she picks up dishes and silverware from the table and countertop and places them on the cart. She then puts her hands on the bar and rolls it out of the room without a trace of emotion on her face. Rozalia lowers my head, looking up through my lashes in a satisfied way. "Hm hm hm *hmm*..."

-Ivy-

"Miss Summers?" I hear a woman say, waking me. I turn over and look at the door, "...Yes?" She comes in with some towels, having a friendly face. It's Pamela.

"Good morning... I brought you these for your morning bath." As she talks, I rub my eyes and check the clock on the nightstand. It's 7am. "Is there anything else you would like?" she asks. I look at her kindly, "Oh, no thank you. I'm good." She bows her head softly, "Breakfast will be served in 1 hour in the grand dining room. Mr. Francis will be expecting you." she starts for the door, "Excuse me." I almost stop her from leaving, wanting to ask what's for breakfast, but no–I let her go. I understand she must have a busy schedule.

I get out of bed, make it up real fast, collect my denim-wash skinny jeans, black sweater, white coat and tan rider boots from my bag. I'm anxious about the horse-riding later. Hopefully nothing will go wrong. It's ironic I brought these boots along, now that I think about it.

After a short yet luxurious bath, I put my hair up in a bun and put some makeup on, then hurry over to the phone and press 11.

"Yes Miss Summers?" It's Angel. I know that voice. Hearing it brings back the memory of what happened yesterday.

Don't give the impression something is wrong, Ivy–A questioning maid is the last thing you want to deal with right now.

"Angel, hi–I would like to put my luggage in the foyer closet so when I'm ready to go I can get it on the way out...is that ok?"
"We can get that for you Ms." She says.
"Oh! Well, thank you!" I say.
"You're welcome."

Alrighty then...it's breakfast time. I glance at the clock. It's 7:50. I leave the bag on the bed and hurry out into the hallway where I see Walter coming toward me. He asks me if I had a good night sleep, which I say yes to, and then he asks if I'm going to the dining room. "Yes I am."
"Allow me to escort you madam." He offers to guide me there.

I go with him downstairs. On the way, I notice Pamela walk by us, headed for the left corridor. She seems a little confused about something. I can see she's trying very hard to mask it.

"Is she ok?" I ask out of the corner of my mouth.
"I'm sure she is." He answers, although at the same time, I think he's trying to understand her behavior too. Hmm...

Pretty soon, we arrive at the dining room. He opens the door, and immediately I find Nick who is actually not sitting yet, but talking with the chef, and he's wearing the old Victorian clothing again; all black Victorian clothing today. He has a black vest with a blood red cravat tucked underneath, a silky black long sleeved shirt, black pants and shiny black rider boots. He looks beyond dashing. He's so fancy. I can't stop staring at him.

He turns to us as soon as he hears the door, and a bright, heart-stopping smile graces his face. I almost melt.

"Ivy, Walter," he bows slightly, then approaches us and takes my hand in his, lifting it up as he nods once at Walter. Walter bows back and goes out, saying, "Very well sir… Enjoy your breakfast."

I look at Nick again.

"I trust you slept well…?" He asks curiously.

"I did… It was very peaceful, thank you." I beam modestly at him.

"Very good, very good." He leads me over to my chair and pulls it out for me. "Miss Summers…you look very beautiful today."

"Why, thank you… You look quite handsome yourself." I watch him join me at the table, joy all in my eyes. He chuckles, then he says, "Well, I am most comfortable in this fashion of clothing…as I have explained before." He gives Fitzgerald a look. I also glance over as the chef rolls the cart up and places our plates down in front of us. "Croissants…and some orange juice." He smiles. Nick does the same back to him, nodding and waving his hand a little. Fitzgerald kindly leaves us to our meals.

I look at Nick in a slightly confused way.

"I recommended we have a light breakfast this morning… I don't want you to get an upset stomach during our time horseback riding." He explains.

"Oh, I see…" That's understandable.

"You know, I have felt like having French toast but it isn't a wise idea. Truthfully, I think French toast has been a favorite of mine...for as long as I have been here." He says, taking his glass of orange juice, having a gleeful glint in one eye. It's that glint that always makes me forget everything around us, I swear. Momentarily, I raise my own glass in agreement, giving nearly the same expression.

"Ivy, what is your favorite thing to eat?-Overall." He asks.

I lift my attention up from my plate to him, a little puzzled. That is an interesting question for me. "I don't think I have any favorites."

"Really?" He's a tad stunned. I think about it some more.

"Yeah, really." I nod. He takes his first bite of his croissant with a wondering gleam, "Yes…there is so much food out there to choose from…I suppose when you give someone so many choices, they will never know what they like best."

"Tell me about it. Waiting in line for coffee at the Lounge 'n Sip is no picnic." I roll my eyes.

"Ah, but waiting for something like that, I can tolerate. When you wait for happiness, it is like an eternity, no?" His question…I can really relate to it. My dreams…

"Most definitely." I agree in a somewhat quiet, sad voice. He goes silent as he looks at me in a way it's almost like he's contemplating something. "You seem to know what I mean by that. Why?" he takes a bite of his food. While he chews, I realize how closely he's observing me. The unnerving feeling…has returned.

"Well I…" I try to talk, though it's not working as well as I'd hoped. He takes his napkin in both hands, still watching me in that same way. I inhale deeply. He puts the napkin down, "You are too lovely to experience something like that." I blink quickly at him. "Tell me, what could make you happy?" I become more surprised. "Excuse me?"

He raises his hands, "What could make you happy? It's a simple question, really."

I close my mouth and inwardly scoff.

"What?" He asks. I move my hand around a little as I think about it, and before getting a taste of my croissant, I quietly say, "It's not that simple. No one has ever asked me a question like that. I don't know how to answer properly."

"Would there be a proper way to answer that?"

"Well," I look at him, "I don't…think so."

He looks down at his glass, "Hmm," then a sudden smile spreads across his face as he props his chin up on his left hand, "Ivy…let me tell you…the proper way is to know yourself and then you will know what you want. Do you know yourself?"

"What do you mean?" I ask. He places one hand over his heart, "Your heart Ivy–What does it tell you? Listen to it–Really listen to it." I am falling speechless again. Anybody could tell me this and I wouldn't give it much thought, but when it's him, it's different. What could make me happy...

The desire I have for him is so strong; it runs my life every minute now. I haven't known him long but ever since the first time I saw him, he's really all I think about. I don't understand this. I just know that when we are near each other, everything feels whole and complete again. I'm happy–Happier than words can really explain. But how can I tell him this?

He laughs quietly without opening his mouth, then takes a deep breath and turns his head, "Love..."

I slowly look up from my plate at his profile. He glances at me out of the corner of his eye, "Love is the answer." He faces me completely with a sort of smile that I don't understand. "Well don't we all want that?"
"Yes...of course." I utter.

Suddenly, Walter comes in and whispers something to Nick. When he's done, Nick nods at him, "We are almost finished here. Thank you." Walter bows his head and leaves again.

Turning back to me and taking his glass in a hand, he says, "Our horses are ready to go."
"Oh," I return to my meal.
"Are you nervous?" he asks, and I think he wants me to say yes.
"No." I say in a small diminished voice.
"You are lying..." Quickly, I shoot him a troubled look.

"It's alright my dear...Mr. Vladoiu's horses are very well-behaved."
"But what if I startle them?"
He winks at me, "You don't worry; it will be fine." I raise an eyebrow as I eat some more.

"Last night, did you hear anything in the halls? Perhaps feel a little chill?" he asks.
"No...I don't think so. I was very comfortable actually." I begin to wonder why he's asking me such a question. I understand he's

concerned but it's a little strange how he says that.

"Hmm…" he finishes his meal and uses his napkin, "Very good."

"Nick," He pauses and looks at me questionably. I become hesitant again; this time it's for a very good reason. I bite my lip. He sees me do that. "What is wrong?"

"Why is the Windsor room so different? You told me you are a psychic and I'm just wondering what's really going on here." I ask. He slowly sits back in his chair, taking another deep breath. Is he bothered?

"There are others here. I see them night and day." He says.

"Yeah…? Are they good or bad?"

He forms a devilish smile, now seeming eager, "Well my dear, define good and bad…" Oh! A sudden mood change! The expression he's making, how his voice suddenly became dark and evil; I feel like sinking into my boots.

"Good ghosts, I guess, would leave you alone. The bad ones…" I can't finish my sentence; I'm not exactly sure how to describe the bad ones.

"The bad ones…" he tilts his head, "what?"

"They would terrorize you." I say.

"Are you saying there might be bad 'ghosts' here?" Oh yeah, he's entertained again.

"No! No I'm not…!"

"Then why do you ask of the Windsor room in that way?" He looks quizzical now.

"Because…it gave me chills, literally. I heard banging within the walls and some women whispering. They were either in the hall or in the walls." I think to myself…wouldn't that be considered bad?

He makes a more interested stare.

"What?" I ask.

"I will investigate that when I can." He says. He takes a last sip of his orange juice and stands up, "In the meantime, our horses are waiting for us… Shall we go?" I glance down at my plate and then at my glass, "Yeah," I also get up and he smiles softly at me. "I

hope you enjoyed your breakfast–As small as it was." I look at him for a minute. "Yes, yes I did…thank you." I lightly bow my head. He offers his arm, winking at me, "It is my pleasure. Come now– Allow me to escort you there Miss Summers." He's just so...different. I love that.
Gently, I take a hold of his arm.

He leads me out into the corridor and we follow it all the way. It feels like it could never end. After a while, I really begin to notice the dark-wood ceiling is lower than I'd imagined, and more rounded off too. It has fancy dimly lit lanterns dangling far apart from each other and the floor is light brown marble. There are interesting designs in the wood on both walls. Along these walls, I see some paintings nicely spread out from each other and also the small almost-black tables with two chairs at each and every one of them. I do wonder why everything is so dark.

"Nick, you live in a fantasy world." I absentmindedly mutter. He looks at me with a bare smile, "No, not really–It could always be better." At that, I want to ask 'how could it? How could it when you live in a castle and have people constantly waiting on you hand-and-foot?', but all I ask is, "How?"

We stop at a single dark, dark-brown door at the end and he takes my hands, "My life is truly a complicated one. It's one that I wouldn't expect you to understand–Or even try to believe." I glance up from our hands to his face, "How can it be so complicated when you live in such luxury?" He starts to smile in a dry sort of way, "Luxury is what you make of it Ivy. This is my life, yes–But it's never perfect." he seems to frown at the last few words, almost like a longing frown. I blink at him slowly, then I take my hands out of his, "Well, I'd say your life, despite your ghost issue, is so much better than mine."
He quickly blocks the door, "Oh, I highly doubt that."
I look at his lips, "I thought you don't like doubts."
"I have plenty reason to doubt that."
"How so?" I ask. He studies my eyes and nearly answers my question but stops himself. He backs up and opens the door

without looking at it. I see past him yet another hall, but this one is brighter and narrower. I look at him again. He has a sort of smug expression. I follow him for a short distance past a single window. The sun is shining brightly and it illuminates the end of the hall.

As he guides me along, I hear him hiss, "So bright today."
"The sun bothers you?"
"A little bit. It bothers my eyes. The hat will help though."
"The hat?" I ask.
"Yes–you will see." He says, not looking at me.
"Ok…"

I change the subject. "Let me guess…you don't ever go to the beach?" I grin slightly. We stop at the door, and as he opens it, he looks back at me, "Oh **no**…you will **never** find me going there. I get sunburned quite easily. Always have–All my life." Ah, no wonder why he's so pale!

We stop at a single lone door across from the window. He gestures me to go first. I open the door and see we're walking into the stable. Immediately, I see 4 beautiful horses in their stalls. Two of them are saddled. I really didn't expect this at all–Surprise, surprise! I wonder who saddled them.

He shows me over to a saddled white mare and pats her side, "This is Amelia; she is 5 years old; an American Saddle-bred. She is a very good horse." He smiles up at her while rubbing her ribcage, "Aren't you a good girl? Yes you are." She really likes him, I can tell. He must coo over her like this often. It makes me giggle to myself. The other horses in here are very tame as well. He pats her two more times and then looks at me, "You will ride her. She's the most calm here. Now, the horse I will ride," he walks over to a saddled black stallion and greets it by petting its muzzle gently, "This is Stelian…it means pillar in Romanian. He's 8 and the same breed as his girlfriend over there." He grins over at Amelia shortly, then he looks at me again. I begin to smile at him. He's good with animals it seems.

"What?" he asks. I give a small laugh, "You are so good with them; these horses." That makes him smile back at me–An after-the-fact smile. "Yes, well," he gazes back up into Stelian's left eye, "They are like my children...when Dmitri is not here. I love them so." he chuckles, "Even when they misbehave." He walks over, opens Amelia's gate and starts checking her saddle, "The hats are over there hanging on the wall." he points with his chin over to the left. I follow his gaze to the other side of the stable. Oh my gosh, they're those black Spanish hats with the feathers at the backs! I go collect them and hand him one.

"Thanks," he puts it on, then flashes a suave smile. My cheeks flush. After putting mine on, I grab my arms and watch him return to fixing his saddle. "So do you want to have kids?" I ask. He pauses, almost looks at me, but only stares down at the ground for a moment, then he returns to what he's doing, "No. I've considered having some, but I don't think I'm able to." he finishes checking the saddle and motions me to mount her. I walk up to her. Before I do anything, he says, "Why do you ask?" I look at him as I take a hold of the saddle, "...You seem like you'd be a wonderful father." He stares at me for a long few seconds; a thoughtful kind of stare. I furrow my eyebrows at him, "Does that surprise you or something?"

He blinks, then quickly smiles and shakes his head, laughing quietly, "Well, I can't be sure. The only way to know if I'm a good father or not is to ask them." he moves his hand around the room at the horses. I briefly smile, but wonder about his sudden odd behavior. "Yeah, I guess so."

He winks at me, "Alright. Well go on–Mount her."
"Um," I'm sheepish.
"Here," he helps me up onto the saddle and I almost fall off with an "Oh!"
We both laugh as I steady myself on Amelia. She stands still and whinnies as if to reassure me.

I feel strange up here; I don't know what will happen next. I watch him go over to Stelian's gate, open it, check his saddle and then mount him easily.

"Follow me."
I blush and nod nervously.

Here we go...

Chapter 26

As we're trotting along a trail lined with many trees, I look around and feel as if I'm in a movie. The scenery is very similar to those I've seen in movies. Much to my surprise, this horseback riding thing is quite easy; Amelia and I are getting along great. Nick is ahead of me, riding with his shoulders back, and his chin is up a little. He's proud. So handsome…

I follow him down a small hill where we come upon a hunchbacked gardener wearing a large, old and tattered brimmed hat. He's digging a hole and throwing the dirt into a small trailer behind a golf cart. We stop to say hello.

"Eduard…good morning." Nick says.
I wait for the gardener to turn so I can see his face. As soon as he does, I know for sure he's the one I saw before. He has an eye-patch and a piece of straw dangling from his teeth.

Squinting, he says, "Mr. Francis, good morning!" Oh, he sounds very much like…very much like Igor from Frankenstein if I do say so myself! Wow! I quickly look at Nick who smirks slightly at him. "Eduard, this is Miss Ivy Summers." He looks at me. Eduard bows while holding his hat over his large belly, "Miss Summers, it's a pleasure to meet you."
I nod once, slowly, "Yes, likewise Mr. Eduard-" "Dillinger." He finishes for me.
"Mr. Eduard Dillinger…" I smile gently, "May I ask…did you saddle the horses?"
He looks at the horses quickly and says, "Are they not right ma'am?"
Nick speaks up and says, "They are as they should be Eduard. What are you doing there?" Eduard glances from me to him, back and forth, then he looks back at the trailer while scratching his balding head, "I'm going to plant an orange tree here."
Nick raises an eyebrow, then scans the area, "There is too much shade here though…isn't there?" Eduard blinks at him, "Sir, it

needs to have half shade."

Nick smiles, "Ah, spoken like an expert."

"Yes, well… Miss Ivy," Eduard laughs a tad as he then points off to a part of the castle, "I know I'm not seen in there much, but I live in that end of the castle. You know–near the greenhouse." He nods up at me. "Oh," I say with a kind smile. Nick sighs softly, "Well...time is slipping away. Let us continue our little tour. Eduard, do not forget that mound you left near the greenhouse."

"Oh! Yes sir–Of course!"

"Very Good" Nick nods back at him and snaps his reigns to head off. As we move away, I look over my shoulder at Eduard and see him smiling like a grandfather at me. I give him a last nod, "Again, nice to meet you Mr. Dillinger!" I wave at him as I follow behind Nick.

"You too Miss Summers!" This gardener guy makes me shiver a bit, but for the most part he doesn't bother me much. He seems pretty innocent-minded.

-Walter-

While walking to Leonardo's boathouse, I look at the partly cloudy sky and around at the trees. I'm enjoying this cool autumn breeze. It won't be long before it begins to snow. I do like that weather.

Upon my arrival at his door, he opens it before I can knock. I lower my hand and smile at him, "Good morning to you Leonardo; I've come to retrieve the mail." He seems surprised.

"Well now, that's a switch." He chuckles and offers for me to step inside.

"Why, thank you." I go just inside the door and wait while he begins talking as he walks to a table where he keeps the mail.

"How are things at the castle? And that girl–Ivy?"

"Nothing quite out of the ordinary… Miss Summers is a nice young lady. Mr. Francis really fancies her. They are out horseback riding at the moment."

He sets the mail aside and smiles slyly, "Maybe he will marry this one. Would you like some coffee?"

"Yes I would...please,"

He raises a finger, "I've got just the thing! Here–Let me show you." I watch him walk through a hall to his kitchen, and I follow.

It looks like he bought some new pictures to hang on the walls. They're mostly coastal scenes. That doesn't make sense to me…we being on the coast, I think to myself.

As we enter his kitchen, he opens a cupboard, saying, "Esmeralda gave me some new kind of coffee. I didn't think I would like it at first because I like to stick with what I know, but I tried it and it was like gulping down heaven. It's a Brazilian blend with vanilla extract. Would you like to try it?" I look at it and then at him, "Well…I suppose it wouldn't hurt."

He points at me and then starts making our coffee in his small coffeepot.

"How are the ladies?" he asks. I pull a chair out from his small kitchen dining table and gently sit down, then fold my hands on my lap, "They are curious about Miss Summers, just as you are…or maybe more."

"Ahh…I understand. What about Mr. Vladoiu?"

"What about him?"

"Does he know of her?"

"I don't know, to be honest." I say.

He crosses his arms over his chest with an eyebrow rising, "Do you ever wonder why he doesn't come here?" I ride my finger up the side of my face, resting my elbow on the table, "Yes, but it isn't my concern."

"Come on, you have worked here longer than me."

I look at him somewhat dryly, "Only two years longer."

He shrugs, "That's plenty of time to start wondering about it."

"Well, we all understand Mr. Vladoiu owns other homes. Mr. Francis has told me that this castle is the place he likes the least."

"I say this is a paradise…but what could be paradise to him?" He scoffs.

I raise a hand a little, "We may never know."

The coffeepot beeps.

He turns and prepares our cups. "Cream and sugar?"

"Hmm…" I have to think about it, since this is a different sort of coffee. "Yes please–Cream and sugar." He makes it for me and then joins me at the table with his cup.

He laughs a bit, "I tell you, it surprised me to see you at my door this morning to get the mail."

I smile, "First of all, thank you for the coffee." I lift it up, "And I decided to do something a little different today. I usually go for a walk in the mornings, you know that."

"True, true." he takes a sip of his coffee. I do the same with mine and look around the room swallowing. My eyes quickly switch back to him, "Oh my, this truly is good."

"Told you!" He grins. I let out a small hum at him, "Yes, yes you did. Tell me, why are you so chipper this morning?"

"What do you mean? I'm always like this."

"I don't know. Maybe I just finally noticed." I drink some more, then I look at my watch as an excuse and finish my coffee quickly. "Well, I must get moving. Thank you again for the coffee. Maybe Esmeralda can get me a pound or two that I can share with the other staff."

"Yes, I'll talk to her. Thanks for coming by." He walks me to the front door and shakes my hand. "Don't be a stranger." He says. I smile at him and we wave to each other as I leave.

"Hm, nice fellow." I smile to myself, walking away.

Now that I've retrieved the mail and returned to the castle, I head to the elevator. Instead of taking the stairs to my office on the second floor, I choose this for once. But I realize that after a moment, it's not working. I sigh, "Here we go again. This thing is older than I am." I see Angel walking toward me with Christine by her side. They look confused. By what–Maybe it's the elevator.

"Walter…" Angel says, "Have you seen Maria? We all have been paging her but she won't respond." I look from her to Christine and then over their heads across the room in thought. "Well no…as a matter of fact, I have not."
"She never returned to the maids' office. She's usually finished and back by 8. It's almost an hour past." Christine tells me. I calmly raise my hands, "Ladies, I'm sure everything is fine. I will see if I can find her. Don't worry. Continue your own duties." The two look at each other, then at me. They nod carefully and leave.

I suspiciously turn back and start for the stairs to the second floor. I try the elevator there, pressing the 'up' button a few times, but nothing happens. "Well…that's odd."

I walk farther down the hall and go around the left corner, up the spiral staircase. Once I am at the 3rd floor elevator, I notice the doors are open. It's dark in there. Apparently, the power is out. I move closer and immediately realize the elevator is not on the 3rd floor at all. Quickly, I go to a utility closet to collect a flashlight, then I return and shine the light down the shaft.

Squinting at it, I can barely understand what I'm seeing down there because it's so dark. Just as my eyes adjust and focus, I recognize there is a body down there with other things around it; a cart and dishware. It looks like Maria! Her body is twisted up among the cables. I clutch my chest; the breath has almost left me. I nearly drop the flashlight. As calmly as I can, I shut the doors a bit, move away from it and take the stairs down to my office. When I get there, I privately page Eduard and tell him to meet me at the stable. Just after, I take a moment to breathe. I am not sure what happened but this is unbelievable.

I page the maids to meet me in their office, then I sigh and make my way downstairs to the first floor. As soon as arrive, I inform them they must remain in their office until I give further notice. They can't know Maria is dead yet. They ask me if this concerns her and also if they are in some sort of trouble. I say "no," and "stay calm."

I hurry out as fast and carefully as I can, going through the corridors to the stable. It takes me a few moments because I never run anywhere.

Eduard and I meet by Amelia's gate; he has a very concerned and slightly impatient look. Quietly, I say, "There has been a tragic accident with one of the maids. I need you to find Mr. Francis and tell him to return to the castle as soon as possible. Tell him to meet me in the rear foyer." He nods quickly, "Of course–Yes sir!" He hurries out to his golf cart and drives off. I turn and rush back inside the castle. "Damn it…damn it!" I still can't believe it. How could Maria have done this? I must contact the harbor police.

-Ivy-

Nick and I ride out of the trees, into a large clearing. Automatically, my sight sets on three archery targets in the middle of the open land. Nick does archery? Sweet!

We slow to a stop.

"I come out here early in the morning sometimes." he says, then he looks at me, "When I need to clear my mind, I do target practice." That's…interesting.

"Are you any good at it?" I ask. He scoffs, "Considering I've done this for decades, I'm skilled enough to hit the center every time." Oh come on, he's only 32! How many decades–2? He sees the face I'm making and shakes his head, "You don't believe me?" Uh oh…here we go with the doubt thing. "How many decades?" I ask. He stops smiling for a second, but then he quickly does it again and looks around, "Well, it feels like many decades. I exaggerate sometimes." I stare at him a little. "Okay." I look ahead again, "Is there anything else you do out here?"

"Well yes! Watch!" I quickly lift my eyebrows. Before I know it, he yanks back on Stelian's reigns, making him suddenly neigh and stand up on two legs, then he shouts, "HA!" Stelian takes off running and Nick starts laughing and leaning in close to his neck. This startles Amelia. She does the same as Stelian and almost knocks me off when jumping up on her hind legs, neighing. I scream, "WHOA, WHOA! NICK!" Amelia rushes forward after Stelian. I take a tight hold of her reigns while trying not to belt out another louder scream.

We almost catch up when Nick maneuvers around one of the targets. Amelia hurries behind and tries to meet up with him again but just as we get close enough, he abruptly stops. Amelia suddenly jumps up like before and I try to snatch the reigns but instead fall off her back. BAM! Down I go, flat on my back. I hear Nick burst out laughing as Amelia runs away. He rides up to look down at me and finds me glowering up at him. It's kind of hard to do with the sun in my eyes.

"Are you alright?" he chuckles. I throw my hand back above my head to snatch my hat from the ground, then I sit straight up and shove it back on, "Oh YES, I'm fine!" He belts out another insane laugh. I stand up and brush myself off while looking for Amelia. Just then, I feel him tap my shoulder. I whirl around to him. He offers to help me up onto Stelian. "There is no way you will get her back after she's found a good place to graze." he gestures me to follow his eyes over to the far, far left. With an upset glare, I do. Oh great–Amelia is way out there near the trees, eating a very green patch of grass. I look back up at Nick, sighing, "Ok." I take his hand and he helps me up, which is a little difficult to do. He turns his head, showing his profile, "You will have to hold onto me." Whoa, wait. Me–holding onto him? I blush.

As I put my arms around him, I can sense he's grinning wide like he just won something. He flicks his reigns and we calmly, and slowly, ride back toward the stables–Or so, that's where I hope we're going... But just then, we both see Eduard coming out of some trees in his golf cart. He's looking right at us with urgency. I look at the curious Nick staring off at him. He starts walking us in Eduard's direction.

"What's going on?" I ask.

"I don't know."

We stop riding and he gets off Stelian, "Excuse me for one moment." He walks up to Eduard and I watch the calm but greatly unsettled behavior of the gardener who speaks very quietly. Whatever they're talking about, I see Nick suddenly grow a little tense and a bit worried. He nods at Eduard and comes back to me.

"I need you to go with Eduard back to the stables. I must return to the castle for a moment. I will be back for you soon."
"What's wrong? What happened?" I ask.
He waves a hand, "One of the maids has been injured."
"Oh my god, does she need to go to the hospital? Maybe I can help...?"
"I will know soon." He offers a hand. I take it as he helps me off the horse, then he kisses my hand and says, "See you shortly." I give him a concerned frown. He dips his head firmly and snaps his reigns, riding off to the castle.

"Miss Summers?" I hear Eduard say.
"Yes, I'm coming." I go to him and get in his golf cart, tucking some of my hair behind my ear, "I hope everything's okay."
"Me too." He drives us away.

-Nicolai-

I get to the rear of the castle and tie Stelian to a tree, then walk across the stone laden decking towards the rear entrance with authority. On my way, Corneliu follows behind me, pestering Rozalia about how stupid it was to murder Maria. She doesn't pay him any mind. Every time I try to look at him, she forces me to focus ahead of us. He's not the only one in my ears; there are others shouting at me—calling me names. I hear giggling everywhere. I flick my eyes to the right and see Jennifer in a black, snakelike mass slithering among the bushes, moving at my pace. I glower, looking ahead again. The hatred Rozalia has toward her has increased. But, she begins to laugh quietly, then her volume rises and rises until it's a loud maniacal cackle. *"She must be*

PISSED! *Hahahaha! Yes! AHAHAHA!"* I slap both sides of my head, "Taci dracului din gura! Ea aduce iadul în castelul asta!" I get through the glass doors to the foyer and see Walter looking out a window, anxiously waiting for me, and Rozalia is still laughing.

He turns, "Sir, I have something to show you. On the third floor." He points up with a stare of warning. "What happened? Tell me first." I demand–Calmly. Rozalia has all of a sudden stopped her insane cackle and now she's listening to Walter intently–It's as if she was never amused. "Sir, I highly recommend I show you." He almost whispers. I give him wary eyes and then look toward the doors that lead to the grand room. "Very well." I follow him out.

"We have to take the stairs." He says.
"Why is that?"
"When you see it, you will know."
"God damn it Walter, what is this already?! Tell me!" He stops and looks at me, "A tragic accident has happened to Maria." I fall silent, staring at him grimly.

*Taci dracului din gura! Ea aduce iadul în castelul asta!

Shut the fuck up! She brings hell in this castle!

We continue moving upstairs, faster this time. Still, the spirits have not left me. At least Rozalia is a little quieter. She is rambling to herself about Maria's jealousy of Ivy. We both know Jennifer magnified it. But why? We will find out soon enough what her plans are. Rozalia and I are becoming a little unsettled that we can't see what might happen next. Jennifer definitely has plans for Ivy.

"I am not a fool; I will solve this before the first event can take place."
'And you will use me to do it?'
"What choice do we have?"
"La naiba…" I grumble aloud as we reach the third floor.
"Excuse me sir?" Walter quickly says.

"Yes, I'm sorry. I just need to calm my nerves." I cough lightly.

He leads me to the elevator and stops to take a breath before he opens the doors. Shakily, he takes his flashlight out of his pocket. I put my right hand on his wrist, "Walter, calm yourself. You are too rattled." His eyes light up and switch back to the dark shaft, "You will understand why!" I hum a little, gently take his flashlight and shine it down the shaft. And there she is…her body mangled and a lot of blood. I see her perfectly; my sight is 10 times better than a normal person's would be. She has plates and other dishware around her. Her head is lying on the roof of the elevator separated from her body. Her legs and arms are contorted too.

Rozalia gasps, *"Oh my goodness! ...What a **KNOCKOUT** job!"* I bite on my bottom lip, "Fuck…" Quickly, I look at Walter, "How did this happen? When did it happen? Do you know?"

"No sir. The maids told me she was missing and that they had tried to page her many times. She was overdue for her shift change by over an hour when they informed me. I was going to my office and tried to use the elevators but discovered they didn't work. I started investigating the elevator problem, and that is how I discovered her."

I lift my chin slowly, "Have you called anyone yet?"
"Yes I have. I called the harbor police. Leonardo is preparing for them to arrive."
I sigh and rub my forehead, "Very good… The maids–Where are they?"
"In their office waiting to hear from me, sir."
"Inform the staff the police are coming and explain why, but be brief about it." I move my hand away and begin to walk back down the hall.

"But sir, are you going to meet the police?"
I stop and turn just a little, "I have every confidence you can handle them. I have to return to Ivy." He makes an understanding face at me as I promptly proceed down the hall.

Chapter 27

Eduard and I retrieved Amelia and found Stelian tied to a tree near the rear entrance of the castle. Eduard tied them both to the golf cart and led them back to the stable. They are now unsaddled and back in their stalls. He is brushing them down and making them comfortable while I stand by the large barn door of the stable, looking out for Nick. He doesn't talk to me much; he's very preoccupied. Of course he's quite friendly to me though, whenever we speak. Many times, I've wanted to pry out the answer on what happened in the castle. At the same time though, I always consider the fact he may not know. I asked him when he thinks Nick will be back. He's not certain. I should have known he wouldn't be. Something very bad has happened; I don't know what it is, but it sure puts my stomach in a knot.

I hear Eduard behind me say, "Would you like something to drink or anything Ms. Summers?" I gulp and turn around to him; my features are perplexed. He points over to a small fridge on a counter way back in the right corner, "I keep things in there–Juice and water mostly."
"Thanks…but I'm fine."

The inner door opens and I turn around to see Nick coming toward me with a worried face. "So what's going on?" I say. He looks over at Eduard and then back to me, "I don't want to talk about it here. I will tell you after we go back inside the castle, alright?"
"Okay...sure." I say.

We walk out of the stable, into the narrow hallway in silence. I can see a look of calculation on his face. As we enter the big corridor, he says, "I could use a drink right now–would you like a drink?"
"Yeah, I think so."

Soon, we go into the grand room and I'm thinking we will be

going upstairs, but no, we make a left turn as soon as we're out of the corridor. He leads me to an archway leading down a few steps to a dim, somewhat narrow hallway that has mahogany walls, no windows–Just paintings, and a shiny, dark brown wooden floor in the middle. The black lamps on the walls are beautifully vintage–Creepy-looking too, but it's exquisite to me. This hall is behind the grand stairs, and we're heading toward the end.

During this walk, I feel a few unsettling things; the atmosphere is heavy and tense, and I feel I shouldn't say a word to him while my curious mind is going in all directions. The suspense–It gets to me so much that I have to ask, "Where are we going?"
He briefly sighs and smiles a little, "There is an office in this hall that has a bathroom in it and I need to use it…if you don't mind."
We stop halfway to the end at a door. He says, "I'll only be a minute, I promise." As I study it, I say, "Yes, of course…I'll just…wait out here."
"Thank you." He looks around me suspiciously before giving one gentle nod and going through the door and shutting it behind him.

I inhale a bit shakily, looking ahead now.
There isn't much more walking before reaching that end. It looks so eerie down there. It might be getting darker…or is that an illusion? The lights seem to be dimming down.

"Ivy, come to the end." I hear Nick say. Wait, he just went inside this office. I don't think any doors opened… Could there be a door that was already opened?

"Ivy, please." He's getting impatient. I gently, uneasily ball my hands into fists and start walking toward his voice, no matter how uncomfortable the air is. I should do what he says.

I see a door opening slowly. Instantly, I pause. Am I being too skittish?
"Ivy." he repeats.
"I'm here." I say.

Suddenly, I feel a warm stream of air slither up my back, nearly taking the breath out of me and relaxing me. Quickly, I turn around. There's nothing. No one. It's still in my back and it's rising to the nape of my neck. I feel like the fear is slipping away. Something is making the atmosphere lighter, calmer, more comfortable. What is it? What is this? Oh… Slowly, I close my eyes, sighing softly. "Ivy?" I hear Nick as he comes back out into the hallway. The strange, relaxing warmth stops. I blink a few times.

"Yes…I'm here…I thought you said you where down here." He looks me up and down, then behind me. When he does that, I get the impression someone's there. I turn but see no one. "Come on." He says, coming to take my hand. I step back once, "Nick, who's behind me?"
He stops in his tracks. Looking past me twice, he forms a look of annoyance.

"Will you tell me?" I ask. He offers a hand, tilting his head a little to one side, "I will if you come with me." After that, his eyes rise above my head in a wary sort of way. Now I figure whoever is behind me is just as tall as he is. I'm 5ft 4". He's like 6ft 5". I put my hand in his and he starts for the end I almost went to. In the moment I take my first steps forward, I feel a sudden pressure in my chest. I have to breathe in quickly because of the pain. He looks at me, "Are you alright?" Putting a hand just below my neck, I stare at him, "I–I don't know what just happened… My chest–It's sore." I rub it with two fingers and wince a bit.
"I do." He utters in a sort of disgusted way.
"What?"
"Come on." He guides me along the hall, around a corner and up a spiral staircase until we get to the 2nd floor. The pain is almost gone now. I don't know how. Why did it happen?

"Where is Walter?-And everybody else?" I ask.
"They should be in the maids' office now."
"Oh… Is that where the hurt maid is?"

We approach a door, he opens it for me and I go inside, then he gently shuts it and runs a hand through his hair while walking over to a desk. "Listen, it's tragic what happened to her. I am trying to collect my thoughts but I really need that drink. Please Ivy, have a seat. Make yourself comfortable."

I slowly look away from him and around at the furniture and decor. Mostly antique, but really well-kept. I get settled and finally look up at him in question. He stands there quietly.

"Are you okay?" I ask. He stares through me...his gaze dropping to my feet, then he sighs, "I am... How are you?"
"I'm fine now. I don't know what happened earlier."
"Well..." He walks to a small table with a phone and intercom, "The wine will surely help you." I watch him use the intercom, telling Fitzgerald to send up the beverages. Maybe because of what's going on here, the maids need to stay together in their office. I'm pretty sure that's where the injured maid is.

He finishes the call and sits next to me in another armchair, rubbing his forehead, "Oh Ivy..."
I slightly raise my hand, wanting to pull his away from his face, but I let it fall back down to my lap. Why am I so afraid to touch him? The closeness just gives me a feeling I can't understand. What do I think he's going to do–Bite me? Get it together Ivy...

He looks at me, "As you heard, I will have to retrieve our drinks from the dumbwaiter in a few minutes." I nod gently. He blinks at me, then pats the right arm of his chair once, "You want to know who was behind you, yes?"
"Well, yeah...I do." I say. He scans my face like he's trying to read my thoughts.
"I'm not afraid." I say. Behind my poker-face though, I truly am becoming terrified. The suspense is murder.

"The one that was behind you was a man named Corneliu." My eyes light up.
He nods, "Ohh yes...Dmitri's brother."
"His brother? Why was he behind me?" I ask.
"You felt...uncomfortable in the hall...didn't you?"
"Yeah." What's he getting at?

"He was protecting you." He says.

"Protecting me… Why did you look at him like that? Like he's your enemy or something? Is he?"

He moves closer to me, "He is not my enemy. I looked at him like that because I want to protect you." I move back slightly out of instinct. Oh my…

"Protect me...from what exactly?" My question makes him halfway grin, then make an agitated sort of look, and he leans back while starting to stare ahead, "It is hard to explain, but I will tell you that it is something you should not concern yourself with."

"What if I get hurt?"

He quickly looks at me, "You would never be harmed. Never."

"…I was alone down there, and something-" I almost admit the weird warm feeling going up my back and the fact my name was being called–not by him, but by something else, I figure. There wouldn't be a way for that to be possible–he would've had to run from one end to the other that fast.

"Something…what?" He quietly asks, brows rising in interest. I become nervous. I put my hands together in my lap, "Well, just after you went into that office, I heard you call my name but I know it couldn't have been you…it was too quick. And you might not believe me when I tell you what else happened."

"I would believe you." He sternly says, staring icily at me. I have to look down.

"It's hard for me to explain but I will say that I felt a stream of warm air slide up my back, to the nape of my neck. Before that happened, I felt vulnerable. But it changed how I felt as soon as it touched my neck; all the fear I had went away. It's still mostly gone. That pain in my chest–you behaved as if you knew what caused that. Do you know?"

"Yes…"

I slowly look back up to him. He is very sure of everything now. He looks like he knows just what I mean. "You were touched." He says, calmly throwing a leg over the other and placing a hand on it.

"By whom?" I hesitantly ask.

"Her name is Jennifer."

"Oh my god... Is she...bad?"

He suddenly slams a fist down on the arm of his chair, "ASTA CURVA!" I instantly sit back, alarmed. He raises his right hand dismissively, "Excuse me...I just really don't like her." I can't blink at the moment; I'm watching him *very* closely.

"Why did you flip out like that?" I whisper.

We hear a sort of bell ring from the desk with the intercom and phone on it. He lifts a finger and stands, "One moment. That's our beverage call." He walks out of the room and returns after a minute with a fancy silver tray, two glasses and a bottle of wine. He goes over to a coffee table motioning me along the way with a simple tilt of the head. I *tentatively* rise and meet him there.

As he watches himself pour wine into my glass, he says, "I 'flipped out' because I am on-edge, Ivy. I didn't mean to." He finishes, hands the glass to me, giving a small smile, "You have my apologies. It was entirely wrong of me to do." Taking it from him, I search his face almost ominously. "It's alright... What did you say anyway?"

He pours his wine and tells me, "I said 'that bitch'." Wow, he HATES her!

He puts the bottle down and raises his glass, "She is. She causes a lot of problems."

"So she is bad." I say. He nods, "Yes...but she won't touch you. Never again." I carefully clank glasses with him.

As he takes his first sip, I ask, "What could she possibly do to hurt me besides touching me? She's merely a ghost." The door opens and slams shut, then sounds of nails scraping up the wood fills my ears. A heavy feeling has taken over the room. I immediately jump closer to Nick. He sets his drink down. Fearfully, I watch him mouth the word 'wait' and then he walks to the door and opens it. He just stands there while the loud scraping noise continues. It's starting to hurt my head! I have to put my wine down and cup my ears.

Suddenly, it all ceases. The heaviness has vanished too. I blink rapidly in complete surprise, slowly removing my hands. He turns to me with a face as blank as a sheet of paper. What in the world…? I'm so confused now! "What was all that? It scared the hell out of me!" I quickly say. "It was her, and someone else." he fixes his shirt cuffs as he goes back over to the table.
"Is she gone? Are they gone? Who was with her?"
"For now, yes. They went to a different place–A different part of the castle. Jennifer does this sometimes. Corneliu was trying to get past her to protect us. He's gone too." He sips from his glass, visibly stressed but holding it in well. I'm really having a hard time wrapping my head around all this.

"What is Jennifer's problem and how long has she been here?" I quietly ask. He takes a deep breath, "A long time. She is…envious." He looks at me. I become silent. Envious of what?– Me? Or life in general?

He looks up at the ceiling shaking his head, "She is not all that. She can't do much. She won't."
"Why do you say that?"
"She is afraid of me because I take control. That's what you have to do."
"But Nick, what just happened there in the doorway?"
"I stared her down…and made her very uncomfortable."
"You do that all the time…?" I question, somewhat hinting around about who or what she's envious of. Could it be him or someone else?

"I do it whenever it is needed."
"So that means not all the time, right?"

He brings his glass up and takes a slow sip of the dark wine. What does that look of his mean? It's like what I said irritates him. He won't stop looking at me in that intense way. Then, I'm not sure why…but Gina's words…'So, how was lunch with Vlad the Impaler? Mr. Vampire-man Dracula…' replay in my head. I run my fingers over my glass, then I look down at it, "Not all the time…well that's good. This wine–it's really tasty, thank you." I drink some.

"You're right…" he says, "It is not all the time. But as it happens now, I must protect you. You want to be here a while, don't you?"

"Yes, yes I do…" I definitely want to–No matter what is going on. Why–I don't know. I just really want to be around him and if anything like what just took place happens again, I don't care–I want to be here for him; to help him and give him all the care and kindness he deserves. How well could he 'protect' me though? How would he do it? To know that…I really need to stay.

"…Nicolai, while I'm here, you must know I have questions about these supernatural things."
"Hmm," he gets a small twitch of the lips; I'm not sure if it's a smile or not. "Well then…I could tell you some things." he licks one of his eyeteeth and then slowly takes a sip of his drink. Seeing him do this sends that familiar tingle up my spine. I swallow a bit hard, "But first though, what happened to the maid that got hurt?" His eyes close. Oh, I have just struck a sensitive nerve.

"I'm sorry. I'm just concerned." I say.
He puts his glass down, "No need to apologize Ivy." He looks at me, "It's Maria. She was collecting some dishes from my private kitchen and when she went to the elevator with the cart, she didn't realize the elevator had gone back down to the first floor and so…she fell to her death."
I cover my mouth, eyes enlarging in surprise, "Oh my god…I'm so sorry this happened! When did she fall?" He lets out a large breath and lightly shrugs his shoulders, "That, I don't know."
"Wow, that's shocking!" I say.
"Yes…the police will be here soon to recover her body and to ask questions. Walter will handle that. I am just…shaken." I let my hand down while watching him. Poor man. He needs all the comfort he can get! That was an employee of his; how will he deal with her family, I wonder? "In the meantime, please Ivy; let us talk about something else. There is some time." He says. "Yes, of course."

"You have questions, yes?" he asks. I nod slowly and begin, "Yes, well, I would like you to tell me about Corneliu…and more about your special gift." He waves his hand toward another set of chairs, "I will tell you about him before I go into detail about my…'*gift*'." The last word he doesn't like. Why in the world would it disgust him when he can possibly do so much with it? "Okay," I take my wine and go sit down there.

"Mr. Vladoiu's brother…" he quietly begins as he joins me with his drink, "A few years ago, he lived here. Life was great then; Dmitri seemed happier. One morning, Corneliu went to get up from a chair and it gave way. A shard of wood cut his arm badly. Dmitri was away, and I did what I could to help patch up his wound-" he stares at his wine, "there was so much blood." He won't take his eyes off it. I start to wonder if he's becoming depressed again.

He quickly looks at me, "I had…help patching it. Surprisingly, he began to heal at a very good pace. However, after a week or two, he became gravely ill; he had gotten an illness–An illness I didn't understand. I took him to the hospital for Dmitri. It was so bad that he fell into a long sleep–A coma. One early morning, Dmitri was called by the hospital. The doctor thought he would die because his heartbeat was so faint. When I could, I came to see him, and when I had arrived, he was awake and fully alert. He seemed alright. I asked him if he was better but he became enraged with me for some odd reason. He blamed his illness on me. I don't know where he got that energy." He trails off at the last few words. I listen intently to this story he's telling me but it's not exactly clicking in my head. What sort of sickness could have caused this slight coma?

"So, when it came time for him to be discharged, Dmitri called a relative that was here on vacation to come to the castle and take him with them back to Romania. Dmitri knew I could not be around Corneliu any longer; the anger he had was so strong."

"Wow… Then…why does Corneliu stay here if he lived somewhere else?"

"Well, it's because he's attached to this place. And he's family to Dmitri, you know."

"But why does he bother you? Is he still mad at you?" I ask.

"He is unhappy because he still thinks I'm responsible for his sickness–and his death. Yes." He says.

"How could that have happened?" He noticeably stills to my words. Soon, he brings his wine up to his mouth, "I have yet to know the answer to that question." I focus on the liquid swishing around in his glass. I really don't know why, but I am getting uncomfortable looking at it. I know though, it must be absolutely crazy to think that way. This is the real world. That's not blood. I'm taking Gina's words about 'Vlad Tepes' too seriously. I need to be alone for a minute. I'm overwhelmed by everything happening.

"Ivy, is there something on your mind?"

I quickly look back up to him, "Oh, well I–I've got to go for a minute, if you don't mind."

He raises an eyebrow, "Where are you going?"

"The bathroom. Would I be followed?" That's a good excuse; the bathroom. "No you wouldn't. I'm sure of that. Go ahead." He waves a hand, "Don't be long though, please... I'll miss you."

I smile and nod at him as I calmly walk out, shutting the door quietly behind me.

I slightly hit the back of my head against the door with a small exhale. I look down both ends of the lit hallway. There's not a soul in sight. I don't know if I should feel safe. There is hardly any fear in me though. Why is that? There's no time for this; I hurry away to find my room. I need to do some quick thinking.

Finding my way there, I slither inside once I see Walter coming around the corner at the end. I don't feel like talking to him right now. I hope he didn't see me!

I walk over to sit on the bed, put a hand on my face and think about the last few things Nick and I were discussing. I just couldn't stop staring at his wine. He treats time like it's nothing to him, sunlight bothers him, he can hypnotize people, he has…long eyeteeth... Oh no. No! I can't think this way! He can't be the kind of person that claims to be a vampire; he can't be the sort of person that has an obsession over vampires. He doesn't have time for that, does he? Well…that is a lifestyle…

I wonder if Maria is a ghost. Could she be talking to him right now? Or would she be in here with me? I could've asked where she is when I was in there with him. It wasn't on my mind at the moment though. Why was she so mean in life? That look she always had…

As for Nick and his 'vampiric traits', I think I should test him. How though…? I look out the window. The sky is clouding up. I need some time to make a plan. This will be no easy task. He's very clever. Hopefully by tonight, I'll have an idea–That is, if I won't be too distracted. Right now, I should be getting back to that room. I'm not certain how things will go when I see him again, but I hope it will all work out smoothly. That might be asking for too much.

With a slap on the knees, I stand up from the bed and make my way over to the door. I open it and suddenly gasp, clutching my chest, "Oh my god–Nick!" He's standing right there; eyes dark and on fire. His head tips to one side and he lightly grins, "I should have escorted you… I don't know what I was thinking. I apologize." he scans me up and down, "Are you alright?" My hand falls and I gulp, "Yes, I'm fine. I was about to go back to that room you were in." He walks toward me, closing the door with his foot, "I somehow knew you would open the door before me."
"How?"
"Prediction, perhaps?" He quietly says. As he gets closer, I keep trying to back up more.
I can't.

"Nick," I almost ask him to stop but I don't. He finally approaches me, "You are so cute." I stare up at him. He notices how shy I look, and it makes him laugh. "Look at you–You are so cute!" My head sinks low into my shoulders. He was sad minutes ago; what is this?

He grabs my shoulders, his smile now as if fascinated, "Ivy, I have something to say; I've noticed that you seem so nervous around me... Look, I want to tell you, you are breathtakingly beautiful in every sense of the word to me. I really find you amazing in all ways describable. You should not feel this way around me, nor should I intimidate you. I am just a person; same as you. You are the most unique flower amongst many within a meadow, and I want to be the one to pick you Ivy...can I do that?" My mouth falls agape. "Well I..." I'm at a loss for words now.

I'm on the spot and he has me locked in place. My body is tense and tingles are shooting up my spine. He looks back down at our hands. A slow smile spreads across his face, "...There is so much to learn." he sighs, "In such little time."

"...Then why don't we start talking now?"
He meets my eyes again, "Stay longer frumoasa mea. Please. I can take care of you; I can give you anything you would ever want."
"Nick, that's-" I don't know how to respond.
"I could give you the happiness you seek." He whispers. I close my eyes slowly, taking in a soft breath. He brushes a finger over my cheek. I turn my head and look down at the floor, "I don't know. I have to think about it."
"Yes, think about it..." He says while admiring my profile and neck.

He sighs, "I will have to–in a while–explain to you how I got my ability to hypnotize. I have some business to tend to. The police are here."
I nod perceptibly, "Of...of course."
He kisses my hand, "We must discuss that in private. Walter will let you know when and where to go. In the meantime, I hate to say this, but I must go. You should remain in your room."
"Would I be alright in there alone?" I ask in a small voice.
"You will not be alone, my dear." He walks over to the phone and calls for Christine. Angel tells him she will be up in a moment. He confirms that with her and then looks at me, letting his finger off the button, "You seem to like her better than the others. I would

very much like for us to be together, but we can't at this time. As for the spirits, consider yourself untouchable for a while…for a long while. Don't worry love, you will be fine." He bows his head at me and opens the door, allowing me to go first, then he follows me out.

We see Walter coming up the hall, and soon he approaches us with a questioning look.

"Yes Walter?" Nick says.

"Sir…ahem," He gives him the 'we have to discuss some things in private' expression.

"Of course," Nick looks back at me, "go ahead to your room." He smiles in a genuine way to assure things will be ok. That's one of the smiles I adore most. When he smiles in that wild way, it makes my heart race. I feel like melting on the spot. It gives me a feeling I've never felt before.

I bow my head some and gingerly start my way back to my room as he and Walter head off. Hopefully he's right, but that makes me wonder why I'm 'untouchable for a long while'. So many strange things are happening so quickly. My head is in a huge whirl!

*Frumoasa mea.

My beauty

-Nicolai-

I sit down at my desk as Walter shuts the office door. The phone is ringing. Quickly, I answer it, holding up a finger to excuse myself for a moment. "Yes…certainly…very good. Confirm with Ms. Vega my intentions are to have that product on the market by January 4th. Yes. That meeting will have to be postponed…it does not fit into my schedule… Thank you Mr. Wesson." I hang up and put my hands together on the desk. At least business is moving along nicely.

Walter straightens his posture, "Sir, the police want to see you. I told them everything I know. They have retrieved Maria's body from the elevator shaft and are almost ready to transport it to the mainland." In this moment, I have a flashback of what happened early this morning. After hypnotizing Maria, I stood in my bedroom doorway, watching her open the doors to the elevator and roll the cart inside. She didn't make a sound, nor did she make a face as she fell. Rozalia forced me to smile in a grizzly way through the whole event as the bangs, crunches, smacks, pops, slices and shatters echoed in the shaft. Only I could hear it. And simply after that, as I backed into my room, I quietly shut the door and went to take a shower. Rozalia was ecstatic. Because she was so thrilled, I chuckled to myself during my walk to the bathroom. She was too strong; her excitement overrode me.

Now, I put on a professional face.
"I will be down shortly to speak with them."
"Very well sir, of course."

I flick a hand at the door, "Oh, and also…make sure Christine has gone to Ivy's room and notify me when she gets there."
"It's 'Ivy's room' now, sir?"
"Yes... Do you have a problem with that?" I ask while taking my pager out of a drawer. He makes a slight smirk, "Not at all sir." I lift my chin at him in a bit of amusement as he leaves.

Chapter 28

I stare at my office door as it gently closes, listening to the single click and the sound of Walter letting go of the knob, then I shut my eyes. "HOW COULD YOU DO THIS TO ME?! HOW COULD I BE DEAD?! I WAS IN YOUR ROOM, UNDERNEATH YOU–YOU WERE PINNING ME DOWN AND THEN EVERYTHING WENT BLACK UNTIL I OPENED MY EYES AGAIN AND YOU WERE GONE!" Slowly, I look up through my lashes at her–Maria–as she yells at me, points at me and stomps her feet. I glance at the clock and see it stop moving, then I rise from my office chair, pressing my palms firmly down on my desk. She growls and starts marching toward me, but then she gasps, immediately stopping midway. Shocked, she backs away asking, "Who is that behind you? That woman?!" I begin to chuckle in Rozalia's twisted way. Her face freezes in disbelief as she sees our mouths moving at the same time. "You're both one entity! What are you?!" she gasps. I slide away from the desk, quickly moving toward her, "I am very much human." Rozalia illuminates my eyes, making them completely white, and she speaks through me, "No Maria–*I* am in control here." She whips my hand at her. Maria screams, covering her ears as she collapses to her knees. I place my hand on her head, and as a black mist engulfs her body, I say in my own words, "Welcome to the afterlife…where hell *truly*…exists." She lifts her chin up with a growing wail and disappears. The white glow in my eyes fades in the silence; I'm exhausted in the moment but apologize.

"I'm..." I let out a small almost-laborious breath, "I'm sorry...Maria."
I look at the now-moving clock and start to remember something. Something very bad.
"Black mist…she's not human. Rozalia, I warned you! She will be as powerful as-" She makes me scowl, "Jennifer." I jerk my head toward the door, emitting a deep ferocious growl. "We have to get

rid of her! Where the FUCK is Jennifer now?! WE MUST BLESS THIS CASTLE!"

"No no Dmitri–blessing this place will not give you any solace."

"There has to be a way. We can't let her or Maria near Ivy! Their energy is not human!"

"Stop your whining! Don't worry, I have control. There is time, and time is our best ally at the moment."

"I cannot wait until you reveal what you truly desire from this girl. You are putting everyone in serious danger, do you realize that?!"

"Let time answer your queries; we have the police to speak to."

"Don't you **dare** dictate to me!"

"I will whenever I wish."

I huff and go out my office door, putting the appropriate front on.

-Ivy-

It's been strange having a maid in here to keep me company. It's only been a few minutes, but still. Christine and I haven't said much about anything other than the weather, what it's like living here for her and some things about Maria. She likes it here. Anytime I bring up her opinions of Nick though, she gets a little standoffish. I understand it's to keep her job safe, but really? When she first arrived at my room, she asked me if I needed anything. I told her no, of course. What I really want is Nick. It can't be like that though.

The conversation about Maria is a very interesting one. It's because I just can't figure out why she despised me from the start. All I did was show up. Christine tells me that Maria has always been quiet, tried to be as antisocial as possible and hasn't slept well lately. She's also had a very large appetite. Either I caused the lack of sleep somehow or she just had something tragic happen to her outside of the castle and it affected her very badly. I had to mine this information out of Christine–sneakily and smoothly.

We suddenly hear Walter knocking on the door. Christine answers it and he talks to her for a second, then he asks me if I'm alright. "Yes, I'm fine. How is everything with Maria and all?" He puts his hands together at the front, nodding once, "All is as it should be Miss Summers. Please don't concern yourself. The police will leave soon; after that, Mr. Francis will have a late lunch and will be expecting you." he checks his watch, "Nearly 1pm, hm." I look at the curious Christine, then back to him, "Well yes, of course…I am hungry."

He smiles briefly at me, "I will return after they've gone." He gives Christine a sort of gesture, which she acknowledges with a single nod and he goes out. She stands up from a table in the right corner near the window and fixes the tablecloth. I lean my back up against the bathroom door, folding my arms, "Was that thing he did a goodbye or something?"
She looks at me, "Yes, in a way."

"How long have you worked here?" I ask.
"A year and a half. When I hit 2 years, I have to find somewhere else to work." 2 years? Only 2 years and then she 'has' to leave? That's pretty strange. I've never heard of that before.

"This must be a great job to have…" I mutter.
"It's very good, yes. 2 years is perfect for me."

"Is that for all the maids–to work here only 2 years?"
"Yes ma'am. Everyone else though, they have it differently."

"What do you mean? Could you explain that to me?" She becomes a bit hesitant. I zip my mouth at this point, now knowing I stepped over a line I wasn't supposed to cross.

"Maids have 2 years, Walter has 10 years, Leonardo and his sister have 5 years, and Eduard, the gardener, he has 5 also." She quietly says. I watch her without saying a word. It was unexpected of her to tell me anyway. But her explanation is interesting.

"Do you ever go on vacation or something?" I ask.
"Yes ma'am. At the end of the first year, we have our 2-week

vacations."

"Oh… Nice."

"Say," I clear my throat a little, "I'm not sure how you would take this, but I'm curious about something; while you're here, do you ever experience anything…supernatural?" She doesn't do anything but keep a straight face–Until finally, she looks down with a small amused 'hm', then she straightens her posture and smiles at me. "I don't believe in that stuff, but unexplainable things tend to happen sometimes during the night. Things fall off tables and doors shut on their own. I don't give it much thought though."

"Ah…"

That's nothing compared to what I've gone through. Why did so much happen to me when she's already been here for almost 2 years? Am I really some kind of magnet for these things? Is it true what Nick said about them being attracted to me? That could be it. I feel really victimized now. This is something I definitely need to emphasize to Nick. Hopefully, he could give me an idea of what is really going on. I should feel unsafe here but I really don't want to leave him or this place. He is more important to me than anything.

I decide to change the subject. "Where is everybody anyway? Gathered downstairs?"

She nods, "Yes ma'am. Every employee except me is down there. I have already talked to the police."

I sigh, "I'm sure this is a huge thing for everybody. I'm shocked by it all."

"Indeed." She sadly murmurs.

-Nicolai-

I arrive at the maids' office and see a uniformed officer standing outside the door. He sees me coming and opens it for me. As I enter the room, there is a plain clothes officer sitting at the maids' office desk looking at his notebook. He looks up, then stands to greet me with a handshake. "Hello sir, my name is Sergeant

Rollins; I'm with the Gales police department. You are
Mr. Francis?" I extend my hand into his and answer, "You are
correct." I squeeze his hand firmly and stare him down. He is
impressed with my grip; he grimaces from the pressure.
"Wow...that's quite a grip you have. A little warm though. Are you
feeling alright sir?" I smile and let go of him, "Yes, thank you for
asking." He takes his seat at the desk again, saying, "You don't
mind?" I sit down in the chair in front of the desk, "No, not at
all...please."
"I'm just finishing up here and wanted to talk to you last. Terrible
thing what happened to that girl." He watches me closely for my
reaction. I know this tactic and was expecting it. He just wants to
make sure this was an accident and not a murder.

I look at him in a matter-of-fact way, "Yes, it is very tragic, but
I must say...I really didn't know her. I am Mr. Vladoiu's executive
assistant and I travel a great deal. I stop here from time to time in
the course of my duties."
He turns his gaze down to his notes, "Walter, the butler, said you
were here when the accident happened–is that correct?"
I level my eyes at him, "Yes, that is correct." He looks at me and
leans forward a little, "Where were you exactly when the accident
happened?" I too lean forward in my chair, "I have no
idea...because I don't know when the accident occurred. I also
don't like your inference sir. Walter can answer all of your
questions better than I." The Sergeant is surprised by my forceful
response and takes a second to regroup his thoughts. "Yes, I have
spoken at length with him...and he has been very helpful." He
says. I stand quickly and extend my hand, "Well then, if you will
excuse me, Walter will see you out." The officer has no choice but
to respond in kind. He stands and takes my hand, saying, "Please
don't do any traveling until we call you with the results of our
investigation...couple of days, I'd say. We'll be in touch."
"Of course." I nod and leave the room.

Walter is standing outside the door when I come out. I motion
him past the other officer to follow me. We walk out of earshot and

I tell him, "Make sure they get everything they need. I don't want them to return."
He nods, "Yes sir."

-Ivy-

While in the middle of me talking about my job, Christine is paged to return to the first floor. She gives me a sort of apologetic expression and excuses herself.

"It's okay." I smile and watch her leave the room. I go look out the window and see Leonardo, Esmeralda and Eduard talking to each other. Leonardo looks up and sees me. He waves and smiles. I smile back and raise my hand on the glass. They finish talking and separate from my sight. It's now that I realize I haven't been messed with by any ghosts. Nick must have really known what he was talking about. Either that…or they mess with Christine. She said she doesn't believe in them. Why would they do anything to her if she doesn't think they exist? She would be boring to play with.

How much longer will I be in this room alone? After she went out, it felt empty in here, then it became warm and welcoming. It's really strange how that works. It makes me think somebody stepped in here. I'm not afraid though. I'm still fearless to a fair degree. There is one thing that unsettles me, however; I've not talked to anyone over the phone in a little while. I really should've asked Christine if there is a phone I can use. This room doesn't have one–just an in-house phone. It isn't exactly wise to use that right now. I don't know where everybody is. I guess I'll have to wait a little longer.

An idea pops into my head–An odd but possibly good idea. I look around the room. "Um…shit." I've gotta be out of my mind. "Hello? Is there anybody in here besides me?" Gosh this feels weird…

I suspiciously scan every corner. There is no response.

I sigh, "Come on, I know I can't be alone. This is a castle for Pete's sake!" A few more silent seconds go by. Nothing…absolutely nothing. Now I know I'm being targeted; I'm some kind of plaything for these ghosts.

Bang, bang, bang. "Miss Summers?" That knock and Walter's voice makes me jump. "Yes? I'm still here." I calmly reply. He opens the door quietly and peers in at me. "The officials have left. Lunch is being prepared. Are you alright?"
"Yes, I'm fine." I nod.

"Miss Summers…" he searches the room with his eyes, "Were you talking to someone?" Oh my god, he heard me. I close my slightly opened mouth and then try to behave as if that is the strangest thing he could've asked me. "No, no I wasn't." He stares at me for a moment, and I do the same back at him. Soon, he's convinced.

"Walter, is there a phone I can use? I need talk to my mom."
"Hm, well…considering the weather is fairly nice, I don't see why not. When would you like to make the call Miss Summers?"
I almost warily smirk at him, "Please just call me Ivy."
He only becomes more expectant of an answer. Fine...

I look away for a second, "Well, if everything is settled down, now would be perfect–If that's okay."
"Certainly miss. Right this way. You can use the phone in the grand room, near the foyer."
"Okay." I follow him out and go downstairs into the grand room.

The maids seem a little lost but are still working. They're all so deep in thought it's like they forgot I'm here.

He takes me to a small table near the foyer and gives me the go ahead wave of the hand. "Press those two digits to get out first," he reminds me, pointing to a small piece of paper taped to the phone, which looks ancient. I nod and he leaves me to it.

I wait longer than expected. It rings and rings, until finally…
"Hello?" Gina picks up. No, I chose her. I would have called mom but she knows nothing of Nick, or me coming here. At first, I

didn't want her to know. However, I've been second-guessing myself.

"Hey Gina, how are you?" Maybe she could help me with that; help me with telling my own mom.

"Wow, I thought you forgot about me! I'm fine, and you? How are things? And where are you? I didn't recognize this number."
"Things are actually okay. I'm at the castle-"
"What?! You're at that castle?!"
"Calm down, calm down! Sheesh!"

"Ivy, what in the world...? I thought you quit the Hospital. What the hell is going on with you?"
I take a deep swallow, "Well...I got fired from the hospital...and Nick invited me to the castle...so here I am."
"Oh wow... Tell me all about it! Please, I'm dying to know!"

I'm starting to think that maybe this phone call wasn't such a bright idea...
Well, now I have to explain. "I agreed to go on a date with Nick."

"Uh huh...?"
Hesitantly, I tell her, "Last night."

"It's dinner time... You stayed overnight and all day?" She sounds excited and astounded at the same time.
"Yes. I might stay longer too. I'm not sure. He wants me to stay."

"Girl, is this a good idea?"
"It feels right Gina." Gosh, it's as if she's like my second mother!
"Well, the guy's rich... What's your family think of this?" she asks.
"They don't know yet. At first, I didn't want them to know, but now that Nick and I are forming a sort of relationship, I'm beginning to think more about telling them. The thing is though, they're worrywarts. They're kinda on the pessimistic side, if you know what I mean."

"Oh... So what are you going to do Ivy?"
"I'm not sure."

"I could help if you need me to. I wouldn't mind." **Yes, that's**

just what I need!

"Okay. Yeah, I would like that."

"Alright—what would you like me to do for you?"

"I'll give you my mom's number and you tell her that I dropped my phone and it broke, so I'll have to get another one. But I won't be doing that until next week. If she says anything about giving me any money, decline that. I will see her when I see her. We're not close by each other anyway."

"You sure this will work?"

"Yeah I am. She lives 40 miles away from me."

"Oh geez!"

"Yep…quite a distance."

"I can see why they worry a bit." She laughs a little.

"Well, you know. I'll give you the number now."

"Sure, go on."

I tell it to her and she writes down the information on the money and phone situation. We go over the plan with each other and confirm it.

She says, "Alright, well I gotta go now. I have to cook lunch for my brother and his girlfriend. They're getting along again—go figure. They have a weird relationship."

Pff, yeah no kidding! I grin at that, "Good luck."

"No Ivy, I wish *you* good luck."

"Very well… Goodnight Gina, and thank you."

"You're welcome."

She and I hang up and then I turn around to see Walter standing at the now-low-burning fireplace with his hands behind his back. He looks at me and bows his head as if asking if I'm done. I nod back, walking his way now.

"Everything alright Miss Summers?" he asks.

"Yeah, everything's fine. My mom didn't answer her phone, so I asked a friend to tell her something."

"Is your mother alright?" he has a slightly concerned face.

"She's fine... just some personal business that needed taken care of." I say, though I know that's something I should keep to myself.

"Ah, I see. So are you ready for me to escort you to lunch? Mr. Francis should be along shortly."

"Oh! Well yes, of course."

"Very good." He waves toward the staircase, "Lunch will be served upstairs in the small dining room."

"What? I don't understand."

"He is in his office on a business call."

"Oh…my apologies."

"It's quite alright madam."

We casually climb the stairs to the second floor, and once we're in the small dining room, he pulls a chair out for me and tells me that he will return shortly with Fitzgerald. I sit down and pull myself up to the table. "You have no idea when Nick will be done?" He puts his hands together, "Miss Summers, he is very busy at the moment. I cannot disturb him." He starts backing away to the door, "I will return momentarily." He goes out, carefully shutting it behind him. Ok then...

I let out a tired sigh and drop my chin into my hands. Nick is right; so much to learn, such little time. About the hypnotism…I hope he won't do that to me. He doesn't seem to be that kind of guy though. Well, just in case, I'll somehow make it impossible for him. I've got a plan. As for seeing if he's obsessed with Vampirism, I've got a plan for that too. He won't be charming me; I'll charm him! Tonight, when we see each other, I will try my best to be myself as I play along. Hopefully, it will start out with my question about his 'hypnotizing', and we'll go on from there. My satisfied eyes narrow as an evil smile slowly forms on my face.

Just then, the door opens. I quickly look at it. I didn't expect that. There's Walter and Fitzgerald. I smell steak. My mouth is beginning to water...

The chef walks up, greeting me with a bow of the head and a "Miss Summers," I smile quickly as he sets the plate and my tea down. "Kansas strip steak for the lady, with mashed potatoes, corn on the cob and a fresh steamed mixture of vegetables." he pauses, "Is tea alright? You didn't ask for it, but…" he looks at Walter. I nod at him, "I haven't asked for half of the stuff you've given me." I chuckle a little, which makes him do the same back.

He finishes setting everything down and then he rests his hands behind his back. Walter clears his throat, "Miss Summers, Mr. Francis has paged me and gives you permission to go ahead and eat. In about 20-30 minutes, I will escort you to him; in the poker room." Poker room! Why didn't he show me that place before?

He notices how amazed I look and laughs quietly, "Yes yes–We have a poker room." I slowly take my glass and sip from it, "That's interesting." I wonder if there's a pool table in there. That's pretty much the only thing I like to do in places like that.

"I will return soon Miss Summers. Enjoy your lunch." He smiles at me again and goes out, Fitzgerald also giving me a last smile while trailing behind him. A ghost of a grin appears on my face, now drinking some more of my tea, "Poker room huh? I don't think that should surprise me but…it's pretty cool, I have to admit." Mr. Vladoiu really, really does know how to live. I wonder what other great places he has here that I haven't seen? I look around the room, the grin never faltering.

I take my fork and knife and begin wolfing my delicious food down, but I start to hear a rattling noise. I look up and around, then back down to my plate. "What the-?" My spoon's shaking. Momentarily, I put my hand down on it. It keeps moving. I quickly look around again. There's a loud BANG in the middle of the table. I jump in the chair, then leap out of it away from the table. Trembling, I whirl my head around to look at the door, "WALTER!!!" I hear thumping noises outside like someone is walking quickly up the hall. The door opens, I almost scream, but then I see that it's Walter. "What's wrong?" He asks. I point at the table. He looks at it. Before we can say or do anything else, we both hear someone stomp their way up the hall and abruptly stop in the doorway. Walter and I shift our eyes over to it. There's Nick; standing tall, eyes on fire and his lips are pressed in a thin line;

he's extremely pissed off. It's scary!

I watch how only his eyes move around the room. Walter takes my arm, "Come Miss Ivy–Hurry." He must know something bad is bound to happen. I allow him, but I can't stop watching Nick. By the time we get the door, I see Nick say, "You and I are going to have a talk Jennifer." Holy shit!

Walter pushes me out into the hall as my mouth falls open in shock. It's her! I was alone in here with HER!

He shuts the door and looks at me in the 'please stay calm' way. I wave my hand out toward the place we came from, "Excuse me but, could you tell me what the hell just happened?" He shakes his hands, "Now now, Miss Ivy-"
"Shit was seriously moving Walter! You have some serious ghost problems! I know I shouldn't talk to you about it but DAMN!"
"You must understand." He sighs heavily, "And please–no foul language." The door opens, getting our attention. Out comes Nick, flicking out his shirt-cuffs and cracking his neck as he walks. "Walter, I will explain this to her..." he looks at the perplexed me, "in the poker room." his eyes slide back over to him. Walter doesn't say anything at first, but after a moment of silence, he nods quickly, "Yes sir, of course. Shall I escor-" "No. *I* will take her." Oh man...

Nick walks up to me. I move away from him. This unsettles Walter I see–and it frustrates Nick. "*Ivy...*" Nick exasperatedly says. I look from him to Walter repeatedly. "You should." Walter mouths with a nod. I lower my head and slightly glance back over at Nick. Fine...I'll let him take me along.

I grab his arm and look at Walter again. Nick tells him, "We are not to be disturbed." I don't know how to feel about that. Walter bows, "Of course." With a last nod, Nick takes me down the hall.

On our way to the poker room, he's quiet. The atmosphere feels very tense. I keep getting the urge to ask more about his ghost issues, but I hold it in. We pass a few more doors, then we stop at one. It's an average-looking door. He turns to me before opening it, "With me by your side, you are safest." He sounds completely certain of himself. "What about Jennifer?" I ask in a small voice. He takes my hands, "Ivy, she would not get past me." I stare at him. He opens the door and pulls me along inside with him, then he turns back around and shuts it. I clutch my arms while looking around the room. It's sort of small; has a couple old-fashioned poker tables in two corners, a pool table in the middle and there are only three Gothic-styled windows.

I face him again, speechless, waiting for something else to happen. He walks up to the end of the pool table that faces the door and takes a cue stick–just to hold, I guess. With a breath leaving him, his eyes flash back up from the table at me, "You are very pale Ivy; pale as a sheet of paper."
I slowly nod, "I…was scared." I hate to admit that.

"I'm sorry… You still are it seems. Oh Ivy, there are many occupants here; live and dead. The live ones come," he looks at the tip of the stick, "and they go. The dead ones are merely guests…who won't leave." He returns his attention to me. I blink expressionlessly. I sense there's something off about what he's telling me. "How many guests?" After a minute, his eyes move around the room like he's thinking about it, then he says, "…Many." he looks back to the cue stick. How is that possible?

"Well what about Dmitri? What does he think of this ghost problem you guys have here? Does he ever experience these things? Is his father here?" He stops rubbing the top of the stick

and looks at me. He's motionless now. My stomach is beginning to turn, watching his grim face. What's going on in his mind right now?

He blinks, softly smiling now, "He has. But he is carefree of these 'ghosts' as you call them. And yes, his father is here."
"Nick…aren't they ghosts?" I ask.
"They are souls. They are *spirits*. When you call them ghosts, that is like belittling the dead."

"I'm…sorry."

"It's okay. You didn't know."

I point down at the floor while looking at him, "You say Mr. Vladoiu, the original owner of this place…is here. Where? In this room?"

He nods slowly, "He is."

"Is he angry like Jennifer and Dmitri's brother?"

"Oh…" he simpers and shakes his head, "No, not at all."

"Have you talked with him?"

"I don't much." he puts the stick down, "In fact…" he looks at me while moving away from the table. I start stepping backward. He says, "I can't remember the last time I spoke with him…but I do know he is in here with us." He saunters toward me and gets so close to me that when my back hits the wall, he stops before touching my nose. My breathing is a little uneasy and my heart is beginning to race. I gulp again, staring into his eyes.

He moves a little bit of my hair away from my neck, making me faintly shudder to his overly-warm touch. He grins at my reaction. I focus on his lips, then look back up again, "Does he want anything from me like the others do?"

"…Just more time being around you."

"What?" I whisper. He leans in and presses his lips to my neck. His hot breath brushes over my skin, making me shiver again. He starts nipping at it. I slowly let the back of my head hit the wall behind me. "How lovely," he purrs. I feel his eyeteeth graze over my skin a little more forcibly. I grab his shirt a bit tightly and a small sound escapes me. He steps closer, putting a hand on my waist as the other slides up a little higher. I pull him up against me, receiving a soft deep-toned growl from him. He kisses and trails his tongue up to my jaw-line. Without thinking about it, I turn my head, allowing him. My eyes lazily open and I suddenly gasp, "Nick!" His eyes suddenly grow, then he whirls around to look at what I'm seeing. As soon as he does, he quickly waves his arms out in front of me, "*Corneliu*!" I don't see Corneliu; I see a monstrous thing! It's a tall all-black worm-like figure! Something else gets my attention–something moving around on the ceiling. My head snaps up, seeing little tadpole-like things slithering away from the top of the door ahead of Nick and I. My whole body jumps and my breathing is getting coarser. "Nick? NICK?!" I panic. He watches it, growling in a low inhuman growl, behaving as if he is a big vicious wolf. What the hell is happening?!

The tadpole entities drip from the ceiling, creating little female screams with each drop. I cup my ears as tears begin to fill my eyes. The black worm figure is just standing there, its form zigzagging as if you'd see on a radar screen when it's out-of-phase. Nicolai's furious face starts to become more of an amused one. First, he snickers in a low tone, then it grows louder and louder, turning into an insane cackle.

He takes in a huge breath to regain his composure and then he chuckles, "WELL *then*!" he waves a hand up to the darkness on the ceiling like presenting it, "You have made a extraordinary entrance Jennifer and Corneliu." he then tilts his head at the tall entity, the entertained eyes draining to severe hatred, "Ivy este a mea! Nu o sa te ascult pe tine, prostule! How many more times must I argue with you over this?" The black thing emits a low snarling noise and the tadpole-things he called 'Jennifer' immediately converge at the door and slither across the floor, all joining together as one body and then quickly stop at the somewhat indifferent Nick. My eyes instantly widen. I watch her jolt up from the floor, suddenly forming her face in the blackness and abruptly lunge forward, screaming in his face. He wrinkles his nose, his eyes glow completely white, and he swings his fist around and bashes through the side of her head. She wails in disgust as her face and then body immediately turn to an evaporating mist, exploding out everywhere. As soon as she's gone, he turns his head to look at Corneliu. Corneliu slowly fades away. He jerks his shoulders back, "Hm!" He turns around to look at me, eyes as normal as I last saw them.

I blink at him, perplexed. A whimper slips out of me as I bring my hand up to my bottom lip. I shake my head after a time of indecision on whether I should run out of the room or stay. I want to leave but I keep reminding myself that he just protected me from them! All of this is so overwhelming. My subconscious overrules me; it pushes me to latch onto him and push my nose into his shoulder. He's amazed at first but he doesn't hesitate to wrap his arms around me.

"You were not supposed to see that."

"You have to deal with this? This is what you go through?" I cry. He runs a hand over my hair, "No Ivy, not always." I look at him, "Is it me being here?" He doesn't answer.
"Nick, is it me-" "They can't hurt anyone Ivy. They can't." he shakes his head.

"Can't they be taken care of somehow? They were not supposed to come back for a long time, remember?" I sniffle. He searches my face in thought, holds my chin in place with a finger underneath it, then he sighs and grabs my shoulders, "I am trying to find out."
"But Nick, there are many *ways* to solve this problem! How can you not be sure of this?"
He wipes a tear away from my cheek, seeming upset that I'm crying. I see his brows come together in a troubled way. Is he sad or confused? Or is he sad because he doesn't know what to do?

"Why can't you have someone come out here to rid this castle of them?" This question I ask makes him turn his head and close his eyes. Grief?

I gently take his face into my hands, "Nicolai..." He stares silently at me, visibly easing up but he also looks like he's getting slightly uncomfortable. "You need to take care of this problem somehow. What does Dmitri think?-The first one?" Again, he slowly searches my face as he takes my hands. His gaze drops to my lips. He looks like he's holding something back. That mysteriousness in his eyes has yet again made me forget everything around us. There is so much suspense. What is he hiding? What is Dmitri telling him if he's truly in the same room as us? He won't say anything; he just continues to study my features in a growing sort of adoration. I just don't know what he could be thinking in this moment. He isn't as worried as he should be. He is so brave and strong. "Ivy…" he forms a small smile, "you are just so beautiful." He's hardly audible, and there is much meaning laced within his voice. What is happening…? He truly isn't worried about anything. How could he be like this? I try to talk a few times but there is nothing I can say or do right now.

He places his hands on my shoulders and gently squeezes them. I watch his eyes as they begin to brighten in color. They're like blue sapphire diamonds…sparkling ones… Is my mind playing tricks on me? I've never seen this before. "Don't worry…Ivy." He whispers while I blink at him once and slowly. My heartbeat is starting to calm down and now it really feels like it's just him and I. To me, the world has vanished. Everything is secure; anything evil has been replaced by the warmth between us.

"Da, draga mea…don't worry at all…time is our best ally." He smiles genuinely. I have lost my breath.

"I have not eaten yet…" he sighs. I still can't say anything. Gosh…he is the most beautiful thing I have ever seen!

He picks up a house-phone and calls Walter. "Two for lunch in the small dining room. Whatever she was eating is fine." He hangs up and smiles. My behavior makes his smile form into a smirk and then he touches my belly, making it jump. "And you…are still hungry." I'm surprised toward his actions. He chuckles at me, "You are anxious, love." The light blue glow in his eyes is fading. I'm beginning to fall out of my strange preoccupation. I don't even think twice about where he put his hand, nor do I have any fear left in me. I'm not worried about the ghosts; he has everything under control.

I gulp before letting out a sound, then I calmly agree, "Yes, yes I am." He again smiles and offers an arm, "Let's go eat then, shall we? We will dine in the small dining room to spare the walk." "Okay…yeah, sure."

He takes me out of here, and away to the room we go.

Chapter 29

Entering the dining room now, Nick leads me to my chair and pulls it out for me. I carefully sit down, then watch him take his seat in the larger chair at the end of the table. I didn't see that coming. Walter is standing back by the door with his hands together at the front of him. He called the kitchen before we got here and now Fitzgerald is about to send our meals up. Nick tells him he's not needed at the moment, so he bows his head and leaves us alone. The magnetic pull between Nick and I is beginning to overwhelm me again. But there is also something I don't feel right about. I just wish I knew why and what it is. Evidently, Nick notices my behavior; he looks expectant of an explanation.

I shut my eyes, thinking over what to say first.
"I know what I saw earlier, and I'm not afraid." My tone is just above a whisper. My words might make him think I'm crazy. Not exactly keen on the idea, I reopen my eyes to see his reaction. He has no expression; strictly emotionless. When he does that, it's so unnerving for me, yet at the same time I'm getting used to it.

He leans forward in his chair, placing his hands over each other. I watch him intently.
"What do you feel exactly...?-Miss Summers." he asks.

What do I feel 'exactly'? That's just the thing! I don't know! It's like this infatuation I have overpowers anything else I feel. When it comes to fear of the 'spirits' here, I'm numb. But when it's just him and I together and we're focused on one another, nothing else exists–nothing at all. And he's all I want. All I would ever want. I'm sure of that.

He sees that I am having a hard time answering his question and he sits back again with his finger over his lips, completely focused on me. That stare...

I rest my forehead in one hand, "I just don't understand why, after all these years, I have no fear of the supernatural anymore. At least, it's not as much as it's always been for me."

"Ah... Well consider me mad, but Ivy, the truth is...you are never alone. You are protected by many here, believe it or not."

"...How many are here?" I ask, a little unsettled.
"Native Americans, people from the turn of the last century and some of Dmitri's family and friends. Some of my loved ones visit me but that is...rare." He says. I'm amazed. I'm on an ancient piece of land...

"When we went horseback riding earlier, along the trail, the Native Americans were watching us. I could not show that I knew they were there. Only you know I have this ability." He tells me.

"Really...? You haven't told Walter anything? You've known him for a while." I'm stunned more and more. He lightly shakes his head, "I am not really an open book. Not even to him–and we are good friends. But our relationship is mostly a professional one."
"Wow," I murmur.
"You are more special to me than you realize." He laughs quietly.
"Well I..." I chuckle back, "I'm flattered." He winks at me.

I sit silently for a moment, then say, "Nick, this about the spirits brings me to a question; if so many are 'protecting' me, how powerful is Jennifer?"
"Not powerful enough to overrule the others."
"And you have control over her." I surely say, though at the same time it is a question.
He folds his arms, nodding, "Yes I do." His answer leaves me in immense wonder and a sort of awe. "How?"
"It is part of who I am." He smiles, then waves a hand out, "Hard to explain."
"Would you ever be able to explain it to me?" I ask. He sits back and lets his hand fall into his lap while only staring at me. By the way he's looking at me, I'm thinking the answer is either 'I don't know' or simply–'no'. Suddenly, there's a knock on the door. He

blinks a couple times, looks down, then glances over at the door, "Yes, come in." I don't take my attention off him.

Pamela wheels a cart in with our meals and a big pitcher of tea. She places everything neatly on the table and starts to pour Nick's drink but he stops her. She is taken aback by that. He says, narrowing his eyes with an odd smile, "No, I will take care of it. Thank you Pamela." She backs up slowly and looks at me. I do nothing but watch her with a faint 'well, that was intense' face. She then excuses herself and wheels the cart back out of the room. Nick and I look at each other again and he dips his head, smiling as if satisfied. I return it with my own light one.

He opens his hand to my glass, "May I?"
I nod softly, "Sure, thank you."
"It is my pleasure." He stands and starts waltzing around the table to me. The closer he gets, the more my body tenses up. He stops by my side and begins pouring my drink–slowly.

As I stare at how carefully the tea flows into the glass, I mumble, "You're spoiling me." Something is going through my mind besides that; Gina's words about Dracula, and my 'plan' to see if he lives the vampiric lifestyle is cycling over and over in my head.

"Is that a problem?" he asks. I look up at him. He pauses, reading my eyes.
"No..." I utter, watching his fanged smile. He sets the pitcher down without taking his sight off me. I gulp.

"What is on your mind Miss Summers?" He's entertained by my nervousness. I take his hand–his very **warm** hand. "Please sit by me." He looks at it, then sits next to me.
"What is on your mind?" he repeats, quieter this time and more curious. I know what I want to say but the words just won't come out. I'm so jittery. Again.

"Why are you always so warm?" I ask.
"I don't know."

"It's part of who you are..."

"Yes."

Now I have run out of things to say. He obviously won't give me more of an explanation. Why–why is he so warm and pale? Why are his teeth that way and why is he psychic? Why does he talk about time like it's nothing? I have to find out! But how will I do it?

"Ivy…"
I stop staring at the pitcher and look at him. He takes my hand and kisses it. My lips part.
"What is really on your mind?" he asks.

"I want to…kiss you." Oh god, did I just say that? Me–kissing him? A man with so much authority? The very one that I constantly feel nervous being around, the one who does weird things like dress in clothes from a different era and has unnatural abilities–I want to kiss him.

He snickers until he chuckles in his deep-toned way. This is what I figured would happen. My cheeks are reddening by the second.

"You are so cute." He smiles wide at me. I can't believe I'm still looking at him and not hiding my face. "How about…I kiss you?" he asks. My eyes widen.
"No?" he shakes his head, still amused.
"Um…" I can't answer properly. He offers a hand, "Stand, Ivy." I look at it, then up to him…and carefully take it. Why am I behaving like this? I'm not a kid. It's a kiss–just a kiss, right? No, no it's not.

Once I stand, he places one hand on my lower back, pulling me close while the other holds the small of it. I don't understand why he's holding me like this. "What are we doing?"
"Your anxiousness is getting the best of you Ivy." he says, "I want you to be comfortable." He sidesteps, winking at me, "And so, we will dance! Forget about the food; we can eat anytime." He twirls me around as I blink blankly at his actions and words, then he pulls me up flush against him, taking the breath out of me. I look at his

lips. He smiles darkly. I blush.

"Off we go," He laughs and we start to glide around the room; his quick and skilled movements are so graceful it's like we are skating on ice. It's so magical. Moving around the furniture is nothing to him. I'm nervous at first but I begin to really trust him. I even giggle a few times as we move.

He slows once we're to the windows and twirls me around one more time, then I comfortably stop with my hands resting on his shoulders. Our faces are so close now, and his eyes…his captivating diamond-like eyes… I watch them lower to my neck as he says, "It is great fun dancing with you Ivy," I swallow carefully while admiring his glowing gaze.

"You dance…like an angel." I say.

"Years of experience…" he whispers.

Rozalia says, *"So soft and fragile… Oh, the ache to sink your teeth into it and drink in her warm blood…you could feel it now; how it would gloss over and soothe your gums, filling you with that sweet body-tingling burst of energy when it flows down your throat. I bet it truly is rich. Bite her…**Dmitri**."* His eyes brighten and flash at the last word. The sight of it causes me to widen my own and my mouth to fall slightly open in more awe.

"Ivy…frumoasa mea," He tilts his head as he brushes his lips over my neck. I breathe in, lightly squeezing his shoulders. Rozalia purrs, *"We will take our time…with her."* A low growl emits from deep within his throat while he tightens his grip on me. The sharp ends of his eyeteeth run over my skin. I shiver. He starts walking me backwards until he pushes me against a wall and pins my hands above my head. My heart leaps. His kisses trail up to my jaw, and he pauses and gazes into my eyes. I again look at his lips, breathing quicker. He smiles in a wicked way and then claims my mouth. In the moment his warm lips touch mine, a more powerful bolt of electricity shoots throughout my body. Is this lust?

I bite his bottom lip and he makes another small growl noise. He does the same back to me, though his bite is more forceful than mine. I'm not even worried if he bites too hard. My hands escape his grip and take fistfuls of his hair. He clutches my waist and hips as he returns to my neck, then I feel him pinch my skin with his teeth. I take in a quick sharp breath. He removes his lips from my neck with a hiss and suddenly stops. I quickly place a hand over the spot he pinched and stare at him, panting. He bites his bottom lip while looking at me, and gulps.

Rozalia snarls in his mind, *"HOW DARE YOU RESIST ME!"*

I am without words; breathless and amazed at how...erotic...that was. He halfway smirks and starts to laugh in a devilish way. He won't stop. I lean my head back against the wall with a sigh to regain my composure.

"Excuse me, I could not help myself..." he snickers. I look at him, wondering what else could have happened.

"Please, take your seat–I will have this food warmed up." I interject, "Actually, I..."

"You are not hungry anymore?" he amusedly asks. I shake my head in response. "Me neither." he says. His eyes give me the impression he's not telling the truth. My cheeks flush. He looks over at a clock on a small table in the corner of the room, "Hm...1:55..." Just then, someone knocks on the door. He turns to it, "Yes Walter, come in." How did he know that? I look over and see Walter coming in.

"Sir, Miss Summers.." he bows his head at us. I manage a faint smile and glance out the corner of my eye at Nick who's smiling cheekily at him. Why the snobbish face–I couldn't know.

"Walter." he nods once at the straight-faced butler that soon approaches his side and whispers something close to his ear. I'm able to pick out...a man named 'Gerald' that will be attending an upcoming event. I'm surprised Nick didn't excuse himself from the room to speak any sort of business with him.

"Hmm..." Nick rubs his chin with an index finger as Walter steps back, folding his hands behind his back. Slowly, he forms a fake kind of smile at him, "Very well." He nods at him. Walter bows again and gives me a nod on the way out of the room.

I look at Nick as he walks up and grabs my hand, saying, "Ivy...ești a mea..." What did he say to me? I put my hand on my chest as his eyes watch my every facial movement like a hungry animal. He's making me feel like a lamb in a cage with a lion. He chuckles, "I said I have a surprise for you."

"Oh," I mouth. He winks at me, "You will love it; I am sure."

When he's sure of himself, he's usually right...

*Ivy...ești a mea...

Ivy...you are mine...

Chapter 30

Nick takes me up some spiral stairs to the third floor where I see everything is darker and the air feels even denser than before. It's the sort of feeling you get when you go somewhere and feel as if something very tragic took place there. I don't move once we've made it up to the top of the stairs. Not far from here, I think I see an elevator with yellow tape crisscrossed over it.

"The elevator is broken, isn't it?"
"Yes, I believe it is." he says. We look at each other.

"Which floor did Maria fall from?" I ask.
"This one." he answers. I look ahead again at the long hallway with those old-fashioned lights on either side. Now the memory of that dream I had of those hands grabbing me and my dream man saving me flashes in my mind. It looks so very familiar.

"Ivy, are you alright?" he asks.
"I'm...fine." I briefly smile at him. He makes that expectant look.

I sigh, "I'm okay. Really, I am."
He waves a finger at me, "No lying Ivy. I don't appreciate that." I don't know how to reply.
He offers his arm, "You are safe with me at your side–remember that." I take it while studying his face.

We start walking. More and more, the feeling overwhelms me. I'm tolerating it very well; he does make me feel secure. It's like he is my protection bubble made of light and everything around is darkness that cannot penetrate his shield. How long will this last? For however long I stay here, will I need him with me at all times?

"What is up here?" I finally ask as we pass the elevator with police tape on it. I don't know if I can imagine how Maria died. It's frightening enough seeing the tape.
"Shh, it's restricted. Dmitri's quarters." I quickly look at him.

"What isn't known will not kill, Ivy." He says.
"You...daredevil." I say, unbelievably.

"As always." He artfully remarks.

"…Are we surrounded by spirits right now? How about Maria?"
"Yes, but they are only watching. Maria is not…here right now."
My god, that's unnerving!

We stop at a door and he puts a finger to his lips with a sly smile. He turns the knob and pushes the door open. I peer in and look around. It's a barely used office. The furniture is the same as everywhere else overall; Romanian designed–and old too.
"Ladies first," he waves inside. I give him a last look before proceeding into the room.

When I stop in the middle of it, I hear him shut the door and say, "This office was once a personal poker room. Dmitri wanted this floor to be less used, because back in the day, he loved having guests over and it seemed to him that all the best things to enjoy were where no one could see them. So, all the fun rooms were set on the second floor." I turn to him as he folds his arms. For a moment, I stare at how he's dressed; how neat he is with those black aristocratic clothes and that fancy blood red cravat. I really can't get over the whole Victorian obsession he has. I wish I didn't stand out like a sore thumb whenever we walk together. Or do I stand out at all? That is all beside the point right now.

I lightly cough, "And when was that done?" He looks me up and down; clearly he knows what I was thinking. "It was done in the early 50's." he tells me.
"Wow, long time ago." I say.

"Well," he unfolds his arms, walking over to a closet door on the right, "yes, I suppose. Here, the surprise is in here." I lift a brow and follow him to it. He opens the creaky door and then pulls the light switch. I look in the walk-in closet. Instantly, I'm thrown off by what I see. I can't speak. There are many Victorian dresses hung on the racks and they're all beautiful. That's not what matters though; what matters is the fact he has them! No, he said a relative collects these things–I must remember that. Oh, it's so strange and coincidental though!

He cuts into my concentration by softly clearing his throat and saying, "Welcome to a closet of history." he laughs. "Here…" He excuses himself as he walks past me, into the closet. I watch him put his hand between the dresses and take out a small black box, quickly stow it away in a pocket, then retrieve a dark blue dress. He looks at it, then at me. I form a faint grin.
"What is that look for?" he asks. I won't tell him the truth. He would think it's preposterous. Maybe it is—but I know what I have dreamt about. My answer is simple; "So much beauty is kept here. That's what." I also wonder what that box has in it…

"Would you like to wear it?" he asks. God…wouldn't I… Yes, but it would be so odd.
"Wear it Ivy; we would be a fine match if you did." He playfully urges. I giggle at him. He shakes it a little, giving me a trying look.

"Ok, I will. But would it fit me?" That—makes him look at it and then size me up with it. He examines me longer than I imagined he would. "Yes. It would fit you perfectly…Miss Summers." Oh my goodness…

"Come, come with me." He walks out of the closet with the dress. "Wait, where are we going?" I hesitantly ask. He pauses before getting to the door, turning his head slightly enough for me to see his profile. "We are going to your room…where else?" "Um… Right." I uneasily reply with a blush. He smiles impishly, "Follow me Ivy."

I quietly go with him out of this office, into the extremely uncomfortable hall. The lights seem dimmer, and the end is the darkest. How much freakier can this hallway get? I search around us as we're walking. There has to be someone next to me or behind me, I swear. I grab Nick's free arm and gently squeeze it while scanning the hall.

"Do not fret, draga mea." He says. Suddenly, the door at the very end of the hall slams shut. I immediately jump and look while Nick slowly turns his head down and directs his annoyed eyes in that direction. I begin backing up for the stairs. He shoots his hand out, stopping me. I gasp. He stares me down, then looks at the end of the hall again, "That door never opened."

"It didn't?" I stutter. The door opens and slams shut. He gives me the dress, pulls me around behind him and forces me to hug him. I bury my face in his back and start to hear a woman not too far from us, breathing laboriously. All of the hair on the back of my neck stands straight up and I feel as if I had lost all my color.

"Nick- Nick, can we please leave this floor? Can we? I want to leave! Why are we staying?" He won't answer. What is he doing?!

He tightens his grip on me, "You don't trust me…?"

"I do, but I'm terrified!" I snap, "Stop them! They're coming!" His eyes narrow and he quietly growls, "Don't move." He steps away from me. I reach for him, "No, please don't leave me!"

"Everything is under control Ivy." He starts stomping toward the end; his pace is getting quicker and quicker with each step as he rolls his sleeves up. What is he going to do? I watch him soon meet the door, fling it open and march into the room where a female scream escapes. He doesn't even turn the light on before whamming it shut.

-Nicolai-

I stand at the door of this curtained sun-room, glaring ahead at Jennifer. Chairs are levitating a couple inches off the floor around her and the curtains are twitching.

"I want her gone!" She barks, "You can't have her!" she throws a book off a shelf at me. I dodge it and hiss back at her, eyes glowing white. She steps back once seeing that but it doesn't stop her. Rozalia shouts in her own voice, ***"ENOUGH!"*** Jennifer grabs both sides of her head, letting out a scream as she drops to her knees. The furniture slams to the floor. I slowly walk up to her and kneel. She pants and looks into my eyes hatefully. Rozalia says, *"You persist…even when you know I can make your whole existence a pit of misery. I'll burn you Jennifer."* I'm forced to get nose to nose with her as Rozalia whispers, *"I will bring upon you the worst entities you could ever imagine."*

"N- No! I have power of my own!" Jennifer snaps, "Maria is all I need!" Rozalia puts my hand through her neck, making my eyes flash, "Pathetic creature…" Jennifer gasps. Rozalia takes the emotion out of my face. "I render you and your protégé *silent*."

"NO!" Jennifer shouts. Rozalia yanks my hand back through her neck and she vanishes in a black mist. The room immediately falls silent, and everything is calm. Only a few spirits are here, hiding behind me. They're construction men. I pay no mind to them at the moment.

"Frivolous bullshit." Rozalia grumbles. I inhale heavily, slowly standing up again.

"I need more energy. You are losing strength."

'I will not bite Ivy.'

"No you won't…but someone else."

'Maria was enough–and the last.'

*"**Dmitriii**…you amuse me!"*

I throw my right hand down, "I RESIST YOU! EVEN IF IT KILLS-" The door quickly opens, revealing the highly concerned Ivy. She is holding the blue dress tightly. I sigh slowly, calming myself. She looks around, "Who were you yelling at?" I stare at her and wish I could answer that correctly. "It's a long story…" I walk to her, take the dress and put my free hand on the small of her back, "Let us return to the previous task, shall we?" She watches me oddly as we head off.

"Nick, please tell me. I heard something about you resisting someone and that it might kill…who?" Without so much as glancing at her, I say, "Ivy, please don't make me explain it here. When we get to your room, I will tell you." I'll have to lie to her. With her, lying feels worse than ever.

She lowers her head, "Ok." I study her profile for a moment as we near the spiral staircase. A memory comes to me of when I almost revealed my secret to the girl I loved in 1983–Lovely Ivana.

I was so close as we sat at my fountain in the atrium. But Rozalia made me change the subject completely; she hypnotized her, and soon, we went to my room where I was forced to do terrible things to her; I bit her so many times and watched how she thought she enjoyed it. Rozalia told me that was punishment. No, this won't happen again.

Rozalia makes me laugh quietly.

Ivy looks at me curiously. I shake my head, "It's nothing. Some spirits are down that way arguing with each other over something meaningless. They are residual, which means they're trapped in time and have no idea what is going on around them. It's alright."

"Are they suffering?" she asks.

"Not at all. Only a piece of them remains here. They are not truly here among us." I say.

"That's–that's interesting."

"Indeed…" I hold hands with her as we go downstairs. She doesn't understand why I do this. I don't expect her to either. These days, such chivalry is nearly forgotten.

Once we're on the second floor, I feel she is more at ease. I can sense it. It makes me feel better but I'm still tense. We get to her room and I hand her the dress, then look around at everyone standing in the hall, giving them a stern 'leave us alone' expression.

"Nick," she says. I narrow my eyes again and slowly turn to her while shutting the door. She notices my behavior, which causes her to fall silent–unnerved and very curious. I know that demeanor all too well.

I point to the dress, "You can set that on the bed for a moment. I must answer your question."

"Oh… Yes, of course." She does as suggested and then gestures to the chairs and table by the window, which I nod at. I join her at the table as she folds her hands up against her mouth. At first, I say nothing. I only watch her, admiring all her features. She brings back so many memories. Some of them seem so unfamiliar to me. They're all short and sketchy though; blurs that I can never focus on. It's similar to having a dream and waking up with very little memory of it. Tears are threatening to leave my eyes. I don't know why. I feel envious all of a sudden.

"I envy you Ivy." That slips out of me as I look away for a moment. Why did I say that? I am not like this. 'Rozalia, why did you say that? You envy her?'
She doesn't answer.

"Why?" Ivy asks. I face her again. There is nothing I can say to that. Instead of answering, I smile softly and say, "Don't worry about it. Now then, you wonder why I shouted earlier…I was angry at Jennifer." She forms a troubled grimace. "And you mentioned the word 'kill'." I turn my nose down. "She is…more powerful than you can imagine." Her eyes light up, now more alert. "She could kill?"
I sigh, "I cannot answer that comfortably."
"Nick, if she has so much power, there is no doubt she could kill." I flick my eyes up through my lashes at her, "But she cannot–and will not–harm you." She sits back in her seat, unable to speak. I add, "And as long as she is under my control, no harm will be done. Believe me when I say that." She disbelievingly shakes her head, "How on earth do you have control over the other side?" I put my other hand firmly down on the table, "I just do." She glances down at it, then back up to me. I do the same as her and remove it, giving a small clearing of my throat. "Forgive me." She silently watches me.

"…I trust you." she says. I let my forehead fall into one hand, "Good…I am glad to hear that." She takes my hand away from my face and gazes at me. In this moment of silence, I think of the party soon to happen; imagining her in one of the finest dresses and dancing with me in the middle of the ballroom floor.

'Rozalia, this must be a surprise. It will be a surprise.'
"What a thrill it will be."

'But I don't understand why you are so drawn to this one.'
"I just am."

Ivy releases my hand on the table and begins to stand. I pull her back down to her seat, "Ivy, wait." She searches my serious face.

"Everything will be perfect."
"It will be perfect…" she says in a questioning way. I lower my head, "I promise you, I will make it so." She watches me stand up and kiss her hand.

"I will not be far if you need me." I say while walking backward to the door. She quickly rises from her seat, "No wait, please don't go." I stop and grin a little, "But you are going to get dressed…Miss Summers…" She slightly looks over at the dress, "Well…"
I wink at her, "I will wait outside." She starts to pout as I step outside and shut the door. Oh how I would love to stay but I can't trust Rozalia and it is not good manners.

Out here in the hall, Corneliu is waiting for me. I shoot him an annoyed look as he folds his arms expectedly and asks, "Why–why is this one so special?" I also cross my arms, not telling him anything. He very well knows I can't talk to him right now. With that understanding in mind, he smirks at me. He leaves and a few more moments pass.

The door slightly opens. I turn to it and see Ivy sheepishly looking through the crack at me. It's adorable.

"Would you…help me with the buttons at the back?" She asks. I quizzically lift an eyebrow. She blushes while opening the door a little more. I see how the dress fits her and it takes my breath away. She's…perfect. Just perfect…

"If you insist…" I quietly say. She steps back, allowing me inside. As she turns around, I urge Rozalia to behave. At this point though, I am really beginning to wonder how she truly sees Ivy.

I inhale slowly as I move her hair over her shoulder. She buttoned it up halfway. I grin. "You have a beautiful back Miss

Summers…" She makes a small amused noise. My warm touch sends a shiver through her. I can hear her heart jump. A chuckle escapes me as I near the top buttons.

"Nick,"

"Hm?"

"I saw you take a black box out of the closet…"

"Yes...what of it?" I finish buttoning the dress and then reach into my pocket. She starts to turn around. "Ah." I stop her, "Stay put. I am not done." I open the box and smile at the item inside. The memory of the day I went to the gift shop at the hospital comes back to me. I bought this from there.

"What are you doing?" she asks curiously. Gazing at the blue sapphire pendant on the silver chained necklace, I broaden my smile a bit more and carefully place it around her neck. She gasps as I gently clasp the chain together, then she holds the pendant and looks at it. "That was from the 'little black box'." I tell her while she faces me in great surprise.

"It's…" she quickly looks at it again, "I can't express my feelings; how beautiful it is." Seeing how happy she is, I'm warmed by it.

"How lovely. It was a good idea after all." Rozalia says.

'Yes, yes it was.'

"You look absolutely stunning Ivy." I say.

"Thank you…" She whispers, still holding the pendant. My pager goes off. I shut my eyes.

"Excuse me…" I check it. Walter has paged me to take a business call in my office. I was caught in the moment. How irresponsible of me.

I tuck it back into my pocket and tell Ivy, "I have some business to attend to…"

She looks at me with suspicion and disappointment at the same time.

"You know… I have an idea… Why don't you explore a little around the castle? I wouldn't mind."

"In this? And unescorted for once? I'm not in any danger…am I?"

she asks.

I look left to right, then at her, "Well, yes… You don't mind, do you? And no, you are not in danger at the moment. I have taken care of it."

"But Nick…the staff will think I have lost my mind. Not too mention–Walter!" she says.

"I will call him right now and tell him what you're doing. It will be ok…I promise."

The corners of her lips twitch up into a quick smile, "Well…alright Nick."

"I will see you later, draga mea." I kiss her hand, gazing into her eyes. Her cheeks redden again.

"What does that mean? 'Draga mea'?"

"It means 'my dear'." I say.

"Oh…how lovely," She likes that.

I bow my head, "Later." She bites her lip as I calmly leave.

Chapter 31
-Ivy-

I leave my room and go to the grand staircase feeling very befuddled. I was given permission to roam the castle freely but after all that has happened, I still don't understand why. I look down into the Grand room and see the maids moving around, changing the curtains to black ones, pinning golden drapes over the archways and setting black, Gothic floor candelabras on both sides of each of them. I fold my arms and rest on one foot, "Well, this is interesting."

I see Angel talking to Christine and Pamela. She looks up the stairs and sees me. She looks at me long enough for the others to see what has her attention. They don't understand why I'm wearing this dress, which makes it awkward for everyone. I briefly wave at them. Pamela and Christine smile a bit back at me. They nod at each other and part. Angel heads for the staircase and starts coming up. She almost passes me when I stop her. "Wait."
She looks at me, "Madam?"
I slightly point at everything happening below, "What's going on exactly?"
She turns around, looks at what I am pointing at and says, "We're preparing for the upcoming event Miss."
"Upcoming event?" I ask.
She nods, "Yes Miss Summers...for the holiday." she starts walking away. I raise a hand, "Wait…!" She doesn't stop this time. I frown and let my hand down. An event for Halloween… Will Mr. Vladoiu be hosting it? Will I meet him at last? I wonder…is this going to be a big party or something? I look at the windows and realize it's probably about 4 or 5pm now. When will this 'event' take place? I'm so confused and out of the loop! Why hasn't anyone told me anything?

I go downstairs and head for the archway on my right; a place I haven't been to. Surely, there's no doubt there are more 'secrets' to be revealed. Yes, I feel quite brave right now.

I make my way for the archway and see it's just like the other corridor that leads to the stables, but this one isn't nearly as long. As I walk the hall, I see a lot of light coming from the right side. I follow it and realize the light is coming through two big glass inlaid doors that have beautiful white drapes. I can't make out what's inside and my curiosity is getting the better of me. Quietly and carefully, I take a handle and pull down. The latch is louder than I expected and gives me pause. Pulling it open, I look behind me to see if I'm being watched. The maids are walking by the archway but no one is paying attention. I slip backwards through the door and quietly shut it.

When I turn around, I instantly lose my breath to the sight of a big majestic dark-gold organ at the other end of this room, a beautiful stage nearby, and then a great clock on the right of it, above the very fancy private balcony. It's like a box-seat area with no chairs. No...this is much more than a 'room'; this is a ballroom for sure! It's huge and round with soft tones of whitish blue and yellow marble floor tiles and there is a massive expensive-looking chandelier in the center of the high ceiling. I must add that the ceiling is decorated almost like you'd see in some parts of Buckingham palace! The windows have blood-red curtains nicely pinned back to the sides and there are a few tables with flowers and chairs spread out in some places. I imagine the majority of this 'event' won't be happening in the foyer as I thought; it'll be in here! I cover my mouth with a hand, "Wow..." Dmitri owns this.

My eyes wander over to the far left and find a dark almost-black door. "Hm," I wonder what's in there. I look at it up and down as I go to it. "Hmmm," The knob is ice cold as I turn it and pull the door open. The only thing I see is a stone stairway leading down. I assume it goes to the basement. I want to go down there but I'm not sure if that'd be a good idea. I glance back for a moment... This ballroom is starting to feel crowded–like I'm being ganged up on. I'm seriously now getting the feeling like I should run away. Something though...something makes me stand here fearlessly.

I hear one of the glass doors open and a voice very familiar to me says, "Esmeralda, are we done in here or what?" It's Leonardo. I didn't know they were helping the maids decorate. It makes sense though. "Almost. The last things we need are the candelabras but we have to get them from Christine too." Esmeralda answers; her voice is a little echoic. "Ah...ok," Leonardo sighs. I quickly go through the door downstairs, and after a minute, I notice the farther I go, the more I hear whispering at the end around the right corner. It creeps me out but curiosity just keeps driving me forward.

Finally, I meet the end of the stairs, very close to the voices now becoming clearer. It sounds like Nick–talking to someone. That can't be! He said he had a business call to take. His voice doesn't seem too happy; more like aggravated. Charily, I peer around the corner. Oh my gosh–it *is* him.

He's walking up the hall alone with his hands in his pockets, his head slightly down as if he's angrily looking up through his eyelashes, and the lights on either wall are beaming down on him, making him look even paler. This is very unnerving to see. I can just imagine horns slowly emerging from the sides of his head and his ears becoming very pointy. He's that devilish.

"No, I can't do that." he snarls. There's a moment of silence until I hear a disembodied male voice laugh the word '*coward*'. There's quite an accent too. My eyes grow a little. That was loud and clear! Who is he talking to? *Corneliu*?

"They cannot touch her. They are silenced! Leave me alone!" He growls. What does he mean? I lean out a little more to listen in better, but now I see it seems like whoever was messing with him has left; he's more focused on where he's going now. I get a sudden feeling he sees me.

Quickly, I move back around and pick up the sides of my dress, now hurrying up the steps. I hear footsteps quickly coming my way. I glimpse back and see him abruptly stop at the end of the stairs, taking a hold of both walls, looking for me. "Ivy?" I pause, extremely nervous.

"What are you doing...?" He walks up the steps and approaches me. Before I answer, I look around in thought of a good way to explain it to him. He takes my chin in two fingers, "Are you alright?" I blink and nod, "Yeah, I'm fine. I was just…exploring. You said it was ok, so I did. I didn't know you would be down here. I thought you were in your office." Hopefully he didn't really see me.

He smirks, "You were exploring alright. I was in my office, but I took a different elevator down here to get something. I saw you peeking around at me." he says, now placing a hand on the wall beside him, crossing his legs and moving his head to one side, "Tell me Ivy…what do you think of the ballroom?" Crap–I'm so busted.

"I…loved it." I say.

"Ahh..." he smiles, "Well come now, I have more to show you. I couldn't leave you alone for long." he chuckles, "You will love this too." I watch him straighten his posture and I still feel uncomfortable about what I saw just a few moments ago.

"Will there be a party happening here soon?" I ask. He looks from left to right, "Why yes…as a matter of fact, there will be. I will be hosting it for Mr. Vladoiu." He smiles slow and genuinely. I blink a couple times. "…Am I invited?"

"Are you *invited*?" he chuckles softly, "Of course you are, my dear!" He takes my hand, winking at me, "Come now." I'm unable to say anything as I let him guide me back upstairs, out of the ballroom, up the corridor and to the other across the way. On our way through, we turn right into a small round room where there is a black spiral staircase going up to the second floor. He leads me up, and then, when we meet the top, I slightly spin around on my heels to look at everything around. We're in a big white room with many Gothic windows, big French-like double doors in the middle, few bright-colored cloth covered tables and chairs, and on the far left corner near the many windows is an easel. He paints in here, I'll bet.

I look at him, mouth open a tad. He smiles with a small chuckle as he slides his hands down into his pockets and walks forward, "This is Dmitri's paint studio. I paint in here–rarely." I move on behind him, admiring all the furniture and the way the room is set up. "Always too busy to paint, I take it?" I ask.

"Yes…" he says, "But when Mr. Vladoiu first gave me all the privileges that I have now, I would spend a lot of time up here."

"I see. It must have been nice."

"It was." he murmurs.

As I meet his side, he forms a thoughtful sort of face and asks me, "Ivy, while I was away from you, did you have any paranormal experiences?"

"No. I didn't have any at all." I say.

"Hmm, good."

"You know, I think they're interesting to learn about." I slightly, slightly hint to him.

At that, he makes an expression like he thinks I'm being cute. "So you want me to teach you some things…"

I give a couple shy blinks in reply.

"Hm," he looks ahead at the windows and waltzes toward them, "A spirit, like everything else over time, gains experience; they learn what they can and cannot do." I follow him until we stop at the double doors. He faces me and looks into my eyes, "If experienced enough, they know how to touch you–make you emotionally or physically sick. If they're experienced enough, they can possess your body and make you feel their pain. The latter Ivy, that's what I mean by control. I keep them from possessing me everyday–all the time that I'm here. This is why I'm constantly going to the coast. But, come the warmer weather, I will remain here." he sighs, "I consider it a burden rather than a gift. The only good from it is, I can use my mind to do physical harm to them." That's…very interesting… I've really never heard of anything like this.

"How does that make you feel?-Seriously." I ask.

A side of his mouth twitches. "It is sometimes too much to bear. I do it though. It keeps me on my toes…" he gets a sadistic smile on his face.

"What?" I slowly ask. He waves his hands, "You will learn of it all soon. No need to kill a perfectly good surprise." He looks pleasured by whatever is going on in his head. I don't think this 'surprise' is safe, considering that expression he's making.

"Soon–as in **when**?" I ask.

"Soon!" he turns and walks over to a closet-like room. "Hey!" I quickly trail behind him.

We go into that room and he starts taking out some painting accessories. I watch, then glance up to his face in wonder, "Painting–now? You don't have business to tend to?" He looks out of the corner of his right eye at me, "I am free for now. Have a problem with that?" "Um… Well no." I laugh lightly. He finishes collecting the brushes and pastel-colored paint bottles. "Come." he gestures me with his chin to go with him to the easel. As he walks away, I say, "I can carry some of that, you know!" He stops, looks over his shoulder with an eyebrow rising. I go to him and take some of the stuff into my hands without looking at him. The feeling of being watched comes over me. Slowly, I look up to his smiling face.

"So so cute you are." he snickers. I blush and drop my eyes a bit. That must be his favorite word for me...

"Come now, let's go paint." he continues walking. I'm painting too? I don't paint very well though! This is going to be embarrassing…

I meet him at the easel and he takes some of the supplies from me, sets them down on a small table near it, then starts opening the bottles. I take one and try to open it, but it's sealed by dried paint. I keep twisting it and twisting it–it just doesn't work. He finishes opening all of them, then he notices me struggling with my bottle. He takes it before I twist it again, "Allow me." Just like that, he opens it–No sweat. He puts it down and grins smartly at me. My lips part for a second. "Whatever." I fold my arms and roll my eyes. "Hm hm hm," he chuckles. Suddenly, he takes my hands and moves me in front of him. "What-! Hey!"

"Silence Ivy. Watch." He fits a brush with black paint on the tip of it into my hand and holds it there, then he leans in close to the side of my face and looks at me, "Ready?" I blink at him. His beautiful eyes scan mine. I gulp at him. "Yeah," I slowly look back to the white easel. "Good." he gently glides my brush across it and starts drawing the outlines of a rose. I watch for a while, becoming lost in awe of his skill. It's so very beautiful…

"Ok," he snakes the black brush out of my hand and gets a fresh one and dips it in dark red paint. "Nick," He pauses to hearing that. I smile at him, "You are so talented…it blows me away." He gradually smiles back, "Why thank you Miss Summers. I greatly appreciate that."

"Years of experience, I know." I nod slowly, slightly humored, "Yes, of course...you're welcome." Just then, we hear Walter come up the stairs, saying, "Sir,"

Nick turns to him as if he's bothered. I give the butler a somewhat stunned 'Oh, hello!' face.

Walter apologetically bows his head at the impatient Nick and proceeds inside. "All has been taken care of sir." he looks at me like I should get out for a minute. "Miss Summers." It's that simple expression that makes me turn to Nick in question, and Nick nods once. I do the same back, gently walk to a door and go out into a small open hallway.

There's a table and some chairs under a picture in front of me. It's nice out here; very comfortable. I almost go to sit down but the idea of Nick or Walter coming out at any time stops me. In this moment, I suddenly get an image in my head; I'm standing in a dark enclosed space. There's a square hole leading down into an abyss. Why am I thinking of this? I feel a cold blade placed at my neck and hear a woman breathe in my ear. I inhale sharply.

"Ivy…ohh lovely Ivy…" she chuckles. I don't know this voice. "Who- who are you?" I shakily say.

"Oh, you know who *I* am…" My eyes enlarge. "Jennifer!" I spin around.

"Oh my god!" There she is! She looks terrible! Her hair is strung out, her eyes are red from exhaustion, she's extremely pale and she's boney. I place a shaking hand over my chest as I watch her run the knife over her arm, cutting it, making blood seep out and drip on the floor.

"*You*..." she says with an insane, murderous glint in her eyes, then she starts snickering, "*Nick* is quite infatuated with you... Oh yes he is..." I fearfully start backing up as she walks closer to me. Just then, the door flies open and then I feel a warm, male hand grab my mouth. I try to scream and fight him. Jennifer hisses at him and readies the knife to throw at us. He pulls me close and whispers in my ear, "Dormi acuma Ivy." his hand quickly slides away from my mouth to my neck and he tips me over his arm to make me look up at his face. I snatch his shirt collar, "Nick wait! Jennifer-" His eyes brighten, "Don't worry draga mea...dormi acuma." I try to look away but I can't; for some reason, I'm locked on his eyes. The room around him is getting darker by the second. "Nick," My grip on him is loosening out of sudden exhaustion. "You need rest." He whispers. Everything is going black. What is happening?! The last thing I feel is him pick me up into his arms, and then I'm out.

*Dormi acuma Ivy.

Sleep now Ivy.

Chapter 32

-Nicolai-

As I hold the limp Ivy in my arms, staring at Jennifer, I snarl through my teeth, "You had **better** watch your **step**." She screams at me and throws the phantom knife past my head into the wall, making a slit in it. My thinning eyes flash white and the veins in my head and neck stress. "WHERE is your **protégé**?" I hiss, voice just below shouting. Jennifer silently stands in place with a stained grimace on her face. I lift my chin slowly, impatiently, holding Ivy closer. Jennifer notices and starts laughing quietly. Rozalia belts a vicious demonic growl out of me, "*KNEEL*!" My eyes flash brighter white and Jennifer is forced to her knees. She rears her head up to look up at me, face now filled with fear. That pleases Rozalia, who then twitches a corner of my lips twice, making me form a smile made of pure darkness. But she's not pleased enough.

She walks me up to the nervous Jennifer and stares down directly into her eyes, "Ivy…is mine." Jennifer gasps. Suddenly the walls surrounding her burst into flames. I turn slowly and head away to my private elevator while Jennifer remains on her knees, screaming and crying uncontrollably. The flames are completely an illusion.

I carry Ivy into my elevator and press the 3rd floor button. As I look down at her, I think of where I am going and that I tried very hard to avoid taking her there. But, no one would dare come up here after what just happened. Hopefully, she will sleep all night. She will be so hungry in the morning…poor girl. Things are beginning to make no sense to me.

"Rozalia…you are losing control?"
"No, I am not losing control!" she grumbles through me. I roll my eyes.

"Don't roll your eyes at me!"
"At least tell me what is happening. I'm in the middle of this and

Ivy is beginning to fall into the same place!"

"I cannot say, Dmitri...I cannot say."
"You rendered them silent, yet...Jennifer found a way to return." I impatiently remind.

"I know what I am doing."
"If you do, Jennifer would not be here."

*"HAVE **PATIENCE**!"* I flinch at her loud screech.

The elevator doors open. I walk out and into my room with Ivy, then carefully lay her down on my bed. "We have to stay here with her." Rozalia makes me say.

"I don't trust you. She is not yours." I muster while staring down at Ivy.

"What choice do you have? I wish to protect her just as much as you do. Words are words; they don't always have meaning."

"Bullshit. You envy her–why?"

"She favors someone...that I used to know. I was slightly envious of that person for their appearance and demeanor. I needed them in my life; I wanted them." I'm astonished. This is something I assumed from the beginning. I slowly turn away and look at the closet, eyebrows curving inwardly. "Why didn't you just take her as you did with me?"

"Well...I work in mysterious ways Dmitri..."
I understand now. I understand it all completely!

'You possessed someone just like her. You looked like her once, didn't you? That's why she reminds you of you! That's why she's so familiar!'

"Why would you think that? That's preposterous."
I almost respond to that but we hear Ivy stir in her sleep.

I turn to watch her. It seems she's starting to have a nightmare. What could be happening to her? I don't see or feel Jennifer's presence. Maria isn't here either. Rozalia makes my eyes go thin in suspense.

-Ivy-

I dream of lying on a bed, staring out a Gothic bedroom window at the crimson moon. There aren't many clouds out. I admire how some of them pass across the center of the moon. But then there is a click followed by a door squeaking. I look over at it. A tall woman is sauntering in. Her hair is brown and long, covering her face, and she's wearing a long white nightgown.

"Who are you?" I warily ask. She doesn't answer; she continues walking toward me. I'm really getting a bad, bad vibe from her. But, for some reason, I only lay here, too frozen to move. "Ivy," She slowly lifts her hand, showing that she's holding a knife. My eyes get bigger and bigger. She gets to the bed and slowly crawls up. I try to back away, but as I do, she gets quicker and quicker until she's in my face. I begin to pant in fear. She snatches my head and shoves it to the side. I scream as I struggle. She strokes her hair out of the way and hisses at me, baring long sharp fangs. I burst out another louder scream as she comes down to bite me.

I gasp, eyes snapping open. Frantically, I scan the room–the large bedroom. I don't recognize it at all! Everything is colorful and Romanian style–like everywhere else in this castle. But this is completely traditional in here. I look at the Gothic windows that show it's dark outside, then I see Nick in the moonlight by a narrow door as he promptly walks toward me. "Ivy, what's wrong? What happened?" He asks. I rub my clammy forehead, soon realizing I've broken into a cold sweat. "I- ...Wait, where am I? How did I get here?" I look around again. He takes my hand and rests it on my lap, "Look at me." I do as I'm told.

"You are in my room. I carried you here after you blacked out. It's 12:30 in the morning. Now tell me what happened." He says. "Your room?" I ask. He nods, "Yes." I take a few more breathes while looking around, then finally I calm down and fall to the bed with a hand on my forehead. "Jennifer..." He clutches the sheets. I glance down my nose at him. He seems emotionless. I don't understand.

"Jennifer what?" he calmly asks. I sit up a little, "Nick," He leans forward, "Jennifer what...Ivy?" His behavior unsettles me to the point I have to back up to the headrest. He notices and backs off a bit. I quietly say, "I think it was her...but I can't be sure. She tried to attack me by...*biting* me. She didn't seem human." He emits a low growl as he focuses down at the bed, "Ohhh...*biting*..." I move closer to him, "Why?"
He looks at me, "She wants you to be afraid. Are you?" What sort of question is that?
"I don't know." I reply.
"I need an honest answer Ivy." He demands. I do nothing but stare at him and think about it.

Only in that dream, I felt most vulnerable. For that short time I was alone yesterday, I didn't feel threatened...except when I neared the basement. I don't know why that is. All of a sudden, it was like I stood in someone else's space. After Jennifer appearing to me twice; once in that hallway and then in my dream, I feel more insecure than frightened of what I might see, hear or feel. As long as I'm not alone, I feel safer. "Please answer me-"
"When I'm alone, I feel vulnerable. I want to stay here with you, but truthfully, my life is at risk. I'm so confused." I say.

"Ivy...I would not leave you. You are safest with me."
"But I was alone to 'explore' the castle. The thing is, I didn't feel anything evil following me. It was normal. Did you make the spirits disappear or something?"
"They got quiet for a short while." He says.
"But was it your doing?"
"I am not...certain." He's quiet for a few seconds. I want to ask him what he's thinking about. There could be so many things on his mind. Or would it just be best if we move on to a different subject?

"I will see to the end of this as soon as possible." He finally says.

"How will you do it?" I frown. He moves closer, making me back up to the headrest again. When he stops, he's a few inches from my face, and he speaks in a low tone; "First...I need your full trust... I need you to trust that I can keep them from you and the fact I have the ability to banish them from here. Confirm this with me Ivy. Now."

I bemusedly sit still, just unable to say anything. Why–why is he behaving like this? I see he's becoming impatient. If I stay quiet for much longer, who knows what will happen next? Do I trust his 'ability' or not? In my world, it's not possible to have these talents he has.

"I have seen you do some very interesting things. I don't think I'm very skeptical now. I will trust you. I will give you all my trust." I swallow hesitantly. He reads my face intently, searching for any uncertainty.

"...Then my research begins now." He backs away to get off the bed.
I grab his arm, "Wait a minute." He looks at me.

"Where are you going?" My voice is small.
"I'm not leaving this room unless you ask me to. Don't worry." He smiles faintly.
"Come back to me." I say. He doesn't move. "I want to hold you." I say, "If that's alright."

"Oh, that's lovely." Rozalia amusedly purrs.
He makes a strange face that gives me an indication he's uncomfortable about something.

I look down to my lap and start to get up. "Stop." He quickly crawls up to me. I stop him, looking into his eyes. He grins, "I will not do anything that you will not like me to do." Oh my god... I blush and smile briefly, stupidly, "I'm sorry..."
"Don't apologize." He chuckles, then he wraps his arms around me and pulls me close to him, placing a chaste kiss upon my head. I utter a small laugh as I bury my face in his chest and squeeze his shirt. Here I realize he hasn't changed clothes or anything–and I'm

still in that dress. I look up at him, "Have you been with me all night?"

"I have–Yes."

"What about your bath and your business calls?"

"It's ok Ivy. Walter has the business calls under control for now. And the shower…" I roll my eyes with a small shake of the head, "I won't stop you."

"I'm here to make sure you're safe though."

I glance over at one of the doors in this room, "I'm sure you have a private bathroom…go ahead." He warily smiles at me, "You are a daredevil as well Miss Summers."

"You should enjoy a nice shower after the aggravation." I insist.

"Fine." he raises a hand, "But you should go before me."

I bite my lip, "And I suspect you want to be with me in there too?" He smiles darkly, "Ivy, go take your bath…I will not be far. The second door ahead of us is the bathroom." He places his hand over his heart, "I promise I will not move from here. You need something, call me." I blink once and quizzically at him, then I start to climb out of bed. He rests his arms behind his head and smiles warmly, permissively at me as I go to the bathroom.

As soon as I'm in and shut the door, I check every corner for something eerie, hoping that nothing will jump out at me. The next thing I do is admire the style of this room. It's just like the bedroom; wooden, colorful and very detailed in the artwork. I love it so much; it's quite beautiful. I stop for a second. Holy shit…I'm in Nick's bathroom and I was in his bedroom too–with him! I purse my lips as my entire face goes completely red.

-Nicolai-

I lean over and use the phone on my nightstand to call the maids' office for Pamela to bring up a nightgown, a green Victorian dress and some Victorian shoes for Ivy, then I lie back down and think of the conversation Rozalia and I had earlier. Ivy looks just like someone she possessed long ago; she is more preoccupied with this one, therefore I've found the answer to Corneliu's question 'why is this one so special'…and finally, I have come to a conclusion–the reason why I have not been forced to kill Ivy–I see it now. As long as this goes on, there will be a sort of peace; a hint of happiness. When this party takes place, which is day after tomorrow, there will be even more of a distraction. Perfect–absolutely perfect. I have a plan–I finally do. This is one of those times I feel so grateful that Rozalia can't read my thoughts.

"Why are we smiling now?" She feels that though…
"A memory, Rozalia…just a memory."

"I want to go to the University Library. We don't have any books here that could help banish these pests."
"I need something that banishes only certain spirits."

"I will no longer tolerate the nonhuman ones."
'Corneliu stays!'

"Tomorrow we go."
I frown.

Then I hear something in my office; past the bathroom.
I sit up quickly and stare coldly at the bathroom door, letting my special sight shoot into my office. I find Jennifer walking with Maria behind her, trying to find a way into the bathroom without me noticing. I rise from the bed but then Ivy opens the door and peeks out at me. Her hair is wet and she is in a towel. I get out of bed, forming a smile, "You can use my robe if you would like." She gives me the 'are you sure' expression. "Use my robe." I tell her.

"Ok!" she goes back into the bathroom.

I then rise from the bed and go through the kitchen into my office in search of those two, leaving the door opened. I can't find them. Not even my special sight can. Splendid; Maria has also returned.

"Rozalia, if I go to the University Library, what about Ivy? She needs my protection." I whisper.

*"**Our** protection Dmitri... I will silence them again. They will return, but for as long as we are out, they will not be here to harm her. She must stay here."*

"Why can't I take her?"

"It's easier if she remains here; I can keep track of her better."
We hear someone knock on wood. I turn and we see Corneliu standing by the kitchen door.

"I am not powerless. I can watch over her. Jennifer and Maria are gone because I am here." He says.

*"You do not have my trust. You think they are frightened of **you**? You are one against two of your kind, Corneliu."* Rozalia says.

"We are of the same blood!" I hiss.

"He tried to frighten her many times already...Dmitri."
I twitch an eye at Rozalia's words.

"**Liar**! I protected her from everything when you were not there. Ever since she arrived here, I have watched over her. Sometimes it's harder, but it's not impossible." Corneliu says. I rub my forehead agitatedly at this whole conversation.

"Nick?" Ivy calls out. I glance at Corneliu.
He bows his head.

"Since we have no choice...once they are silenced, you will protect her." Rozalia tells him. He slowly backs up, disappearing in a black mist along the way. I inhale softly and walk back through the kitchen into the bedroom, quietly shut the door and scan the surroundings again.

Once I look over at the bathroom door, I see her wearing my dark red robe. It's large on her...and she looks amazing in it.

"Excuse me, I thought I heard something." I say. She watches me in concern. "Your clothes are on their way." I assure.

"What will I be wearing?" She asks. I smile artfully, "A nightgown and something for you to wear tomorrow. It's a surprise…that you will love, I guarantee."

"Hmm, ok."

"Sit…" I wave toward the bed, "Make yourself at home." She shyly pulls the robe closer to her form. "I'll stand."

I slightly narrow my eyes at her. She sighs, "Ok, I'll sit down." I watch her walk over and gently sit on the bed, then I smile in satisfaction.

I lift my chin, "You like my robe?"

She looks at me for a moment, "Yes, it's quite comfy…and smells good too." Her cheeks turn pink. I grin halfway at her. There's suddenly a knock on the kitchen door. I hold up a finger, "That's your clothes. Let me get them."

"Ok." She says.

I walk to the door and go in the office where Pamela waits for me. She is curious about Ivy but won't say anything.

As I take the short white gown, dress and shoes, I whisper to her, "I need you to accompany Ivy while I take my shower. Don't ask any questions. I will let you know when to go in there. Also, after I am finished, make sure you leave a note for Fitzgerald; he will not make breakfast until I am ready."

"Yes sir." She bows and turns away. I stare icily at her back as she goes to sit down, then I turn around and go back into my bedroom. As soon as Ivy sees the dress and gown, she gasps.

"My dear," I laugh, "what is the matter?"

She removes her hand from clutching her chest, "Another Victorian dress! And those shoes!"

"Yes…you don't like them?" I ask. She rises, holding the robe mindfully, "I do! I really do like them." I approach her and hold them out, "Then wear this dress tomorrow. Here, take your gown." She looks down at it, then up at me. Carefully, she takes it, eyes not leaving mine.

"I will hang this dress up in my closet and put the shoes under it, then I will go take my shower." I point at her, "Stay here. If I come out and see you are gone, expect me to hunt you down." She dips her head in acceptance. I take the dress to my walk-in closet, hang it up and come back out to see her standing in the middle of the room, examining the gown.

"Is that ok to wear?" I ask. She quickly looks at me, "Oh, it's good–Thanks." She makes a calculative expression, "For the next few hours, will we sleep? Where will I sleep?"

"Yes, if you are tired…you can sleep in my bed." I tell her.

"And you?" she's surprised.

"I will sleep there too." I see a spark of excitement fill her eyes, and she's trying hard to hide it. "Oh! Ahem...you won't do any-" "I will behave myself. I promise." I snicker.

"Okayy." she says with a little skepticism in her voice. I bow at her, get some black shorts out of my dresser and my pager off the top, then I go to my office and tell Pamela to go ahead in my room in 2 minutes. She accepts. I then go to the bathroom and start taking my shower.

As I bathe, I watch out for Maria and Jennifer and keep a close eye on Ivy. She's cautiously watching her surroundings.

Over the years, Jennifer has gotten worse and worse with her jealousy. She and Maria both don't understand why Ivy is special, but I do–I do now. Corneliu still doesn't know, and I will not tell him why. Rozalia knows it too but I must be very careful now. She's being more observant about my actions. Though her behavior isn't changing, I'm sure she's becoming a tad anxious.

I cannot believe I took an interest in Jennifer. What a dumbass I was. That was the 40's; the decade of total emotional failure for me. We fought too much and hardly had any good times together. After a while, Rozalia had enough of her and made me kill her. My guilt over that has left me completely. Maria is becoming a problem too, considering she is also quite envious of Ivy. I know it when I see it. And I am seeing it again–in this era–but it's worse than ever. I will destroy them.

I quickly finish bathing, dry off and put my shorts on, then stare in the mirror at Rozalia. She makes me grab some cologne and spray it over my chest. *"I want to smell nice."* I sigh slowly and put it back down, then shut my eyes.

"Dmitri, let's go. Stop dawdling." My brow creases, then I look in the mirror again and head back out of the bathroom.

I see Pamela standing near the bed where Ivy is laying with the covers up to her neck. My robe is hung up on a nearby coat hanger. Both of them blush at me. A toothy grin spreads across my face. Pamela coughs lightly and leaves the room, bowing her head at me along the way.
I look at Ivy and shrug.

She says, "I didn't know Pamela would come in here."
As I walk toward my bed, I say, "I don't want you alone. It's too risky."
"Well, thanks." I raise an eyebrow at her for that.

Hesitantly, she moves over and I join her in bed.
"Oh! You smell good! And…nice muscles." she bashfully laughs.
I smile at her, "Thanks…you smell lovely as well."
"I had to use your soap..."

"You smell like a man." I remark to her, which makes her smile somewhat shortly. I kiss her cheek, "Sleep now Ivy." I gaze at into her eyes for a long time, admiring her beauty. She leans up and kisses me on the lips, then lays her head back down on my chest, "Goodnight Nick." She snuggles up to me, but then stops. "…Your heart." Wonderful–She has noticed my unusual heartbeat…

I take a deep breath, wrapping my arms around her, "Yes, it beats a little faster than the average person."
"Are you alright?"

"It is a condition I have lived with for a long time. I'm fine, don't worry."
"Do you take anything for that?" she asks.

"I have to be very careful with what I take." I answer. "Well, maybe that's why you are so warm all the time." She jokingly says. I smirk, starting to stroke her back slowly, "Perhaps so." I close my eyes and continue to think for a long while, until eventually fading into a deep sleep.

Chapter 33

There is darkness, then I notice I'm in the basement of my last home with Corneliu; the big manor in Albany and the year is 1907. Just as I remember it, the large room is dim; candles are lit. I habitually ball my hands into fists while looking around. But then I stop at one corner. It seems to be unusually darker than everywhere else. I eye it suspiciously. That area gradually lightens up soon enough for me to see there's a bronze kerosene lamp swaying gently back and forth above a long table. What I see on the table makes me immediately step back. It's Corneliu's dead body, and he's wearing the same thing he did the day he died. Now I know for sure this is a memory–Not a random dream.

Quickly, I look up at the ceiling and then over to where I remember the stairs being. They're not there. I turn around. Where are they? There's no way out. Frowning, I look at Corneliu again. Something is going to happen. I'm waiting for it; I can expect nothing else. But, everything stays calm and still. I decide to go to him.

I was right; he looks exactly how I last saw him; eased face, eyes and mouth slightly open, and his somewhat small fangs are just about to touch his thin bottom lip. It's dark around his eyes and his lips are purple. I take his arm and turn it, roll his sleeve up and look for the bite marks I had left. There they are–I see them. Sighing, I put his arm back down and place my hand on my forehead. Not long after, I choke on a small cry and sniffle a few times. "I'm so sorry Corneliu...I'm sorry...sorry about everything!" I inhale deeply before I lose my breath to this painful feeling and slowly peek through my fingers at him. If only I knew better. Things could've been different and life could've gone how it was supposed to.

I wake up and stare at the ceiling. Wonderful...another dream of my past, haunting me some more. I blame this on Corneliu; the dream manipulation. He always does this. He doesn't even have to be in the same room to do it. These dreams are always about death and guilt. I should think less of it now, but I know...that is my humanity, and it still somehow exists. I'm not what Rozalia wants me to be. No, I'll never change. The past should remain where it is.

Turning my head to look at the window, I notice it's still dark out. I glance over and find Ivy half-covered with the blankets, curled up into a little ball at the edge of her side. She looks so beautiful in the moonlight. Her porcelain skin is so fragile and perfect, and her fine curves... She's just gorgeous. I smile slowly and scoot myself closer and trail the side of my index finger down her arm around to her back and then down to the lower area. She stirs in her sleep. I switch my eyes up to her face. Her grip on the blankets tightens. I smirk and then kiss behind her ear. She softly sighs, "*Nicolai*," I stay quiet. She turns over onto her back, turning her head toward the window. My attention falls down to the calmly beating pulse in her neck. My lips part. So smooth, so fragile, so kissable...so...bitable.

"Yes," Rozalia's echoic voice murmurs, *"...It won't hurt her at all."* I leisurely lower my head to her neck and gently kiss her. She utters a little sound. My now-glowing eyes drag open to half-lidded and we make eye contact for a second. I softly smile, "Don't worry...everything will be alright. Sleep Ivy... **Dream**..." She lazily smiles back, closes her eyes and falls asleep again. I begin to nip at her neck, then gently take a hold of the area above her waist and carefully climb over top of her. She turns her head as I lean back down, sliding my hands up her body to hold her arms down to the mattress and then I start licking the place of her quickening heartbeat. *"We must take our time with this one."* Rozalia purrs. Ivy moans quietly, pleasured by the sensation, making Rozalia curl my lips up into a wild smile. She makes me say, *"**Finally**...I can taste you now...**Ivy**."* She closes my eyes, opens my mouth while

tilting my head and then she starts to close me in on Ivy's neck. Suddenly, Ivy gasps, eyes flying open. She clutches the blankets as tight as she can as her heart races faster, "Nick! What are you doing?! Let go of my hands!" Her legs shift around behind me and try to knee my bottom. Holding her in place, I blink and then quickly jump off and sit with my back facing her. My face falls into my hands, "God, no." She backs up to the headboard, panting, feeling her neck. I turn around. She gulps, "Did- did you bite me?!" she pats it. I shake my head, "No." She points at me, "Don't come any closer to me!"

"Ivy," I sigh. She hisses, "I mean it!" With a roll of the eyes, I crawl toward her. She pushes herself closer to the headboard, "I'm warning you!" To avoid getting kicked, I suddenly make a quick advance on her. She squeals as I take her shoulders and push her back down to the bed. Now we're face-to-face. Her breathing is fast and mine is a bit above comfortable.

"I will not harm you."
She nervously puts her hand on her chest. I grab it, "I mean it." My hand slides off hers, down her stomach and stops at her navel. I can feel her jerking reaction to this.

"Calm down Ivy." I whisper.
"How can I?!" she quickly asks. I lightly brush her hair back while looking into her eyes, "I can make you calm down."
"No." she shakes her head repeatedly, "Don't hypnotize me!" I gaze down at her lips for a few seconds. My hand stops and moves away slightly. She takes it in midair, "How close were you to biting me? I dreamed everything." I raise an eyebrow and tip my head to a side in wonder. She releases my hand and tries to pull the covers up over her chest. I stop her. She looks at me isapprovingly. I inch in closer to her face, almost touching noses with her as I return my eyes to her lips, and I soften my voice, "What did you dream of...?" She's goes silent, visibly disturbed, but also beginning to blush.

"Well..." she quietly says, "I dreamed that you were on top of me, kissing me..." she looks up from my nose into my eyes,

"I…enjoyed it…and kissed back, wanting more–to go further. But deep inside, something was telling me not to. I am not sure what side of me was more powerful." To go further, she says… "What do you really want?" I whisper. She gives me a blank expression. I can see it though; I can see she's really thinking about it. She sighs and throws her head back into the pillow, "I don't know." I don't really think that's true. I lie down next to her and stroke her cheek in admiration with two fingers. She turns her head toward me. I slowly smile, "You are so beautiful Ivy." She watches me, and after a moment goes by, she mumbles, "Nick…I kissed you like you were someone I've missed for a very long time. What does that mean?"
I pause, then look at her and warmly smile, "I think it means you want to stay." What I say makes her look like she doesn't believe me. I arch an eyebrow at her again. She returns to staring at the ceiling.

"I...have a question..." she says.
"Hm?"

"Will you hold me?-Kiss me like you did in my dream?" Her cheeks are darkening. That request is a dangerous one. I really would love to give her what she asks for. What will it do though? How far could I go? I suppose I will…chance it…

"Ivy," I pull her close, "of course." I cup the back of her head and stare down at her lips, "Of course." She looks at me with such innocence and curiosity; it's very cute. I lean in and press my lips to hers. She slowly wraps her arms around my neck as my right hand rides down her ribcage to her waist and gropes her bottom, receiving a surprised 'mmh' from her. My fingers clutch her tighter while I softly bite her bottom lip, granting a quiet moan from her. My left hand runs down her leg, around to her inner thigh. She makes another surprised sound and takes it before I do anything else. I grin at her and she gives me a smile of disapproval. "Not so easy," she breathes. I tilt my head, "You are challenging me?" She must not understand me very well. I grin wickedly and suddenly roll her over on top of me, then I broaden my smile to a wolfish gleam, "Go on and try me. Let's see what you've got." She immediately stares at me with wide eyes, blushing redder. My own narrow almost impatiently, and intensely. "I'm waiting." She looks down my chest. I smirk, "Time's up." I grab the back of her head, she gasps, and I pull her down to me and start kissing and gently tugging at her bottom lip again with my teeth. She's hesitant yet quick to respond and slides her hands down my chest while I trail mine down her soft, curvy midsection to her waist, and I let out a baritone hum. Again, I clutch her bottom tightly and pull her lower body flush against mine. Yet another moan escapes her as she feels me pressing against her. I grin into the kisses. Her hands move down my chest as she rises off me a little. I gape up at her lustfully, breathing a bit heavily. She starts to smirk, and again I see such innocence in her features, but it's *slowly* going away.

She seems to have more confidence; it's in her eyes. I watch her run the sharp tip of her index fingernail down my chest, stomach, and slow down when she nears my pelvic region. I huff as my heart jumps. I snatch her hand, "No." Oh, I want her so bad! I can't risk this though. I frown sadly, "Ivy, we can't do that." Things will go too far and I might kill her. I almost say something but she runs her hand down and stops near my crotch. I grunt in surprise. "Ivy," I breathe coarsely, "Don't!" Oh god, no. She moves closer to it. Where is this sudden daring behavior coming from? Is this not her but Rozalia making me think it is? No, I'm not ruining this by thinking that! I suddenly snatch her hands and flip her underneath me, and I warningly look down into her eyes, "You want this?" She pants, "Yes." That's not good enough for me. I firmly place my fists down on either side of her and more seriously say, "Are you *sure*? You have no idea who you are dealing with." She goes breathless, "I am." I suppress a sudden chuckle from Rozalia. She grabs the back of my head while leaning up and kisses me romantically. I purr lustfully. Freedom…this is a little taste of freedom. I've yearned for this for so long.

I move away from her lips and kiss along her neck to her ear, making her breathe faster. I sigh into it, "Ivy, my love–remember what I said before." She moans, "I do," I kiss below her earlobe, "Then we will risk it–Now." She moans again, holding me closer. I quickly sit up, take my shorts off and snatch the straps of her gown and tear it apart, then throw the clothes across the room. She gasps at the pain. I look down at her again and see her body...is perfect. *Absolutely* perfect.

I beam darkly at her, "You are stunning... I will take you now." She again goes breathless. I thrust into her and she suddenly gasps and I groan in pleasure. Once I realize it was painful for her, I ask, "Ivy, are you alright?" She takes in an unsteady breath, "Yes," "Should I stop?" I ask. "No," she shakes her head quickly, "don't stop." I make a sudden fanged smile, briefly closing my eyes. I ease farther inside, being careful, granting another moan from her, and she leans the back of her head down into the pillow again, fingers drilling into my back, forcing a somewhat pained groan out of me. I move in close to her neck while beginning to pull in and out of her. She whines out in pleasure, clenching my back tighter, almost breaking my skin with her nails. I gradually quicken my speed, groaning more. I can hear her heart beating quicker by the second, her breathing getting more and more excited; how mouthwatering. I huskily say into her ear, "Let me know if I am too rough." My answer is a fragile sort of whimpering; "Ah-hm,"

"Shh, Ivy," I lick her neck and drag my fangs across it when I take little bits of her skin in between my teeth. I feel her muscles begin to tighten around me. Her body is starting to buck into mine and she lets out an, "Ah!" I let out a throaty sound to her pulling me farther in. My pace hastens more; in and out, faster, faster. Her nails drag across my back as she loudly cries my name. Her heart is racing madly now, deliciously pounding in my ears. I can just taste it now; her sweet warm blood caressing my gums and running down my throat... Oh, so tasty! I need it–I need it *NOW*! My suddenly-glowing eyes fly open again while my nose wrinkles; I open my mouth with a hiss, eagerly tilting my head and clamping my teeth down on her smooth, pale, soft skin. Instantly, her blood fills my mouth. Ohh, *YES*!

She screams, "AHH!" her head jerks farther back and her body lurches forward as her chest rapidly moves up and down, "Nicolai!" She's so delectable! Her body, her neck, her blood– She's perfect! By her doing this, I roar in delight, eyes squeezing shut to her pushing herself closer again while I drink in her **absolutely** delightful blood. It's much richer, now that her heart is pumping so much faster. Rozalia's haunting laugh is beginning to fill my head but I ignore her. I keep slamming Ivy over and over, lust and passion just **consuming** me. Ivy whines again, turning her head the other way while she suddenly scrapes her nails down my back, drawing blood. I fling my head back with a shout as I find my release. She also belts out a loud moan, climaxing along with me.

Breathing heavily, I slow down, slowly pull out and fall over next to her. I rest my hands on my fast-moving chest and then look at her. Her neck is still oozing blood and she's completely drained of energy; very sensitive too. I scoot closer to her, "Ivy," She looks at me with her hand reaching for her neck, "Nick, my neck-" I stop her, "I will clean it for you." She blinks at me and pants, "Ok," I lean in and lick around the bite marks. "Ohh," she breathes, arching her back only a bit. I finish licking it up and then gaze into her eyes, hovering over her face. She puts her hand on my cheek and slowly smiles. I hold it there, returning her loving smile. "You wore me out," she says. I grin at her, then lean down and whisper close to her lips, "Then I believe we should sleep." I give her a chaste kiss and then tap her nose. She tilts her head at me and smirks faintly, "I agree." I smile at that.

"Here, lay down," she pulls my head to her chest. I inhale deeply, softly rub her shoulder and stare ahead at the wall, blinking slowly while listening to her calming heart.
"Goodnight, dragostea mea." I murmur. "Goodnight…my lovely Nick." Hmm…her voice saying 'my lovely Nick' like that… I smile in content. Too bad she can't say my real name. What an evening this is. I did not expect all this to happen. In fact, I never did expect to go so far. The thought has always been there to do

this, of course. Every time I'm around her, I want to do all kinds of bad things to her. I am a gentleman though–with her anyway.

"Thank you for all that pleasure." Rozalia chuckles wickedly. My eyes slowly open, narrowing in hatred. She chuckles louder, evilly excited about the energy gained from Ivy.

I awaken a couple hours later to the sun beaming through the window. Squinting at it, I look over and see Ivy is almost uncovered. I halfway smile and pull the covers up to her shoulders and kiss her hair near her temple, then slide off the bed. Yawning quietly and stretching, I look at the window again and start to realize that I'd slept better than I have in at least 20 years. My clock says it's 8:30.

I start getting my clothes; a white shirt, gray button-up vest, gray formal pants, black shoes and a burgundy tie, all the while thinking of early this morning. I give Ivy an amused side-glance. 'She was fun.'

I take a quick shower, put some cologne on, then after I put everything on, I check myself in the mirror and leave.

"Dmitri." I hear Corneliu while walking to the other end. "Yes uncle?" I glance at him.

He bows his head slowly, "I will make sure she will not be tampered with."

I point at him, "Good... Do not ogle at her." He folds his arms. I nod once and firmly at him, then I see ahead of me Walter is coming up the spiral staircase. I soon meet with him.

"Good morning Walter."

"Good morning sir. I realize you didn't come down for breakfast at your usual time."

"Yes…something different today." I say. He smiles shortly, then straightening his posture, he becomes more professional. "I must speak with you in private sir."

"Of course," I wave my hand toward the direction of my office, "Let's be on our way then, shall we?" He follows me there, shuts the door carefully, then he walks toward me as I sit down at my desk.

He says, "I received a phone call from the sheriff's office at 8:15 this morning. They have finished their investigation and deem Maria's death a suicide. They will not be returning to the castle sir." I put my hands together and give a sign of acceptance. "Very good… I am glad... This entire situation has been stressful for everyone."
"Indeed sir. Shall I put the elevator back into service?"

I glide my eyes across the desk to a mirror placed on a corner. *"You are actually quite chipper this morning."* Rozalia says while beginning to contort the mirror. I slowly narrow my eyes.

"Sir?" I blink, then look at him, now back into reality, "No. Remove the police tape over the doors and lock it up until I say otherwise."

Leisurely, he tilts his head, murmuring in a somewhat apprehensive voice, "Something is wrong." Yes. Something is always wrong…in my life. I start to grind my teeth while dragging out an inhale.

"There is something on my mind; do you ever notice that sometimes, things go bump in the night?"
He forms a slightly confused face. "Mr. Francis, I have witnessed some things I cannot exactly explain. As a personal rule, I do not usually engage in conversation about things of this nature, but because you asked…" I tap the table in anticipation, "You are my friend, and I'm very interested in your thoughts." I flick my serious eyes back up to him, "Please continue."

"…There have been times I've heard voices from someone that isn't there." He utters above a whisper. I grin and rest my chin on my hand, "I believe in the supernatural."

"What are you doing?" Rozalia says.
'You will see.'

I look at him sternly, "We are not alone. We never are. There is evil here–I feel it all the time." He widens his eyes, which really gets my attention.

"You are suggesting there are spirits here?"
I raise a hand, "I am not sure what it is-"
"How clever of you. He is of no help." Rozalia's voice gives me a sudden migraine; my ears are ringing because of it. I grab a side of my head with a wince. "Sir, are you in pain?" I shake my other hand at him, "No, I'm fine." I clear my throat and readjust myself in the seat, "Every waking moment, I am tormented. I have headaches." I lean forward, "They are real Walter–as real as I am to you. I have gotten used to these headaches."

"My god..." he muses. I know he's skeptical but I think he trusts me. He has the whole time he's worked for me.

"Where did these 'spirits' come from?" He is very curious and on the edge of not believing and trying to believe. I sigh, "That is something I don't know. What I need is peace. I desperately need it." He half-crosses his arms and places his left hand over his jaw in a contemplative manner, "Well, may I suggest you doing some research on 'ancient' supernatural beings?"
"What for, I wonder?"
"There is a certain kind of book in a certain place..."
I rub my forehead, "Enlighten me."
He nods, "When I was in town, I went to Gales' University Library and asked about some books on that subject. Because truly, I have noticed strange events taking place of late. Ever since Ivy came into in our lives, the castle has become an eerie place." I pause and stare at him, "And...?"
"I believe they might have what you are looking for, sir. I spoke with a gentleman by the name of Albert Strauss who told me about a book named 'Mythological Creatures of Ancient Times', and he mentioned that it was written in 1863. It was sent to the university from England about 15 years ago. Currently, it's on display."
Interesting...that's very interesting. I knew Walter would know something. He visits that library from time to time.

I tap my chin and then rub across it as I look off to the right at a bookcase. I've been to that library many times before, but have never had such luck finding anything like that. In fact, I cannot remember the last time I visited it; it's been at least 30 years–more or less.

"Would you like me to visit the library again?" he asks. I stop rubbing my jaw and look back to him for a minute. Putting my hand down, I give him another stern look and then I say with a slight dip of the head, "No. I will go myself–today."

"Cleverly planned... Though I do question why the word 'mythological'." Rozalia is entertained.

'I have not lost my interest for that subject and I am curious about what other people have believed in.'
"Hmm."

Now Walter is more concerned. I move my head to one side, "Problem, Walter?"
"No sir." he shakes his head, "It's just…as I said–Ivy and the 'ghosts'. Also, the event tomorrow evening... Sir, she hasn't anything proper to wear. You didn't quite make arrangements for her."
I roll my eyes and then stand up, "Walter, you question me?-On this? I know exactly what I am doing." I approach him, "You know where I keep the most formal dresses. Find a dark red one with diamonds and a lot of black lace–one of the most beautiful dresses we have. She likes those colors and looks amazing in them. This is a grand surprise." I pause, then ask, "What do the spirits do when I'm gone?"
"Well… Not really anything…sir." he mumbles. I shoot my finger up, "Yes! Now, I ask you to do something for me; make sure Christine leaves a rose on the pillow next to Ivy and this note." I go to my desk, lean down, take a pen and notepaper and write on it, then I reach it out to him. He takes it, and I go to the door and look over my shoulder at him, "When she wakes, she will ask where I am; tell her I am out looking for this book. As far as speaking of the event, don't give anything away." He raises an eyebrow, "Yes sir, of course." I leave the room, taking my black trilby hat off the hat rack near the door.

As I walk quickly up the hall, I say "Good morning," and bow my head to Angel as she dusts off a lamp. She smiles and curtsies. As soon as I am ten feet away from her, I start to hear someone following me.

"Dmitri," It's Corneliu. I continue walking fast. He appears in front of me with an angry face. I go through him, "Out of my way Uncle." He shows up in my path again, "DMITRI!" I stop and growl, "Why do you disturb me now?" My voice is quiet enough for no one to hear me.

"Get rid of her *now*! She is too much for you!" he says. I point at him, "I said I refuse to listen to you! I have plans and they will work! You made a deal with me; don't fuck it up!"

He slowly shakes his head, "But don't you see it? You cannot love, nephew. This is becoming ridiculous." Just after he says that, I hear Jennifer belt out a bloodcurdling scream, "YOU'RE A MONSTER! A MONSTER! GO ON AND KEEP THREATENING ME! I CAN TAKE IT!" She starts laughing madly. I dart my eyes to the right and see her phasing through the wall. I clutch my hat as my head falls to one side in distress and horror to seeing her face twisting into a waterlogged scowl. I almost make tighter fists but my stiff, trembling fingers stay the same. Angel notices me and thinks I am in some kind of trouble. She walks toward me in a hurry and asks if I'm ok. In my mind, I'm screaming at the top of my lungs. I slowly lift my chin, giving them a death look as I loudly say out of the corner of my mouth, "I'm fine…Angel." She stops just behind me. "Excuse me but, what are you looking at sir?" She's unnerved.

I turn to her, "See to it Ivy has a good breakfast. I have to go to the mainland for a little while." I pick my hat up and start walking away while she bewilderingly stares at me. "Yes sir." she says.

Chapter 34

-Jennifer-

While Corneliu and I watch Dmitri leave the castle, we stare at the dark shadowy Rozalia encompassing his entire body. She resembles a dark aura you might say. Her sheer size frightens all the dead here; she's not a human spirit at all.

"With enough power, I'm sure I can defeat her. She must know this. Why won't she do anything though? Is it Ivy? What's so great about that bitch anyway? She's nothing."

"You...will do nothing." Corneliu says behind me.
I turn around to him and see others at his sides; early pioneers, some of the men that helped build this place, a few women and three Mohegan Indians glaring heavily at me. They know I'm not a human spirit in the same sense they are.

I stare at Corneliu, "You can barely speak English old man." I look at the Natives, "All you people do is sit around and watch everyone else. You can't understand a word I'm saying either! I will put an end to this; just watch me!" I vanish with a thought and go to the 3rd floor conference room. Noticing I'm alone, I begin to pace back and forth, thinking more and more about Rozalia's change in behavior.

"She's never so mellow or reserved. Something is happening and I really hate not knowing what. I have spent so much time and energy trying to unseat this witch that I have missed something. There must be a way...some way of getting rid of her! What is it about Ivy that keeps her interest? Why has she not made him kill her?! Maybe the others have seen or heard something useful." That's it. I know what to do. I will gather those women that have died because of her, and have them meet me in the files room immediately. I know the files room is a safe place to have a meeting because it's off-limits to all except Dmitri. I grin as my feet become mist and soon my entire body, then I quickly move throughout the castle, touching each female victim and giving them notice. "Meet me in the files room now." I say to each of them, and they listen. Maria is the last I notify. I find her in Dmitri's room, standing at the end of his bed.

"Maria, I need your help in the files room."
She slightly turns her head and faces me. "The files room? No one is allowed in there."
"No one will know." I say, "Don't ask questions. Let's go." I take her hand and vanish in the shadows, heading down to the basement.

Once we're there, everyone stops talking. Maria and I look around the dark, brick room at them standing near the back wall in a group. She looks at me, then slowly walks over to join them, a little uneasy about my behavior.

I put my hands together and form a smile, "Ladies, please line up together so I can see all of your faces. Thank you." As the women line up, Madeline, from the 1920's who has been here the longest says, "What is this all about Jennifer? Still having issues with Rozalia? Maybe you should do as all of us have and accept your situation as it is." The others nod in agreement except for Maria. I continue, ignoring her, "I have gathered you here to discuss something important to all of us. You know who Ivy is, correct?" They all look at each other.

"Yes we've seen her." One of the ladies replies.
I wave a hand slightly, "I'm sure you all have noticed how Rozalia's behavior has changed since Ivy arrived here." Maria becomes aggravated by that and the others fall silent as they think about it.

"Have any of you seen how she makes Dmitri treat her?"
Maria's eyebrows instantly rise. "Dmitri?"
I sigh, "Yes...Nick has played you, Maria, as he has all of us." She glances around at everyone who is either looking down in a sort of shame or is completely blank-faced. "But...I don't understand." She looks at me again.

"Don't you see? Don't you get it? Dmitri never comes here.

You know why? Because Nick IS Dmitri!" I walk toward her and stop, pointing at her face now, "Rozalia controls him; she is not a human spirit and never has been. The cold hard truth, Maria: she has possessed and perpetuated the youth in his body for 105 years; he is the original Dmitri. She is the reason we are all here and is a force that must be dealt with. Together, we will stop her. You all need to be stronger. You *will* be stronger!" Maria is astounded and speechless; between believing and highly skeptical. She continues to look down at the floor and at me.

Emily, a woman killed in the 1960's steps forward. "But what if we can't? She will only inflict pain on us as punishment for angering her. She's very powerful." I turn my head toward her with an icy stare, "We are doing this together. With the power I have, and all of you ladies combined...she doesn't stand a chance. You all want peace, don't you? You want the chaos to end!-Don't you?" They search each other's faces for reassurance.

"Let's make it happen before the party!"
They return their curious, almost agreeing eyes to me.

I watch them intently, becoming satisfied.

-Nicolai-

I go to my private elevator and walk inside it. As soon as the door is closed, Rozalia stops me from pressing the button. *"Wait."* she says.

"Wait for what?" I exasperatedly look up.
"We must go to the files room in the basement."

"I have no need to go there Rozalia."
"I do!"

"Fine...I'll see you're amused, then we can go?"
"Yes indeed."

I press the button for the basement and wait as the elevator moves in a slow descent and stops. The doors open to the dimly lit brick hall. I'm just beside the room containing all my personal and confidential files. I can hear whispers coming from inside that room. I walk up to it, and as I place the key into the lock, the whispers cease. Slowly, I open the door. In the middle of the room, I see Jennifer standing in front of all the women I've killed, including Maria in a line abreast.

I kick the door shut with a heel and they see Rozalia over my shoulder with glowing expressionless eyes; it frightens all of them except Jennifer. Maria backs away and hides behind her, shooting a finger out at us, "WHO ARE YOU?!" The others quickly tell her to hush; Rozalia is too powerful. Jennifer's eyes light up furiously, "I KNOW WHY YOU HAVE COME HERE!"

"SILENCE!" Rozalia shouts, causing me to twitch and Jennifer to fall to her knees in great pain. Maria reaches for her arm as Rozalia refocuses on her, emitting a demonic baritone growl through me. Maria gasps, stepping away as Jennifer moans quietly. The other women start vanishing through the ceiling after witnessing this.

"I…am not…afraid of you!" Jennifer winces.
"Oh you make that quite evident Jennifer." Rozalia says, nodding slowly.

"Hey, she doesn't deserve this!" Maria points at us again.
I do the same at her, "Her kindness is a façade!"

"You can't make us leave!" Jennifer barks while forming her shape into a black misty ribbon. She quickly slithers across the floor and jumps up in my face, baring her fangs with a loud hiss. I drop my hat as Rozalia snatches her by the neck with my hand. She gasps in surprise.

*"You will not be **heard!**"* She looks at Maria, illuminating my eyes to bright white. Maria begins to tremble uncontrollably. Suddenly, while still looking at her, she symbolically crushes Jennifer's neck and then marches me toward Maria. "No! No!" Maria tries to turn away but Rozalia has immobilized her by manipulating the energy within the room. On approaching her, Rozalia shoves my hand down and squeezes her neck until she

bursts into a black mist and fades away. The room immediately falls silent–dead silent…and somewhat peaceful. I take in a long breath and let it out.

"They are in a different realm for now." Rozalia says.
"Yes…the realm of nothingness, as you call it…but for how long, I wonder?" I breathe a little roughly.

"Do not doubt me Dmitri. Ivy will be fine."
"For the last time, give me a break! Let's go find your damn book." I flick out my jacket cuffs, pick up my hat and make a swift exit out of the room to the elevator.

Momentarily, I'm at the first floor in a small room. I go out and walk up the hall behind the grand staircase until reaching the doors to the back walkway of the castle.

"Sir?" I hear Walter behind me. He just came out of the kitchen. I turn to him.

"Christine has left the rose and note, and breakfast should be ready in about an hour. Are you alright sir?" he says. I nod, "Good, good. Yes I'm fine, thank you. I will be on my way now."
"Are you all set?" he sounds a tad suspicious.
"Walter, I'm in a hurry."
"Of course sir. My apologies." He bows his head, folding his hands behind his back.
I again nod, then turn around and open the doors.

The sky is gray. It'll be snowing soon.
"Sir…one more thing…" My eyebrows lower.

"You forgot these." His words baffle me. I face him and see he has taken my pair of black sunglasses out of his right breast pocket. I reach for them, "When did you get these from my office?"
He smirks, "Just after you exited the room. I was going to give them to you before you left for the mainland. You never leave without saying a final goodbye sir. And you never leave without these tucked away in your pocket."
I slightly smile, "Yes…yes that's true. Thank you."

"Already a long day?" he asks.

"It would seem so." I laugh.

He smiles softly, "Good luck with your trip."

"Make sure you keep a close eye on Ivy." I quietly say.

"Yes sir."

I put my hat and shades on, tip it down and head off to Leonardo's boathouse.

-Maria-

I suddenly feel within the darkness, after what seems like a long time of nothingness, a hand grab my wrist, and I'm pulled forward. As I'm led along, dim light is starting to illuminate around me. "Maria, come with me...come out of this abyss." It's Jennifer's voice. The light finally shows where I am; back in the room Nick and that demonic woman banished us from. The hand releases me.

I quickly scan around and find Jennifer a little to my right. "Jennifer, you saved me...you brought me back." I mouth. She walks closer, smiling a little at me, "As always." She puts her hand on my shoulder, "We have work to do."

"Like what?" I quietly ask.

"We will have our revenge...and we will start with Ivy."

A smile slowly traces my lips to the idea, and her own broadens. Revenge is exactly what we need, and deserve. I *want* this!

-Ivy-

I wake to hearing a woman knocking on the door. Squinting from the morning sun shining on my face, I look over. Nick isn't here. I sit up and see there's a rose on the pillow and a note that says:

Good morning beautiful. I left this for you as a small good morning kiss. I didn't want to wake you because you looked too peaceful. Christine will be there at the door for you.

Love,
Nick

I smile at the fancily written note, then look at the rose again.
"Miss Summers?" Christine knocks again.
"Yes! One moment!" I get out of bed with a wince. Turning around, I glance down at the sheets and see two spots of blood from my neck and from…losing my virginity. The memory flashes in my mind; how everything happened. Oh my…
I hesitantly dab the sore bite marks. The slightest touch sends shivers up and down my spine and my stomach tingles.

Cautiously, I rise up off the bed, take his robe from the coat hanger and put it on. "Christine?" I say, opening the bedroom door.

There she is…with a kind smile and somewhat impatient eyes that she's trying to keep friendly, but then she sees I'm wearing his robe and it causes her to suddenly go expressionless.

"Miss Summers, I've come to tell you breakfast will be served in 45 minutes. Is there anything I can get you?"
"Um," I look behind me, around the room. Here I begin to think of Jennifer, Maria…and Corneliu. I don't feel threatened…I don't exactly feel right either. Something unnatural is here; yet at the same time, it's nonthreatening and more of a protective presence. …Corneliu?

I turn back to her, "No thank you. I will be down there shortly. Could you tell me where Nick is please?" She puts her hands together in front of her in a modest way, "I don't have the answer to that Miss, but you can ask Walter."
"Oh…" I wonder what he's up to.
"Ok, thank you." I say, grabbing the side of the door.

"You're quite welcome."
I shut the door and go to take a quick bath.

After that–and my swift primping–I collect the green Victorian dress and shoes from the closet and fit it all on. The shoes are black and have little heels–just how I like them, actually. I notice the attire inside the closet; it's mostly filled with navy blue, grey and black suits. Nick **really** loves those colors... How dashing. I blush, imagining how it looks on him. And then I think of how muscular he is. "Ahem," I snicker to myself. He's **very**...sexy. Very.

Now the last step; I put my hair up into a bun, then take the necklace with the blue sapphire pendant Nick placed on the dresser and look at it for a moment. I could get lost in its beauty forever it seems.

The air is slowly getting thicker. It's the feeling like eyes are coming in, leering at me. I still myself. What's happening? I don't want to look back.

As I lower my stare down the dresser to the floor, my body stiffens more and more. I breathe in slowly through my mouth. Before I do anything else, a hand touches the place Nick bit me. I gasp and spin around to see Jennifer with Maria behind her. "Holy shit!"

Jennifer grins wide, "Hello princess…we couldn't leave you for long."
I gasp again, "What do you want from me?! How dare you call me that?!"
"You look delicious." She starts walking toward me. "W-" I try to say 'what' but the fear is too much. She stops and looks to Maria, who is starting to smile and laugh at me. I quickly back up and hit the dresser, then the wall beside it.

"Won't you join us Ivy? You would love being one of us." Jennifer says. I put a hand on my chest, "I don't know what you mean!" Maria takes a comb off Nick's dresser and clenches it in a hand, pointing the handle of it at me, "I don't want you looking at

him anymore!" Jennifer smacks it out of her grasp, "No, not yet."
Just then, the bedroom door opens and the two shift their heads in
that direction. I see a black mist standing there. My eyes grow
larger. Before anything else happens, Walter appears through it.
The black mist disappears and I quickly look ahead of me again to
see Jennifer and Maria are now nowhere in sight.

"Miss Ivy, are you alright?" I look at him, horrified. No, I'm not
alright! How in the hell can I explain this to him?
"I heard you talking to someone." He says. 'Talking' to someone?
That makes no sense! I have to keep as calm as possible. Fuck!

I swallow and scratch my head a little, "Oh, well uh, what did
you hear?"
"Something about breakfast." **I said nothing about breakfast...**

My god…these 'spirits' can manipulate what you hear too?
Who was that in the doorway? Corneliu? Is he the reason Walter
heard that instead?-To make sure he didn't hear the struggle? He
must have followed him up the hall. If he did that, I am thankful.
Without Walter coming in here, who knows what else would've
happened?

"Miss Summers…are you ready for breakfast? You are a little
late, you know." he says. I regain more of my composure and nod
slightly, "Yes…yes, I'm sorry. Excuse me, Walter, could you tell
me where Nick is?"
"He went to Gales University Library to find a book."
"What?"
"Ahem…" he looks out into the hall, closes the door a little more
and approaches me, "He wanted me to relay this message to
you…" He sounds a little like he doesn't believe what he's about
to say. I stop him before he says anything else, "Walter, what is
this book about? You don't seem to agree with it." He sighs
slowly, "This book I speak of is about ancient supernatural beings,
and he went to study it." A book on ancient supernatural beings?

This will help him with banishing the spirits? Why can't he just
bring a priest of some sort out here? How powerful are these spirits

really? Too powerful for a holy person...? I wish I could have gone with him. I should have gone with him but it's obviously not what he wanted. I am so in the dark.

"When will he be back?" I ask.
"Not long, I assume."
"You assume?" I repeat.

"Miss Ivy, I will escort you to your breakfast in the small dining room. You will be served with Mr. Francis' favorite morning dish–French toast, fruit, bacon and orange juice." He says. The look in his eyes tells me he won't let me go anywhere alone. I'm glad, yet frustrated about this concern for safety. "Ok..." I say.

-Nicolai-

Leonardo has docked the boat at Esmeralda's. Now, as we stand outside the car garage, Esmeralda hands me my car keys and my cell-phone. Leonardo is standing behind her with folded arms and a look of ease.

"Mr. Francis, how is Ivy?" she asks. I maintain a straight face while tucking the phone into my jacket, "She is fine. All is well." I smile, though I am second-guessing myself. If I had it my way, I would still be at the castle.

"See you soon." I say. She and her brother watch me step away and walk toward my Aston Martin.

"Be careful!" Leonardo says. I raise my hand with the keys in it and soon approach my vehicle. Taking the door handle, I mumble, "That's all I am." Once I'm inside, I adjust my mirror and then speed off. Just to think if I did get in a car wreck, death never sounded so sweet. It would never happen though...I can't die at all!

A good minute of silence goes by, then I hear Rozalia tell me, *"Let me see our eyes."*
"No thank you." I say.
She laughs, *"Very well. You know, I have been thinking...I wonder*

if others of my kind have done the same as I have…"

"What do you mean?" I glance at the mirror. She yanks my glasses off and then I see her; her bloody face smiling maliciously at me, brown eyes glowing brightly, "There are others like me all over the place, doing the same as me. But Dmitri…I have possessed you **halfway**. You are different." she winks at me. I shift away, "I am not a child. I know that!" Then my eyes narrow on the street. She laughs again. *"Possessing you fully would have been too easy."*

"Just shut up." God I really hate her face. I should destroy all the mirrors at home. It's so agitating that every time I look in one, there she is–reminding me of that day I killed her. The mirrors are for the maids and Walter though.

I look in the mirror again, lean forward and whisper, "Fuck. You. Okay? Fuck you."
She lowers her head and starts chuckling.

Now refocusing on the road, I put my shades back on. Soon, I slow down and look up at a tall white brick building. From what I can remember, it was built around 1915. There's a bronze sign at the turn-in entrance that says in golden Edwardian lettering: *Gales University Library.*

Carefully, I find a parking space and get out, put my hat back on and look from left to right, then in front of me. Good, there's hardly anyone around.

I walk on and as soon as I get to the French double doors, a woman comes out of the building and almost runs into me. "Oh! Sorry!" she giggles shyly, flips her hair and smiles briefly. First, I stare at her oddly, but then I take my glasses off with a smile and simper as she backs away. "Not a problem." I bow my head at her. She sees my eyes suddenly flick up to her and flash bright blue. She almost stumbles off the curb. I give her a quick flirtatious look and then turn for the doors and my eyes return to their normal color. 'Rozalia, no. I said I'm not doing that again.' I grimace at the doors.

"Wait!" the woman calls out. I stand in place for a second while she walks up. Turning around, I watch her look up at me in a way it seems she's about to say something but can't seem to do it. "No." I hypnotize her into thinking she never noticed me. A puzzled expression forms on her face and then she starts walking away, "Um, sorry." she fixes her hair with a small uncomfortable laugh. I grin halfway and then go inside the library.

"What is one drink?" Rozalia sighs.
"One drink...is one too many." I reply as I look around.

So I see, the place is beautiful and silent. There are very few people in here. It's old, has a high ceiling with a few big chandeliers, many tables and chairs are spread around, and farther back, there are the book aisles. "Hm," There is nothing over there for me.

As I continue to the empty front desk, I slowly take my hat off. I can remember the first time I set foot in here. It was the summer of 1917 to be sure. Of course, things don't exactly look the same now. It's amusing to me how the people of today are running this place; trying to make it look as it did back in its early days. Whenever I came here–which was often at first, but soon became very seldom–I would refrain from speaking to anyone for very long. Back then, I thought I couldn't control myself well enough; Rozalia was most brutal to me in those times and I had no real courage to stand up to her. It was only 10 years after her 'death'–or I should say, her 'release'.

I stop at the desk, looking around again and sighing to myself, "The good old days..."
"Sir?" A woman's voice says. She sounds elderly. Arching an eyebrow, I turn and face her, then I smile professionally, "Good morning."
She puts her hands together at the front, "Can I help you sir?"
"Yes," I say, "I am looking for a man named Albert Strauss. Is he here today?"
She nods, "Yes sir. He is on the third floor." she then makes an interested face, "Is there something I can help you find?"

I smile once more and then say, "No thank you madam, only him–
Albert."
Her right eyebrow quirks up slightly. She waves her arm out,
"Alright. Right this way."
"Thank you." I follow her to some gold elevators.

She presses the 'up' button and then waits with me for the doors
to open. I look out of the corner of my eye at her once getting the
feeling I'm being stared at. She's trying to understand me, I guess.
"How long have you been in the US?" she asks.

The doors open. We both look in there.
I turn to her, "A little while. Thank you for helping me." I wink at
her. She slightly smiles, "It was my pleasure sir." I dip my head at
her, then go inside the elevator. When the doors shut, I look up at
the ceiling in a sort of amusement. She's a cute little old lady.

The doors open again. Now I'm on the third floor. I walk out
into a big room where there are bookcases everywhere on the left,
and on the right, a sitting area. In front of me is a large desk with
an old man looking down at something. He looks like a well-
educated professor. There is no one else up here (visitor-wise) that
I can see. That's good.
I go to him.

He glances up past the top rims of his old-fashioned glasses,
"Can I help you sir?"
I get up to the desk and nod, "Indeed you can. I'm Nicolai Francis;
I am searching for a man named Albert Strauss."
He gently smiles, "Well, you are talking to him." he stands up and
reaches out for a handshake, "What can I do for you good sir?" I
shake his hand, "I am looking for a book with the title
'Mythological Creatures of Ancient Times'. I heard you have it on
display. Would you mind if I have a look at it?" As he puts his
hand down, he thinks to himself and nods, "Of course. Here,
follow me." He walks around the desk and leads me toward the
book aisles. We go down one into another area, and then ahead of
us, I see the stand with the book set there upon it. He takes me over
to it and quietly says, "If you turn the pages, you must use these."

He takes some white gloves and hands them to me. "Of course." I say as I take them and put them on.

This book is big and looks older than I am. Very good...very good indeed. A small satisfied smile spreads across my face and then I turn to him, lowering my head in thanks, "Thank you for your help Mr. Strauss."
"You're quite welcome sir. I will be around if you need anything." he nods and then strolls away with his hands folding behind his back. I hear him greet someone coming in and I smile shortly again.

Before I begin my reading, I stare at it for a moment. I have a feeling of dread; as if Rozalia will force me to do something wrong. My eyes close as a memory comes to my mind.
The year was 1958...

I drove my red Chevy impala up to a cliff and parked it. At the time, I had my sights on a pretty girl, but I wouldn't dare talk to her for long. I couldn't–wouldn't–get close to her. Not after what I did to Jennifer. I did the same thing to Jennifer as Rozalia; cut her head off, but I threw her remains down my oubliette.

I just sat there in my car with the side of my face resting on my left hand, thinking about life. The best thing to do was to drive off and drown myself. I was ready to go. I figured I couldn't be stopped that time; everything would move too fast.

I snatched the column-shift, rolled up my window and then said, "I'm done. I'm ending this now." I yanked it into gear and went to floor it, but then suddenly raced backward and hit a tree. My head slammed into the steering wheel and knocked me out. I woke up to hearing a police officer tapping on the window with his flashlight. It was an hour into twilight. I looked at him and squinted my eyes from the light. It made my headache worse. Wincing and rolling down the window, I said, "Evening officer... Can I help you?" He slightly peered into my car and then looked at me, beaming the light in my face, "Yeah, I see you wrecked your car. You alright buddy?" I quickly turned my head, "I'm fine. I just didn't hit the brakes in time. Could you please keep that light out of my eyes?" "Uh huh…" he said as if he had a pinch of disbelief, then he asked while letting the flashlight down, "You need a ride to the hospital?" he gave my car a brief inspection, "How about a tow-truck?" I quickly looked at him, "No thank you. I'm fine." He stared at me. "Son, how long have you been out here?" Him calling me 'son' ticked me off a little, but I was very much out of it. I had a hard time focusing on things. And because of that, I kept my squinting eyes on him once he started seeming suspicious of me. I finally blinked and repositioned myself in my seat, clearing my throat, "Sir, I'm fine. I came out here earlier in the day. I've been unconscious for a while, but I feel alright. I'm only a little sore." I rubbed the back of my neck.

Again, he stared at me, watching me almost intently. He then backed up some and checked the rear end of my vehicle, shining the flashlight on it, "Well, the damage isn't that bad." He glanced at me, "It looks drivable." I slowly put my head against the headrest and closed my eyes, "Good. Thank you."
He nodded, "No problem. You sure you're ok?"
"Yes." I said.
"Ok…" he began backing away, "Stay safe out here, alright?"
"Yes, of course officer."

Once he left, I started thinking about things. I remember putting it in drive, but how did it go into reverse…?
Rozalia…

Right then, I gradually squeezed and pulled on the steering wheel. I was doing it so hard I thought I would break it, then I jumped out of the car and screamed out all the rage I had to the world. I kicked the car, ripped the back doors open and began throwing everything out, down on the ground. The guitar I had, I threw that off the cliff with a last infuriated shout. It was brand new and I was trying to learn how to play it, but in that moment, it didn't matter to me. After all of that, I fell to the ground, sobbing in defeat. Rozalia always wins–always. I couldn't hear her but I knew she was quite ecstatic.

Snapping back into reality, I blink a couple times, soon frowning. 55 years later, here I am doing the same thing again; trying to get rid of her with almost the same desperation. I'm taking things slower though; the contemplation.

I put my right hand on the book and sigh. Here I go. I open it and look through the table of contents. There's a chapter called 'Demonic Expulsion' and the page number is 536. I still my attention on it, engrossing the title. While doing that, Rozalia says, *"Demonic expulsion? We don't have any demons at home..."* She may be amused–I can't tell.

"Hm," I make a quick smile, "Why yes, you must be right Rozalia. I just found something that interests me. I wonder again– are you so vain that you have forgotten my fascination for mythology?" I start flipping through the sections of the book to get to page 536.

Once I get there, I begin reading...

Demonic Expulsion -

Demons are capable of possessing an unwary person's body. This is accomplished by-

"No." She suddenly makes me shut the book. I glare at it, then reopen it and try to read again. She does just like before when I find where I left off. I grumble, "Enough Rozalia. I am just curious." I open it and then quickly fold my arms and read on. *This is accomplished by moving its energy from a body near death, to one that is-*

She forces me to turn the page. I take in a deep breath and grab the hand she used and pull it away. While doing that, I happen to glance over and see a young man with glasses staring at me strangely from one of the book aisles. I give him a smile, though it turns out to be an ugly one. He doesn't do anything but turn and walk away. I sigh, then look back down at the book.

"I know what you are doing. I am not a fool."
'I am doing research!' I mentally snap. With an agitated shake of

the head, I turn the page back and do as before; put my hands away and continue reading.

This is accomplished by moving its energy from a body near death, to one that is not. This does not exclude animals. Once the demon has moved to another host, it must stay until the host dies – or is near death. Only then can a demon freely move to another host.

However...

My eyes grow slowly in curiosity.

The most commonly accepted way to expel a demon from a host body is through ritual exorcism. This can take up to several months to accomplish and is not guaranteed. Many people believe the ritual drives the demon to another host by giving it permission to leave the current host.

I step back in a sort of astonishment. Several months, it says. And it's not guaranteed. That would be the last option for me. I can't let this happen. I won't.

I take my phone out and take a picture of the page, then stuff it back into my pocket, all the while scanning around to see if I'm being watched. I've got to get out of here now. There are things I need to do at home. I already know how to get rid of Jennifer and Maria. Corneliu–I can't let him go. Once I banish Rozalia, everyone else will have more of a chance to leave.

I stand up, flick out my shirt cuffs and go on my way to the exit, giving Mr. Strauss a 'thank you' and a goodbye nod. He does the same in return but has an odd way of doing it; he has an unnerved expression; he must have seen Rozalia causing me to act up. While I'm leaving through the door, I check the ceiling corners and see cameras almost everywhere. I block my face with my hat.

Of course.

Chapter 35
-Ivy-

I've finished eating but haven't left the dining room. Walter and I talked for a little while about how he likes his job and then he had to go take care of some business. Just a couple minutes after he went out, Christine came in and we've been talking ever since. I ask her if she has other things to do; I don't want her to get into trouble. She says I shouldn't concern myself and that it will be fine.

For some reason, I have a strong feeling Walter doesn't want me to leave this room right now. I don't understand why, besides the 'safety issue'. After all, he is a little worried about earlier. Twice now, he's told me I was very pale and shaken when he came to find me in Nick's room. Still, I haven't revealed the truth. It's very hard to hold it in. But I will tell Nick. I'll definitely do that. At least no one knows what happened–or so, I hope they don't.

Just before Christine finishes her sentence having to do with her sadness over Maria's fatal accident, she gets a page. "Pardon me, I'll be back." She says.
"Sure, of course." I rub my shoulders, then stand up from the table. I'm motionless until I feel the need to go look out one of the windows. Right away, as I peer down at the roundabout, I'm stunned. I see Nick down there a little beyond the fountain. He's looking off into the trees with his back turned to the castle. It confounds me a little; he would have already let someone know he's returned. This seems quite out of place.

I give the door another look, then I decide to walk out into the hall and keep a close eye out for Walter as I hurry downstairs to the main entrance. I don't want to be stopped on my way out to Nick. Though, it's almost impossible that somebody won't see me.

On nearing the main staircase, I see Angel and Pamela are down the hall where the Mont-Saint Michel room is, talking and dusting. What a relief!

Finally, I get outside and find him still standing there. I raise a hand, holding one side of my dress up with the other while hurrying to him, "Nick!" He turns around and I suddenly halt in surprise. It's not Nick; it's an old man! I watch him look up at the windows I stood at and then he starts walking to the right side of the castle. The stables are that way. Who is this guy and what does he want?

"Sir," I say, but he doesn't listen. I check behind me for Walter, then quickly follow him. He goes all the way to the stables and then vanishes before reaching the front of the building. I stop in my tracks. Whoa, he wasn't a physical person?! Hold on a second...
I walk into the stables.

In the moment I look around the place, I see only Eduard at the other end by that little fridge, drinking juice. He acknowledges me and sets it down, also seeming surprised I'm here. "Why, hello Ivy–! I mean Miss Ivy! What brings you out here–in a long dress like that?" I remain without words, still trying to understand who that man was and why he led me out here.

"Miss Ivy, are you ok?"
I finally realize he's talking to me.

"Well, it's sort of strange actually..." I answer.
As I start walking to him, he rests an arm on the counter, asking, "What do ya mean?" I stop a few feet from him and check behind me again, "Did you see an older gentleman walking around out there?"

His head droops while he searches the ground in thought.
I take that as a no.

He says, "No, I haven't seen anyone in a while."
"Interesting." I mumble. Could that have been Corneliu? It looked a little like him...maybe. I don't know for sure; all I've seen of Corneliu is that portrait in the grand room. Or maybe it was him after all but he changed the way he looked to confuse me. Why? Why would he do that?

"Is there some kind of event before the party that I don't know about?" Eduard asks, pointing my dress out again.
"Oh, um-" I briefly smile, "No, it's just…it's kind of a long story. You know Nick wears old-fashioned clothing; he has Victorian dresses and I wanted to try one on, so I did and he gave me permission to wear these dresses."
"Yeah," he scratches his head, "he does have a strange obsession for Victorian stuff for some reason." I smile again, then I remember the party. "Eduard, are you excited about the party?"
"Oh," he laughs, "I don't do Masquerade parties."
"Masquerade!"
"Yeah, you didn't know he's throwing a masquerade party?"
"No…but I do now."

"I think you would like it. You seem like that kind of person." He takes his drink and raises it, then sips some. I gradually begin to nod, "Yeah, maybe so."

We hear a phone ring. I look over and see it on the wall. He holds up a finger, "One second, hang on." He walks over and answers it. "Eduard speaking! Ivy…? Yes, she's here with me… No, she-" he glances at the curious me, "she came out here, saying there was an older gentleman walking around outside… Alright then… You're welcome." He hangs up.
"Walter asks you to meet him in the main entrance."

"Ok. Well…I'll be going then."
He tips his hat to me, "See ya later! Oh, would you like me to escort you back?"
I shake my hand at him, "No, I'm fine thank you. See you around." I leave the stables, going back the way that man led me. I don't exactly have enough confidence to go through the hall and large corridor.

When I get inside, I see Walter by the big fireplace. He must have just lit it or had somebody else do it. As soon as I approach him, he says, "Miss Summers, are you alright? I noticed you left the dining room before Christine returned."
"Yeah, I'm ok. I just looked out one of the windows and thought I

saw Nick near the fountain." He slowly lifts an eyebrow.

I sigh, "I know he's not here. It was…someone else. It was an old man in a suit."

"That's interesting. We are not expecting anyone today." I only watch him. His pager suddenly goes off.

He checks it. "Ah, Mr. Francis is about to arrive." **Oh, good!** "I'll stay here by the fireplace, if that's ok."

"I would recommend it." He says with a nod, "Here, have a seat while I greet him."

I do just that and sit on the sofa in the center.

Weird things are happening. Weird things indeed. I expect him to go to the foyer, but instead, he goes to the right side of the grand staircase into that hallway. Here I am—alone again. Somewhat. For how long, I wonder…?

-Nicolai-

I walk up the stone path at the back and see Walter coming out before I can reach the doors. Taking my shades off and tucking them in my breast pocket, I dip my head firmly at him. He offers to take my hat, "Mr. Francis, welcome back." I give it to him once I'm inside the back foyer.

"Thank you. How is everything? Where is Ivy?"

"I just can't believe it! You made us look like a fool! See what happens when you resist me? You behaved as if you had some sort of fit leaving the building! I demand we return to that library AT ***ONCE****!"*

'You made me walk like that. I know what it will take to get rid of Jennifer and Maria.' I think to Rozalia as Walter says, "Miss Ivy is in the grand room sir. So far, everything is fine."

"Good…" I say under my breath, looking past him in search of Corneliu, Jennifer or Maria.

"You know nothing. These creations of mine are ***rare****!"*
'I will treat them as demons.'

She growls at my comeback.

Walter says, "We have things to discuss sir, if you are not too busy." He looks at me like he's trying to understand my unreadable face.

I switch back to him, "Indeed we do." He slightly bows his head, tilting it a little, "Ivy was a little late this morning for breakfast, so I went to find her. She was in your room; quivering and very pale as if she had seen a ghost. I don't know what happened, but I am quite concerned sir. This is not all that occurred either. During her meal, I stood by, but had business to tend to. I had Christine accompany her. A while later, Pamela and Angel had a mild emergency that Christine had to assist with, then after assisting them, she returned and saw Ivy had left. I checked the security cameras and found her at the stables. I called Eduard and then asked her to return to the main entrance. When she met me there, she claimed she saw an older gentleman in a suit outside by the fountain. I was just about to call Eduard and have him search the grounds for an intruder."

Rozalia is shocked and angry. I try very hard to be calm with her emotions nearly overriding mine. 'I knew I should have stayed here!' I mentally hiss.

"It was the best choice to go!"

I tell him, "I think I know what's going on old friend. Don't bother Eduard for now. I must talk to Ivy right away. I think I found what I needed at the library; I will have all this under control very soon." I pat his shoulder and walk on, placing my hat over my chest along the way.

"Asta se întâmplă când îmi pun încrederea în tine." I grumble to Rozalia. "Să pui încrederea în *mine*? Nu ai de ales." She makes me whisper. Soon, I'm in the grand room. I see Ivy on the middle sofa, watching the fireplace. A sigh leaves me.

*Aceasta este ceea ce se întâmplă atunci când mi-am pus încrederea în tine.

This is what happens when I put my trust in you.

*Când ai pus încrederea în mine? Nu ai de ales.

When you put your trust in me? You have no choice.

"She must leave this place for now."
'What?'

"We will tell her to go home. We have preparations to make. She must have things to do as well."

'She would not be followed…would she?'
"Bodiless souls cannot pass the sound."

'I know that. I mean Jennifer, Maria or-"
"NO ONE!" She shouts, causing me to wince.
"Very well…" I whisper to myself, and begin walking toward her.

I stop next to the arm of the sofa and clear my throat softly. It seems she knew I was coming; Rozalia can make me feel her anxiety. As she turns her head a little, I smile, "My love, I am back." She looks up at me in that innocent manner she always does. I automatically assume she didn't expect me to call her that.

"I missed you," she lightly laughs. I kiss her hand, "I've missed you also. How are you?" Rozalia is intent on watching her eyes. Ivy notices my stare. It makes her blush. Lowering her head, she mutters, "Well, I had an interesting time while you were gone. How about you? Did you find the book?" My smile vanishes to a thin line.

"Do tell. I'll explain myself later." Rozalia makes me say. Ivy looks around, then back up to me, "I would rather discuss my situation in private." I continue to observe her expressions until leaning close to her ear to whisper, "Then we will talk in my office, ok?" As I back away, she becomes silent. I offer my hand, "Shall I escort you Miss Summers?" She finally blinks. I slowly grin at her behavior. "Yes, of course." She places her hand in mine. I wink at her and begin our walk there.

"You are ravishing in that dress."
"Thank you," she quietly says.

"I'm getting hungry."

I look ahead. 'I've noticed. No, you can't have her right now.'

"Hmmm..."

I roll my eyes.

Soon, we reach my private elevator and go inside. I try to press the 3rd floor button but Rozalia is resisting me and forcing me to focus on Ivy's heartbeat. I gulp, closing my eyes.

'Please don't do this to me. Not now.'

"Nick, are you ok?"

I bite down on my lower lip, then take a deep breath, "Yes, I'm fine. Sorry, I have much on my mind."

"It's ok."

I press the button.

"I said I'm hungry. I will have my drink."

'Is there **really** time for that?'

"You are going to our office to have a conversation, aren't you? She will be leaving soon. Let's have a...farewell drink to that."

'No, please no.'

*"You will have fun! I'll be **gentle!**"*

I slowly look over at Ivy standing beside me. My gaze lowers to her soft neck and the memory of my first taste of her blood sends a shiver throughout my body. How long can I go on like this?

I grab the phone on the wall beside me, press three digits and say, "I will call you when I need you." I hang up.

"Was that for Walter?" Ivy asks.

"Yes, he has a voice pager."

"Ohh, cool. Excuse me but, what were you thinking about, if you don't mind me asking?"

I look at her, "...I will explain when we are completely alone."

"There's someone else in the elevator with us right now?" she asks nervously.

"Yes... No need to be afraid." I smile, taking her hand and gently squeezing it.

The doors open.

I hesitate to leave but she's eager to walk out. This lust I have is becoming more intense by the second. Calmly, I slow my breathing and go to open my office door. The first place I go after releasing her hand is the wet bar in the corner on the left. Maybe I can drown out the temptation by having a drink.

"Would you like some champagne?" Rozalia asks kindly through me. Ohh…something bad is bound to happen.

"Yes please." Ivy says while walking to the front of the island counter. I get two glasses from a shelf and pour hers first. "Alright then…" I set it down in front of her and suddenly smile, "You may begin." She smirks at me as she slowly takes it, "Thank you." I dip my head and start pouring my drink.

She says, "I think Corneliu was leading me around outside." Putting the champagne bottle down, I raise an eyebrow up at her from the counter, "What makes you think that?"
"I was in the dining room downstairs and looked out the window. I thought I saw you, because this guy was dressed in a suit. Only, he had his back turned. I went outside and called out to him. When he turned around to me, I realized it was an old man. It confused me quite a bit. I followed him halfway to the stables and he vanished into thin air. I haven't seen him since, but seriously, I'm thinking it was Corneliu. Why would he be leading me around like that?"

I swallow my first sip, "Protection."
"Wouldn't I be followed outside by the others?"

"No, Jennifer and Maria can't go outside."
"Why is that?"
Rozalia impishly lifts a side of my mouth up into a half-grin, "Because I disabled their ability to go that far when I crushed them." Ivy eyes me curiously, sipping from her glass.

"I cannot explain well enough for you to understand. Just take my word for it." I mumble, slightly looking away for a couple seconds. When I slowly return my attention to her, Rozalia refocuses on her heartbeat. I squeeze my glass.

"What about the book?" Ivy asks. At her question, I try to smile again as I put my drink down. *"Enough waiting!"* Rozalia brightens my eyes. I immediately turn away from Ivy before she can notice.

"Nick, are you ok?"
I uncomfortably blink at the floor a few feet ahead of me.

'No! This is not going to happen!'
*"You do as I command. You are **mine**."*

"Nu o voi mai muşca." I say under my breath.
"Want to bet?"

"What did you say-?" Ivy comes around to me and tries to look at my face. I raise a finger, turning away some more, "Wait, I'm forgetting something."

"Nick." she sighs, "Please–what's wrong?"
"Are you going to keep a lady waiting?"

'Leave me alone!'
Rozalia laughs at me, but stops just as soon as she started. She whispers in my voice, "There is nothing wrong Ivy." I fill with fear.
'NO!'

Rozalia makes me turn back to Ivy and my glowing eyes are revealed. Ivy's mouth falls open, "Oh my god,"
Rozalia snickers, "What is it?"

'You are making a mistake!'
She ignores my thought and increases my hunger.

"Your eyes-! They-! They're so...wow..." Ivy can't speak clearly. Rozalia gently places my hands on her shoulders and speaks quieter, "What's that about my eyes?"

'Stop this torture!'
In this moment, I realize am unable to leave; she's keeping me here, forcing me.

'Please, I beg you!'

*"Oh shut up. You want her. Your lust is so intense I don't know how much longer you will be able to **resist**."*

Ivy stares up at me speechlessly as Rozalia slides my hands down her arms and around her waist, then she pulls her up against me and whispers in her ear, "I want you now." Her heart jumps. Now my mouth is watering. The temptation–It's too much!

"In here…?" Ivy nearly mouths.
"In here. Right now." We kiss the pulse point of her neck. My body tenses up, eyes flashing. 'Oh god, I want her!' Ivy squeezes my jacket as I lock lips with her, forcefully unzipping her dress and quickly taking her through the kitchen and into the bedroom.

*Nu o voi mai muşca.

I will not bite her again.

I spin her around, yank her dress and panties off and throw them while pushing her down on the bed. Quickly, I start to undo my pants. *"No! Just a bite! **Bite her now!**"* Rozalia hisses.
'I want more than a bite!' I bark back.

"Too bad. We have no time for that!"
'No, I won't keep a lady waiting! Look at the glowing desire in her eyes!' I finish my pants, quickly take all my clothes off and toss my watch over onto the dresser, then I pause to admire her curvaceous form for a moment. A wicked beam fills my face. Quickly, I climb up the bed and then trail kisses from her shoulder up to her ear where I huskily say, "You're *mine* Ivy." She instinctively moves as I roll her over onto her knees. She rears back like a wild mare, gasping, "Yours," Then she belts a surprised moan as I take her from behind and move quickly. Rozalia growls fiercely. She lunges me down and bites her shoulder, instantly drawing blood, making her nearly scream and almost fling her head back. I drink it in like there is no tomorrow. *"She is mine; all **MINE**! This blood is mine and you are my puppet **TO TAKE IT**! AHAHAHA!!!"* I keep moving faster and faster as the intense sensations of her being around me and her blood overriding

anything else I feel consumes me. How fast her heart is beating; it's like a roller coaster racing down for me. I can't get enough of this! I go down again, licking and sucking around the bite mark. The more I have, the more powerful I *feel*!

"Nick!" she moans, pleasured and pained at the same time. I feel myself getting even closer. I groan louder. Before I climax, she has her release, shouting "Oh Nick!" Yes! That's what I want to hear! I follow after her, flinging my head back with a roar. My head falls down as I breathe heavily and lick my bloody lips.

"See? That wasn't so bad after all." Rozalia says, making me smile arrogantly. I suddenly stop that expression.

Ivy falls onto her stomach and relaxes, soon uttering with a sigh, "What was all that...?"
"Are you complaining? You want more?" I ask. As I fall over next to her and place my hands over my chest, she turns on her side and cradles her face in her hand while watching me in bashful amazement. Thank goodness she doesn't give the biting a second thought. Rozalia made sure she wouldn't–again.

"More? Hm, could I handle that?" she asks.
"You have no choice." I chuckle.

"I have no choice?" She's stunned.
I smile darkly, "None whatsoever." She studies my face while her cheeks get pinker by the second. God, those pale blue eyes of hers...how innocent she is. She deserves so much better than me...but I need her. Slowly, I lean in and kiss her lips tenderly. She takes a hold of my hair and squeezes gently, kissing back deeply, passionately. Then we slow to a pause.

"Nick," she sits up and lowers her head a little, "I'm not safe, am I?" Her words sadden me. I rise and pull her close, wrapping my arm around her and frowning, "As long as you are with me, you are safe." I kiss her temple, then get off the bed and start putting my clothes on. "Don't worry my love, I have everything under control now. I have everything required to put an end to this chaos. But I want you to do something for me." She pulls the sheets up to her neck and lies back, "What is it?"

"You should spend some time with your family. I have many things to do that will keep me from you, from this afternoon until tomorrow."

"The party is tomorrow." She says in a reminding way.

"In the evening, yes. Please Ivy, they would be worried about you. Have you called anyone while being here?"

"I called Gina…"

I shake my head, "Not good enough. I will take you home this afternoon."

She stares at me. I do the same to her, sternly.

"Ok…this afternoon." She says.

"Good girl." I sit on the edge of the bed to put my shoes on, "So the only thing that happened to you was being led around by Corneliu?"

"Uh…" she gets quiet. I pause what I'm doing.
Now I'm all ears.

"Not long before breakfast, I had an encounter with…'those two'." She says that very hesitantly. She wanted to hide this from me.

"Go on." I whisper while fitting on the second shoe.

"…They appeared to me and Maria tried to stab me with a comb. Jennifer stopped her, telling her 'not yet'. They threatened me Nick." After hearing that…I take my watch off my dresser. Rozalia's anger is building now and it makes me squeeze it until it shatters. Her feelings have magnified mine to infuriation. Ivy blinks repeatedly at me, shocked.

Glaring down at the pieces around my feet, I hold in my anger as much as I can. "I will drive you home. They cannot follow you off this island…Ivy." I look at her with cold piercing eyes. She gulps and nods slowly, then definitely.

"I must speak with Walter now. You can make yourself at home in my room. No one can get past here. But I do suggest you get dressed quickly. I will have your bag brought up to you."

"Ok, but spirits can't pass through walls?" she asks.
I laugh softly as I go to the kitchen door, "No no my dear, they only do that if there was a door there once."
"Spirits aren't physical though."

I point to my head, "It's all in the mind."
She forms a thoughtful face, then glances over toward my mess.

"Don't worry, it will be cleaned up later." I say.
"Alright, I'll be in your room." She mumbles.
I wink at her and leave.

Immediately, as soon as I'm back in my office, Rozalia throws a tantrum.
'NO, DON'T START IT NOW! I KNOW! She is leaving soon; your wish is about to come true!'

"Something must be done!"
'There is nothing you can do yet!' I page Walter to come to the office.

"Oh, is that so?!"
'You better watch yourself; I will make this conversation audible.'
"HOW DARE YOU!"

I wait a few minutes. Finally, Walter knocks on the door. I invite him in and he smiles lightly at me. I wave to a chair at the front of the desk, "Please sit down. Tell me—how many guests are we expecting tomorrow evening?"

"Approximately 200 sir." He says while sitting.
I suddenly smile, "Hm, that's quite a lot of energy, no?"

"Indeed. I can't wait." He's being sarcastic.
"I think you will be just fine." I sardonically say, indicating his heart issues. He returns that same look with his own.

"Sir, the library—how did that go?"
I think back on what all happened.

"It went well." I smile.
It wasn't pleasant.

I continue, "I got the information and even took a picture of it

315

with my phone."

A gradual smile appears on his face, "Ahh, very nice sir."

I gladly take the phone out of my pocket and set it on the desk, "Yes. Now to access that photo and save it to my files." I turn the computer on and let it boot.

"What exactly is this about, if you don't mind?" he asks. Watching the monitor, I quietly answer, "Something you don't deal with everyday." I then smile at him again, "It's a way to expel…evil. This book is quite old, and I trust it."

"I see." He murmurs, not entirely believing me. I change the subject, "Ivy will be going home in about an hour and will be returning tomorrow afternoon. Page one of the maids to bring her bag up here to my office and make sure to let Leonardo know."

"Yes sir. And Esmeralda?"

"No no, I will drive her home."

"Of course." He laces his hands together down on his lap, chuckling slightly to himself.

I make a somewhat humored face at him.

Chapter 36

-Ivy-

After taking a quick bath in Nick's bathroom, getting dressed in my skinny jeans, black sweater, white coat and rider boots, I get my stuff, say goodbye to Walter and the maids, then Nick and I leave for Leonardo's boathouse.

During the walk there, Nick seems tense. I think I know why though; it must be the spirits out here. But I thought they were friendly. I hesitantly ask what's wrong out of the corner of my mouth. He doesn't reply, which makes me look at him in concern. His eyes are searching all around in front of us in a suspicious sort of way. He turns his head slightly to the right but immediately returns to staring ahead.

"Nick, are you ok?"
"Hm? Oh, I'm fine."
I watch him oddly.

We get to Leonardo's, have a small chat with him about the weather, the party tomorrow night and then we board the boat. Nick double checks to see if I have everything. I assure him that I do. It's cute yet annoying.

It seems Leonardo keeps this boat ready to go all the time. I guess he would have to. He never knows when someone will need him. For some reason though, that's something I half-expected. Still, I forget how life works on this island. Except for Leonardo, everything is planned out; everything has a schedule; everyone is doing something all the time. Such busy lives these people have.

As we're leaving for Esmeralda's place, Nick and I sit down on the cushy white seats and watch the wake from the bow as we cross. He and I are strangely silent–until he takes my hand with a gentle squeeze and looks at me with a sort of loving smile. That beautiful heart-stopping smile…

"Are you feeling alright?" he asks.

"Yes, I'm fine. You?"

He kisses my knuckles, "I'm feeling wonderful."

I tuck my hair behind my ear, furrowing my eyebrows some, "What was that back there? Who or what were you looking at?" He blinks once at me and concentrates on my face, boring those extreme blue eyes into mine. It's becoming too much to handle…again.

"I don't want to explain it. Forgive me." Oh…

"A tragic thing happened…" I questionably say.

"You can say that." He gazes at the water again.

I gulp slowly and join him in doing that.

He looks at Leonardo, leaning in close to my ear, "Alright, I will tell you. I'll be honest. A murder happened there over a hundred years ago." I quickly look at him again. He places his finger over his lips, shaking his head slowly. I blink many times. He pauses, then smirks, "Just kidding." My mouth drops.

He winks at me, slapping his knee, "Just kidding!" he laughs. I hit him, "You're terrible!"

"I know!" He continues to laugh.

"Ok, but seriously…why did you behave so oddly?"

He looks down, slowing his laughter, "Indians doing strange things with each other."

"Like what?"

"It's personal." He shoots me a devilish gleam. I cover my mouth, blushing. He sits back, wrapping an arm around me and pulling me close, "It will be ok Ivy. Everything will be just fine."

I sigh, "I won't live that down; what you said."

"You are going to have to."

"Yeah, ok." I giggle.

Soon, we arrive at Esmeralda's. She greets us with a wave just before catching the rope from Leonardo and begins to tie the boat. Nick gets off the boat first and extends his hand to me. As a silent joke, I bow before taking it. Leonardo is amused with my actions and laughs a little. We all go inside the house and Nick tells me to wait in the living room. He and Leonardo leave me to talk to Esmeralda in an adjacent room off to my left.

As I hear them talking, I admire how the place is set up. It's nicer than I thought. Like before, I imagined it to be dark and eerie but it's quite nice; very comfy with the western American style. I compliment her on her home and she gives me a warm smile in thanks. "This home was built in 40's, actually. It's been renovated a few times." She glances up and around at the room in a thoughtful way. "Oh wow, that's cool!" I say. A few more moments go by and then I hear Nick say, "Alright then." I turn toward his direction as he comes back. Once again, watching him, I just cannot stop staring at how handsome he is, and the memory of how animalistic he was earlier just keeps playing over and over in my head. I try very hard to hold a straight face and I try not to blush–but it's pretty much impossible to control the last thing.

"Well, Miss Summers," he smiles at me kindly, offering his arm before we go out the door, but once the other two aren't looking, it becomes quite a dark smile. I purse my lips before grinning and look away from him as we walk outside to his car.

He whispers in my ear, "What did I say about hiding your smile?" I slightly look up at him. He's watching me dead seriously. Very, very intense. Oh my gosh. He's so intimidating!
I don't know how to reply.

"Smile more; hide it less." He says as he opens the passenger side. I'm quiet–until finally I say, "And if I don't?"
"You will find out later." He smiles that arrogant smile. Ah great...he's leaving me in suspense again. I give him a type of skeptical face while getting in the car.

He shuts the door and starts going around to his side. As I watch how authoritatively he walks, his words from earlier 'You're *mine* Ivy' and when he said 'You have no choice. None whatsoever' repeat in my head. This isn't the first time that's happened to me. I'm 'his'–the rich man who lives in a castle and lives an extraordinary life–I'm his. However did I get here? Wow!

He gets in, starting the car right away and looking at me. He won't say anything; he's just observing me. Why does he do that?

I quickly smile, "What?"

He smiles back in his fanged way, "You are blushing *again*, and...it's adorable." I immediately look down with a giggle. He takes my chin in two fingers, "Look at me." I blink at him, lips soon parting. He gazes at my mouth, then he kisses me slowly. In the middle of the kiss, he shifts the car in gear. Moving away from my face with a daring expression, he asks in a low tone, "Ready to go?" I breathe in slowly, "Yeah, yeah I am." He looks ahead with a deep soft laugh, thrilled by how I react toward his behavior.

We're off with his lead foot. I grip a part of the door and try to remain calm.

"Ivy," he chuckles.

"What?"

"Your heart is racing."

I quickly look at him as he repeatedly glances out of the corner of his eye at me.

"How do you know that?" I ask. He shrugs a shoulder, "It's just a feeling." Suddenly, he lets off the gas. Now we're cruising up the lonely road.

I stare at him, "Really?"

"What? You don't like this pace?" he asks.

"You...don't have to slow down that much." While watching me, he presses down on the gas pedal a little more at a time. He's not even watching the road!

I check in front of us many times.

"Nick!" I finally snap. He throws his head back with a big evil laugh and then he focuses on the road.

"Don't worry babe, I've got it under control."

I fold my arms, rolling my eyes to what he says.

We approach my apartment door. Nothing seems out of the ordinary. I unlock it and go in first. He follows slowly behind with my bag, which he insisted on carrying. I didn't want him to do that but he did it anyway.

I tell him to set it on the couch in the living room as I place my keys on the counter and inspect everything to make sure it's how I left it. You can't trust anyone these days–especially in an apartment complex.

While standing here in my kitchen, I stop everything, beginning to feel the familiar sadness I had after the first time I left the island. Knowing he'll be gone...it tears a piece of me away. I don't want to be alone. Why am I so insecure with him? It seems almost unnatural. It's just overnight.

"Ivy..." he comes up behind me and hugs me, "It won't be long."
I close my eyes, taking a deep breath, "...I'm such an idiot."
"Don't you ever say that."
I turn around to him.

"You can't help what you feel. I don't want to leave but I must."
I understand what he says but it's not right to be so clingy like this!

"Nick, I totally get that but-" "Stop." He says. "Watch these." he points to his eyes, "Don't be sad anymore. You must rest, have time to yourself and time with your family, ok?" As he talks, there's something weird happening with his eyes; it's like they're glowing and the room is getting darker. "Nick...your eyes..." Wow...I'm in...complete awe of them; such beautiful blue diamonds shining within the darkness.

He smiles softly, "I know..." I gradually smile back in the same way. He wraps an arm around my waist, pulling me up against him and lifting my chin with the other hand, "Everything will be ok, yes?" I find myself gaping up at him again, and I bite my lip, "Yes," My god...he's like an angel. "Good." he slowly tilts his head, brushing his lips over mine. I pull him closer, kissing him back with more passion; the sort of kiss where it would seem him and I would never let go of each other. But he slips away, and goes to the door.

"I will pick you up tomorrow afternoon. Around 2 o'clock."

I rub my arms, nodding, "Tomorrow afternoon."

"Take care of yourself and have a good time." He says.

"Ok, I will. You too."

He bows his head and leaves.

I bring a hand up to my mouth, staring at the door and stand in silence trying to collect my thoughts. "Ok." I get my phone from my bedroom and turn it on. Immediately, it shows many missed calls from family members, a couple from Eric and some from Gina. Well, who should I call first? Since I made a kind of deal with Gina about convincing my mom to think I broke my phone, I'll call her first.

Because she might be busy... I text her: 'Gina, I'm back home now. Can you talk?' I wait a minute, then put the phone down and shrug out of my white coat.

Here I notice over the last few days, I haven't worried about my makeup like I usually do. What–is Nick changing my attitude about that too?

My phone beeps. I grab it and see Gina's reply: 'Hey hey! If it's not Princess Ivy of Castle Dracula! No, I'm not busy. I'm on lunch break.' I roll my eyes with a scoff and stupid smile, then call her.

It rings twice before she picks up.

"Hey Ivy, what's happening? How ya doin'?"

"I came home for the rest of the day." I smile, "I'm ok. How are you?"

"For the rest of the day? Oh, I'm alright. Thanks for asking."

"Yeah, but I'll be goin' back tomorrow. I have things to take care of here on the mainland."

"So you're staying with this guy now?"

"Well..."

"Ohhh, you're not sure." She laughs.

"No, I'm sure. Quite sure. I am staying with him."

"WHAT?"

"Gina, calm down!"

"Ivy…" she gets quiet, "You just met him. Is this a good idea?"

"He's perfect for me. I strongly think I've fallen in love with him…but I'm not revealing that until he does first."

"He has you under some sort of spell…" she says.

"Maybe so. I just know that he's become everything to me."

"Ok Ivy…if you say so."

I nod to myself, "I do say so. Gina–My mom–what happened between you and her?"

"Well she said ok, though it was a little hard convincing her about everything. She wanted to see you but I insisted that you have it all under control and everything will be ok. Excuse me for asking–is there a reason why you won't tell her and your dad about your boyfriend?" My 'boyfriend' she calls him. Is that what he is? Or more than that?

"Ivy, you there?"

"Yeah…" I squeeze the phone a little, "No there's not. Don't worry; I'll tell them. It shouldn't be a secret anyway."

"Not anymore!" she says.

"Well thank you for doing that for me. How can I repay you?"

"You don't need to do anything." She says, "I hope the best for you, as always. Anyway, I'm sorry to cut things short, but I have to go back to work."

"Ok then. Have a good day."

"Thanks. You too."

I look at my phone and press the end button.

As much as I love my parents, I think I might be dreading calling them. They worry quite a lot. It's the right thing to do though. No, I'll visit them–tomorrow. Right now, I need alone time.

I go in the kitchen to grab a snack out of the fridge and smell something rotten. "Ugh, yuck!" Checking around in the fridge, I find a bag of old seafood I forgot I had and toss it in the trash. After spraying some air freshener and washing my hands, I get a box of crackers out of the cupboard and go turn the computer on. I have to check my bills and bank. As I wait for it to boot, my mind wanders off into the conversation I just had, and all through it, Nick's face continues to pop up. He brings feelings out of me that I thought I would never have. He's the one I've dreamed about in a sense. He is…like my prince charming or something. I flush, placing a hand over my forehead and chuckling to myself, "Prince charming… How different it is for me to talk that way. It's just how I feel though."

I finish checking everything and look at the clock. It's about 4. Wow, Gina took a LATE lunch. There's no possible way I could go to my parents' place and come back before dusk.

"I'll write in my journal." I get up and go find it in my room. Honestly, I didn't imagine having nothing to do.

Let's see… Where did I leave off? I put pen to paper right away, losing myself in the bliss of writing about 'my prince charming' and what all has happened to me there at the castle. But then there are the dark parts of it…the dangerous 'spirits'. Jennifer and Maria are more than that; they have to be. I stop what I'm doing and look to the window in growing worry. Nick is dealing with them alone. Well Walter is there… No, they concentrated on me and it kept him safe! Stop Ivy, this is crazy. What do you think he did before he met you? Jennifer was there *long* before you.

"No, god damn it!" I shoot up from my bed, clutching the sides of my head. He's not safe! He's not safe with both of them there. Surely Jennifer is teaching Maria how to be like her! Corneliu is a peacekeeper, but only him against those two? They seem like demons. He might even be one. I don't know what the hell they are but they are *very* dangerous!

I snatch my phone and search everywhere for Nick's number. Oh, I really hope he still has his phone! "Shit! Where's his number?!" I empty my purse over the bed and scatter everything out but I can't find it anywhere. I collapse on the edge of the bed, a heavy sigh of hopelessness leaving me.

Gnawing on my knuckles, I look at the window again. Please be ok Nick–please.

Suddenly, my phone rings, startling me. I quickly take it, hoping it's Nick. I'm stunned when I see who it is.

I answer, "Mom?"

"Ivy! Your phone is working!" I blink a few times, confused at first. Oh yeah, my phone was supposedly broken. This anxiety ruined my focus. Automatically, I know Gina told her I'm able to use the phone. I'm not happy about that; it wasn't for her to do. But I'm glad to hear from her.

"Yes it is!" I say, "Well no, actually–I got a new one. Same model." I really dislike lying to cover my ass...

"Oh, wow. Was it expensive?"

"No, not really."

"Good, I'm glad to hear that. So everything is ok now?"

"Yeah, everything's fine. All is back to normal. The whole thing of getting a new phone though, it sure was aggravating."

"I bet. You know, Gina called me not too long ago and told me about your phone. I'm surprised you didn't call me."

"I just got it." I slightly laugh.

"Ohh, calling friends before family now, eh?"

"No no, it wasn't meant that way." I say.

"I'm joking." She snickers.

"Oh, sorry. Hey listen, I've got a major thing to tell you. First, where's Dad?"

"He's not home yet." She says.

"Ok. You remember the guy I saw in the coffee shop that I told you about?"

"What about him...?"

"I uh...kinda..."

She sighs, "What Ivy?"

"We're together..."

"What the hell! I mean, what in the world?!"

"Mommm…"

"You said he annoys you and you seemed to really dislike-! Ivy, that's just weird. Did you hit your head or something?"

"No! Mom–please!"

"Who is this guy?"

"He's the executive assistant to the owner of a heavy machinery corporation."

"Oh my god…"

"Yeah, I know."

"You hit gold girl!"

I scoff, "A minute ago you weren't saying that."

"Well you know. Oh, hold on–your Dad just got home."

"Mom, how about I visit you tomorrow and tell you more about this guy then? I have something to tell you." I knew this would catch up to me–I knew it.

"You sure?"

"I'm positive. I've got *plenty* to talk about."

"You're really making me wonder what you've been up to Ivy…"

"You'll find out." I say, "Now enjoy your time together."

"Alright. I'm about to set dinner on the table; fried chicken, corn and mashed potatoes."

"Sounds delicious! I might cook spaghetti."

"Eat well tonight. I love you."

"Yes mom…" I then laugh, "I love you too."

We hang up and I go find the ingredients to make my spaghetti. The worry about Nick's safety is not as much as before, but it's still there. I can't wait to be with him again…

Chapter 37

Later into the night; I toss and turn in my bed as I dream of being at a castle. It feels completely real. I'm in a grand room with a butler, some maids and my dream man. But this isn't right...it's not right at all. I don't recognize anyone, but this is Dmitri's place–I know that for sure.

"Ivy, are you alright?" My dream man asks. I don't answer as I scan his face like I'm lost. I love him but...

"Miss Summers?" I hear the butler. I look and see Walter.
Oh my god.

Quickly, I turn back to my dream man. He still looks the same. What's happening here?
"Excuse me," I say to him, "I need to speak with-" I step closer to Walter, "you, sir...if that's ok." The butler seems a little confused, yet he accepts and walks with me toward the grand staircase.

"Walter..." I say.
"Yes madam?" **Oh! It *is* him!**

"Who is that man? And those maids–who are they?" **Just to be sure...**
"Miss Summers...?" He's astounded. I'm not joking, and he sees it.

"Why, that's Pamela, Angel and Christine...and that is-" He says the man's name but it's muffled. "Pardon me?" I question. He repeats himself, "Madam Ivy...that's Nick." My mouth falls open. NICK! I dart my eyes over at him. He's smiling at me warmly, genuinely.
My lashes flutter, "...Nicolai..."

Suddenly, I hear a phone ringing. I squint, open my eyes and smack my lips a couple times. I realize I've been drooling; there's a pool of spit on my pillow. Wow, I must've slept really good! Oh my god...it's him! It's always been *him*! Holy shit! I finally have my answer!

Reaching over and grabbing my phone, I wipe my mouth and blink a few times to help adjust my eyes quicker. Wow…I'm so shocked, and happy! It was him all along. I cannot explain all the mixed emotions I have at the moment; I'm between confused, stunned and ecstatic.

The caller ID says it's Mom.
I answer, "Hey, good morning," I look at the clock. Oh geez, it's 9:50am!

"Good morning! You sound like you just woke up… You slept in a long time!"
"I did." I smile with a small laugh.

"Well, sorry I woke you. What time are you coming over?"
"Oh! Sorry I didn't specify when! Well I still need to take my shower and get ready to go."

"It's ok Ives. I actually have to go out today; do you want to meet at Lounge 'N Sip for a few minutes?"
"Yeah, that sounds great. I'll get ready to go real quick and then I'll call you."

"Alright, talk to you soon. Love you, bye."
"Love you too, bye."

I toss the phone on the bed and hit the shower. The hot water feels great over my shoulders and the steam clears my head. I have to wipe the mirror because I left the exhaust fan off.

Still smiling from that dream I had, I put diamond earrings on and then start on my makeup. I have all these choices of eye shadows and my favorite dark red lip gloss staring at me. I don't have time, nor as much interest in putting all that on. I put on a light-blue long sleeved shirt, dark jeans, black high-heeled boots and then decide to only use mascara, the powder and the lip gloss.

I finish up with the blow dryer and go look in the fridge for a snack on the way to the coffee place. Nothing looks appetizing. Not even that yogurt I always like to eat. Nick has spoiled me indeed.

I shut the fridge door, grab my purse and give everything a last look before leaving. On my way down, I run into my favorite neighbor, who's holding a cup of coffee. He does this every time, no matter the time of day.

"Ivy, long time no see." He sips from his cup.
I smile shortly, "Yeah, I've been looking into moving."
"Oh wow."
I nod, "Yep. But I have to hurry now to meet my Mom somewhere. Talk to you later."
"Ok, see ya. Drive carefully out there."

I raise my hand with the car keys and keep going down until I'm at my mailbox. I find nothing but more junk and a bank statement. I stuff it all in my purse, take my phone out and head outside for my car.

Once I get in my jaguar, I call Mom and wait for her to pick up. In the meantime, I think of Gina and what she said about Nick 'having me under a spell'. He sure does. He's the most interesting person I'll ever know, no doubt about that.

Then I start thinking about finding another job. What do I do about that? I only have limited medical skills.

She finally answers her phone. "Hi Ivy."
"Hey mom. I'm outside my apartment, in my car."

"Alright, I'm about 10 miles from the coffee place."
"I'll head that way now and buy our coffee when I get there." I say.

"Ok. I'll have the pumpkin drink."
I confirm that, end the call and begin my drive there.

Now at the shop, I check my face in the rear view mirror one last time before hurrying inside. The first place I look is where Nick sits with his journal. Yeah, it's an instinctual thing for me to do. I go through the short line, buy her ice-blended pumpkin coffee and a hot pumpkin coffee for me, then I go to Nick's place and sit down. It seems like a good idea to sit here.

After a few minutes, I see her park her van and come inside. She searches for me and sees my hand raised. She comes right to me like she's the only one in the room and sits down, smiling. I push her coffee to her, "Morning Mom." She takes it, thanking me with a very relieved look in her eyes. She loves this coffee. "Good morning. Thank you. So…" she starts taking the wrapper off her straw, "Tell me about this mystery man you got together with." Yep. Right down to business. That's my Mom.

"Well, his name is Nicolai Francis. He comes here all the time. And guess what? That strange building on that island we saw–he lives there."

Her eyebrows rise, "Ohh, really?"
"Yeah. Mom, listen…I haven't told you anything. I'm sorry. The weekend of my birthday, I actually had Gina go there with me. That guy has a butler and everything–well, sorta… The owner of the castle–Dmitri Vladoiu–everything there is his and under his employ, but Nick is his executive assistant. So you know what that means."

"Wow Ivy…that's quite a thing to keep from your parents." She is very amazed yet at the same time, a bit ashamed.
"I know." I sigh, taking a drink of my coffee.

"And you too are together?" she asks.
I nod. She looks quizzical. "This leaves me speechless, honestly. It's so bizarre to me. It…it doesn't seem real at all."

"But it is!" I say, "Trust me, when I really think about it, it's like a fairy tale. But it's really happening Mom. It is."

"You don't need to repeat yourself. I do believe you. I just want you to be safe. You don't feel strange about this at all? You were avoiding him, weren't you? You behave as if you never knew him." I sit quietly after she asks that. Then I let out a slow sigh, "I'm sorry Mom…I lied. I was so intimidated by him that I felt like he was going to follow me or something. I couldn't handle being here any longer with his eyes on me like that, so I told you he annoyed me and I wanted to get away from him as fast as I could.

Please don't be mad. He's really a great guy and I judged him all wrong." She stares at me, then raises her hands, "Ivy, it's your life. I'm not mad. I want you to be careful. I'll only give you my opinions."

"I'll be fine." I assure with a single nod.

"Your Dad would be completely stunned."

I scoff, "No doubt. But I'll tell him in time."

"I won't say anything for now." She says.

I slightly point at her, "Like I said; I'll tell him. But anyway, I'll be going back to the castle this afternoon. Nick is going to pick me up around 2."

"You're going back? In his car? What's he drive?"

I grin arrogantly to myself. "A dark-red Aston Martin."

She gasps, "Oh wow…those are expensive and classy! I imagine you've been in it already…?"

"I know." I laugh, "Yes I have. It's fast and really smooth." She warily smiles, "Girl, what am I gonna do with you?" I playfully shrug my shoulders, drinking more coffee.

"Well it's 10:40 now." She says, looking at the clock above my head. Her telling that reminds me of tonight. This is going to be quite a day to remember.

"Yeah," I slowly smile.

"So Ivy…you say his name is Nicolai. That's not an American name exactly. What is he?"

"Romanian." I'm smiling wide in my head right now.

"That's a Romanian name?" Now she's disbelieving.

"I don't think so… Maybe he had his name changed." I say. She hums, "I wonder why he would do that."

"Beats me. You know, I haven't even considered that." She shakes her finger at me, "Well…consider it."

"Ok Mom." I look away, finishing my coffee. Something comes to my mind. She doesn't know what happened with my job. Oh, what would she say about that? But, it's my life…not hers.

"What's wrong?" she asks. I look at her and set my coffee cup down, "There's something else I held back from you and Dad."

"What? Are you pregnant?" Her brows rise. Whoa now, I didn't see *that* coming!
"What the-? Mom, no!"

"What is it Ivy?" she laughs.
I sigh and let my head hang low, "I lost my job. Last week."

"You did? Oh my god... What have you been doing since then?"
I look back up to her, "Well...I've been at that castle."

"You're living with him?" she surprisingly asks. "Well...yes...I guess. It sounds bad, I know. I didn't ask for it; it just happened. After we got to know each other, I told him what happened and he suggested I stay there, and I agreed. We really like each other, Mom."
"But Ivy! Again–you hardly know the guy!" I quickly stand up from the table but then realize how defensive I'm getting. I calm down and take my cup, muttering, "I'm still alive and well, aren't I? If he was bad news, I would've told you." I go throw my cup away and then come back.

As I sit down, she nearly glares at me. After I look at her for a few seconds, she loses that face.

"Are you moving out of your apartment?" she asks.
"I don't know yet."

"Well, let me know."
"I will, don't worry."

"Hey..." she gently grabs my hand, resting it over the center of the table, "You know I want the best for you. Follow your heart, but also notice any red flags that might start showin' up, ok?" "Ok Mom."

She glances at the clock, "It's 11 now."
"I have a little time left." I say.

"We can go clothes shopping if you want."
I stare at her.

She smirks, "Just kidding. But seriously, you do need more clothes."
I groan like a child, "I don't want to go clothes shopping!"

"What are you going to do for the next few hours?" I pause. Then my eyes go into two thin lines, "Clothes shopping."
She smiles again, "Good! Now," she stands up with her coffee cup, "let's go. Follow me." She motions me to stand, "Come on, get up!" I roll my eyes and do as I'm told. She puts her hand on my back, leading me out, "Stop being such a prude. It will only be for about an hour or so." She drinks more of her coffee.

"Hmmmph…"

Finally, the shopping is done. It's now 12:55. I have to rush back home. We're now standing by our cars outside an outlet store. Thank goodness we're not far from my apartment. We made a deal to stay within that area. I only got a few items, whereas she got much more. I got some earrings, a pair of shoes, two shirts and a pair of skinny jeans; all of which were marked down. I bet if Nick were with us, he wouldn't let me get that stuff. He would want me to wear expensive clothing. I'm definitely ok with that.

"Well, it was nice shopping with you." She says.
"Yeah, it turned out better than I thought it would." I admit, chuckling some.

"Alright, go on home. I've got things to do at the house." She hugs me and then adds, "Be good and be safe, you hear me?"
"I will Mom–I promise."

She winks at me while we both get in our vehicles, then she starts her van and leaves before me. I get behind her at the exit. When it's clear, we beep at each other and go our separate ways.

During my drive home, I'm so preoccupied by everything that's happened to me within the last few weeks. The way I'm watching traffic; it's like I'm just naturally wavering through, not paying close attention.

What is Nick doing right now? What is anyone at the castle

doing right now? Surely they're getting ready for this evening... And I wonder what I'm supposed to wear. Wow, this is such an awkward situation. You'd think everything would be taken care of by now, right? Or maybe...maybe these 'preparations' have something to do with the spirits...

I really, really hope he's ok. Walter obviously has no clue what's truly going on there. Neither do the maids; they probably don't concern themselves with anything. It's just Nick and I.

On a different note, something tells me Mom will tell Dad about Nick very soon. It's nearly impossible to hold something like that back for a while.

"Oh well...that's not really something to worry about." I muse.

Finally, I'm home. I climb the stairs as quickly as I can, go in my apartment, toss my purse on my bed and start unpacking my bag, then I refill it with other clothes and more accessories. Two bags; I'm better prepared this time! Yes indeed!

It takes me about 15 minutes to do all this.

I stop, thinking I'm finished when I glance over at my journal on my nightstand. I didn't take it last time. Do I take it this time? I might be too busy for it now. I've never asked myself this question before, honestly.

My doorbell rings. My belly clenches. I know who it is. I go out of my room and look through the peephole of the door. Nick... I bite my lip with a growing smile and open the door.

He winks at me and presents a dark red rose, "Buna ziua, iubirea mea," He makes me blush. I daintily take the rose, "Multumesc." At least I know what that means. It means thanks! Me saying that surprises him. "Very good..." he says as I invite him inside.

"But do you know what I said?" he asks, walking into the kitchen.

"No, I sure don't." I laugh.

He grins at me, "I said good afternoon my love."

"Ohh," I snicker, "Well good afternoon to you too."

He starts that strange contemplative stare while I sniff the rose and try to decide whether to put it in a vase or not. "What is it?" I ask. A mysterious smile creeps at the corners of his lips as his head slowly tips to one side, "You were worrying about me last night…" I suddenly halt everything. How does he know that?

"You seem bewildered." He simpers.
"Well I was worried." I murmur, "How did you know?"

"I know that face."
"You know what face?" I repeat in an oddly amused way.

He steps closer, "I know it."
I look up at him silently.

"I told you I have everything under control." He says. Oh…I feel so on the spot now.
"You always have this stare…like it's straight into my soul." I say, very quietly.

"Are you *questioning* me?"
I gulp, "I am."

He smiles darkly, "It's just how I am." My heart jumps a little as he brushes his warm fingers across my cheek. "Stop worrying…because I am taking you home now."

"Home," I begin to smile. He winks and kisses my hand. Watching him, I forget everything; just lost in this state he's put me in, but then I come back to reality. "Ahem," I lightly laugh, "My bags…"
"Go on," he waves a hand, then slides both of them into his pockets. I again flash a bashful smile. Carefully, I set the rose down and go into my room to get my stuff.

As I'm collecting the bags, looking around for other things I could be forgetting, I hear him stop in the doorway. I glance over my shoulder at him. He flashes his eyes up to my face.

I suddenly smile at him, "What were you looking at?"
"What do you think? Miss Summers, you have a nice ass…staring me in the face."

I stand up slowly with my heavy bags, sarcastically blinking at

him. He walks up and takes them from me, "I will carry these."
"But-!" "Ah!" he lifts them up in the air effortlessly, "I will carry them."

"Oh my…" I absentmindedly say. He chuckles, "Come now."

I giggle, following him. Before heading out of the apartment, I grab my purse, the rose and lock the door, then we're gone.

As we're driving along, I feel completely content being with him again and his pace is so smooth, I could just fall asleep. It's so peaceful watching how we pass the trees and the sunlight feels wonderful on my face. While I'm admiring the scenery, he talks to Esmeralda on the phone, letting her know we are almost to her place. He puts his phone down between his legs and sighs softly. I take his hand, slowly smiling.

"I am glad to have you Ivy. Without you, I honestly don't know how life would be." I look at him, and he does the same with me. It's a strange thing to say; I am not sure what to think of it. Though, it warms me and makes me happy.

I have to admit my feelings… As many as they are, where do I even begin?
I focus on our hands, thinking about it.

"Nick," I look back up to his face, "you make my world a whole different place…you make it so much bigger and extraordinary." My voice is small, sincere. He only studies me in adoration. Because he doesn't say anything, I feel I have to turn away; back to looking out the window. I've stated my true feelings; I've taken that leap...

"I adore everything about you Ivy." I shut my eyes at that, smiling stupidly.
For a few more seconds, there's silence between us.

I start talking again, "This morning…I had coffee with my Mom at the coffee shop."
"And…?"

"I haven't told anyone about us." I say.

He becomes more interested. "You told her?"

"Yes I did."

He smiles ahead, "What did she say?"

"She is stunned mostly." I nervously laugh.
"Heheheh…how cute. You have not said anything to your father, I assume."

"No."

He pouts, "Well why not?"

I start laughing at him, "I…I don't know!"
"Oh yes you *do* know."

"I do know, huh?" I fold my arms.
"Of course you do. You are his daughter. It's natural."

I look out my window again without saying anything else.
"Don't worry sweetheart; that only means you come from a good family."

"Yeah, perhaps. What about your family? Where are they?"
He sighs in a matter-of-fact way, "They are all in Romania."

"They won't come here?"
"No. They love their country and prefer to stay there." He shrugs.

"Huh, interesting." I say.
"Indeed." he halfway smirks, "I am the…black sheep of my family."

"So am I." I say, amusing him. Then I start straightening up in my seat as we pull into Esmeralda's driveway and park the car in her garage. She's waiting outside for us. She sees me in the car and smiles at me.

Nick parks the car and gets out quickly. Before I can open my door, he's opening it for me. Esmeralda looks amused but doesn't say anything. He hands her the keys and cell phone and she tells us Leonardo is inside the boathouse.

"Alright then." He lightly shakes her hand and guides me there. She follows us.
When we get there, Leonardo greets me happily. He and

Esmeralda must really like my company. They don't talk to us for very long though, since they know Nick is in a hurry.

Nick holds my hand while stepping aboard and then Leonardo follows behind us. Just before we go, Nick makes sure everything is secure; my luggage and me. He's so protective.

Esmeralda casts off the lines and we back out of the boathouse.

While crossing the Sound, I gaze at the top of that big castle filled with so many secrets. I no longer wonder why Dmitri never goes there. I can understand why. But the place is also so luxurious.

I lower my gaze but then smile at Nick as he wraps an arm around my shoulder.
"So...I've got quite a surprise for you." He says.

"What is it?" I ask, grinning daringly.
He mysteriously thins his eyes at me, "It's a surprise."

I clam up.
"And I will not allow any hinting either." He lifts his chin, looking down his nose at me.

"Ohh-kay," I giggle. He kisses my temple and then looks out at the water. I wonder what's up his sleeve this time.

Soon, we arrive at Leonardo's boathouse. Before we get off the boat, Nick talks with him about tonight. From watching and listening to what they're saying, I learn the ferry has been hired to run from 6 to midnight. 7 o'clock is when the party starts, and Leonardo will be available in case any of the guests have any emergencies. Sounds like a good plan to me.

Nick picks up my bags and starts to get off the boat. Leonardo slightly points at the bags in his hands, "Would you like some help with those?" Nick laughs with a small shake of the head, "No no, I've got it. Thanks."

"No problem." Leonardo salutes him, and then we start heading for the castle. Yeah, he's got it alright. I smile shyly to my secret joke.

Chapter 38

Waiting in the grand room as Nick speaks with Walter and hands the bags to the maids, I see the final touches for the party; a red carpet with the classic red rope fence along it, leading to the left archway. The ballroom is that way. I can't wait for tonight. It excites me so much! I turn around to Nick with a juvenile smile. He thinks it's cute and funny.

Offering his arm, he flirtatiously flickers his eyes at me, "Your surprise awaits you in your room, Miss Summers..." I bite my lip. He thumbs over it, "I love it when you do that. I'm going to bite that lip." That takes the breath right out of me; what a hot thing to say! Once again, I smile in that stupid bashful way. "Come." He takes me upstairs, and then I start to get that heavy feeling; the closer I am to the Bojnice room, the worse it gets. Why though? That is the calmest room I've been in. All of a sudden, just before we reach it, the heavy feeling disappears.

I instantly look at him, remembering when he said he has control over this sort of thing. He has the same vicious scowl as he did when I saw him walking up the hallway in the basement. It's so threatening and unsettling. He's not quite...himself. His muscles are tensing too. What am I missing?

Before I can ask any questions, he lets his arm fall, turns in front of me and opens the door with the sort of smile as if nothing ever happened. "Your room, Ivy." I stay put, watching him. He waits silently for me to go in. Finally, he asks, "What's wrong?"

"Please tell me what all that was about. I'm not stupid; I know something just happened."
He doesn't answer.

"I don't want to be in the dark anymore Nick." I shake my head. He breathes in slowly. Now he's bothered. It's making me want to sink my head into my shoulders. "Nick, tell me!" I say.

"No no no–you come with me!" He grabs my hand and pulls me

into the room, shutting the door with his heel, then he sits me down on the end of the bed and drills his eyes into mine, **very** close to my face. I try to back up. He puts his hands on my legs, "You don't let things go, do you?" I grab them, "Not when I care as much as I do–no!" Why is he being like this? His lips go into a thin line. "Anything I tell you…it's too much." he says, "And I don't want those images in your mind Ivy."

"Are they that horrific?" I agitatedly ask.
"They are worse." Oh my god…
I scan around us uncomfortably.

His hands slide off my legs as he stands, "Please…don't ask me to explain my life."
I innocently peer up at him, "Your life?"
He runs his fingers through his hair, "I won't do it Ivy. I just can't."

I also stand up, "But for as long as I'm here, I need to know what to look out for!"
He shoots me a glare, "This fight is mine and mine alone. When it's over, we will no longer have these discussions." he whispers, "This war is about to end." he slightly raises his arms, "All of this torment will be gone–at last!" He says that like he's been putting up with it for way longer than he's told me. It also seems there is more to this than I have imagined.

As his arms fall to his sides, he notices my wondering and calculative expression.
"Then I will ask only this; how will it end?"

"Demonic expulsion." He says.
Rozalia hisses, *"There are no **demons** in this house!"* He winces.

"Nick, are you ok?" I ask.
A heavy sigh leaves him as he raises his eyebrows down at the floor, "Oh there are… Yes…there are."

"What…?"
"Demons…" he blinks at me, "Or so…that is what I am certain of." That's…not what I asked him.

340

I place a hand on his shoulder, "Ok, have the castle exorcised-" He cuts me off, beginning to laugh. "How is that funny? It's a serious matter!"

He softly clears his throat, "It isn't funny at all. I do apologize. I'm just...overwhelmed."
What's wrong with him?

Rozalia draws out a sigh, *"Dmitri...I am growing so tired of your **insolence**."* He gently grips my shoulders and smiles, "Let us put this aside, ok? The party will begin very soon. As I said before; your surprise awaits you."

"Nick, this isn't easy to just 'put aside'." I sternly point out. "Shhh," he guides me over to the closet, turns the doorknob slowly, then flings it open, "Tada!" I gasp, looking in and seeing a long, blood-red Victorian dress with black lace and sparkling white diamonds hanging alone in the middle of the little room.

I turn to him, awestruck. My expression entertains him quite a bit. He moves behind me and holds my shoulders again, whispering in my ear, "Do you like it?"
"Oh, I love it."

"I cannot wait to see you in it."
I instantly imagine wearing it and dancing with him in the ballroom in the middle of the floor as the music plays and the other people just seem to disappear. The timeless, joyous feeling. How magical...

"I'll have one of the maids come and assist you in getting prepared for tonight." He says. I purse my lips, then smile, "Ok," He suddenly spins me around and puts his hands on both sides of my head, "Tonight, Ivy...I want you to forget everything and have a great time–am I clear?"
I nod quickly, "Yes, yes of course," He taps my nose, "No spirits, no worries, no harm at all...just you and I at Dmitri's party. This night will be unforgettable, I assure you."
"Unforgettable indeed..." I quietly agree. He grins, then kisses my lips. I grasp his vest, lightly pulling him closer, kissing him back.

His hands slide down the door and he slowly backs away, "I must also prepare." I bite my lip as he bows his head and starts to leave.

"Nick," I stop him before he goes out the door. He pauses there and looks over his shoulder at me. "You stopped them in the hallway. You made the heavy feeling disappear, didn't you?" I ask.

He looks ahead. "…You will not be bothered in this room."
He leaves.

I bring a hand up to my mouth, holding my elbow with the other, trying to conclude what really happened. He won't tell me anything. Why–why can't he?

-Nicolai-

Walking the hall to my private elevator, I think of what I saw coming at Ivy. Darkness crawled up the walls and Jennifer was in her snakelike form, slithering toward Ivy with her fangs bared, ready to do as much damage as she could. Maria was not there, but behind us. They are becoming braver and more daring. The good spirits surrounded Ivy and I, and Rozalia tried to force them aside because she wanted to fight, but I resisted her. I resisted her! They protect Ivy…they like her. She's different. She will survive, and I will endure as much as I have to, to keep it that way.

I take my elevator to the third floor and go inside my office where I page Christine to assist Ivy with her preparation. At the time I finish that, I get the feeling someone is standing at the door. I look up from my desk and see Madeline.

Rozalia tenses my body, *"She is unwelcome."*
I rub my forehead, "Madeline."

"Unwelcome...Rozalia? Since I helped shield Ivy from those witches?" Madeline then looks at me, "Corneliu is with Ivy."

I dart my attention back up to her.
"I have nothing more to say." She vanishes.

*"I don't need her help. I don't need **anyone's** help!"*

"Consider it a favor." I say under my breath, standing up from my desk to go get ready in my room.

"How is it a favor?"

"They 'took the load off your shoulders'."

"Intolerable. I am feared and shall remain that way."

"Whatever you say Rozalia…whatever you say."

I check my watch and see it's about 5 now.

She makes me say, "You had better hurry old man."

"Stop. Behave yourself." I scold. She laughs at herself, calling me an old man again. I slap my head, "Shut it!" I suddenly giggle in her way, "Ohh, **ouch**!" I squeeze my eyes shut.

Now dressed and all ready for the party, I see it's 20 after 6. I make my way to my dark northwest tower and observe the people getting off the ferry and following the path to the castle. Fixing my red handkerchief in my right breast pocket, I begin to lightly smile to myself. From what I can see, everybody looks very stunning.

"I can feel this is going to be a very powerful evening." Rozalia hums.

I nod, "The world is a bigger, more socially involved place these days."

*"All the more **fun**."* She simpers.

"So much energy…" she purrs and runs my tongue across my teeth, having me emphasize, "I can almost taste it." I shake off the sudden blood-lust and leave the tower, headed back to my room; there's something I want to do.

And I have a little more time on my hands.

-Walter-

As I read my watch in the foyer, I say, "Finally, it's time." The front doors are open and Angel and Pamela are standing behind me, ready to take the guests' coats. The first to come to the door is someone I immediately recognize. I smile at him with a nod, "Mr.

Wilson sir, very good to see you." He smiles back, invitation in hand, "Walter, hello. It's good to see you too." I take his invitation from him and motion him to give his coat to Angel. "Please allow Miss Angel to take your coat and follow the red carpet." "Thank you." he walks in and the next couple guests come up to show me their invitations.

I check their names against the list and smile back up at the two, waving inside, "Mr. and Mrs. Kowalski, glad you could make it. Miss Pamela will take your stole, and your coat sir. Please follow the red carpet and enjoy the party." They thank me and the man asks, "When will the ferry return?"

"It will return at midnight, sir."
"Thank you." He nods and continues inside.

"You're quite welcome." I say. Then, I greet more of the guests. Everything is moving smoothly so far. This will be a night to remember. I smile. Everyone is in good spirits, but I do wonder what Mr. Francis and Miss Summers are doing at the moment... Hmm...

-Nicolai-

I enter my closet and open the panel to the oubliette. As I stare down the dark hole, a childhood memory of Corneliu and I weeding out his garden comes to mind. I was almost finished pulling weeds when suddenly a snake slithered out of the nearby shrubbery and hissed at me. I fell back with a startled gasp. Corneliu pointed at his shovel and glared at me, telling me to face my fears. I was frozen in place. Before the snake could get to me, he quickly took the shovel and chopped its head off. My eyes grew very large to seeing how fearless he was. I would always consider him heartless for doing that. But in truth, it was necessary.

Now once again, I am facing a fear; I always tell myself not to stare down this hole because it isn't just a hole; it's a portal. I know I have created something more powerful than I can handle. Rozalia may have control over things like this but she wouldn't prevent anything from happening unless it had a direct effect on her.

I start to feel this room slowly dropping in temperature and I'm also getting a bit of vertigo. My stomach twists and I begin to see the bottom of the oubliette lighting up. My eyes narrow, engrossing it. The bottom of it suddenly flashes white, showing me all the women I've killed and dismembered on the sharp metal below. They're all in different states of decomposition. I quickly turn my head away as I become sick to my stomach. I know this is an illusion and my guilt is creating these images in my mind…or are they? My eyes raise a little as a female arm slumps over my shoulders and slowly pulls my jacket up. I grit my teeth to the sensation of cold lips touching below my ear and sharp eyeteeth tickling my skin. A freezing cold hand suddenly rides up beneath my shirt. I turn my head and see Jennifer standing beside me with a mocking smile.

"You *disgust* me!" Rozalia makes me say. Scowling, I back away, press the button and close the oubliette. I turn and march back into my room and see the door slowly opening. My brows rise in disapproval.

"Nick, are you in here?" Ivy. My expression softens. I'm also amazed that she came here. I move closer toward the door and see she's wearing that red dress with black evening gloves. Her hair is perfect with lovely diamonds and she has on a beautiful choker. She looks so mouthwatering. *"I could devour her right now."* Rozalia purrs.

I blink, swallowing a little hard.
'I don't think so.'

Ivy almost speaks but I raise a hand while starting to grin and beckon her in with two fingers. She bites her lip and looks back into the hall. I really love it when she does that. And how she blushes so much. I smirk, "Shut that and come here, my love…" She looks at me again. Something is hiding in those angelic eyes of hers. She shuts it and walks up to me. I bring her hands up to my lips, "Good evening sweetheart." She smiles slowly at me, then looks around, "You're in here...and not down there."

"It's not time yet."
"Nick," she sighs, now looking down. I lift her chin, "What is it?" She slightly frowns, "Why? Why did you hide the fact you were throwing a *masquerade* party? Christine told me she was going to get you. I couldn't wait any longer and I didn't want to. I don't-" she shakes her head, "I don't like that." To what she says, I sense Rozalia is a little amused.

I glance down at her lips, "Are you mad?"
She closes her eyes, seeming aggravated, "Just tell me what I should do next. You're the host." Tell her what to do... Hmm. I grin again.

"Sit on the bed." Her eyes open wide and her brows furrow. "Nick, the time-?" I hush her with a finger to her lips and raise an eyebrow, "Sit on the bed Ivy." She looks troubled, then she rolls her eyes and goes over and sits down. I lift my chin proudly with a smile of satisfaction and walk toward her. She warily watches me stop in front of her and get down on my knees. I grab her hands, look into her eyes and say, "Whatever happens tonight, I want you to be happy." She goes silent.

"What?" I tilt my head.
"You already made yourself clear."

"I know." I smile.
"Do you think something bad is going to happen?" she asks.

"Oh," I shake my head surely, "No, of course not."
"Then you must think I'm not amazed so easily." She assumingly mumbles.

I watch her, my smile broadening. With a scoff, I say, "Perhaps so."
"Don't worry Nick, I'll have a wonderful time." She kisses my nose and then stands up. I put my hands in my jacket pockets, "Alright Miss Summers...I will believe you. In the meantime, you should join the party. I will be there soon to make an appearance,

then I will see you on the dance floor."

"That is, if you will dance with me." She winks at me and leaves.

'Right…' I throw my head back with a silent laugh. How cute.

"We must go. You are running out of time."

'Fine…'

I walk over to my dresser, collect the black and red devil mask that one of the maids left for me, then I exit my quarters and go down to the second floor, follow the hall to the left end and reach a nondescript door that opens out to my private ballroom balcony. I quietly slip through it and stand behind the tassels of the open red curtain, peeking out a little. I'm able to see all of my guests assembled below and Walter is trailing after them. He's headed for a platform the maids put together at one end of the room and he's wearing a very detailed white mask. The man has style.

A few moments later, I see Ivy going inside, looking all around–most likely for me. I lightly smile at her; she keeps pulling her dark red and black mask away from her face every few seconds. It's adorable.

Slowly then, I lose the amusement to an all-business look, and I glance at the clock. Time is moving right along. Everything is going well. I switch back down to Walter. He nods at me and I nod back. Then he ascends the platform and faces the guests with a hand raised in my direction, "Ladies and gentlemen, your host–Mr. Nicolai Francis!" They turn and applaud at my appearance with much excitement. I smile through my mask, lift a hand slowly and bow my head.

"I always enjoy the spotlight." Rozalia says.

I ignore her.

Waving my arms out around the room at the people, I loudly say with a happy tilt of the head, "Welcome, welcome! Welcome all! Please enjoy yourselves; there is much to eat and much to drink! I will join you shortly." I flick my hand at the maestro of the orchestra at another corner of the room on a more decorated stage,

"What is a party without music? Let the music begin, and do not let me find anyone standing still for long!" The leader bows his head at me with a big smile and conducts the musicians to start playing classy big band music. The guests joyfully turn away and return to their mingling. I lower my hand and smile once more as I move away from the golden rail of the balcony.

As soon as I go through the door, the smile is gone and I'm heading back up the hall to Walter's office. When I reach for his doorknob, Rozalia asks me why we're here instead of the grand room. I go in, shut the door and murmur, "I am taking a detour." I walk up to his desk and check the drawers, then I find a bottle of nitroglycerin pills. I shake it around in my hand a couple times, studying it. These are really effective; Walter only needs one. But me, I'd have to take at least half of it.

"What are you doing?"
I pause. "These are breath mints."

"They don't look too tasty."
I empty the bottle into my hand with a growing smirk, "Oh, they are."

"I don't like your tone of voice."
"I am not lying to you. I never do." I tuck the pills into my jacket pocket, place the bottle back in the drawer and go back out of the room. Rozalia quietly huffs.

As I walk swiftly up the hall, I see the spirits coming out of the walls on either side; some questioning me. I turn my nose down. When I'm nearing the end, a black orb appears in midair, shape-shifting into a long pole and soon creating a head and shoulders while the feet and legs are forming, and then the middle is last to manifest. There he is–Corneliu. I stop in front of him. The spirits are grouping up behind me and I'm staring indifferently at him.

He asks, "Is this party any different from the last ones? You won't be taking anyone in a backroom, will you?" A corner of my mouth rises, "It certainly is different this time. And thank you for the interesting entrance, show off."

"Dmitri, I want only what is best for you." he says. The tension in the room grows as the ones behind me become more doubtful. I turn my head slightly enough for them to see I truly don't care, then I look back to Corneliu again with serious eyes, "Tonight will be different. You wait and see." I go through him, then he and the others slowly turn, watching me.

While I'm on my way down, I remember the first party I had here. It was a lot like this one. These sorts of parties never change. Only, back then my plate was nearly clean. Corneliu was alive, but a monster. I hadn't killed very many people at all. Rozalia kept our blood-lust under control as much as she could. Corneliu was harder to manage.

That particular party is the one I murdered Madeline. I took her up to the second floor and seduced her. She was drunk and I played along. She wanted to be erotic, so I was, then things started getting out of hand; I became a true animal–a hungry wolf, I would call it. She died thinking I was playing when I was truly a monster drinking her dry.

Corneliu did the same thing at that party with a girl named Lucy. I couldn't let him do it again. I couldn't...

I walk through the grand room where the maids bow their heads at me in respect. I nod once at each of them, smiling kindly, then I go through the double doors into the loud ballroom, eyes searching left and right at the many people laughing and talking with each other while sipping on cocktails. Right away, I find Ivy and smile to myself. She turns slowly with a drink in her hand as I walk her way. Some of the guests notice me and raise their glasses in a toast to the party. I wave a few friendly hellos, and then one man I know approaches me.

With a smile, he slightly lifts his drink and says, "Wonderful party Mr. Francis."
I nod, "Thank you. I'm glad you're having a good time."

He tilts his drink and head in agreement, then he steps a little closer, "There are some market items I would like to discuss with you." I place a hand on his shoulder, giving a friendly expression in return, "Not tonight my friend. This is a party–enjoy yourself. We will talk again Monday." I pat his shoulder and walk on. He bows his head at me.

Another familiar man stops me along the way and compliments me on the party and then he says, "I heard there was a tragic accident here. I'm so sorry for your loss." he frowns sympathetically. I nod sadly, "Thank you… She is greatly missed…" I put my hand on his shoulder, "…This is a party…we must enjoy ourselves."
"Indeed."

I firmly dip my head, "Good talking to you sir."
"Likewise," he raises his glass. I smile a bit and then we part ways.

Finally, I meet up with Ivy and take her hand and kiss it, "Hello again."
"Nick," she warmly smiles. I offer my arm, suavely asking, "May I have this dance?"
She lowers her head, "Of course Mr. Francis." Her glistening eyes rise to my face. I look at her for a moment, "…You are so beautiful." She chuckles and I start taking her to the middle of the room. Many people watch and stare as they slow-dance with each other. They are obviously curious.

Before we get to the center, a man and woman come out of a small group, up to us. Ivy looks up at me, then back to the couple. The man extends his hand while the woman slightly behind him smiles.

He says, "Mr. Francis, hello!"
"Ah, yes–Mr. Viktor Dobrescu. Good evening to you." I look at his date. He kindly waves to her; "This is my personal secretary, Lucy Wood."

"Ahh, lovely." I gently take a hold of her hand, bowing my head a little, "Pleasure to meet you Madam." She glances at Ivy with a small blush adorning her face. Ivy does a curt twitch of the lips, trying to smile. I back away a little as Viktor says, "And who is this lovely creature?"

I then look from him to Ivy, "This is Ivy. She is with me."

"*Oh*…" he smiles at me, then at her. I chuckle softly, "Yes, yes. Well anyway, it was nice seeing you again," I lower my head a little at Lucy, "and wonderful meeting you Ms. Wood."

She gives me the 'likewise' smile. I lift my arm back up, and as Ivy takes it, I tell them, "Enjoy the party." She and I walk off to the middle of the floor and begin our nice slow dance.

"You were so eager to leave them." Rozalia says.

'Of course.' I reply.

"Who is that guy?" Ivy asks.

Looking ahead, I say, "Viktor is a CEO of a yacht corporation."

"Yacht Corporation?" She's baffled.

"Da…" I grin and dip her over my arm. When I bring her back up, I gaze into her eyes, "Many have come to this party to be seen. Social politics, you know."

"Are any of them close friends?" She quietly asks.

"I haven't any true friends; I am a private man. You should know that by now."

"True," she looks at my lips.

I pull her close and whisper in her ear, "So you are having fun, I see."

"I am…" She sounds very eager, anxious too. "This is beyond anything I would've imagined going to. I'm surprised no one is taking any pictures." She says. I smile warmly to her words and close my eyes, "There will be no picture taking tonight my love… I am very happy to hear you are enjoying yourself." Carefully, I slip my hand into one of my pockets and take some of the pills out. She doesn't sense this. She speaks more about how amazing the party and everything here is. While listening to her, I throw back the meds and continue dancing.

"…Nick…" she backs her face away from the side of mine as I swallow them.

"I have a question." She says.

"What is it my dear?" A corner of my mouth rises into a type of smile.

"Does anyone here know about Maria's death?"

"Dmitri, these do not taste like mints." Rozalia uncomfortably says. I flare my nose a tad, eyes stilled on her face as I ponder over a way to answer.

"Yes." I say. She starts searching my face with more curiosity once noticing I don't say anything else. "Ivy…" I grab her shoulders. Suddenly, I pause. "Oh," I put my hand on my forehead, "Oh, my head." There's so much pain…! It's worse than a migraine and equal to what Rozalia gives me–but it's not her, I know. She isn't taking it too well either, but only because she is losing control over me.

"Nick?" Ivy worriedly raises her hands. I wave it off, taking a step backward, but then my eyes roll back in my head and I collapse to the floor with Rozalia panicking in my mind. I am aware of everything but cannot move or open my eyes; Rozalia is keeping me conscious the best she can.

"Oh my god!" Ivy gasps, instantly catching my head before I hit the floor. She checks my pulse, then whirls her head around at the people hurrying toward us, "Is there a doctor here?!"

A woman breaks through the crowd, "I'm a nurse!" She takes me out of Ivy's arms, presses two fingers to my neck and puts her head against my chest to listen to my heart. Her brows rise and she snaps her head back up to look at Ivy, "He is in serious trouble." She looks over at Walter promptly coming up, "He is going into cardiac arrest. We have to get him back to a hospital ASAP!" He turns to Eduard, Esmeralda and Leonardo behind him, "Leo, prepare the speedboat right away." Leo nods quickly, pushes past the staring Esmeralda and Eduard and rushes out. Walter turns around with his arms rising, "Everything is under control. Mr. Francis is not feeling well and we have to get him to a doctor. The ferry will return at midnight, so continue the party." He points over at Christine, "Christine will be in charge. Enjoy yourselves and thank you for coming. Have a good evening." While he does this, Ivy flutters her scared, teary eyes down at my face. Eduard and Esmeralda race up, get me off the floor while Ivy slowly stands and wipes her eyes. Walter tells her, "Go out with them to the boathouse." he glances at the nurse, "You too." She hesitantly nods at him.

Ivy grabs his arm, "You're staying?"
He shoots her a disbelieving look, "Of course not!"

She repeatedly blinks at him, "Oh- Oh!"
"Come on, we have to go!" The nurse abruptly pats her on the shoulder and rushes out.
Ivy anxiously follows behind.

"Shit, shit, shit! God damn it, no!" she panics.

Chapter 39
-Nicolai-

Everything is dark. There's nothing. Nothing at all. But then…I start to feel something I have never felt before…perhaps one could call it a sense of relief. It's a weightless feeling that starts at my fingertips and my feet; the sensation is as if my arms and legs are slowly rising and I'm slipping through a cloud that's cool to the touch. Now I see nothing but white light. It's so bright I have to cover my face. "Ugh," I hiss. Hold on–the pain isn't there. My eyes don't hurt…?

My eyebrows furrow as I slowly move my arm away from my eyes. I can hear an angry woman speaking but her voice is muffled.

The light fades, then I gasp.
I see myself!–Lying motionless on a bed in a hospital emergency room with nurses at my sides, giving me fluids through an IV. The privacy curtain is closed around us.

Slowly, I bring my hand up to my chest, "So this is what it is like… This is…death?"
I hear her but where is she? Where is that woman?

"You are not dead! PAY ATTENTION!" I hear slightly behind me. Looking to my right, I see her–Rozalia. She's in full form and looks just how she did before I killed her. I lose my breath, perplexed. After so many years, I see her in full form again. I could not have imagined this.

*"You are not **dead**. I have not left you!"* she says with a black look, "Where is Ivy?" her flaming brown eyes scan the room. Why does she want to know that right now? Shouldn't she be angry with me for trying to commit suicide? Wasn't she the woman that sounded angry?

I momentarily look at my body again, "I'm not dead…?" Right then, I hear another voice to the left beyond the curtain. It's clearer now. It wasn't Rozalia; it's a woman scolding herself for the life she's led.

"PAY NO ATTENTION TO HER!"

Suddenly, I notice everything around just stops; every person and working machine is frozen in time. I lock eyes with Rozalia again, glowering at her.

"What is going on?" My voice is harsh.
"Where is Ivy?" she's beginning to worry.

I point at her, "Tell me!"
"You answer me first!" She shouts.

I tilt my head, "To be honest, I have no idea where she is, and I can't help you." I point at her, "You will not have her!"

She opens her mouth to say something else, but before I hear her next words, the lights go out and it's like before; nothingness. All I know is, I feel like I'm being drawn in and condensed into a small space.

My eyes fly open as I take a huge breath. I look around and see that I'm back in my body. I can feel things again; my heartbeat, a little bit of hunger, cotton mouth, a bad headache, and some soreness. Right off, I search for Rozalia.

She is nowhere to be seen.
'Where is she...? Am I alone? I don't feel any different. The weight is still there.' I think to myself as my eyes dart around the room, not paying much attention to the nurses talking and asking me questions. I'm unable to respond. They assume my body has stabilized and decide to leave me momentarily to check with the doctor.

"I am here."
I gently close my eyes, feeling almost defeated.

After a few seconds go by, I reopen them and see a woman in a black pantsuit standing at the foot of the bed, staring directly at me in a cold, deathly way. Her eyes are piercing green, her hair is jet-black and her skin is smooth and pale. She's standing there in an intimidating way. Immediately, I get a sick feeling in my gut and my entire body tenses up. Rozalia is very disgusted. This is not a regular person…no–this is a powerful medium.

I take in a labored breath and manage to muster through my teeth, "My friend…you have abilities, yes? I ask-" It's so difficult to speak; there is an ***immense*** amount of pressure in my chest.

The woman raises a hand and stops me in mid-sentence, "I can see...her." The last word is said in an unnerving way, as if she is staring at a creature made of pure evil rather than me. My stomach twists and my face goes a little sour.

"She has been with you for a long time. Is there anything I can do for you?" she quietly asks. I give her a long stare, slowly beginning to wonder how she found me. I fell unconscious once I returned to my body. It's somewhat hard to think clearly. But I am focused enough to have my special sight wander away to find Walter standing at an admission desk in a large room not far from where I am.

"There is an older gentleman-" I quietly say, "standing at the admissions desk. He's tall, thin, and wearing a black suit. His name is Walter. Please find him and tell him Mr. Francis asked you to speak with him about cleaning my home." I breathe in coarsely and let it all out. It hurts so much.

*"No! **NO! STOP!** HOW **DARE** YOU?!"* Rozalia shouts, now pounding on the insides of my eyes as if they're glass windows. I try to shut them but I can't.

I turn my head to the left at a medicinal cart and blink uncomfortably, wincing, "I will pay you for your services…" I look at her again, "whatever you need."

"We'll talk about that later. You rest now." she nods slowly at me, backs away, then turns and heads out of the curtain. I sigh and lift my gaze up to the ceiling as I slowly reach into my pants' pocket and clutch the remaining pills I stole earlier.

*"No... I will make you pay for that! Do you **really** think I am going to allow you to eat the rest of **those**?"* Rozalia growls and fights me for control of my arm. With every last ounce of strength I have, I manage to place the pills in my mouth and swallow.

"…Too late."

*"NO! NO! **NO!**"*

'Goodbye…Rozalia.'

A few seconds pass and then my body begins to convulse. The pain is unbearable but I'm ready for the end. I close my eyes tightly, feeling my heart trying to survive as it pounds uncontrollably. Rozalia screams at me in terror, *"WHAT ARE YOU DOING TO ME?! STOP THIS, STOP THIS NOW!!! **NOO!!!**"*

I reopen my eyes to the lights in the ceiling that suddenly become extraordinarily bright in a flash but they don't hurt my eyes. This is it.

Just like that, in less than a second, I find I'm now standing up, looking down at my body. And I'm not in pain. I look up and see Rozalia on the other side of the bed, staring at me with a heinous glower.

*"Now I loathe you **twice** as much."* She hisses and falls backward as if being pulled away and vanishes through the curtain. I blink in a bit of surprise. The woman on the other side that has been scolding herself screeches and then falls silent in almost the same voice as Rozalia.

My lips twitch into a scowl, "Good riddance you filthy bitch." I shift my gaze back to my body and realize there isn't any life in my face. The machines around me are alarming as I'm beginning to fade. A nurse quickly draws the curtain open while calling for a crash-cart and the doctor. Quickly, I step out of her way when she comes to my side and checks for a pulse, then she motions someone to assist her. The other nurse searches and finds a set of shock paddles and the first nurse tears my shirt open. The doctor plunges a large needle into my chest, injects something, then quickly draws it out. I feel the stab even though I'm not in my body. The paddles are charging as the doctor says, "Clear!" I feel the shock and witness my body's reaction. He quickly checks for a pulse and then shocks me again, "Clear!" The electrical surge overwhelms me and I see myself begin to take a breath. Then suddenly, the room flashes into blinding light. My eyes enlarge as I take in one last deep breath through my mouth.

Beep. Beep. Beep. Beep.

I moan from the pain in my chest and hear the doctor speaking to me.

"Mr. Francis?" he says, "Stay with us buddy." I drag my eyes open and see him look up at the nurse at my right side, nod once at her and move away slightly to check and prepare the medications on the nearby medicinal cart.

Finally, I blink.

I take a large breath and look around. I'm back–in my body–not dead…I am back. And I don't feel the same. No…I'm drained of energy and my mind…it feels… Could I say 'clear'? Where is the persistent nagging, the constant anger and the lust for blood? Gone…all gone. Oh my god, I must be aging rapidly now! Immediately, my eyes dart around, looking for a reflective surface. I can't find anything. I quickly try to feel my face, struggling a little. It doesn't feel any different. No wrinkles? Nothing? I notice I still have these sharp eyeteeth. Scars–they're my scars.

I look at the nurse anxiously, "Miss, do I look any different?" She takes my hands and rests them on my stomach, "No sir. Here, you should rest."

I shake my head at her, "No no, you don't understand! Have I aged at all?"

She blinks at me strangely, "Sir…you haven't been here long."

I stare at her, becoming slightly confused. Slowly, I look past her, "She lied to me…" The nurse stands there silently watching me, trying to understand. I ignore her as my eyes slowly narrow and begin to water. I'm trying to form a smile but the relief is so great that I have forgotten how.

'I am in terrible pain...but…I am alone at last! I have my life back!' Finally, I am myself again after enduring nearly a century of hell. Ohh… Ohh, thank **GOD**!

-Walter-

I finish writing Mr. Francis's information on the registration papers and the woman behind the counter takes them with a nod and a thank you, then tells me to wait a moment.

"Sure." I nod back and sigh deeply while glancing over at the entrance to this large room with many occupied seats. I check my watch. It's 8:34pm.

"Okay sir, you may take a seat over there. Here is a visitor pass. When we call you, you can go in to see him." The receptionist says. I turn to her and take the visitor pass, "Thank you."

As I tuck it in my right breast pocket, I see a small black-haired woman dressed in a black pantsuit walking and looking around as if she is searching for someone. Her sight falls on me and right away, she starts coming toward me. I slightly lift a brow.

"Excuse me sir..." she says on approaching me, "Are you Walter?" My eyebrow rises a tad more while I look down at her. This is interesting.
"Yes... Can I help you miss?"

She takes a step closer, eyes very serious. "My name is Susan Winters. May I speak with you in private?" Who is she exactly? My face softens a little and I wave my hand toward the large hall leading away from the emergency entrance, "Of course. Let's talk in the waiting room down the hall." She nods in agreement.

As we enter the room, she stops abruptly and takes a deep breath as if she were experiencing a stabbing pain in her chest. Her eyes are wide open and glaring as she looks at me. She is gritting her teeth very hard and lets out a groan. "Are you alright Miss?" I reach for her, but she backs away from me and says, "Wait...just wait." She takes a deep breath and relaxes. "I'm fine." she says.

"For a moment I thought you were having a seizure of some kind. Are you sure you are alright?" I ask.
"Yes, I'm sure. Hospitals are a little hard on me."

...How odd–I think to myself.

"I'm sure I have no idea what you mean Miss. What is it you want from me?"

"Mr. Francis has asked me to do a spiritual cleansing of his home."
A spiritual cleansing…? Preposterous. This woman just wants attention.

"I see…" I nod slowly, "And you want me to do what?"
"I need you to make sure there is not a living soul on the property before the cleansing."

I fold my arms, "When were you planning to do this…cleansing?"
"I must make some arrangements with a holy man and then I will be in contact with you. No more than 24 hours from now."

I raise my chin a little, "Mr. Francis authorized this?" That seems out-of-character for him.
"Yes he did." She sounds quite sure of herself.

Hmm…

"And how is it you were able to see him? You are not a nurse or a doctor, are you? Or did you discuss this arrangement before he became ill?-On the telephone perhaps?" I await her answer with interest.

She gives me a strange, dry sort of look, "I saw him a few minutes ago. I was drawn to his bedside." Drawn to his bedside?

"I see. You realize I must discuss this with Mr. Francis?"
"Yes, of course." she says in a friendlier voice, "Here is my cell-phone number. Please call me as soon as possible. Thank you Walter." She gives me a small piece of paper, a professional smile and then walks out. I arch an eyebrow and look at it, then stuff it in my pocket and quickly make my way back to the admissions area. I don't see her anywhere in the halls. Very strange…

I return to the registration desk, check with the receptionist again and ask if I can go back to see Mr. Francis. She says, "One second. Please wait while I check." she rises from her chair and

goes through the door behind the desk. About a minute after she leaves, another receptionist appears and sits down in the seat beside hers. I bow my head at him, "Good evening."
He smiles, "Hey, how ya doin'?"
"Fine, thank you."

The woman returns and tells me, "Mr. Francis is ready to see you. Just go through those doors to the right, follow the hall, make a left and then go through the double doors. There is a number written on your visitor's pass. The bed you will be looking for is number 6, okay?" I tip my head the positive at her, fish the pass out of my pocket, "Very good." and I head for the doors.

I follow her directions and eventually find my way into the area a nurse called Resus–short for 'resuscitation'. Locating bed 6 is easy, noting the numbers on the floor.

As I walk toward that bed, I see Mr. Francis lying there with his eyes shut, seeming quite relieved. A doctor stops me before I reach him and says, "Excuse me sir, are you Walter?"
I nod at him, "I am."

"Okay. I am Doctor Burton, the attending physician. How are you doing tonight sir?"
"I'm fine, thank you. How is Mr. Francis?" I ask.

"He is stable. I must ask–are you the next of kin?"
"No sir, I am his personal assistant. He has no family to my knowledge."

"Well then…Mr. Francis has been through a traumatic episode; he suffered cardiac arrest and his heart stopped. We were able to bring him back, so now he is resting. Currently, he's awake and has asked for you. You may see him now." My stomach jumped at the mentioning of his heart stopping but now it's only in a knot. Why is this happening to him? There was nothing wrong with his health that I could tell, and then all of a sudden his heart failed?

"Dr. Burton," I say, "could you find the reason for his heart failure?" He lifts a shoulder with a matter-of-fact shake of the head, "We have retrieved the blood test results and all came back normal. His temperature was feverish and he wasn't sweating. His heart was going into hyper-drive. We have yet to come to any conclusions but it appears he was under extreme stress." My brows slowly furrow, "That is completely unlike him."

The doctor shrugs, "We are still trying to figure it out sir. I'm going to keep him for at least 24 hours for observation. We want to make sure he's alright."
I nod finally at him, "Thank you doctor." He backs away and then I proceed over to Mr. Francis.

Before I can say hello, he opens his eyes and looks down near his feet at me. "Walter, hello." He smiles lazily. I step closer to his bedside, push my hands down into my pockets and look at him from head to toe twice, "Feeling better sir?"
He takes a deep breath, "Yes…better now."
I stare at him, then clear my throat with a small smile, "I heard you went through a lot earlier."
He halfway smirks and laughs a little, "Yes. Believe me, it was worth it."
I form a surprised face. "You look pretty happy for someone who died earlier, if I do say so myself."

He then looks at me seriously, "If you only knew."
"I wish I did sir, but you are stubborn." I form a small wry grin.
He rolls his eyes, "Yes yes…well..."

"Sir…I must tell you, a young woman came to see me in the registration room a few minutes ago."
His right eyebrow rises, "Was she wearing a black pantsuit?"

"Yes sir."
"Ahh," he nods certainly at me, "I sent her to you."

"Then she is not lying?" I'm stunned…!
"No…" he snickers, "I need you to handle this for me old friend."

"Yes sir." I say with a little question in my tone.
He moves his head to a side, "What is her name?" My eyes briefly light up.

"Her name is Susan Winters. You surprise me sir."

"Well..." he looks away for a minute, "I was a little busy when we talked." then he returns to me, "Give her whatever she needs and keep me informed." he sighs slowly, "I may be here for a while."

I lower my head, "Yes sir. Is there anything else I can do for you?"
"Tell Ivy..." he pauses, lost in thought for a moment. He says, "Tell Ivy I'm fine...and that I will see her tomorrow. Make sure she does not stay at the castle tonight. That will be all."

"Yes sir...of course." I smile warmly at him with a confirming nod and then I leave for the waiting room to see Ivy.

My walk back is a quiet and thoughtful one. In all my time as a butler, I have never been in such a position as this. Maybe it's time for me to retire? Well...not yet...my tasks are unfinished, and I have enjoyed the drama and adventure since Ivy came into our lives.

As I enter the waiting room, Ivy anxiously stands up from her chair, getting nearly everyone's attention. I let out a sigh and go to her.

"Is he okay?" she searches my face nervously. I wave my hands in a gesture, "Shh, everything is alright. The doctor says it's late and he will be keeping him overnight. You will be able to see him tomorrow. I will call you a taxi so you can go back to your apartment and get some rest, alright Miss Summers?" She blinks at me, then suddenly shakes her head, "Walter wait, why can't I stay at the castle?" I take her hands in mine, "Miss Summers, he doesn't want you to stay there tonight." I give her eyes that say 'You wouldn't want to be there without him anyway, would you?' She scans my features for a good while before she lowers her head and nods softly, "Of course... I understand." I slightly smile and pat her hands, "Let's go then." She takes my arm as we exit the room and head out of the hospital.

There is a taxi stationed just down the drive from the outside doors. I gesture at the driver, trying to get his attention while Miss Summers rubs her arms, shivering from the cool air. I remove my jacket and settle it over her shoulders, "For the time being, wear this." She is a little surprised that I do this but she doesn't hesitate to hug it closer.

"Walter," she says.
"Yes?"

"What exactly happened to Nick?"
I'm silent.

I look at her, "I cannot go into detail about that until tomorrow. I'm sorry Miss Ivy."
"You can't tell me anything at all?" She's becoming agitated.

I shake my head sadly, "I'm sorry. I can't. It's not my place to do so–you understand."
She raises a finger, "Walter, I need to know what's wrong with him! Can't you see I'm in love-"

The taxi pulls up, stopping her before she can finish her sentence. We both look away from it, back to each other. I tilt my head a bit and step closer to the car, "Ivy…go home and rest. You need it." As the driver opens the rear door, she stares at me, eyes welling up and bottom lip quivering. She's also stunned I finally called her Ivy. Finally, she balls her hands into fists, then takes the jacket off, hands it to me and gets in the car. The driver shuts the door and scurries back to his seat. I smile at her in an assuring way through the frosty glass and watch her tell the driver where to go.

With a sigh, I put my jacket back on as they drive away and I take Susan's number out of the pocket and look at it.

I must call her.

Chapter 40

-Susan-

While visiting my nephew in the intensive care unit at the hospital, I listen to my sister speak with the attending nurse. However, my mind is straying away from what is going on in front of me into the memory I have of my encounter with that creature that attracted me to Mr. Francis's bedside. Her presence was so strong I didn't have to look around–I went straight to her. I have never actually seen an entity like that possess someone and manipulate their body like this. The only entity I can match her with is a succubus. I don't think she's a demon though; she must be an inter-dimensional being or something so rare no medium has ever encountered her and shared the information.

I've studied succubae and incubi and what their capabilities are; they invade humans' dreams and have sex with them, draining their energy during the entire time of intercourse. They don't ever possess people, and if they do, it's quite unheard of. If my assumptions aren't mistaken, before she possessed Mr. Francis, she could very well have gotten her energy the 'usual' way for a succubus. But she's using him to survive. Why is that? Why him, I wonder?

On top of this, I also sense she is very strong and very possibly wields power over other types of entities.

Suddenly, my phone rings. I blink, pull it out of my pocket and check it, then I tell everyone, "I'm sorry, please excuse me–I have to take this." I step away and walk out into the hallway. The number doesn't look familiar but I answer it anyway.

"Hello?"

"Ms. Winters?"

"Yes, this is she."

"Hello Susan, this is Walter speaking. How are you?"

I slightly smile, "I'm well. And yourself?"

"Good, good. I am calling in regards to the spiritual cleansing of Mr. Francis's home. I have spoken with him about this and have been authorized to provide you whatever you require to successfully render your services. Have you left the hospital yet?"

"No, not yet. Would you like to meet somewhere here?"

"Yes, how about outside the hospital coffee shop in 10 minutes?"

"Sounds good."

"Very well. See you soon."

We hang up.

I return to the ICU, over to my nephew and sister. My nephew looks up at me, "Aunt Susan, my leg isn't hurt that bad after all." he smiles a little, "It's only got a small…" he glances at his mom, "What did the doctor say?" She smiles back and rubs his head, "He said it's a small fracture in your shin." He looks up at me again, "Yeah, it's only got a small fracture in my shin area. And they gave me some kind of painkillers, so now my leg is kinda numb. It's scary but cool." I smile and nod, "Well good. I'm glad to hear that." I give my sister a slightly wary face after smiling down at him, then I take a step back, "Well, I should be getting home now. Tomorrow is going to be a very busy day." My sister rolls her eyes at me, and tilts her head to the right giving me that 'I need to talk to you look'. She follows me to the door and we step into the hall.

"He has to stay in here until tomorrow. He's got a pretty big knot on the back of his head. I guess he can't feel it. That's why they want to keep him." She says, then shifts herself and leans against the wall, grabbing my arm, "You need to give it up already Susan; this visiting places and confronting supernatural things will seriously wear you out. Every time I see you, you have bags under your eyes." I pull her hand away and straighten myself. "I'm fine sis. You take care of that boy and I'll see you later." I give her a hug and look back into the room at my nephew, "See ya later alligator! Love you!"

"Bye! Love you too!" he says. I then head out of the ER.

While on my way to the coffee shop, I observe people moving

through the halls and see spirits of all ages. Some are from the early 1900's when this hospital was new. They're stuck in time. But a boy notices I can see him. He isn't residual energy; he's very much here. He can see the living and sometimes interact with them.

I try not to pay him any mind as he hurries up to me and says, "You can see me!" He asks the same question over and over; "Can you help me? I have lost my parents. I can't find them!" It saddens me to experience situations like this. Poor little boy... For almost a century, he's searched for those that have moved on. I can't help him–not right now. So...I choose to ignore him the rest of the way up the hall. As painful as it is.

Finally, I get to the coffee shop and find Walter waiting outside the door.
I walk up to him, "Hello Walter."

He bows his head, "Ms. Winters," He motions me inside to join him at a nearby table. I nod and we go to sit down. He pulls a chair out for me.

"Thank you." I say.
A waitress approaches us.

"Coffee please." I say before she opens her mouth, "And you Walter?"
"Yes, coffee please. Thank you."

"Okay. Anything else?" The woman asks.
We both say, "No, that will be all."
She nods and leaves us alone.

"So Miss Winters, what do you require?" He asks. I put my hands on the table, now concentrated on his eyes, "I will need complete access to the entire property and as much time needed to do a thorough cleansing. I will need you to be there–but only you. There will be one other person present when we perform this task. We will begin at 10:30 a.m.. Is that alright?"
Keeping a serious face, he replies in a casual but all-business way, "Yes, of course. Is there anything else?"

I lean forward just a little, "Are you a religious man?"
"No Miss Winters, I am a practical man." he forms a look of
curiosity, "Why do you ask?"

"I just need you to keep an open mind when we perform this
cleansing." I say.
The waitress returns to our table with our coffee and we stop
talking for a moment.
She sets the cups down, "Here you go. Is there anything else I can
get you?"

"No thank you." I tell her.
"Okay then. Enjoy." She smiles and goes to another table.

As I take my coffee, Walter asks, "This other person you
mentioned—who is it exactly?"
"He'll be the one doing the cleansing and I'll be assisting him."
"I see." He takes a sip.

Before I swallow, he hands me his card and says, "Go to the
landing; hand this card to the ferry master and he will bring you to
the castle." I arch an eyebrow as I take it, "Mr. Francis lives in a
castle?" He forms a small grin, "It's a small castle."
I slightly smile back, "Ah… Well, I'll see you tomorrow then." I
drink more of my coffee and finish it quickly.

He watches, and smiles, "Yes, see you tomorrow—and thank you
for the coffee."
"You're quite welcome."

I then leave enough money on the table to pay for the coffee and
a small tip, then I smile at him once more and go on my way.

-Ivy-

The taxi driver drops me off in front of my apartment and I call
Gina immediately. I can't stay here tonight. I can't be alone. I
surely don't want to go to my parents—though it was my first

option.

She answers her phone, seeming wide awake.
"Wow Ivy…you sound really shaken! Are you ok?"

"I'm- I'm fine," I wipe an eye to fight back the tears. I've done well during the trip here but hearing her voice–talking to someone I know–It's getting harder for me.

"You're not telling me the truth." She says.
"Nick is in the hospital."

"What? Why? What happened?"
"We were together…and…and he suddenly went into cardiac arrest." I take in a calming breath, trying to keep my composure.

"Oh my gosh! Is everything ok?"
"I don't know," I bite my thumbnail, looking around, "I haven't heard any more from Walter." My eyes start watering. "I just…I hope he's not-" I sniffle a couple times and soon find myself unable to say anything else; my heart is tearing apart to the thought he might be dead. I picture it and I lose myself in quiet sobbing. Him lying in a hospital bed with nurses and doctors at his sides; the head doctor would be calling his time of death and the nurses would be turning the monitors off. It would be over. No more Nick.

"Oh Ivy… Hold on, I'll come over there. I'm not working tomorrow, so it's ok."
I squeeze my eyes shut and lean against my car, "I'm so shocked Gina. I just don't know what to do. I'm so scared and torn… It hurts."

"I'm coming to get you. You can stay at my place tonight."
I breathe in slowly, reopening my eyes and focusing ahead, "…You don't have to do that Gina."

"But I want to. And I will." She says, and I hear her grabbing her keys.
I wipe my face again, "You are so good to me. I've done nothing to deserve that."

"You're a good person Ivy."

I inwardly scoff, trying not to cry any more. "Thank you so much..."

"See you soon." She says.
"Ok. I'll be here." I swallow the lump in my throat and hang up.

Squeezing my phone, I turn around and gaze up at the apartments, eyes dancing in sorrow. "Nick," I sniffle again, "Stay with me...please."

I drag my feet all the way to my apartment and then collect some clothes for tomorrow and put everything in a grocery bag, then I quickly change my clothes to boot-cut jeans, a warm plaid sweater, brown boots and I put a black beanie hat on. The dress...that will just have to stay in my closet... I carefully stow it in there. After giving it a last admiring, teary-eyed look, I go back outside and sit on the hood of my car for a few minutes, watching, waiting and sniveling. Still, no phone calls. I wish this misery would just end.

Finally, she pulls into the parking lot and drives up to me. I stand up straight and walk up to her window. She studies my face, "Damn Ivy…you look like hell." I frown at her. She gestures me to get in. I don't hesitate to do that.

Once I'm in, she asks, "You have everything you need?"
I nod without looking at her, "I'm fine."

"You sure?"
I shut my eyes, "I'm positive."

She grimaces sadly. "…Okay."
We start driving away.

Chapter 41

-Ivy-

I open my glazed-over eyes and stare at the clock for the thousandth time. It's 8 in the morning now and Gina is cooking breakfast. I didn't sleep last night. She tried to get me in a better mood. I did laugh a few times but this depression is close to eating me alive. We ate some Italian food for dinner and watched a couple movies, then she let me use the spare bedroom upstairs and I tried countless times to fade away into sleep. No, that would be just too fortunate for me.

I sniffle as I sit up from the bed and rub my forehead. My hair is a mess from all the movement I did through the night. I still don't know if Nick is alive or not.

All I want to do is stay right there where he is, hold him, comfort him and try to make everything perfect. I can't be here any longer. I need to go.

I hear footsteps and then a knock at the door. "Ivy...?" Gina opens it. I try to mask this hurt expression I have but it's not working. She slowly frowns. I purse my lips at her, lower my eyes and then I look to the window on my left.

She proceeds inside and joins me on the bed.
I'm unexpectedly hugged. My eyes well up and I pull her close, "I'm so in the dark."
"I know. But you need to have hope."
I shake my head, "All night I've been fighting to believe everything is okay–if everything *will be* okay. The very one I thought I could trust won't tell me a *god damn thing*!"
She takes my shoulders, "Ivy, it's most definitely for a good reason. You think that old man Walter doesn't have everything under control? Believe me–he does. Now," she stands, "come down for breakfast. I know you've been crying all night." she points at my stomach, "You need to fill that thing up." I stare at her worriedly, then I think over her words. Walter is a good friend to

Nick and his right hand man... But he could at least try to get a hold of me, knowing Nick and I are together!

The only way for me to end this suffering is to go to the hospital.

I put a hand on my forehead, sighing, "Okay...I'll try." I really can't eat. My stomach is *all* out of whack. She offers me a hand, I take it and we head downstairs.

As I sit down at her kitchen table, I watch her prepare our plates. She gives me waffles, bacon and scrambled eggs. I take my fork, push the eggs around and stuff a few in my mouth. My stomach jerks. I grimace. Ever since last night, she's been paying close attention to how affected I am by Nick's situation.

She gently puts her fork down and pushes the pitcher of orange juice closer to me. I pause, then look up from it to her in question. She tilts her head a little, "Just drink the juice. It's best for a jumpy stomach." I study her face a while. Carefully, I reach for the pitcher and pour some of it into my glass and drink it. She sits back while grabbing a piece of bacon, "You're really in love with him, aren't you?" It sounds more like a statement rather than a question. I raise my eyes up to her and nod slowly. She tears the bacon away from her mouth, slightly smiling. A few seconds later, she says, "I'll take you to the hospital after this, okay?"

I stop in the middle of taking a sip. "You will...?"

She nods, "I will."

Oh god, now I'm REALLY anxious!

"Ok," my voice is little. I can't wait...

-Susan-

After having a small breakfast in my kitchen, I check my clock; it's 8:30. I call my shaman friend Chayton. We are somewhat close. He's about 60, he's old-school and he's a Native American.

He answers the phone, "Hello?"

"Chayton."

"Susan! Good morning. How are you?"

"I'm okay, and you?"

"I'm well, thank you."

"Listen, I'm in a bit of a situation here; I need your help with a cleansing."

"Where?" he asks.

"You know the castle in the Sound?"

"Ahh...yes..."

"I've been asked to do a cleansing of that castle."

"What do you need from me?" He sounds quite curious.

"You're the expert on these things and I sense a particularly nasty set of spirits attached to this place. There's one more thing; I encountered a sort of entity close to a succubus controlling the spirits there."

"You aren't sure what it is?"

"No...but it's definitely very powerful and dangerous. I'm assuming it came from another world or a realm we aren't familiar with."

"Well then...when and where do you want me?" he asks.

"Meet me at the ferry at 10 and bring your bag of tricks."

"Okay. I'll see you soon."

I end the call.

As I turn to go to my bedroom, I see my grandmother standing in the doorway with a worried look on her face.

She's been dead for 10 years.

"What's wrong?" I ask.

"They know you're coming and why. Be careful." She says.

I blink a few times and bow my head, "I will grandma." I walk through her and into my bedroom.

Slowly, I get dressed as I mentally prepare myself for what lies ahead.

-Ivy-

Now at the hospital, the first thing we do is talk to a woman at the front desk in the lobby. She momentarily tells us Nick is upstairs on the 7th floor, and gives us the room number–7138. My heart leaps into my throat. I'm so stunned and relieved! I can't explain how much lighter I feel right now! But then again, he might be critical…

We thank her and then Gina and I walk up a fairly long hall until getting to a set of elevators at the very end. Once the elevator doors open, she tells me, "Ivy, you go on up there. I'll be getting some coffee. Room 7138 right?"
"Yeah. That's it."

"Okay. Good luck." she pats my shoulder.
"Thank you." I smile at her and go inside, pushing the button for the 7th floor along the way. The people in here are loud, all talking about different things like sports, the weather and work. I move closer to a corner and keep my head somewhat down. The elevator stops 3 times until finally getting to the floor Nick's on.

I get off and go up a long hall to find the rooms numbered between 7120 and 7170. It doesn't take me long to get there; I'm in a hurry. I look at the hours listed on the wall; they're from 9am to 12pm. "Good…I'm just in time." I press a button on the caller on the wall. A nurse comes back, "Yes? Can I help you?"
"I'm here to see Nicolai Francis."

"How many people are with you?"
"It's just me."

The doors open and she says, "Wash your hands on your way in. The sink is on your left." "Thanks." I go inside.

Passing a few rooms, I look in each one for him. Some patients are in critical condition–something I expected, but when you have a loved one on the same floor as the ones barely clinging to life, it makes you feel sick.

I slow when nearing room 7138 and pause as I ready myself to see the worst. Hesitantly, I peer around the corner. I see him. My heart stops and my throat instantly goes dry.

His eyes are shut; he's sleeping peacefully. The sunlight is beaming through the window down on his calm, beautiful face. I swallow hard and walk inside.

For a long time, I watch him—just stand here by his side and wait. Waiting for what, I don't know. Maybe I'm waiting for something terrible to happen. But his breathing is normal; everything about him seems so perfectly healthy. He's not as pale anymore. His skin has a healthy glow to it now. What happened to him...? There's not a single trace of last night's incident. Nothing at all.

Carefully, I reach for his hand.
His eyes slowly open and find me. I lose my breath.

"Ivy..." A glad, genuine smile graces his face. My eyebrows come together while a tear rides down my cheek, "You're okay..." I gradually smile back. He slowly nods with the same content smile and tries to sit up. "No." I shake my hand at him. It confuses him.

"Nick..." I can't take it anymore; I suddenly lean over the bed, hugging him close. He envelopes me in his arms, "Ivy, I'm okay. Everything is fine now."
I sniffle, "You were in my thoughts all night. It was hard bearing the time away from you. Here I am; I'm here now Nick." He kisses my hair a few times, "I am glad you are with me again." he takes my face in his hands and searches my eyes, "Do not cry Ivy. Here," he puts my hand on his heart, "feel this?" My lips part, my lashes flutter, and I drop my eyes to his chest. The rhythm is calm— as a normal heartbeat should be. His hands aren't hot like before either.

I meet his gaze again and say with amazement in my voice, "You are healthy again...?"
He nods comfortably.

"What happened? How?" I curiously ask.

He grins and puts two fingers over his lips, "I will explain that later. As for now…" he brushes his knuckles across my cheek, "Let us enjoy this moment." I scan his expression and slowly smile again, "Okay..." I lean down to hug him again but then there's a knock at the door. I look back and see a woman with a breakfast tray. She slightly smiles, "Breakfast?" He bows his head and beckons her in. I let off the bed, almost stand aside for her, but I can't help the need to take the tray from her and give it to him. We say thank you and she leaves. As I look away from her, back to him, I see he's watching me with amused eyes.

"What?" I quietly ask. He shakes his head, chuckling a little, "Nothing at all. How motherly you are. Come–join me."
"Yes sir." I go stand by the bed and look around for a chair. He clears his throat. I look at him and then he grabs my arm and forces me to sit beside him. I really didn't expect that! He laughs at me, making me start to giggle some.

"So…let's see." he opens his breakfast and frowns slightly. I pull the lid back farther to see grits, toast, 3 pieces of bacon and some low-carb breakfast pudding. It's sort of strange.

"Not pleasant, is it?" he mutters.
"Well…" I tilt my head, "I know you like bacon." I halfway grin. He rolls his eyes, "Very well. You win."
I quietly laugh, take a piece and tell him, "Open up." He gives me a dark smile, then opens his mouth. I carefully place the bacon on his tongue and before I can move my hand away, he clamps down on it like a shark. I gasp in surprise. He laughs as he chews, then he looks over at the window, "Well, I am to be discharged once the doctor comes in and looks over my chart." he turns back to me, "He is at a conference meeting at a different hospital as explained by my nurse. She doesn't exactly know when he will be here and she didn't want to give me inaccurate information. So…I am still here for now." he sighs, "…I need another piece of bacon." He points at his mouth. Hm, spoiled brat.

I amusedly shake my head and reach for more bacon. He snatches my hand and yanks me into a kiss. I gasp as he teasingly licks my lips and bites them. Before I can really do anything, he stops the kiss and slowly reopens his eyes, "I have waited too long..." **What?** I leisurely raise an eyebrow. He whispers close to my lips, "I know there is something you have been hiding from me; something you have wanted to tell me that is very important between you and I." Oh...

He pulls me closer and quietly says in my ear, "Ivy...I want to tell you that I love you...very much...because you are the one person that has kept me going, and you are more than I could have ever asked for. You are everything–*my* everything. And I want to be yours too." he kisses behind my ear, "I really love you Ivy." My mouth slowly falls agape; I think I've just forgotten how to speak or even how to think of where we are. He said it. He said it! I bury my face in his shoulder and hold him close in that way I wish to never let go. "I love you too Nick...more than I could ever explain. I do." A warm smile rife with ecstasy graces my lips. He leans his head against mine and slowly closes his eyes, content. This amount of happiness I have right now...all I can say is, I'm absolutely, positively...*complete*.

Chapter 42

-Susan-

Chayton and I walk up to the ferry ticket office and I place the card Walter gave me on the counter. The clerk notices Chayton's ritual robes. Though it's unusual to him, he doesn't comment on it. He looks at the card, then says, "Yes ma'am, we've been expecting you. The ferry is ready for your departure." Oh?

"Well that's a surprise. Thank you." I smile. We turn and head for the gangway. The ferry master is standing onboard at the other end, waiting for us. When we reach him, he says, "We will be underway momentarily. Please sit down." He waves his hand at two men standing on the dock. They remove the gangway and untie the ferry. The ferry master picks up a microphone and announces over the speaker system, "Underway." The ferry begins to move away from the dock.

While we're crossing the Sound, Chayton and I take this opportunity to summon our spirit guides for special guidance to help open ourselves to the spirit world and to protect us from any harm. Mine is a distant relative and his is a shaman from the 1700's. In doing this, we will be able to see whatever is on the island.

We arrive at the landing, get off the ferry, thanking the ferry master along the way, and immediately follow the path leading to the castle.

As we're walking, our senses are stirred by the presence of spirits long past. Some are American Indians. None of them speak; they only watch us. Chayton slightly bows to a few of them, paying respect to them. They peacefully gesture in acknowledgement.

Soon, I begin to sense hatred and the feeling as though someone planned to murder someone close to them. It's coming from my right, in the trees. This is residual energy; a replay of things from the past. I look in that direction. There's a woman in a formal white and yellow Edwardian dress, walking with a man, holding hands with him. His face is blurry. Sometimes this happens; sometimes their faces are not fully revealed–or at all. I narrow my eyes as I try to understand what I'm witnessing. My spirit guide brings the scene closer to me in a vision that's almost like watching it live.

The woman seems very familiar but I can't place her yet. There's white light coming out of her eyes and her mouth every time she opens it. Her skin is perfect; everything about her projects angelic. Even her body has a white aura around it. But I can feel this is all a lie. She's bad–very bad. Anytime I see something like that, it ends up being the opposite of what it portrays itself as. Everything is happening in flashes now.

The man pulls her down to a blanket and whispers something I assume is romantic to her, which draws a smile from her. They both have secret plans, now I'm realizing. She wants energy–his energy, and **more** of it–and he wants to kill her because he knows she's eventually going to kill him. Now I'm really beginning to think she's that thing inside Mr. Francis.

Chayton stops to join in the vision, then he utters a low disturbed grunt.
The man and woman start to kiss, and in the middle of that, he reaches behind him and pulls a pistol out. She doesn't notice. Suddenly, he shoots her in the temple. As she falls back, he glowers at her, watching her blood stream onto the blanket. In an instant, I see a bolt of white energy leave her mouth and go straight into his head. At that same instant, the spirit of the woman rises and stands a few feet away silently glaring. She then fades away like a mist blown in the wind.

He backs away and stands up from the blanket dropping the gun with a painful shout and grabs his face, pressing on his temples hard. It does no good. He falls to his knees and then hits the ground, unconscious.

I squeeze my eyes shut, then look to a different place. One of her victims. I do wonder how many she's had.

"Medea." Chayton mutters.
I questionably glance at him, "…That woman out there?"

He nods ahead, "You didn't hear it?"
"Hear what…?" I slowly ask.

"The whispers within the trees said the imposture's name is Medea. She possessed someone living here at this castle." He then looks at me, "Her name is not Rozalia; her name is *Medea*. That is her *true* name. She is an ancient entity from another world; an inter-dimensional traveler. She came here because humans are easy prey. The people of this land learned this and told me."

"Oh my god," I murmur. "You said possessed…not possesses. She doesn't anymore?"
"She has moved to a new host." He says.
"I wonder if we will meet again…" I say.

As we're getting closer to the castle, we start to see Walter patiently waiting outside the front doors. I study the place up and down, admiring it, but also watching some other residual spirits. Some of the men that were hired to help build this place are still hammering nails into wood and the stonemasons are still laying bricks down. A few of them died on the job over the few years it took to build this magnificent building.

Finally, we reach Walter. He bows in greeting. Chayton does the same back and I smile. "Good morning Walter, this is Chayton. He is a shaman from one of the greater tribes of New York. I will be assisting him in the cleansing. I must say…this is a very beautiful castle."

He smiles proudly, "Yes it is. Thank you and good morning to you. It's a pleasure to meet you sir." Chayton smiles briefly at him, then forms a very serious look as he stares straight ahead.

"Is there anyone in the castle or on the property?" I ask.
"No Ms. Winters, as per your instructions."

"Good. Before we get started Walter…there are some things I

must warn you about."

"Yes Miss Winters?"

"We ask that you keep an open mind during this cleansing and you may experience some discomfort."

"Discomfort? How do you mean?"

"You may be touched, or feel extreme cold or heat; also, you may feel ill or dizzy. These spirits can make you uncomfortable in an effort to make us stop the cleansing. We ask that you do what you can to get through this."

"Miss Winters...I don't believe most of what you say. But, I will get through this regardless of the circumstances." He opens a door and waves us in, "Please come inside."

I nod, Chayton firmly dips his head, and we move on.

My first step inside sends a highly overwhelming mixture of emotions through my body. I don't like this at all. I turn to see Chayton coming through the door and I hear a gush of wind. Suddenly I have a feeling something ferocious is filling my personal space. I look in front of me and see a very, very tall coal-black entity suddenly materialize. It bends down into my face then quickly switches to Chayton while forming the facial features of a malicious vampiric woman. She takes in a deep breath and screams, "*WHAT ARE YOU DOING HERE?! GET OUT*!!!" Her voice is extremely shrill and rough. It *hurts*! Walter cannot see or hear any of this. I gesture him to stay behind me just in case.

I've never seen anything like that before either!

Walter notices us reacting to something, but sees nothing.

Chayton takes a peacock feather out of his bag and swipes it at her. She vanishes immediately with an angry wail.

He turns to me, "We begin the cleansing now. Is there a basement?"

"Yes there is... This way." Walter says. We follow him across the grand room to a hall on the left side of the staircase. We walk up it until he stops at a nondescript door and opens it. There inside, is a single-man set of stairs leading down. He offers to go first, but

Chayton says no. Walter stands by and waits for Chayton and I to proceed down when I hear him say ouch. I turn around and see him reaching around to his lower back. "Are you alright Walter?" He has a look of confusion and seems to be a little out of breath. "I believe I feel a burning sensation."

"Do you want me to look at it?" I ask. He straightens himself and looks me in the eyes, "No Miss Winters...let us continue." Chayton lets out an impatient sigh and turns back around. "We go now." he says. I light a sage stick and blow it out so it smolders. The smoke is prevalent and has an immediate effect on the general feeling of the area. I also have a spray bottle containing holy water just in case.

We get to the bottom of the stairs without any other incident and begin to go into every room in the basement. There are many, and Walter is unlocking every one. Most of the rooms are empty, and some have old furniture in storage. We come to a door that he hesitates to open.

"Is there a problem Walter?" I ask.
"This room is the private files room. Ordinarily, I would not open this door for anyone, but...Mr. Francis did say complete access..." He unlocks the door and just when he turns the knob, it flies open with great force and a gust of hot damp air hits all of us in the face. The air smells like road kill. Then we hear all manner of noises coming from the room. Screaming, laughing, banging–just total demonic unrest! Walter hears and sees all of this, and now he is as white as a sheet of paper. I tell him, "Please stay here in the hall if it helps you." He looks at both of us in amazement–probably because we don't appear to be frightened. We know this is all for show, but he doesn't. He decides to stick with us and follows us in.

Chayton's attention is focused on the far left corner of the room. We turned the lights on, but that corner is completely dark. I can hear some breathing coming from there. The darkness begins to envelope the room one inch at a time. It's moving toward us and we feel the temperature dropping. Chayton stands his ground and begins to chant. He holds the feather toward the darkness and I see his eyes narrowing. I start retreating to the door with Walter but stop short of backing into him. Chayton is chanting faster as the darkness reaches him. I see the face of a woman in the middle of it and she is screaming at him. He chants even louder to match her voice and then he disappears inside the darkness. I panic and scream at it. My spirit guide reaches for me in my mind and tells me, "Do not be afraid…it is an illusion." Walter is holding my right arm very tight and it's beginning to hurt. The light from the hall is starting to glow brighter and all of a sudden I can see Chayton again. He is standing in front of me with his hands together holding the feather.

"This room is finished, let's move on." He says. I cannot explain what happened. I just know this is why I asked him to be here. The rest of the basement is quiet, but we still must do every room.

We return to the grand room and continue on the main floor. Chayton reaches into his bag hanging from his shoulder and takes out a rattle. It's handmade and looks pretty old. Next, he takes out another feather and a bottle of water. Walter asks, "Is that Holy water?" Chayton then smiles and says, "No…sometimes I get a little thirsty when I do this." Walter looks at me as I smile up at him. Chayton hands me the feather and says, "For protection." I take it and we continue to follow the shaman around the grand room as he shakes his rattle, gently sways his feather and chants something in the language of his people in a low voice. While he's doing this, I fan the smoke from my sage stick around with my feather.

There are many ghosts from different eras here; most of them are friends to Mr. Francis. But they're like the men outside; they're residual. They're walking around, holding beverages of all sorts, smoking cigars and behaving like there is a party going on. At least they're happy. The few friends that are aware of their surroundings come to me with warning; "You shouldn't be here! Rozalia will return soon!" I look at them and say through my mind, "You don't have to worry about her anymore. You're free." They get quiet and very curious.

They follow us past the grand staircase, into a hallway and through a door that leads into the Ballroom. There, we meet an older Romanian man named Corneliu. He is very protective of the castle and is concerned for Nicolai. He speaks broken English; but it's well enough for me to understand.

His problem is…he believes his life ended way too early and all he wants now is for 'Rozalia' to be gone. Or so he should know— her name is Medea. I tell him everything will be taken care of and not to worry.

He follows us around, constantly in my ear about making sure I do this right. It's a little annoying. He also mentions the one that got in my face earlier is Jennifer and he strongly advises that I should be careful about her.

The farther we go, the more we start to hear banging, pops, screams, glass shattering and things sliding across the floor. The screams are from two distinct female spirits. I recognize one from earlier at the front door but the other is unknown as of yet. I get a strong feeling like someone was held against their will down here. My wrists are getting a little sore as this becomes clearer to me. I can't understand it fully.

I'm seeing something about a woman from the 1920's being pushed up against a wall by a big man. He pins her wrists against the stone wall, aggressively kissing and licking her neck. He thinks she's funny. She gasps and screams as he suddenly clamps his jaw down on her neck. My eyes light up. He throws his head back with a deep throaty laugh as she slides down the wall, holding the bloody bite mark and crying. He stops laughing and yanks her back up to lick her neck again. Then suddenly, the episode ends.

I realize I haven't taken a breath for some time now. A few more times, I rub my wrists and choose to keep this to myself. I'm curious to know who these people were. What a strange, evil, twisted man. I hope he's paying for what he's done. That girl is residual, thank goodness. She's moved on. This scene is a memory that will never leave the castle. Terrible–just terrible.

We leave the Ballroom through a side door and enter a long hallway. There is a sitting room just across and over to my right. When we go in there, we all notice the pictures on the walls are tilting sideways while the vases on the table near the fireplace tremble. There are two chandeliers swinging back and forth and an ashtray keeps sliding around in a perfect circle on the floor. It amazes Walter. He's watching it all with wide eyes.

"Keep an open mind Walter." I remind him.
His response is a mere nod.

Chayton never stops chanting or shaking his rattle. Sometimes he raises his voice. The smoke from my sage stick makes each room we go in feel so much heavier than before. It's a little hard on my body. All this activity stops before we leave each room. Chayton will not move on until it does. The last place we go to on this floor is the kitchen.

We step inside and immediately, the hanging pots start to shake, the cabinet drawers open and slam shut as well as the cupboard doors, and the lights are flickering on and off. I hear bare feet slapping the floor around the counter closest to me. I raise an eyebrow. 'I hear you but I can't see you...' I think to myself. I get a sudden flash of a dark-haired vampiric woman in my mind. It's a different woman; this one is vicious but not nearly as bad as Jennifer. I ask her name–in case she might still have one. My answer is a scream and a jab in the nape of my neck, making me wince and grunt. I wait for a few seconds. Nothing. I sense she's left the room. The pain from the jab makes me want to rub my neck, but I can't put my feather or sage down. This is too important.

Chayton doesn't lose his focus, though I know he is a little concerned by what just happened. Walter is trying to stay as calm as possible but he wears a worried expression as he looks at a double sink. The water is coming out of the faucet but it's curving into the other sink.

"I've never seen this happen before." he says in a voice as if trying not to gasp while he watches everything moving in random ways. He then asks me, "Are you alright?"

Fanning smoke toward the counter, I glance at him and say, "I was poked in the back of my neck but I'm okay." He becomes a bit fazed.

We leave the kitchen and head upstairs to the second floor. The bedrooms aren't as active but we are *definitely* in the presence of those malevolent ones. They really don't want us here and are trying to do everything in their power to force us out. The mattresses on the beds shake and slightly jump up and down, and the curtains blow around. Corneliu stands by us with little to no emotion on his face, but I know he is disgusted by what is going on. This is not Jennifer causing all the chaos in here; it's the one that poked me. She's back to hiding herself. I already know she hasn't been dead long; it truly stuns me that she has advanced so quickly in such a short amount of time. Even with help from other spirits, it couldn't work. Spirits learn in their own time. But then again, I don't think this one is human. I don't know *what* she is.

Every room on this floor is quite extraordinary, I must admit. Walter explains that each bedroom represents a castle Mr. Vladoiu, the owner of this castle, has been to. Some of them are very unique; so exquisite I fall in love with them right off the bat. Chayton seems to like them too. However, we don't have much time to admire them like we want to. This floor is just mad with a feeling of vertigo. Balls of bright light come at us at terrific speeds just missing our bodies as they go by. These spirits really *hate* us.

We leave one room and start to enter another but we stop in our tracks to seeing ourselves walking at the other end of the hallway.

"How is that possible?!" Walter asks. Chayton looks at him and I, saying, "Sometimes, they can make you see what they want you to see. They want you to think you have lost your mind and want to leave this place. I have seen this many times. We will continue and finish what we are here for." Hesitant, Walter nods and puts his hand on my shoulder. He was very skeptical before we started, but now I am pretty sure he has no doubts about any of this. He looks quite worried, but in a positive way.

We go upstairs to the third floor. Some rooms are very eerie, less active and give off the gut-wrenching, sick feeling. In almost every one we step into, we're greeted by different odors. Some are pleasant; like flowers or perfume...and others are just terrible with the scent of rotting flesh. But nothing really happens–except the walls sounding like they're going to bow in on us. Little shadows continue to jump from one side of the hallway to the other. They're making the lights flash. Overall...I would say everything is calm before the storm...

We go to the last door in the hall first. It's locked. Automatically, I feel sick to my stomach. I turn to Walter and gesture towards the knob. He lets out a heavy sigh, "This is Mr. Francis' private quarters..." Oh...I see.
I remind him, "We must have full access." He purses his lips and nods, unlocking the door.

I step in first and my attention immediately focuses on the bed. The bedspread in on the floor and there is someone or something writhing under the sheets. Chayton sees this and quickly goes around me, raising his voice and flicking his feather at the bed. The sheets go flat and tight to the mattress. He turns to me and smiles like a little kid who just did something wonderful. "Let's move on." he says. I think he is really enjoying himself now.

The things making me feel sick are black entities everywhere in all shapes and sizes, created by the living and the dead. They're called PK manifestations, which are confused as poltergeists but are made by humans who have abilities. They are complete darkness; never were human; all made of negative energy. It's up to Chayton to get rid of them. But he needs me with him in the areas they stay in most. Both he and I use our feathers on the masses. I make sure to fan extra smoke at them. They don't like this at *all*. Their forms contort and squirm along the walls, toward the closet. We follow them into it. Another wave of uneasiness sickens me. It's very, very strong now.

I smell and feel death straight ahead. The words **'kill'** and **'murder'** keep going through my head. I don't understand it but I know this–it's really bad. The masses are gone. I would voice my opinion on this stuff but I don't want to scare Walter any more.

We walk into the adjoining kitchen suite and notice something rattling. Our eyes trace the sound to the glasses and dishware in the cabinets. A plate flies off a shelf and smashes into a wall, a loud bloodcurdling screech filling our ears at that same moment. I wince and quickly wave sage smoke toward the counters and shelves. A low grumble starts vibrating the floor. It sounds like something is building up. My attention trails over near the sink where a bottle of wine is starting to boil. I continue waving the smoke in that direction, more seriously now. Chayton puts his rattle away and sprays holy water at it. There's an infuriated hiss and a door swings open, almost coming off the hinges.

The room has now fallen silent.
Whoever that is, they've just left.

Staring wide-eyed at the boiling wine, Walter clears his throat and nods once at us.
He then leads us into Mr. Francis's office.

Everything is calm in here–despite the nonstop banging, door slamming, pops, creaking and screaming outside. I look around suspiciously. There's a very odd sound coming from the desk; something like stepping on and off an old squeaky floorboard. It looks like it isn't moving, but I'm positive that's where the noise is coming from. Walter is focusing on it intently. Suddenly, it jumps and slides across the floor toward him. He gasps, quickly backing up. I hurry toward it, swish smoke at it and we all hear a loud growl. He holds his chest, "Oh my!" I place a hand on his shoulder once the desk stops moving, "Keep as calm as you can." He inhales deeply and blinks a couple times in amazement.

"Aaaaa*AAAAHHH*!!!" The lights brighten as the glass-shattering scream shakes the windows. Suddenly the bulbs burst, and the door to the hall slowly opens. I hear a breath behind me. Slightly, I turn my head, but just as I do, something shoots into my back and squeezes my heart tightly. "*Ugh*!" I clutch my chest, wincing, breathing quickly. I'm surprised I'm not dropping to the floor. "Miss Winters, are you alright?" Walter gasps. I scowl, "No, I *will not* let you IN!!!" I cross my feather over my heart and flick it at the door. I'm instantly released and nearly fall to my knees. Chayton approaches me and searches my face. I breathe heavily a few times before I sigh, "I'm fine." Staring at me, he gives me a gentle nod and then Walter an assuring, permissive expression. Hesitantly, Walter bows his head and we follow him out.

For a little bit, each room we go in only feels heavy. It's the feeling of being targeted by something lingering in the shadows, toying with us. Some rooms are extremely uncomfortable. I think I'm being targeted most of all. On and off, I'm getting images of my worst fear; shadow people murdering my family and imprisoning them in the afterlife. My family would be tortured and used until they fade to nothing. Very powerful entities or spirits can do that. It's very hard to continue with this happening to me. I almost want to stop, but I remind myself of the poor man in the hospital…and that creature I saw. No, this is just a threat–a threat that I choose not to believe. *Nothing* will stop me!

We go back out into the hallway, now halfway to the end. Chayton and I can hear coarse whispers and labored breathing. We're starting to see black muddy water sliding out from the tops and bottoms of each door and zigzagging up the hall from one door to the next. Some of it is sliding across the walls and ceiling. It's one of the freakiest things I've ever seen!

Suddenly, in the center of it all, we see Jennifer shoot up out of the floor. She drops her head to a side while her form is beginning to flicker like a clicking, snapping flame.

"Do not go any farther." Corneliu warns.
"That's what she wants." I whisper. I walk forward with Chayton at my side.

Walter only hears things and shivers from the temperature dropping.

Waving the smoke out all around us as we go into the darkness, I stare at the unmoving Jennifer. She doesn't think we'll pass her. How arrogant she is. Because of the look I'm giving her, she is becoming more furious with me. My focusing on her will allow me to see certain things about her that she's trying to keep secret–and she *really* hates that.

I'm able to see one of her memories of when she was alive. She walked out of a bar with a drunken businessman who was having serious issues with his wife. They were supposed to go to her hotel room. I see now; she was a high-end prostitute. This was about 5 years before she met a man named Dmitri…or so, that's what I'm getting so far.

They walked down a dark, empty alleyway, laughing. Then he pushed her against a wall and clumsily locked lips with her. She behaved as though she enjoyed him fondling her body and kissing her like this, but then she suddenly plunged a knife into his heart. He gasped and grabbed her hands on the handle. She twisted the blade slowly. His eyes grew while he struggled to breathe. I feel this and it's hell on my body.

She got in his ear to whisper with a crooked smile, "It would've been fun." she yanked the knife out and looked at it in a sort of adoring way. Just to see more fright in his eyes, she dragged the slick side of the bloody knife over her tongue. He gasped again, sliding down the wall. She wiped the rest of the blood off on the inside of her black blouse and then went to pull his wallet out of his pocket. Footfalls and laughing started getting close. She stood back up, took her small heels off, tossed them, pulled him behind a cluster of metal trashcans and then ran off after picking her heels up again.

Now back into reality, my eyes narrow.
This psychopath *definitely* has to go before she tries to kill again.

Chayton walks ahead of me toward her. She stiffens in

annoyance. Her body shrinks into a needle-thin shadow and darts in my direction. She disappears for a second, then all of a sudden, she's in my face, screaming, "GET–*OUUT*!!!!" Leaning my head back in amazement, I almost forget what I have in my hands, but quickly though, I wave my sage wand at her and swipe the feather through her head. "*RAHH*!!!" She wails, vanishing from our sight. All the lights shut off at once. We hear a hissing noise at the very end. It's coming toward us. Before it meets us, the lights click back on and there's nothing there.

I quickly sigh and glance back at Walter. He's surrounded by the non-residual ghosts from the grand room. They're protecting him, making him feel more comfortable as he looks around in search of what is making the noises.

We move on and soon get to the farthest point of the castle–The Sunroom, Walter calls it. We can hear creaking inside there. I look at Walter. He nods. We proceed, but then the door slams shut, startling us. My eyes widen and narrow shortly after. Walter takes a key out of his pocket and carefully goes to open the door.

Once he pushes it, our jaws fall open to the sight of orbs bouncing off the walls, the lights flickering and the furniture piling up in strange ways. The whispers are very strong in here, more vehement with their quick incomprehensible speech. Chayton and I see shadows crawling all over the place on the ceiling, looking like little spidery entities. They're causing the room to have an intense feeling of vertigo. And we see Jennifer in half-shadow form, standing in the middle of it with her head down, eyes staring up through her lashes. The woman that poked me earlier is climbing up the wall. I slightly grimace. She starts laughing at me when she gets to the ceiling. Walter can only hear her. But Chayton goes inside fearlessly with his dancelike walk and his tone is getting lower, more serious.

I proceed with Walter cautiously following behind, then he quickly decides to go stand against a wall in the clearest corner as Chayton and I begin to circle the room.

The woman on the ceiling disappears and Jennifer blocks me and attempts to enter my body every time I try to move closer to a window. I continue to take a step back but I never stop moving forward to finish this task. This is by far one of the most challenging places I've been to. The spidery creatures fall from the ceiling like rain, a female scream per drop. It really hurts my ears. Chayton only flinches a little. Walter hears it but doesn't see them. It doesn't harm him much. The chairs and tables start shaking more rapidly as I get closer to the farthest window.

The woman that vanished from the ceiling reappears at both sides of me and shouts, "YOU WILL NOT GO ANY **FARTHER**!" The room fills with wind and the windows begin to tremble. The furniture twitches, then it all flies toward the windows like pieces of iron slamming into magnets. The glass shows cracks moving up about midway. Walter clutches his chest and repeatedly looks from me to the door, "Susan, I can't take this!" I quickly look at him, "It'll be over soon!" I turn back and wave what smoke is left from my sage wand around while heading for the window again. Jennifer slides up from the floor into my face, hissing at me like a snake, "Didn't you hear Maria? YOU WON'T GO ANY FARTHER!" I look down at my feather, she follows my actions, then she shouts at me, "*NO*!" I try to swipe it at her. She snatches my wrist, shooting her negative energy into me, making me gasp and drop it. I quickly wave my smudge wand at her while digging in my pocket for the holy water. The smoke causes most of the darkness about her to grate away, forcing her to collapse with a scream. I snap my head up and spray her with the holy water. Her face begins to come apart as she falls. I see Chayton opening the window. Breathing quickly, I look at Walter and then hurry over to shield him from what damage is likely to occur.

Chayton finally pushes it open and his chanting is **ROARING** with authority. He swishes his feather from the room to the window, back and forth many times. Maria wails as the shadows around her begin to fade into ashes and blow toward the window.

She drops to her knees with her hands reaching up, "JENNIFER! SAVE *ME*!" The lights are brightening as if about they're to burn out. Coming through the door, white streams of light race toward the window, going past Corneliu who is inspecting his hands in a very worried way. Slowly, he looks up at me and then we both look at Jennifer and Maria. Some of the lights are circling around their feet. Maria hisses while trying to fight them and Jennifer uses the remaining shadows to defend herself. But the two aren't strong enough anymore. The lights force them to the floor and they slam their hands down to hold on as their bodies are being pulled away; shadowy embers are splitting away from their forms. My eyes have widened greatly and my mouth has fallen open, now that I realize these lights are the non-residual ones from the grand room. And they are pulling the evil out with them.

I look for Corneliu and find him in the same state as Jennifer and Maria; only he's being pushed to walk toward the window. A few white figures are on both sides of him. I hear Jennifer and Maria scream once more, along with loud scratching noises. Quickly, I look at them again. They're clawing at the windowpanes as the darkness lastly slips away from their faces, revealing them as women who never seemed nonhuman. The force becomes so strong they can barely hang on anymore. Jennifer shouts "*NOOO*!!!" and Maria cries, "JENNIFER-!" They're pushed out, disappearing outside the window. Corneliu stumbles over himself on his way to it, trying not to fall. "*DMITRI*!" he splutters. As the darkness tears away from him, he yells in pain. I watch him closely, furrowing my brows in wonder about who 'Dmitri' is.

In the moment he meets the window at last, I get a vision from him of the past he had with this person–Dmitri–how he adopted him from his brother and sister in-law.

They were returning to his manor in a horse-drawn carriage after going on a trip somewhere. He waited outside with the restless baby Dmitri in his arms. He could hear them coming up the hill on the dirt road. But then there was a disturbance with the horse. His brother suddenly shouted, his wife screamed and the horse was neighing in fright.

Corneliu hurried toward them, holding Dmitri close all the while, but when he got close enough, he noticed the horse was startled by a wild animal and caused the carriage to flip over, crushing everything inside. He was extremely devastated; he didn't know what to do at first. His brother's wife was still breathing but his brother had a wooden pole through his neck. She was also impaled; in the stomach and heart by pieces of the roof. She told Corneliu to take care of her son. He held her hand and agreed as tears filled his eyes. She looked at the silent Dmitri and slowly managed one last smile. Corneliu watched the light in her eyes fade away and he hugged Dmitri closer.

I blink, but now he's gone. The shadows are gone and two more white figures are last to go out. The wind is slowing down, the orbs have vanished and the heavy feeling isn't as intense as before. When the final spirit leaves, the furniture drops and the wind ceases completely.

All the air in my lungs belts out of me as my eyes wander the room. I look at Walter, forming a small, stunned type of smile, "…Now the castle is clean and everyone is free." He stares at me in amazement, then we look at Chayton.

Tucking his rattle and feather away in his bag, he says, "Cleansed, yes–*spiritually*." he looks at the mess of papers, an overturned desk, chairs, bookcases and other pieces of furniture spread out or piled in corners.

Walter sighs as he puts his hands on his hips and inspects everything, "Well…I don't think the maids will like this…"

Chayton and I then glance at each other.

Chapter 43

-Nicolai-

"Ok, I'm getting tired of watching these stupid soap operas. I'm about to go make a complaint." Ivy says, putting the TV remote on the end of my bed. I smile at her as she walks over and sits beside me again. How amusing...

I grab her hand and gently squeeze it, "I was never really watching it anyway, so it's fine."
She slightly frowns.

There's a knock at my door, making us instantly look at it. My doctor, David Thornton, has finally arrived. And it's 3:30. For a young man like him, I do wonder how long he's been a doctor. Probably not long.

Ivy stands up, very relieved yet aggravated. I just smile. Nothing can upset me very much right now.

He says hello to Ivy, then nods at me, "Mr. Francis." I make a friendly gesture at him. He proceeds inside with a clipboard in one hand and extends the other to shake my hand. As we do, he says, "How are you feeling today?"
"Perfectly fine." I reply.
He forms a matter-of-fact smile, "Well my friend, that is certainly true. I've looked over your chart and spoke with the nurses; you're healthier than a horse. Quite a miracle, I must say! You came in last night knocking on death's door, but today is a whole different story. Were you trying to...kill yourself?" he chuckles. I snicker back, "Yes, a miracle... Indeed it is. Well no doctor, you wouldn't believe it if I told you, but I took those pills thinking they were mints. Once I realized they weren't, I had already swallowed them!"

He shakes his finger at me knowingly, "Well alright then...but be more careful next time and stay away from those pills–you don't need them." He then takes a pen out of his pocket and starts writing on the forms on his clipboard, "I'm going to release you now. No need to keep you here any longer!" He finishes up and gives me a last smile on the way out the door, "Take care of yourself sir." He nods at Ivy as if saying the same thing to her and then he leaves.

Ivy immediately shoots me a confused look.
I inhale deeply, lowering my eyes, "Yes, that was the reason…"
She sits on the bed again, "You tried to OD on nitroglycerin pills? How many did you take and why'd you do it?"
"…It was an accident–like I said."

She lifts my chin to make me look at her and says, "Nick, you're a little too smart to have any accidents as simple as that." I blink expressionlessly at her.

"Mr. Francis…?" We both hear a woman in the doorway. Ivy rolls her eyes, then looks over at her. We see Susan standing there. She unsettles Ivy a little with her stiff posture and emotionless stare.

"Ahh, Miss Susan," I wave her inside.
She shortly smiles, stepping forward.

Ivy whispers to me, "Who's this?"
I don't answer.

Susan stops in front of the bathroom, nodding at Ivy, "Hello there."
Ivy raises her chin in reply.

I look from her to Susan twice, beginning to simper to myself, then I breathe in slowly. "Ivy, could you get me something…? A regular coffee with two spoons of sugar? "She looks at me for a moment, then finally stands and accepts, "Sure. I'll be back soon." I take her hand and kiss it, winking up at her. She is so concerned right now and a little jealous…it's cute.

As soon as she goes out, Susan says, "Mr. Francis, the cleansing was a success. The castle is free of all spirits now." Her eyes grow some, "You had a lot of people there…so much history too."
"Thank you." I quietly say, and to her saying 'free of all spirits', I

think of Corneliu. My heart sinks a little, though I keep the same serious expression. "It was much to handle, I must admit."

"I bet. I saw some interesting things." She slowly nods. I gulp down my forming sadness; imagining returning home and never seeing my uncle again. He's been with me forever–my whole life. He's all I've ever known. I know though, since Rozalia is gone, I have my life back–and it will finally end with old age. Then I will see him again in the way it was always supposed to be.

"That entity inside you…" she begins. I grimace. "I don't see her anymore." She says. I blink and look up at her from absentmindedly watching the people outside this room, "Yes…yes she is gone."

"If you don't mind me asking–what did you do?" she asks curiously. I search her eyes, then I slowly smile, "I died and came back." She stares at me speechlessly. It's quiet for a long time as she waits for me to explain more, but instead, I reach for her hand and say, "Thank you so much for everything you have done. What do I owe you?" She shakes my hand and clears her throat, "You don't owe me anything, but I would like you to make a donation to the Gales' cancer society." I arch an eyebrow, "Ahh…very well then. I will do as you ask as soon as possible."
"Thank you." She smiles, stepping back a bit, then she seems thoughtful. "You are a very interesting man; maybe we could have coffee together someday…?"
I tilt my head with a kind yet professional smile, nodding once, "Interesting? No…not like before at least. Perhaps one day we could." She wondrously eyes my features. "…It was nice meeting you sir."

"Likewise…Miss Susan." I say.
She goes to the door, waves at me and leaves.

Right as she disappears from my sight, I see Ivy coming up the hall, watching Susan on her way to my room. I have to grin; the way she's looking at her is funny.

Once she comes in, she gives me my coffee, asking, "So…who

is she?" Taking the drink, I sigh in relief and move around to sit on the side of my bed, "Ohh, thank you... That woman? She is a medium." That surprises her.

"Did she help you with your ghost problem somehow?" I hum the positive, sipping from my cup. She puts her hands on her hips, "Huh. I wonder how that went." I put my coffee down and again smile up at her, "I will explain everything when we return to the castle, ok?" She turns to me and looks over my gown, "Yeah, you need to get dressed."

I wink at her, "You could help if you want." She blushes, and I laugh quietly.
"Ok," She says with an impish smile. I get up while she begins collecting my clothes and then we both go in the bathroom.

"So you don't want to tell me anything about Susan now?"
I look at her a bit sardonically as I pull my gown off, "I've got a lot to explain. Walter knows more than I do about this, really." She takes the gown from me, becoming even more curious,
"Wow...then I imagine he'll have a lot to say. That castle is hopping mad with activity."
I smirk and tap her nose, "Not anymore love–not anymore." She blinks, amazed–also repeatedly glancing at my muscles. I'm only in black shorts. I laugh, snatch her into a tight hug and kiss her many times, making her giggle and playfully struggle in my arms. "No, no, you have to finish getting dressed!"

"No, you need to kiss me back!"
"You won't let me!"

I grab her chin. She flutters her eyelashes up at me. I whisper, "Kiss me Ivy." She blinks again, then pecks me on the lips and escapes me. I fling my arms out, "You call *that* a kiss?!" She brings her hand up to her mouth, trying to contain her laughter. I beckon her with a finger, "Unacceptable. Come here. Now." She shakes her head. I lift an eyebrow, "Disobedience? Hm, well then." She starts to back up to the door. I slightly smile, then march up and pin her against it, lustfully taking her lips. It stuns her, as it always does. I soon let go of her wrists to hold her waist and she wraps her arms around my neck, giving me a passionate French kiss. Oh I wish we were back home…!

I slow to a stop and tell her with a smile, "Much better. But sadly, we have to go."
She only watches my face, not wanting the kiss to stop but she eventually accepts.

I take my pants and start fitting them on as she picks up my shirt and shoes.
I have plans for when we return home…

We've left the hospital and are now riding in the backseat of my car. Esmeralda is driving us to her house. I don't like using hospital phones but it's what I had to do to let her know I was ready to leave.

During this ride, I realize how different life truly is for me. No, I shouldn't say 'different'; I should say 'normal' and 'wonderful'. I don't sense Ivy's heartbeat but I'm quite positive from the way she behaves, she is anxious to know what I will tell her. Her grasp on my hand says it all; how she squeezes it from time to time and looks at me with a smile that hides so much curiosity.

I squeeze back a little firmer, whispering to her, "Don't worry my love; I promise everything will be perfect now." She nods slowly, moving closer and resting her head on my chest. I look out my window happily, watching the trees and enjoying how the sun warms me and doesn't hurt my eyes. Life is…*grand*.

"Mr. Francis, I just can't tell you how stunned I am. You scared everybody, you know?" Esmeralda says, looking in the rear view mirror at me. She has already said something like that twice. I'm amused.
"Me too Esmeralda–me too." I laugh.

"Well then! We're here now." she says as she pulls into her driveway. Ivy and I look around and see Leonardo standing near the house, smiling, watching us arrive. We park in the garage and come out where the he greets us happily.

"Mr. Francis, good to see you on your feet and well again!" He shakes hands with me and then tips his hat to Ivy. I chuckle softly, "Yes, thank you. It was quite an adventure for me, I tell you." "I'll bet!" he smiles again at us both, "Miss Summers, Mr. Francis, I won't keep you waiting any longer; I'll take you to the island now." He salutes us and starts for the boathouse. Esmeralda joins him, waving at us as she goes on her way.

"Come now," I place my hand on the small of Ivy's back and follow behind them. She's surprised at how happy Leonardo and his sister are. I do agree it is a little out of character but something big happened last night. Now with that in mind, I can understand their behavior better.

We start crossing the Sound, and I think of Walter. What did he experience? I am very, very curious to know what happened during the cleansing. Did he see anything, was he harmed at all and what did he hear? Have the spirits shaken him enough to make him a firm believer in the supernatural? If they did, what will our future conversations be like? Will he live the rest of his life in fear? All these questions... I guess I will just have to wait and see...

Soon, we reach Leonardo's boathouse and as Leonardo ties the boat off and secures it, I tell him, "Tonight...join Ivy and I for dinner. Tell your sister to come."

Ivy glances up at me, holding my arm, "This is different. What's the occasion this time?" she makes a humored face at me. I smile down at her, "In celebration of life itself." That makes her smile back, though at the same time I'm sure she doesn't understand this fully. That's ok.

"Well sir, I'll give her a call." Leonardo says with surprise in his voice, again tipping his hat.
I raise a hand, "See you this evening my friend."

"Yes sir!"
I nod at him and then we start for the castle.

On the way there, I pay close attention to my surroundings; watching the trees, bushes…that certain area I always refuse to look at. No one–nothing–is there anymore. Not a soul. The terror is replaced with the beauty of nature. I can actually hear the birds chirping, I can feel the cool breeze caress my face and hair, and I can listen to the wind blowing through the trees. It's been so long since I could experience these things–since I could take it all in without any distractions. The feeling is like taking a breath of sweet fresh air for the first time. My eyes are beginning to water a little. I slowly lift my head, shutting my eyes and just breathing it in. A couple minutes pass and then we're at the front doors. They open, revealing the warm-smiling Walter. Ivy is unsure and hesitant to go in. I already know it's safe, so I assure her that it's ok.

"Mr. Francis, Miss Summers…welcome home." He bows slowly and steps aside.
"Walter, my friend…it's good to be back." I smile back as we walk inside.

In the foyer, I search around and try to feel for the spirits. It's silent. Nothing. It feels like an actual home. Hold on…

I realize Walter is asking for my jacket. I shake a hand at him politely, "Excuse me for a moment; let me do this." I walk forward into the grand room, leaving him and the puzzled Ivy there. I see the maids are not far ahead, standing in a line, smiling at me. They were in the middle of cleaning up after the party. I return the smile with my own, but I mostly focus on this feel of the castle. God, it's so empty. So…so empty and… I really can't explain this feeling properly, other than to say I haven't felt so at peace in…all of my life, pretty much.

"Sir, is everything alright?" I hear Walter behind me. Slowly, I look up at the top of the stairs on the right, searching for Corneliu or anyone else. There's no one. I know I don't have the sixth sense anymore, but that certain feeling is something anyone could get. I don't have it at all. He's gone. My eyebrows start coming together, my eyes well up more, and I swallow. "Dear god…" I'm alone in my home. At last.

I cover my face with a hand, holding back all the tears of this great relief. No Jennifer, no Maria, no more poor souls of all those innocent women I've killed. The ones who built this place and my friends who have stayed here all these years; they are all now at peace. And Corneliu…my uncle…my *father*–he can finally rest in peace too.

"Nick…" Ivy approaches my side, taking a gentle hold of my arm. I sniffle, keeping my hand over my face. I can't let her see me like this. But the maids and Walter are watching too.

I let out a slow sigh and almost whisper, "I'm ok." I swallow again and then smile warmly at her. She sees how glassy my eyes are and how red my face is. Before she can comment, I pull her into a hug and look at the slightly frowning Walter. He lowers his head.

I shake mine, "No no Walter…look at me." He does. I smile contently at him, "We have things to discuss–in the ballroom." "The ballroom…sir?" he asks, a little bemused.

"Yes! That is where I want to speak with you." I say.
Ivy oddly looks up into my eyes.

"I've got a surprise for you." I tell her, which makes her stare curiously at me.
We look at Walter again. "Alright then…very well sir." He says while raising his eyebrows, slowly looking away.

I step back from Ivy, lift her hand up and kiss it, then I turn slightly and bow my head at the maids, "Ladies, forgive me for being so rude. It's wonderful to see you all again. Thank you for welcoming me home." My words warm them, and Angel blushes. I smirk as I remember the idea I had at the hospital. "Excuse me darling," I say to Ivy, then I walk up to Christine and whisper something in her ear. She looks at me, stunned, then she nods and starts walking for the stairs on the right. I then point toward the left archway, "The ballroom, shall we?" I offer my arm to Ivy. Slightly confused, she takes it. Walter is a little bewildered too. "Of course sir." They *really* don't understand my behavior. That entertains me.

"Very good. Ladies, you may continue with your day." I tell the maids, now guiding Ivy and Walter to the archway. In unison, they say, "Yes sir…!"

We go on to the ballroom, and during the walk there, we're quiet. Walter is uncomfortable about talking in there, I can tell. Everything will be fine though, I'm sure.

The ballroom is still decorated, as I expected. When we get to the middle of it, I tell Ivy to wait on the organ's bench and that I will be with her shortly.

"You're going to play it?" She quietly and excitedly asks. "Yes I am." I grin. She bites her lip with an innocent smile and then goes to sit down.

I slide my hands into my pants' pockets, now turning to Walter, "So, tell me how the cleansing went." Though he keeps a professional attitude, he becomes hesitant.

"Sir, I must tell you–I saw things that I once considered impossible and unimaginable. But I will explain the most important details first. Miss Winters arrived with a shaman at 10:30 this morning and began right away. I followed them as they went into each room, fanning the smoke from Miss Winters' sage wand. The shaman was shaking a rattle and holding a feather. I'm still not certain what they were doing, but it was working. It stirred the spirits sir, and the castle came alive in a very strange way. There were women screaming, things were moving, sometimes the rooms would suddenly fill with different odors. Your room, sir…it had the smell of death so strong, it was almost unbearable for me but I held my breath and endured it the best I could. The last room–the sunroom…before we could go in there, the door slammed shut. I had to unlock it, and once I opened the door, we all saw balls of light bouncing around the room. Furniture was piled up and the screams were louder. Oddly enough though, during all this excitement, I felt somehow a bit safe–as if something was guarding me. Strange to say, I know…but I must be honest. There was a battle there that I couldn't see and Miss Susan and the shaman were winning it. In the midst of all that, we suddenly felt wind blowing around us. Where could that have come from? The furniture that was piled up before suddenly slammed into the windows, and cracks went halfway up the glass. It was a big mess. When it was all over, I called Leonardo to take them back to the mainland. I would say…the service was quite successful. Nothing else has happened." He sighs, and doesn't say anything else. I can't say anything either. I'm relieved but a little pissed. However, knowing the spirits are gone, I can't be too angry. I had no idea things would get this bad. He witnessed a lot! I have a very good idea on what Susan saw. I used to see things like that every day.

I pat his shoulder, "Walter, I am sorry you endured this much…but now, the castle is free of it all. Everyone that was here before can finally rest in peace. And we can learn how to enjoy life again." His head drops some, "Indeed sir…indeed." We both hear one of the double doors open. Christine is coming in. I slowly smile, then look at Walter again. In this moment, I think of tonight and how I would like everyone to dine with Ivy and I.

"This evening…have Mr. Fitzgerald prepare a large dinner." I say.

"Yes sir. How many guests are you expecting?"

I lift a hand in a matter-of-fact type of way, "*Everyone*!-You and the staff. I think it's about time I return the kindness you all give me. You are family." I wink at him.

His brows rise, "Why, yes sir–of course! I will speak with Mr. Fitzgerald immediately and announce tonight's dinner to the maids and Eduard."

"Very good!" Gleefully, I pat his shoulder again twice. He smiles back at me and then heads for the doors.

I glance at Ivy and see she is becoming a little suspicious…and impatient. Hm…

Christine approaches me with a small black box. I gladly take it,

"Thank you dear." She blushes, slightly looking over at Ivy, who then tilts her head. "You're welcome sir." She turns and leaves with a secretive smile.

I stuff it in my jacket pocket and move toward Ivy with a dancelike stroll. She stares me down warily, curiously. That really entertains me.

As soon as I'm close enough, I slide down onto the seat beside her and gaze into her eyes, "Hello love." Her cheeks redden and she looks down at the pocket with the box in it. I shake my finger at her, "Ah ah ahh…" I lift her chin, "I will play for you."

"What's in the box-" I put my finger on her lips, stopping her. "I will play for you first." I say. She blinks at me. I dip my head, turn to the organ and crack my fingers, also winking at her out of the corner of my eye, "Alright babe, don't drool too much." She rolls her eyes. I lift my hands, then slam my fingers down on the keys, striking a loud and powerful chord, making her jump, and I laugh while looking around the room enjoying the great sound.

She clutches her chest, shouting, "Oh my god! That's awesome!"
I let off all of a sudden, leaning in close to her, "No, not yet."
"Huh?!"

I then flip the page on the book of sheet music–even though I won't need it. "Watch," I focus down at the keys and start playing Magnificat by Sebastian Bach. Her mouth starts to fall agape. I glance at her and begin to smile, continuing to play.

Among the many pieces he's done, this is a favorite of mine to play. And I've even made my own musical compositions with the organ. Without music, what is life?-but a dull colorless existence.

Soon, I finish the piece and look at her. She slowly raises her eyes up to mine, "That's…that's amazing… No, **beyond** amazing! That's **extraordinary**!"
I make a tsking noise, "No my dear, I already told you what is…"

"What do you mean? That's **mad** skill there and you didn't even use the sheet music!"

I stand up and offer a hand. She daintily places hers in mine and I help her off the seat. I reach into my pocket, "A gift you say. I seldom think of it that way. Hmmm…maybe so…but it means nothing if you are not pure of heart. You Ivy, have the purest heart of anyone I have ever known and are more special than any gift in the world." I take the box out and kneel slowly. She gasps, starting to raise her hands over her mouth. I smile and open it, presenting a beautiful diamond ring, "You are a gift so special, I would do anything, and everything…to have you. We were made for each other, Ivy…and I want us to live a relaxed and happy life together. Would you give me the honor to be your husband?" She covers her face, letting her head down and trying to keep her composure. I hear her starting to sniffle and make little noises.

"…Oh, Nick…" she chuckles a little, turning away slightly. I only smile. She slowly looks at me again, "Oh my *gosh*…!" My smile widens into a toothy one.

"Of course I will. I love you!"
I bow my head, then look up at her again. She gives me her hand, and I gently slide the ring onto her finger. As she watches, she whispers, "Wow…it's so…it's so beautiful…" she sniffles again. I finish and quietly say, "It was my mother's…long ago."
"Long ago?" she asks.

I slowly stand, "Yes…"
"What happened to her?"

I think back on what Corneliu told me. How she and my father died. And when it happened.
So very long ago.

"Here–come, come," I sit her down on the bench, "Since you have seen so much here at this castle, you are more believing of unnatural things, yes?"

"Yes…" she says, bemused.
"Well I have a story that you will have a hard time believing but you can't tell anyone. It's just between you and me."

"Your mother was a werewolf or something?" she jokes.

"No no…" I laugh, "No not at all." I then sigh and gently rub my forehead, trying to find the best way to explain this to her. Ahh…I just gave her a ring! Tell her the truth about mother, and tell her about the past over time or whenever it feels right.

I rub my chin and then stop.
"She was here the whole time and wanted me to give you that ring. She died a long time ago when I was a baby." I say.

"Oh wow…! Aww… But Nick, how could that be something hard for me to believe?" She asks. I shake my head with a small laugh, "I don't know."
She stands up and hugs me, "I love you so much."
I hug her tighter, "I love you more than you could ever imagine…my Ivy."

Maybe I can't tell her who I truly am right now, but in time, she will know everything. I will teach her all I know, take care of her and we can live on together in my castle like a king and his queen. This is truly all I have ever wanted.
But there is one thing that will never leave me…

I will always be unnatural.

www.ingramcontent.com/pod-product-compliance
Lightning Source LLC
Chambersburg PA
CBHW031417240626
47154CB00001B/85